Learning Keyboarding and Word Processing for Kids

Illustrations by Ryan Sather

Chris Katsaropoulos
Suzanne Weixel
Grace Jasmine

Acknowledgments

To Mom, Stella, Sophia, and Lydia. We'll miss you in New York. Also, a special thanks to Monique Peterson, editor extraordinaire, for going beyond the call of duty. – *Chris Katsaropoulos*

I'd like to thank everyone at DDC, especially Monique Peterson, Jennifer Frew, and Chris Katsaropoulos. – *Suzanne Weixel*

To my darling husband, Alton, my wonderful mom, Julie, and my daughter Daisy, who knows she is my very favorite person in the world! – *Grace Jasmine*

PROJECT MANAGER
Monique Peterson

ENGLISH EDITORS
David Lott
Kristen Behrens
Monique Peterson

TECHNICAL EDITORS
Barb Terry
Jennifer Frew
Danny Dries

EDUCATIONAL CONSULTANT
Barb Terry

STUDENT REVIEWERS
Molly Jean Mann
Julie Adams
Nathaniel Weixel

EDITORIAL ASSISTANT
Diane Watnee

COVER LAYOUT AND DESIGN
Amy Capuano

LAYOUT AND DESIGN
Barbara Han
Midori Nakamura
Amy Capuano
MaryEllen Hopper
Kirsten Berger
Shu Chen
Paul Wray

ILLUSTRATIONS
Ryan Sather

ISBN: 1-56243-626-0
Cat No.: Z33HC
ISBN: 1-56423-623-6 pbk.
Cat No.: Z33

10 9 8 7 6 5 4 3 2 1

Printed in the United States of America.

TABLE OF CONTENTS

INTRODUCTION

So, you want to learn about keyboarding and word processing? You've come to the right place! I know you're eager to get started but don't skip this section! It gives you the ins and outs of how to use this book. If you understand all this stuff, you won't get confused later.

This is the Book for You if...

You want to learn how to type using the computer keyboard.

You want to create all sorts of cool documents using Microsoft Word—everything from letters to school reports to Web pages.

Macintosh and PC Platforms

We faced a unique challenge with this book since many of you use Macintosh computers at school and PCs at home (or vice versa) and we wanted to serve you in both places. Luckily for us and for you, all of the concepts and most of the steps are the same for both the Macintosh and the PC running Windows. The only difference may be in the name or appearance of a button, dialog box, or some other slight difference. In most instances, we show the PC version of the screen, though we show the Macintosh screen if it looks especially different.

If you use a PC, you know that the software often shows underlined letters on the menus and in dialog boxes. This gives you a way to access a feature using your keyboard. You can press the Alt key and then press the underlined letter. Since the Macintosh doesn't use underlined letters, Mac users can simply ignore the underlined letters.

Some exercise steps have PC-only directions and others have Mac-only directions. In cases like this, you'll see 🪟 in front of the PC-only directions and you'll see in front of the Mac-only directions.

To Use This Book, You Should Already ...

- Have access to a Macintosh with Microsoft Word 98 or a PC with Microsoft Word 97 for Windows.

- Know how to start your computer.

- Know how to find your way around your Mac or your PC.

How to Use This Book

- The book is divided into Seasons, and within each Season you'll complete several Games, Meets, or Events to help you learn about keyboarding and word processing. Coach Carrie and her assistants will help you find your way around the book, train you, and offer tips and hints along the way.

PARTS IN EACH MEET, GAME, OR EVENT

On Your Mark, Chalk Talk, On Deck, or **Suit Up**. These sections introduce you to new topics, concepts, Microsoft Word features, and new lingo.

Get Set, Free Throws, Practice Swings, or **Getting Your Feet Wet**. These sections let you try something right away. Here you will get to try what you just read about to see how it works.

Go!, Tip-Off!, Play Ball, or **The Competition.** These sections are where you really get to put what you've learned to work! These sections are easy, step-by-step exercises that give you hands-on practice working with Microsoft Word.

Gold Medal, The Final Four, The World Series, or **The State Finals**. These sections challenge you to come up with your own cool ways to use the stuff that you just learned. Use these for extra practice or just for fun.

And Now a Word from our Sponsers...

Check out the various characters on each page for key concepts, hints, tips, and warnings:

Coach Carrie gets you started with all the key concepts and basic steps for a winning Season!

Trainer Terry gives you exercise instructions for you to "work out" and get you in tip-top shape.

Look out for Jeff the Ref to give you warnings or important things you need to know.

Meg the Mike will give you the report on terms and definitions you need to know.

Mascot Max will always be there to cheer you on when you reach victory!

What's on the CD-ROM?

YOU'RE IN!

ME?

- The **Student Data** folder
- The **Teacher** folder
- The **Bonus Pack** folder
- The **Acroread** folder
- The **Software** folder

Read the following sections to find out more about what's in each folder.

The Student Data Folder

You will find data files in the Student Data folder for completing many of the exercises in the book. The data files include Word 97 and Word 98 documents that you can use in the exercises. The PC files are in a subfolder inside the Student Data folder called *PCData*. The Mac data is in a subfolder inside the Student Data Folder called *MacData*.

Solutions to the exercises in this book may be purchased separately through DDC Publishing. You may use the files on the Solutions disk to compare your work with the final version on disk. Each solution filename begins with the letter "S" and is followed by a descriptive filename, such as *S03info*.

You will find a complete directory of data and solution filenames in the Log of Exercises section of this book.

The Teacher Folder

If you are a teacher or a parent, make sure to check out the Teacher's Manual in the Teacher folder before you begin teaching the lessons in this book. In it you will find a number of interesting ways to make teaching the lessons in the book easier and more effective for you and your students. The Teacher's Manual is in Portable Display Format (PDF) for viewing and printing with Acrobat Reader.

The Teacher's Manual has been set up to work with the text to increase your students' understanding of each lesson. Each section of the Teacher's Manual has these special features:

OVERVIEW

This section provides a quick overview of what students will learn in each lesson.

TECHNO-TEACHER TIPS

In this section you can get some techno tidbits to help you along as you teach. Look here for brief reminders, special tips, or red flags.

EXPAND THE LESSON

In this section Trainer Terry offers easy-to-prepare lesson extensions to reinforce the Game, Meet, or Event that students have just completed.

STRETCH THE LESSON

Coach Carrie helps you stretch the lesson to incorporate what students have learned in the lesson with other subject areas. You will have the opportunity to have your class form student Publishing Companies, which will allow your students to work together in cooperative groups on many exciting and relevant activities. This section will increase your students' ability to work as a team, as well as provide many lesson plan ideas for you.

ENRICH THE LESSON

Everyone has a few high-achieving or gifted students in class who just can't seem to get enough of any learning experience. This section of the Teacher's Manual offers interesting activities that not only give them something important and unusual to do, but often help you out, too!

The Bonus Pack Folder

The Bonus Pack includes nine Warm Up exercises that you can use to practice your typing and improve your speed. These additional exercises are saved as Adobe's Portable Display Format (PDF) for viewing and printing with Acrobat Reader.

The Acroread Folder

This folder contains Adobe Acrobat Reader for the Mac and PC. You'll find installation instructions in a file called *readme_w.wri* for the PC and *readme_m.txt* for the Mac. Use Adobe Acrobat Reader to read and print the Bonus Pack files and the Teacher's Manual.

The Software Folder

We've included a cool software package called **All the Right Type** which is designed to help you build your typing speed by doing fun games and exercises on the computer. You can test your typing speed by taking timed writings, which **All the Right Type** automatically records. This way, you can keep track of your scores and progress as you practice.

From the main screen, you'll find a **Testing Center**, which has the **DDC Timed Writings** that are included in the keyboarding exercises in this book. Here, you can set the speed and timing goals that you want.

The **Learning Lab** teaches correct technique, posture, and finger placement.

The **Practice Pavilion** lets you race in a rowboat and compete against another rowboat.

You can go to the **Word Processing Plaza** if you need a blank document.

The **Skill Building** has typing drills that let you practice one line of text at a time.

The **Records Library** gives you a report of all tests taken to date.

INSTALLING THE ALL THE RIGHT TYPE SOFTWARE

Have a teacher or parent read these instructions to help you install the software.

System Requirements

Software	Windows 95, Windows 3.1 (or higher), or Windows NT 3.51 (or higher)
Hardware	386/33MHZ or higher (486 or higher recommended), 8 MB RAM, 256 color monitor, and CD-ROM Drive
Disk Space	10 MB available hard disk space for a "Typical" installation.

1. Click **START** on the desktop. Click **RUN** and then type:
    (CD-ROM drive letter):\TIMINGS\SETUP.

2. Click **NEXT** to go to the Choose Directory Location screen.

3. Click **NEXT** to accept the default directory
    (or click **BROWSE** to select another directory) for installing program files.

    *NOTE: **TYPICAL** is recommended for most users.*

4. At the Setup Type screen, click a setup option based on your system needs
    and click **NEXT**.

5. At the Select Program Folder screen, click **NEXT** to accept the default folder
    (or select another folder) for storing the program icons.

6. At the Setup Complete screen, click **FINISH**.

START ALL THE RIGHT TYPE

*NOTE: Steps 3, 6, and 7 are only necessary the first time you log into the program
or if you wish to make any program adjustments.*

1. If program and program icons were installed to the default locations, click **START**
    on the desktop, click **PROGRAMS**, then click **All the Right Type DDC Edition.**

2. When the introductory screen appears, click anywhere to continue.

3. At the Sign On screen, click **EDIT USERS**, then click **ADD**, type your name,
    click **OK**, and then click **DONE** to add it to the program.

4. Click your name in the User list and click **SELECT**.

5. Click **CONTINUE** at the welcome screen.

6. Click **Options** on the menu bar and select Set **Options**.

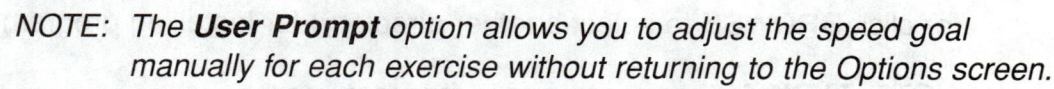

7. **TO SET A SPEED GOAL:**

   (a) Click **Speed Goal**.

   (b) Select a speed goal from the

   drop-down list and click **OK**.

   *NOTE: The **User Prompt** option allows you to adjust the speed goal manually for each exercise without returning to the Options screen.*

   OR

   TO SET A TIME GOAL:

   (a) Click **Timed Writing**.

   (b) Select a time goal from the drop-down list.

   *NOTE: The **User Prompt** option allows you to adjust the timing goal manually for each exercise without returning to the Options screen. However, the User Prompt option does not enable you to select 30 second timings, whereas the Timed Writing drop-down option does.* **THE TIMED WRITING, USER PROMPT OPTION IS THE RECOMMENDED SETTING FOR THIS PROGRAM.**

8. At the FACULTY OF A.R.T. main campus screen, click the TESTING CENTER to access the timed writing exercises that accompany this book.

9. Double-click the exercise for which you wish to be timed.

10. Follow the online instructions.

REVIEW TYPING RECORDS

1. Follow steps 1-5 above to access the FACULTY OF A.R.T. main campus screen.

2. Click **RECORDS LIBRARY** to access an updated report on timings, speed, accuracy, etc. for each exercise completed.

3. Click **Return to Campus** on the menu bar when you are finished viewing your records.

NETWORK VERSION OF ALL THE RIGHT TYPE

A network school version is available as a separate purchase from DDC Publishing. The network version allows you to install the program on an unlimited number of computers in your computer lab. It also provides the ability for instructors to view and monitor each student's progress and the ability to create timed writings tests from external documents.

LOG OF EXERCISES

Season	Exercise	File Name	Data File	Solutions
1	Meet 4	practice	none	S04practice
1	Meet 5	triple	none	S05triple
1	Meet 6	keyword	none	S06keyword
1	Meet 7	time	none	S07time
1	Meet 8	score	none	S08score
1	Meet 9	rim	none	S09rim
2	Game 1	league	01league	S01league
2	Game 2	cutpaste	none	S02cutpaste
2	Game 2	schedule	02sched	S02schedule
2	Game 3	packet	03packet	S03packet
2	Game 3	info	03info	S03info
2	Game 4	coach	04coach	S04coach
2	Game 4	roster	04roster	S04roster
2	Game 4	todo	none	S04todo
2	Game 4	list	04list	S04list
2	Game 5	basket	05basket	S05basket
2	Game 5	pacers	none	S05pacers
2	Game 6	pass	06pass	S06pass
2	Game 6	defense	06defend	S06defend
2	Game 7	offense	07offense	S07offense
2	Game 8	tryout	08tryout	S08tryout
2	Game 8	parent	08parent	S08parent
3	Game 1	scout	none	S01scout
3	Game 1	legend	none	S01legend
3	Game 2	scout2	02scout	S02scout

3	Game 2	stats	02stats	S02stats
3	Game 2	notes	02notes	S02notes
3	Game 2	legend	02legend	S02legend
3	Game 3	keypad	none	S03keypad
3	Game 3	legend	03legend	S03legend
3	Game 4	roster	none	S04team
3	Game 4	legend	04legend	S04legend
3	Game 5	scout	05scout	S05scout
3	Game 5	legend	05legend	S05legend
3	Game 6	scout	06scout	S06scout
3	Game 6	legend	06legend	S06legend
3	Game 7	scout	07scout	S07scout
3	Game 7	legend	07legend	S07legend
4	Event 1	workout	none	S01workout
4	Event 1	datalist	none	S01datalist
4	Event 1	cyber	none	S01cyber
4	Event 2	poster	none	S02poster
4	Event 3	newslet	none	S03newslet
4	Event 4	datalist mainletter parents	04data	S04parents
4	Event 5	program	none	S05program
4	Event 5	inside	none	S05inside
4	Event 6	web practice	none	none
4	Event 6	team page	none	S06team page

SEASON 1
TRACK AND FIELD
BUILDING SKILL AND SPEED

In Track and Field Season, stretch your fingers and work up to speed by learning about the computer and its keyboard. Find out where to put your fingers, and how to type without looking at the keys. Also learn how to create a document and get comfortable with the various parts of Microsoft Word. By the time you finish this season, you'll know how to type the whole alphabet as well as key words for each finger on your hand.

During Track and Field Season, you'll run in various Meets. If you're ready, let's start building some speed!

MEET #1
GETTING OFF TO A
FAST START

In this Meet, you'll limber up with your computer, keyboard, and mouse. You'll find out how to get off to a fast start with Microsoft Word. Put on your gym shoes and let's learn:

- **About Your Computer**
- **What is Word Processing?**
- **Using the Mouse**
- **Starting Word**
- **Identifying Screen Parts**
- **Minimize, Restore, and Close Buttons**
- **Closing a Document and Exiting Word**

ON YOUR MARK
About Your Computer

If you're like most kids, you've probably used a computer before. If you have, that's great, but let's go over a few basics before we hit the track and start running!

Your computer has five main pieces: the screen, the keyboard, the mouse, the Central Processing Unit (CPU), and the printer. These pieces are called the computer's *hardware*.

MEG THE MIKE

CPU stands for Central Processing Unit, the hardware where the computer stores and works with information.

Computer programs such as Microsoft Word are called *software*. Software lets you get things done using the computer's *hardware*. Think of the computer hardware as a CD player, and think of the software as the music CDs you listen to using the player.

Printer Screen CPU

Mouse Keyboard

Figure 1-1. Main parts of the computer

GET SET

What is Word Processing?

Coach Carrie Says:

Microsoft Word is a word processing program. It helps you work with words to create documents such as school reports on the computer. Using Word's commands, you can easily make changes on screen, such as moving, copying, or getting rid of words and letters. These kinds of changes are called *editing*.

Word also allows you to change the size and style of the letters and even include pictures. These kinds of changes are called *formatting*.

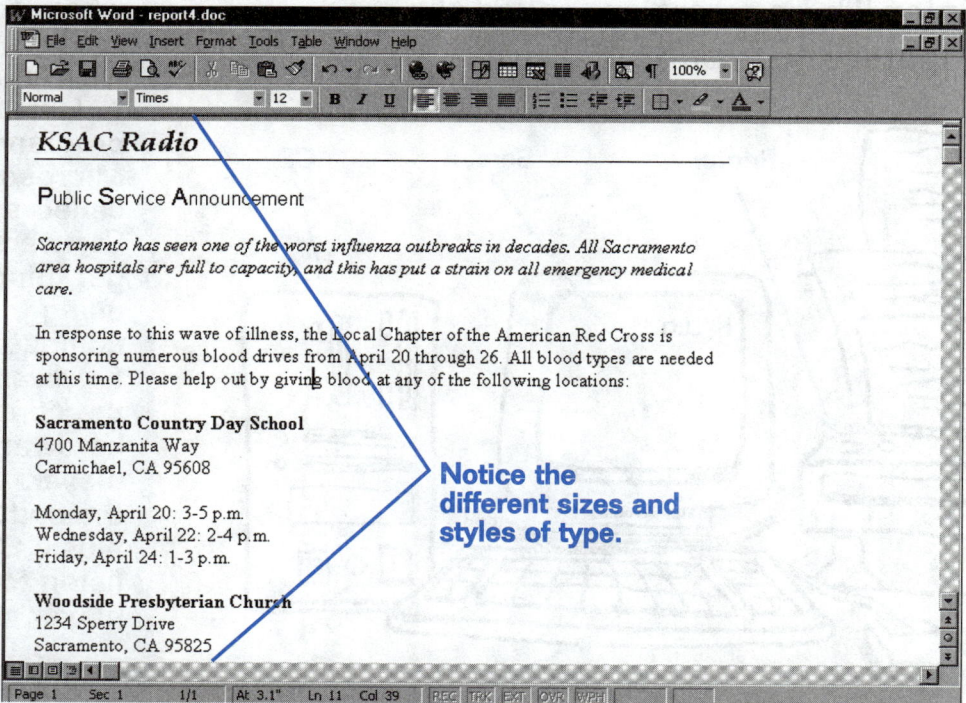

Figure 1-2. Word document with formatting

After you have created your document, Word makes it easy for you to print it out on paper. You can even save a document you create as a Web page for posting on the Internet!

GET SET
Using the Mouse

MASCOT MAX

You'll learn how to create a Web page in the Swimming section of this book!

Coach Carrie Says:

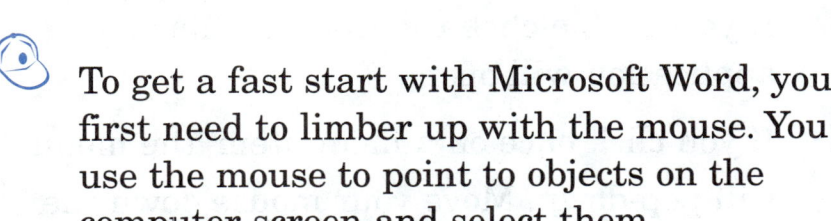

To get a fast start with Microsoft Word, you first need to limber up with the mouse. You use the mouse to point to objects on the computer screen and select them.

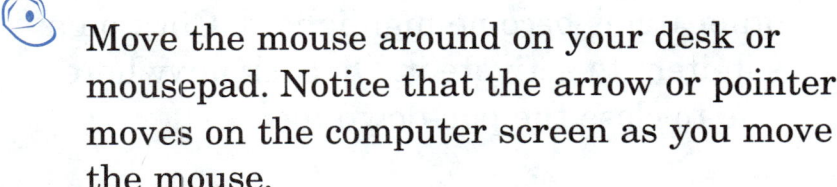

Move the mouse around on your desk or mousepad. Notice that the arrow or pointer moves on the computer screen as you move the mouse.

JEFF THE REF

Be careful not to click on the Start menu or pop-up menu. If you do, another menu will open.

For PC Users

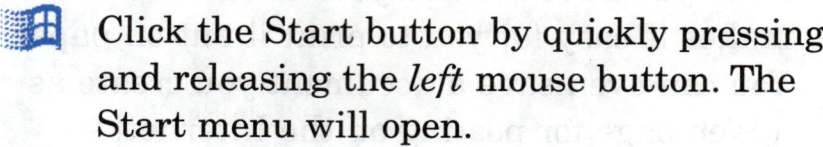 Click the Start button by quickly pressing and releasing the *left* mouse button. The Start menu will open.

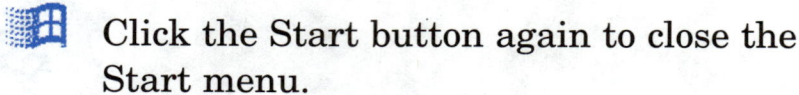 Click the Start button again to close the Start menu.

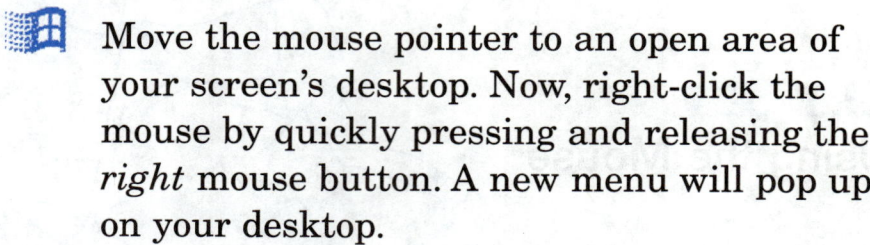 Move the mouse pointer to an open area of your screen's desktop. Now, right-click the mouse by quickly pressing and releasing the *right* mouse button. A new menu will pop up on your desktop.

Click again at another open area of the desktop to close the pop-up menu. Remember to use your left mouse button this time!

For Mac Users

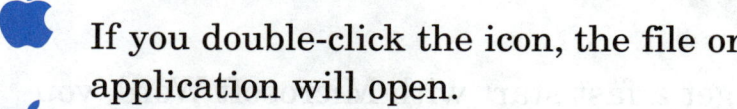 Using your mouse, point to an icon. Then click once. The icon will become highlighted.

If you double-click the icon, the file or application will open.

If you click once on a menu item, the menu will pop-down. Move your mouse down the menu or across the menu bar and watch the other items become highlighted. Click on a sub-item to activate it. Or, click anywhere else to close the pop-down menu.

Go!
Starting Word

 Coach Carrie Says:

Now that you've warmed up with the mouse, it's time to take off from the starting line and run your first race! To use Microsoft Word, you first have to start the program.

Mac	PC
• Locate Word98 folder. • Double-click Word98 icon.	• Click the Start button. • Click Programs. • Click Microsoft Word.

Click Start   **Click Programs**   **Click Microsoft Word**

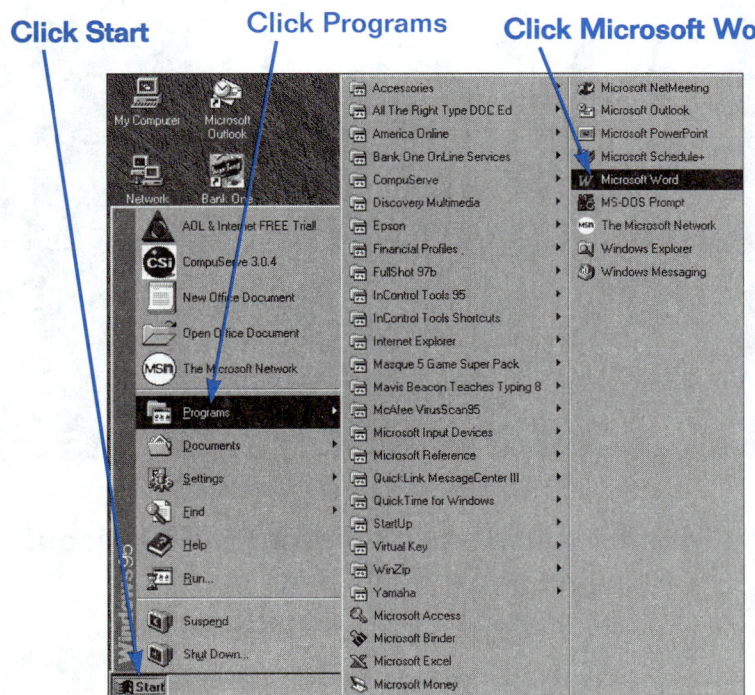

Figure 1-3. Use the Program menu to start Microsoft Word on the PC.

MEG THE MIKE

The *desktop* is where you see the program *icons* and program *windows*. Icons are small symbols that show you what programs or commands are available.

For PC Users

Double-click an icon to open a program window and work in that program.

The *taskbar* shows you what programs are open. Click on a program in the taskbar to go to that program window.

For Mac Users

In the upper right corner of your desktop, you will see the icon for the currently active program. If there are no programs running you will see the icon for The Finder. You can switch between open applications here or just click on any open window.

For Mac Users

You can create an Alias for Microsoft Word (called a Shortcut in Windows.) Click the file once, then press Command+M. You can then drag the Alias to a convenient spot on your desktop or your AppleMenu Items folder inside your System Folder. Double clicking this Alias is the same as Double-clicking the original.

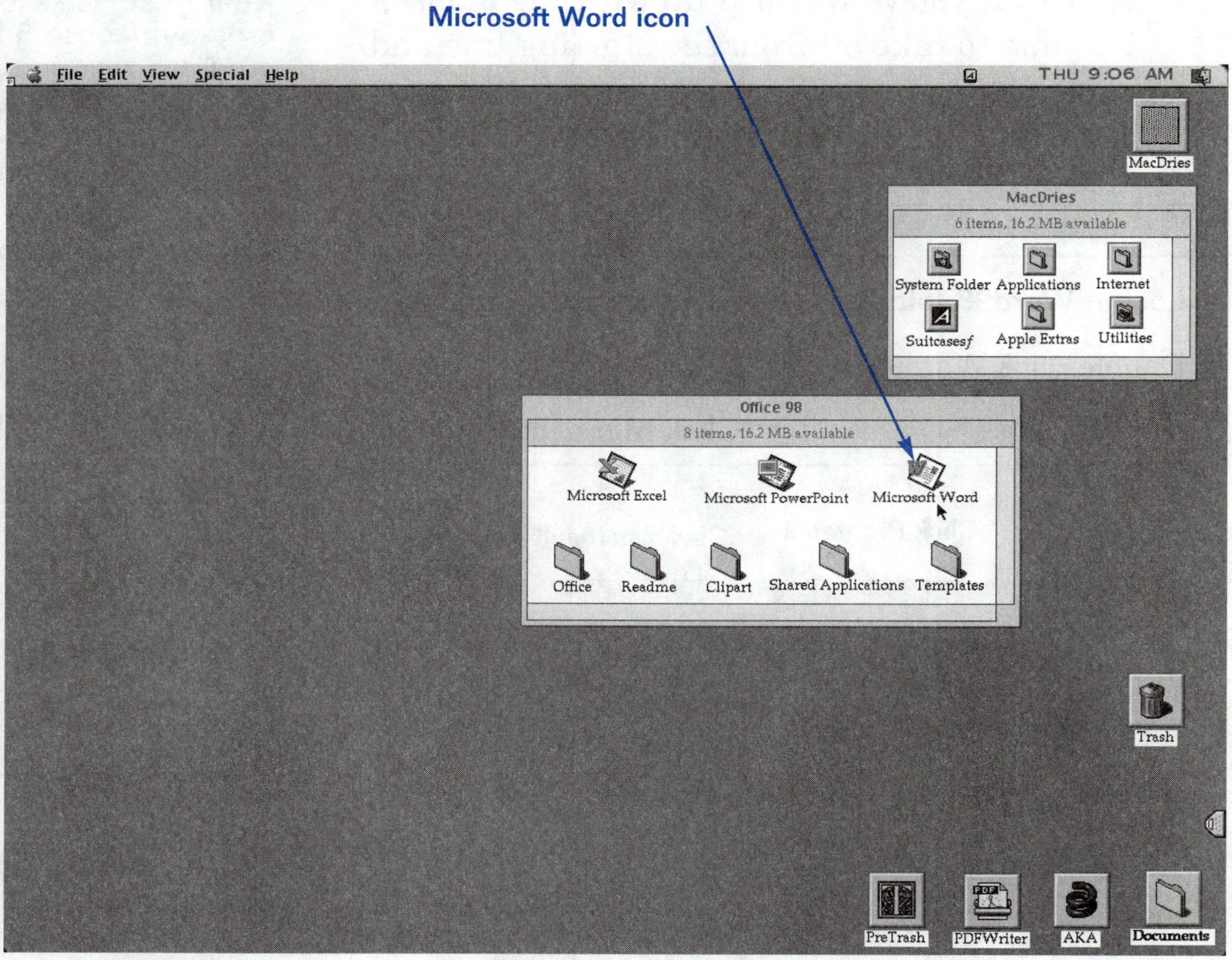

Figure 1-4. Start Word on the Mac by double-clicking the Word98 icon.

Identifying Screen Parts

Coach Carrie Says:

With Word up and running on your computer, you're charging full steam ahead. Take a moment to look at the Training Table on the following page. It tells you about the most important parts of Microsoft Word's opening screen.

If you don't see a new, blank document on your screen, click the New Document button ☐ on the Standard toolbar.

New Document button

For PC Users

Use Figure 1-5 on page 11 to match each part of the screen to its description in the table. Some elements displayed in Figure 1-5 (such as the Office Assistant) may not appear on your computer screen. That's because Word may be set up differently on your computer.

For Mac Users

Check out Figure 1-6 on page 11 to locate the parts of the screen in Word for the Mac.

MEG THE MIKE

Buttons have small pictures or symbols on them that show what will happen when you click on them. Sometimes it's easy to figure out what a button does just by looking at the picture. If you hold the mouse pointer over one of the buttons for a second or two, an explanation of the button may pop up. Buttons are also called *icons*.

Toolbars are groups of buttons, usually arranged in a row at the top of the screen.

Screen Part	What It Does
Title bar	Shows the name of the program running (Microsoft Word) and the name of the active document (Document 1).
Menu bar	Shows a list of menus that you use to get things done in Word. You can click on a menu item such as File to open a list of commands.
Minimize and Restore buttons	Find these buttons at the right of the Title bar and Menu bar. Use them to change the size of the program or document.
Close button	This button is at the right of the Title bar and Menu bar in Windows and on the left of the window on the Mac. Click on this to close the program or window.
Standard toolbar Formatting toolbar	Click the buttons on this toolbar to use menu commands. Click the buttons on this toolbar to change the size or style of letters on screen, change the way the words look on screen, and add pictures to a document.
Insertion point	Shows you where you are in a document. Any commands you use or letters you type will begin at the insertion point.
Scroll bars	Click these to move up and down or right and left within a document.
Status bar	Tells you where the insertion point is in the active document.
Office Assistant	Helps you work with Word.

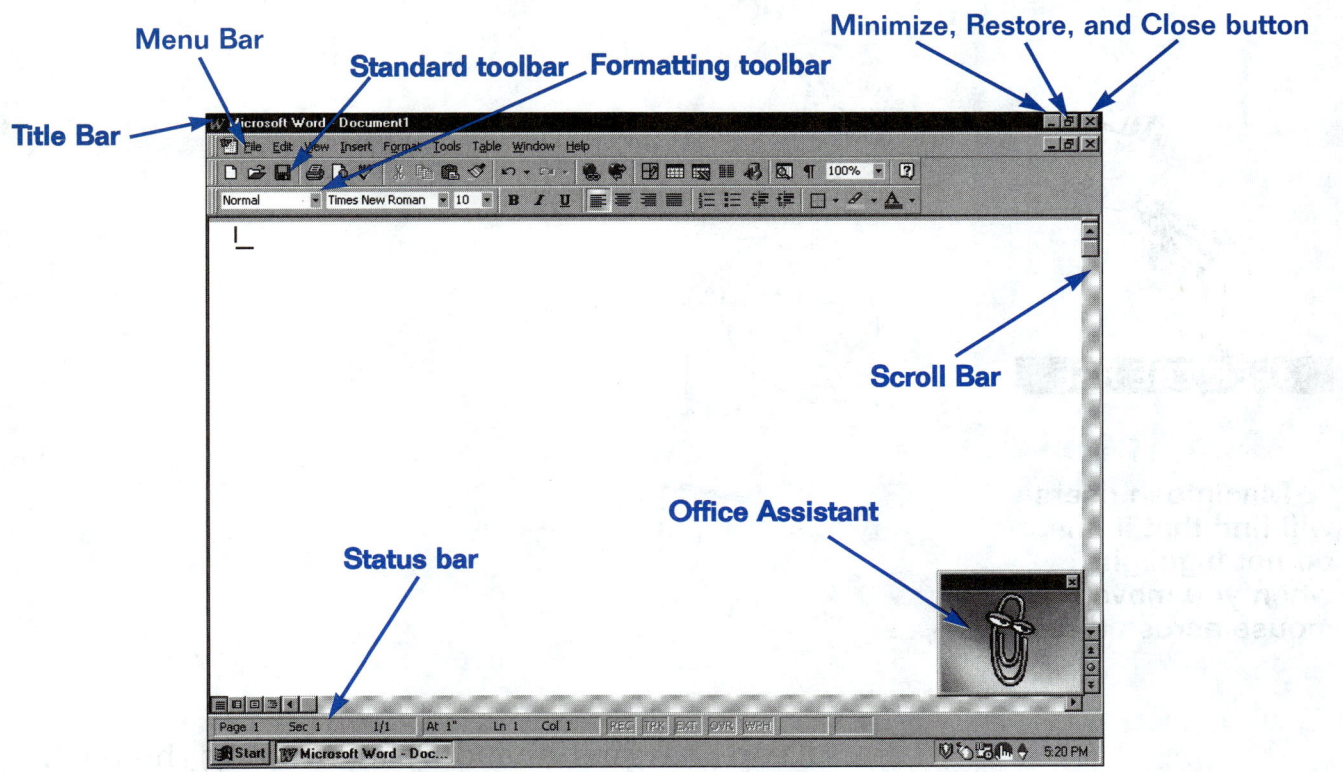

Figure 1-5. Important parts of the Word for Windows 95 screen

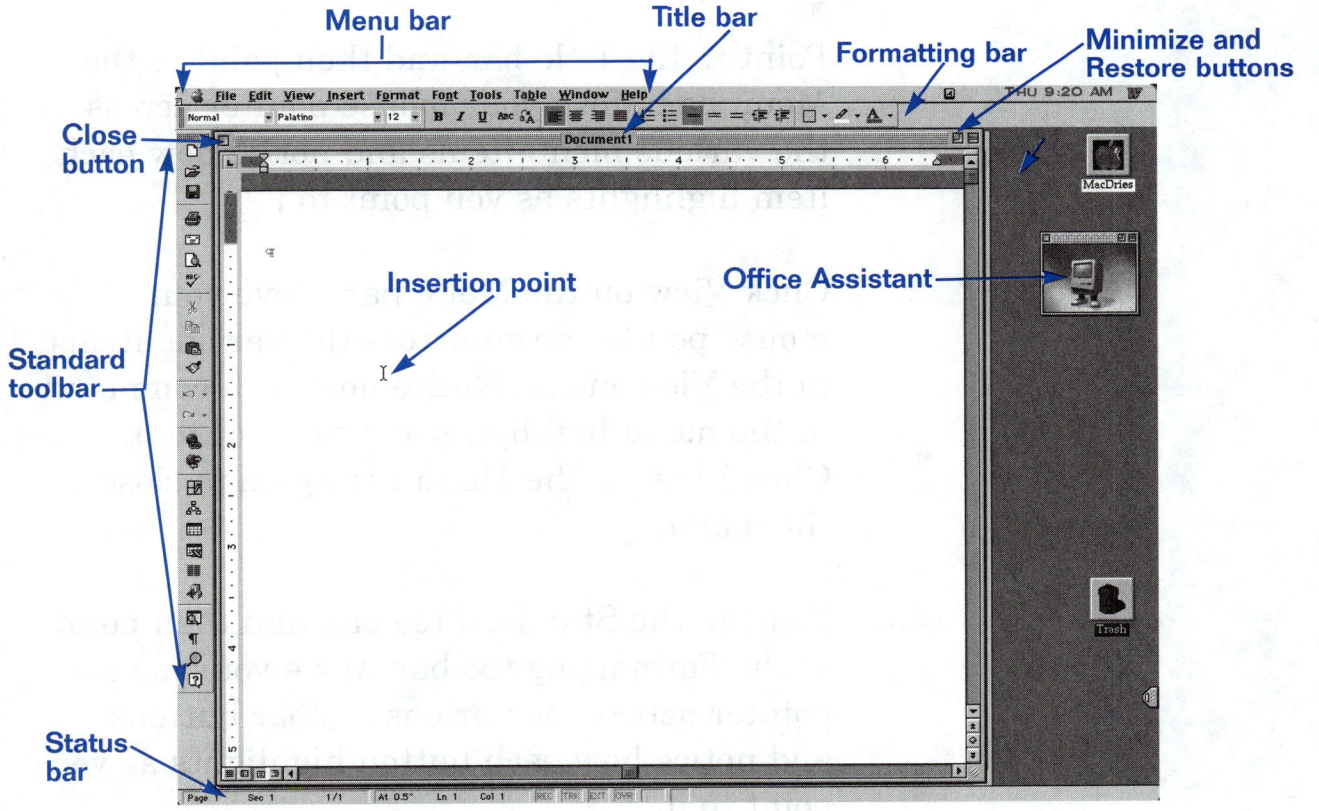

Figure 1-6. Important parts of the Word for the Mac screen

JEFF THE REF

For Mac Users

Macintosh users will find that items do not highlight when you move your mouse across them.

Trainer Terry Says:

Keep charging ahead by identifying the parts of the Word screen. Use your mouse to point to the various parts of the screen.

1. Point to the Title bar, and then point to the Menu bar. Move your mouse pointer across the various menu items and notice how each item highlights as you point to it.

2. Click View on the Menu bar. Move your mouse pointer down across the various items in the View menu. Notice how each command in the menu highlights as you point to it. Click View on the Menu bar again to close the menu.

3. Point to the Standard toolbar, and then point to the Formatting toolbar. Move your mouse pointer across the various toolbar buttons and notice how each button highlights as you point to it.

Minimize, Restore, and Close Buttons

Coach Carrie Says:

Okay, you've identified some important parts of the Word screen. Now, what if you want to change the size of the Word window or the document window? To do that, you click the Minimize ▬ or Restore ▣ buttons, which are at the right end of the Title bar and the Menu bar.

The Minimize and Restore buttons on the Title bar change the size of the Word application window. The Minimize and Restore buttons on the Menu bar change the size of the document window. A fourth button, the Maximize button ▢, appears when a window has been reduced in size. You can also just double-click the Title bar to maximize/minimize any window.

The Close button ☒ will close the application or document.

Check out the following Training Table to see what each of the buttons does.

Button	What It Does
Minimize button ▬	Shrinks the application or document window to an icon that appears at the bottom of the screen.
Restore button ⧉	Changes the application or document window to a reduced size.
Maximize button ▢	Changes the application or document window to full size.
Close button ✕	Closes the application or document window.

JEFF THE REF

See if you can tell the difference between closing a document and closing Word altogether.

Trainer Terry Says:

You're picking up speed now. Try changing window sizes to get ready for the home stretch of this race.

1. Click the Restore button ⧉ at the right of the Menu bar. The document window shrinks to a smaller size.

2. Click the Maximize ▢ button at the right of the Document 1 Title bar. The document window returns to full size.

3. Click the Minimize button ▬ at the right of the Menu bar. The document window shrinks to become an icon at the bottom of the screen.

4. Click the Maximize button ▢ on the Document 1 icon. The document window returns to full size.

Closing a Document and Exiting Word

Coach Carrie Says:

You've worked out hard and the finish line is in sight. Close out this race by closing the document on screen and exiting Word.

When you finish your work, you can either save it or close it without saving. If you have not saved your work before you close a document, a dialog box will appear asking if you want to save changes to your document. Click <u>Y</u>es to save changes. Click <u>N</u>o if you don't want to save changes. Click Cancel if you decide to return to the open document.

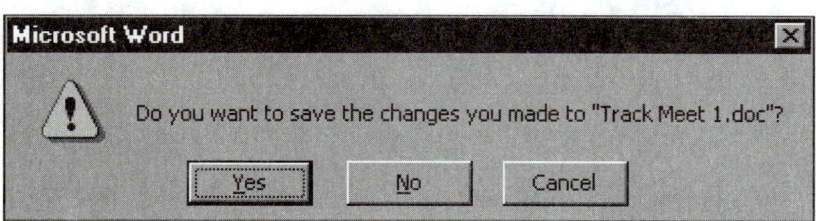

Figure 1-7. A dialog box

You can also use the Close button ⊠ on the document Title bar to close a document. Click the Close button on the Word Title bar to close Word.

MEG THE MIKE

A *dialog box* is a small box that pops up in Word to ask you for more information about what you want to do.

JEFF THE REF

Remember, the Close button ⊠ is on the upper-left corner of the Title bar on the Mac and the upper right of the Title bar on the PC.

Follow these steps to close your document and close Word:

Macintosh	Windows

1. **Press Command+Q.**
 	
   OR
 	
   Click the File menu.
 	
2. **Click Quit.**
 	
3. **If you quit Word when a document is open, you will be asked to choose Save or Don't Save. The document and Word close.**
	1. **Click File on the Menu bar.**
	
	2. **Click Close.**
	
	3. **A dialog box may open asking if you want to save changes to your document. Click Yes to save changes, or click No if you don't want to save any changes. The document closes.**
	
	4. **Now click File again.**
	
	5. **Click Exit.**

MEET #2
THE HOME STRETCH

Okay, now you've gotten off to a fast start by opening Microsoft Word. In the second track meet, you'll begin to learn using your computer keyboard. You'll also learn about:

- The Home Keys
- Finger Stretching
- First-Finger Reaches
- First-Finger Key Words

ON YOUR MARK

The Home Keys

Coach Carrie Says:

On the keyboard, the home-row keys are the keys where you keep your fingertips. Every time a finger leaves this row to press another key, return it to home position quickly.

Think of all keys that are not home keys as being very hot. You want to press them with a quick motion and get back to the cool home-row keys. Keep your fingers on the cool home-row keys!

Figure 1-8. Home-row keys

Finger Stretching

Coach Carrie Says:

Put your fingers on the home-row keys, as shown in Figure 1-8 on the previous page. The fingers of the left hand go on these keys:

- Index finger on the **F**
- Middle finger on the **D**
- Ring finger on the **S**
- Pinky on the **A**

The fingers of the right hand go on these keys:

- Index finger on the **J**
- Middle finger on the **K**
- Ring finger on the **L**
- Pinky on the **;** (semi-colon)
- Your thumbs rest on the spacebar

From the home-row keys, your fingers reach to keys above and below to type other letters.

Notice that all reaches up from the home row are slightly to the left; all reaches down are slightly to the right.

Your first, or index, fingers are stronger than the others, so they also make one reach to the center of the keyboard on each row. Take a moment to run each of your fingers up and down their pathways and see how simple it is!

 **GET UP TO SPEED**

If you want, you can start using the All the Right Type software program on your book's CD for more practice. Start the program and then click the Learning Lab building.

Click the Posture Review button to learn about the proper way to sit at your computer. Click the Hand Position Review to see how your hands should position over the home keys.

All the Right Type is a fun way to practice your keyboarding skills! Throughout the book, we'll let you know where you can use the software to build speed. If you need help starting the software, flip back to this book's Introduction.

GET SET
First-Finger Reaches, Left Hand

Coach Carrie Says:

Look at Figure 1-9 below and think of your *f* finger as being in the center of a car's wheel. Think of this as a clockwise motion even though you go back to f each time.

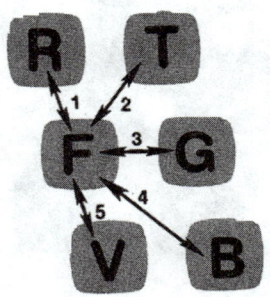

Figure 1-9. First-finger reaches, left hand

Trainer Terry Says:

Put your fingers on the home keys.

1. Touch *f*, move up to *r* and back to *f*.
2. Move up to *t* and back to *f*.
3. Move over to *g* and back to *f*.
4. Move down center to *b* and back to *f*.
5. Move down to *v* and back to *f*.

SEASON 1, MEET 2

First-Finger Reaches, Right Hand

Coach Carrie Says:

Look at Figure 1-10 below. Think of your *j* finger moving in a counter-clockwise motion.

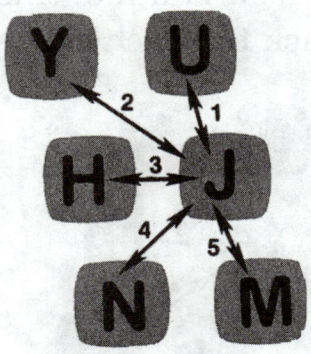

Figure 1-10. First-finger reaches, right hand

Trainer Terry Says:

Put your fingers on the home keys again.

1. Touch *j*, move to *u* and back to *j*.
2. Move up to *y* and back to *j*.
3. Move over to *h* and back to *j*.
4. Move down to *n* and back to *j*.
5. Move down to *m* and back to *j*.

22

Go!
First-Finger Reaches

Trainer Terry Says:

 Now it's time to try your first fingers on the keyboard.

 As you type the following letters, say each letter to yourself as you tap its key. Think of this as a race your fingers are running. Try to type the letters as fast as you can while staying on course.

Between groups of letters, press the spacebar once with your right thumb. Continue, even if you feel you have tapped a wrong key.

1. Start Microsoft Word.

   PC users, click Start, Program, Microsoft Word.

   Mac users, double-click the Word98 icon (or the Alias on your desktop).

2. Ready? Go!

---

frftfgfbfv frftfgfbfv frftfgfbfv frftfgfbfv frftfgfbfv

jujyjhjnjm jujyjhjnjm jujyjhjnjm jujyjhjnjm jujyjhjnjm

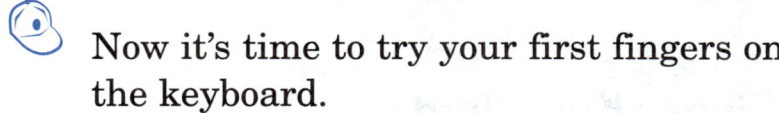

MASCOT MAX

If you say the letters to yourself as you tap the keys, it will help you learn them faster!

JEFF THE REF

This race uses all the letters tapped by your first fingers. Each set of letters appears five times. When you reach the end of a line, Microsoft Word will automatically wrap the letters you type down to a new line.

JEFF THE REF

After you complete the race, check what you typed against the book. Retype any portion that you typed incorrectly.

3. Now type the race again without looking at your computer screen. Check your accuracy when you're finished.

---

frtfgfbfv frtfgfbfv frtfgfbfv frtfgfbfv frtfgfbfv

jujyjhjnjm jujyjhjnjm jujyjhjnjm jujyjhjnjm

jujyjhjnjm

First-Finger Key Words

Coach Carrie Says:

The next race uses all the letters tapped by your first fingers. If you don't remember the location of a key, look at Figure 1-11 below.

Figure 1-11. First-finger keys

In the following race, first-finger key words appear five times. Say the following letters to yourself as you tap the keys. Try to increase your speed each time you repeat a word.

Trainer Terry Says:

1. Open a blank document in Word.
2. Now type the next two races.

fur fur fur fur fur fun fun fun fun fun

gun gun gun gun gun

gum gum gum gum gum

guy guy guy guy guy buy buy buy buy buy

but but but but but hut hut hut hut hut

jut jut jut jut jut vug vug vug vug vug

3. Now sprint to the finish by typing each word as it appears below!

fur fun gun gum guy buy but hut jut vug

4. Check your work, and retype any portion that you typed incorrectly.
5. Close the document without saving it.

MEET #3
BUILDING SPEED

Your fingers are familiar with the home-row keys. Now it's time to build speed by reviewing the first-finger keys and learning the second-finger keys. Lace up your track shoes and learn:

- Second-Finger Home Keys
- Second-Finger Reaches
- Second-Finger Key Words
- Review First-Finger Reaches
- Review First-Finger Key Words
- Review Second-Finger Key Words
- Practice First- and Second-Finger Key Words

On Your Mark

Second-Finger Home Keys

Coach Carrie Says:

Start building more keyboarding speed by learning about the second, or middle, finger and its reaches.

The second finger on your left hand taps *d* on the home row. That finger also reaches up slightly left to *e* and down below the home row slightly right for *c*.

The second finger on your right hand taps *k* on the home row. That finger also reaches up slightly left to *i* and slightly right down to the bottom row for the comma (,).

Figure 1-12. Second-finger home keys

JEFF THE REF

Always space one time after a comma. Do not space before a comma.

GET SET

Second-Finger Reaches

Coach Carrie Says:

Build speed by practicing the second-finger reaches you just learned. Put your fingers through these motions without tapping the keys.

1. The second finger of your left hand touches *d* on the home row.
2. The second finger of your left hand touches *e*, up and slightly to the left.
3. The second finger of your left hand touches *c*, down and slightly to the right.
4. The second finger of your right hand touches *k* on the home row.
5. The second finger of your right hand touches *i*, up and slightly to the left.
6. The second finger of your right hand touches the comma (,), down and slightly to the right.

Second-Finger Key Words

 Trainer Terry Says:

The following race uses all the letters tapped by your second fingers. Each word appears five times.

1.  PC users, click Start, <u>P</u>rogram, Microsoft Word.

    Mac users, double-click the Word98 icon (or the Alias on your desktop).

2. Try to increase your speed each time you repeat a word. Say the letters to yourself as you strike the keys.

---

jim jim jim jim jim dim dim dim dim dim

kid kid kid kid kid red red red red red

cue cue cue cue cue my, my, my, my, my,

---

3. When you're finished checking your work, close the document without saving it.

JEFF THE REF

After you finish typing, check what you typed against the book to see if you made any errors.

Go!

Review First-Finger Reaches

Trainer Terry Says:

Okay, now it's time to really zoom around the track! Try reviewing the first-finger reaches you learned in the last meet.

1. Open a new blank document.
2. Say each letter to yourself as you tap its key.

frftfgfbfv jujyjhjnjm frftfgfbfv jujyjhjnjm frftfgfbfv

jujyjhjnjm frftfgfbfv jujyjhjnjm

3. Check your work, then close the document without saving it.

Review First-Finger Key Words

Coach Carrie Says:

Keep building speed by typing the following first-finger key words. These are the words you learned in the last meet. Think speed!

Trainer Terry Says:

1. Open a new blank document.
2. Type the following first finger key words.

---

fur fun gun gum guy buy but hut jut vug

fur fun gun gum guy buy but hut jut vug

fur fun gun gum guy buy but hut jut vug

fur fun gun gum guy buy but hut jut vug

fur fun gun gum guy buy but hut jut vug

---

3. Close the document without saving it.

SEASON 1, MEET 3

JEFF THE REF
After you complete the race, check what you typed against the book. Retype any portion that you typed incorrectly.

MASCOT MAX
Later on, you'll type faster, if you don't look at the keys!

Review Second-Finger Key Words

Coach Carrie Says:

Now you're hitting your stride! Break into the lead of the race by reviewing second-finger key words.

Trainer Terry Says:

1. Open a new blank document.
2. Don't look at your fingers or at the computer screen as you type the following words.

---

jim dim kid red cue my, jim dim kid red cue my, jim dim kid red cue my, jim dim kid red cue my, jim dim kid red cue my,

---

3. Check your work, then close the document without saving it.

32

Practice First- and Second-Finger Key Words

Trainer Terry Says:

It's time to win this race! Get ready to round the last turn and finish strong by typing these first- and second-finger key words.

Before typing each new word for the first time, put your fingers through the motions of typing the word without tapping the keys.

After typing a word once, try to speed up your typing the next time. Pause briefly before each new word—as if you're taking a short breath.

1. Open a new document.
2. Type the following first- and second-finger key words.

---

fur fur fur fur fur fun fun fun fun fun gun gun gun gun gun gum gum gum gum gum guy guy guy guy guy buy buy buy buy buy buy but but but but but hut hut hut hut hut jut jut jut jut jut vug vug vug vug vug jim jim jim jim jim dim dim dim dim dim kid kid kid kid kid red red red red red cue cue cue cue cue my, my, my, my, my,

---

3. After you check your work, close the document without saving it.

MEET #4
BUILDING SKILL IN THE FIELD

In the last two meets, we've focused on building speed. But there's a reason the sport is called track and field. Field events such as the discus throw and the pole vault require skill and top athletic ability. In this Meet, you'll build your skill with Microsoft Word by:

- Creating a Document
- Saving a Document
- Previewing a Document
- Printing a Document

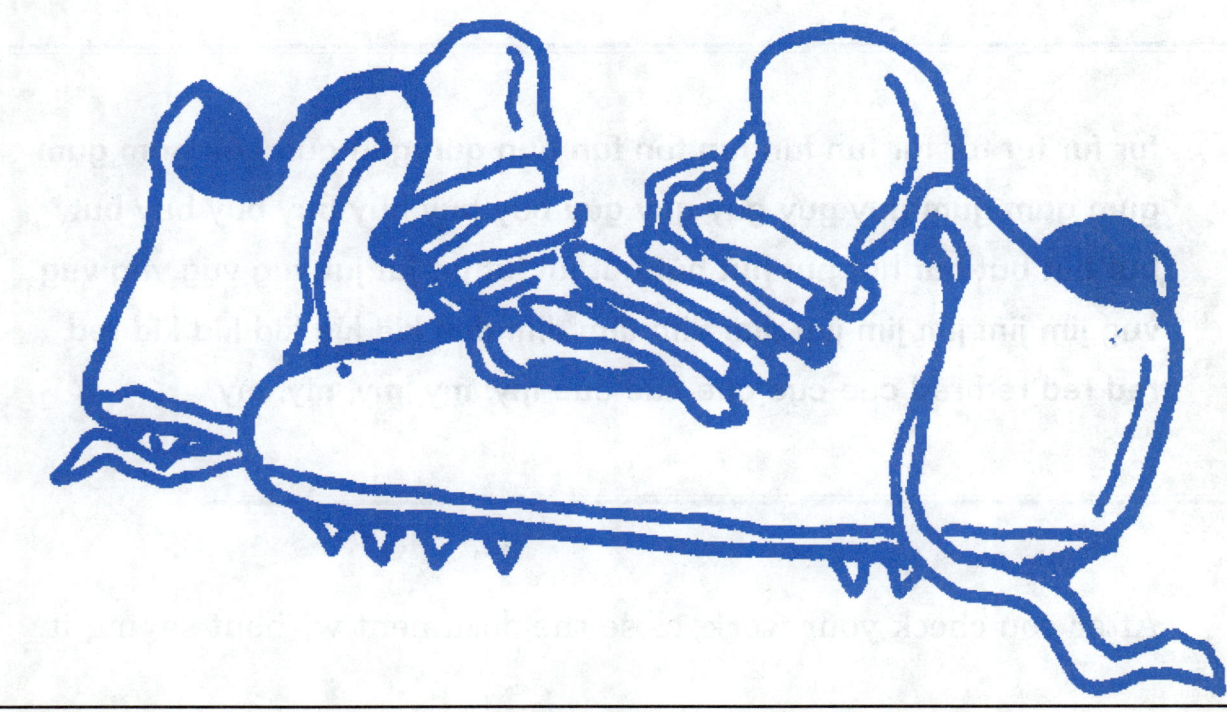

ON YOUR MARK

Creating a Document

Coach Carrie Says:

 Take your first shot at working with Word by creating your own new document! You can open a new document by clicking the <u>F</u>ile menu and then clicking <u>N</u>ew. Another way you can create a new

document is to click the New Document button on the Standard toolbar. (We learned this in Meet 1, remember?)

New Document button

Figure 1-13. The New Document button on the Standard toolbar

PC users, you may also press Ctrl+N to create a new document.

Mac users, you may also type Command+N to create a new document.

Trainer Terry Says:

Let's go ahead and try it!

1. Click the <u>F</u>ile menu and then click <u>N</u>ew. Or you can click the New Document button .

2. As you type the following lines, say each letter to yourself as you go. This time, press Enter at the end of each line using your right pinky! Remember to press the Spacebar with your right thumb.

---

frftfgfbfv jujyjhjnjm frftfgfbfv jujyjhjnjm

fur fur fur fur fur fun fun fun fun fun

gun gun gun gun gun gum gum gum gum gum

guy guy guy guy guy buy buy buy buy buy buy

but but but but but hut hut hut hut hut

jut jut jut jut jut vug vug vug vug vug

jim jim jim jim jim dim dim dim dim dim

kid kid kid kid kid red red red red red

cue cue cue cue cue my, my, my, my, my,

---

3. When you're finished, leave your document open. *We'll come back to it later!*

GET SET

Saving a Document

Coach Carrie Says:

The new document you just created is one you want to keep. Saving the document lets you keep it to use again later.

To save a document, you have to give it a name. You can give a document whatever name you want. Just make sure the name makes sense for you so that you can remember it.

For example, you could call the document you just created **practice**.

PC users, Microsoft Word will automatically add a dot and three letters (.doc) to the end of the name. These letters show that the file is a Microsoft Word document.

Mac users, the dot and three-letter extension is not applied automatically in Word for Mac.

MEG THE MIKE

The three letters at the end of a file name are known as the *extension*.

MEG THE MIKE

The *hard drive* is a big disk inside your computer where all the information and programs are stored.

A *floppy disk* is a plastic case containing a small disk that holds information and documents like yours. You can use a floppy disk to move information from one computer to another, such as from a school computer to your home computer.

To save your document, just click the <u>F</u>ile menu and then click <u>S</u>ave. You can also click the Save button ▣ on the Standard toolbar.

PC users, you may press Ctrl+S to save your document.

Mac users, you may also press Command+S to save your document.

After you do that, the Save As dialog box will open. You use the Save As dialog box to tell the computer what file name you want to use and where you want to store the file.

If you don't give a document a name when you save, Word will give the document a name for you. Word will use the first word or phrase in the document as the name.

You can either store the file in the computer's *hard drive* or on a *floppy disk* that you can take with you.

PC users, first choose where you want to save the file by clicking the Save in menu. The Save in menu will show you a list of drives and *folders* you can choose. See Figure 1-14.

 After you choose the drive or folder you want, type the file name you want in the File name box.

MEG THE MIKE

Folders are used to organize documents stored on the hard drive or on floppy disks. Think of storing your document inside a folder, which is then stored inside a filing cabinet (the hard drive or floppy disk).

When the name and location for the file are correct, click Save. Word does its thing, storing the document with the name you chose.

Choose drive or folder.

Floppy disk   Hard drive

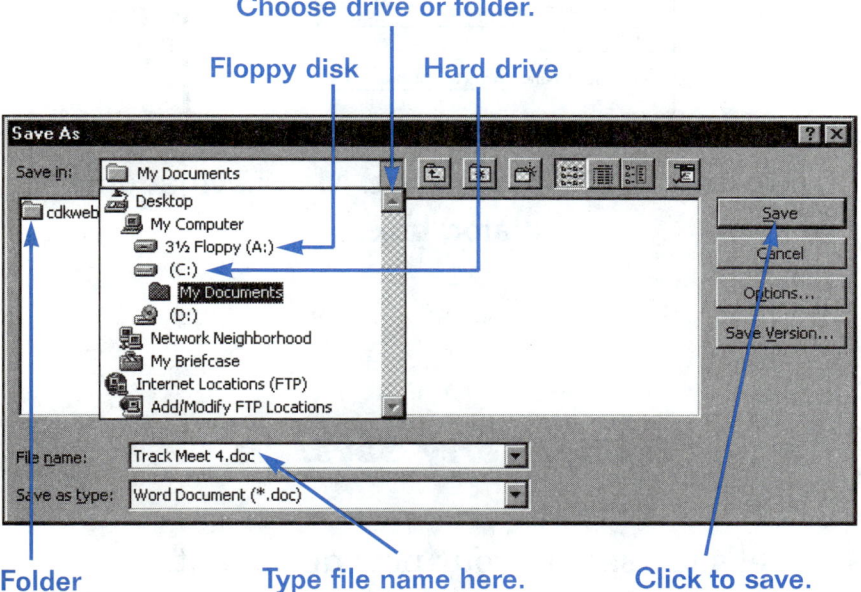

Folder   Type file name here.   Click to save.

Figure 1-14. Use the Save As dialog box to save your new document.

Mac users, when you save a file in Word for Mac, you will be shown a standard navigational dialog box. See figure 1-15. You can scroll to and double-click the folder where you want to store your document.

 Then click the Save button. Or, you may click on the Desktop button and save it there or in any other hard drive, removable drive, or floppy drive on your computer.

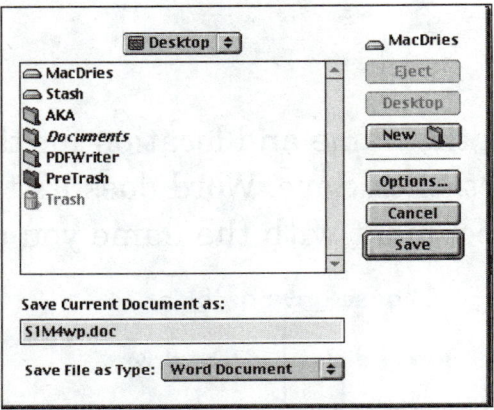

Figure 1-15. A standard Mac navigational dialog box

Trainer Terry Says:

 Let's try saving your new document.

1. Click <u>F</u>ile and then click <u>S</u>ave.
2. Select the drive and/or folder where you want to save the file.
3. Type *practice* in the File <u>n</u>ame text box.
4. Click the <u>S</u>ave button .

JEFF THE REF

If you have any trouble or you see a dialog box that's not the Save As dialog box, just click the Cancel button and try again.

MASCOT MAX

Ask your teacher if you're not sure where to save your files.

Go!

Previewing a Document

Coach Carrie Says:

Your document now has a name and a place for you to save it. You can print a copy of the document using the computer's printer.

Before you get ready to print, you should take a look at how the document will appear on paper by using *Print Preview*. To see your document in Print Preview, click <u>F</u>ile and then click Print

Pre<u>v</u>iew. You can also click the Print Pre<u>v</u>iew button on the Standard toolbar.

Figure 1-16 shows what a document looks like in Print Preview. Notice that you can see a whole page at once. If your document has more than one page, you can click the Multiple Pages button

to see several pages at once.

You can click the Zoom box to change the size of the page in preview. Click the arrow and then click the size you want. To go back to your document, click <u>C</u>lose .

One Page   Multiple Pages

Zoom box   Close   Print Preview toolbar

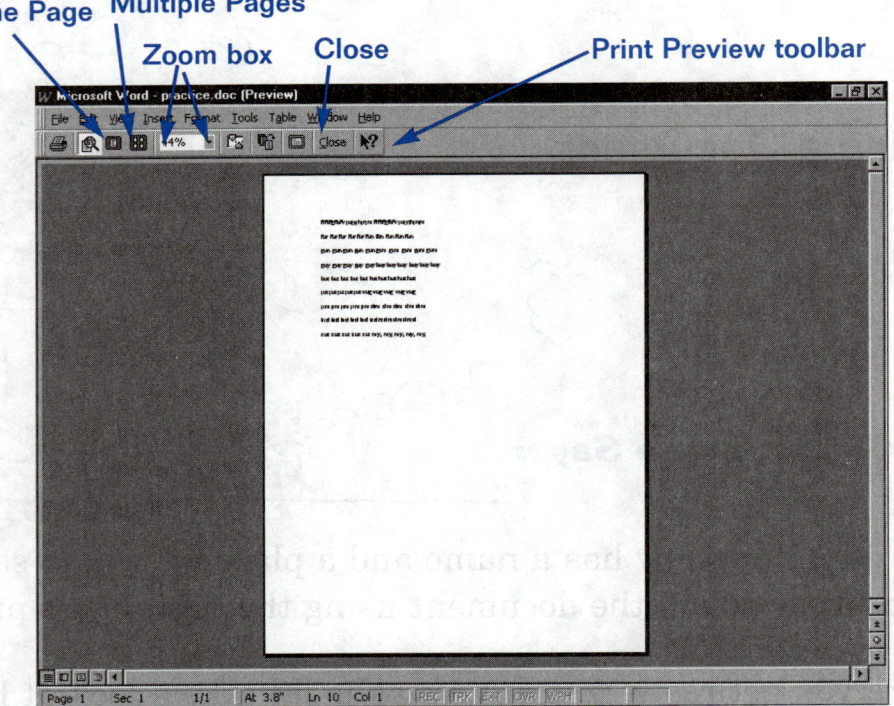

Figure 1-16. Check your document in Print Preview.

Trainer Terry Says:

Your last typing race should still be open on your screen. Now take a look at your document in *Print Preview*.

1. Click <u>F</u>ile and then click Print Pre<u>v</u>iew.
   The document opens in Print Preview.
2. Click the Zoom list box 44% . Click 50%.
   The document gets a little bigger.
3. Now move the mouse pointer over the document and click.
   The document changes to full size.
4. Click on the document again to return to Full Page view. You can now see the whole page again.
5. Click <u>C</u>lose to return to the normal view.

Printing a Document

Coach Carrie Says:

When you have previewed the document and everything looks ready to print, click the File menu and then click Print. The Print dialog box appears.

The Print dialog box offers a lot of choices. Look at Figure 1-17.

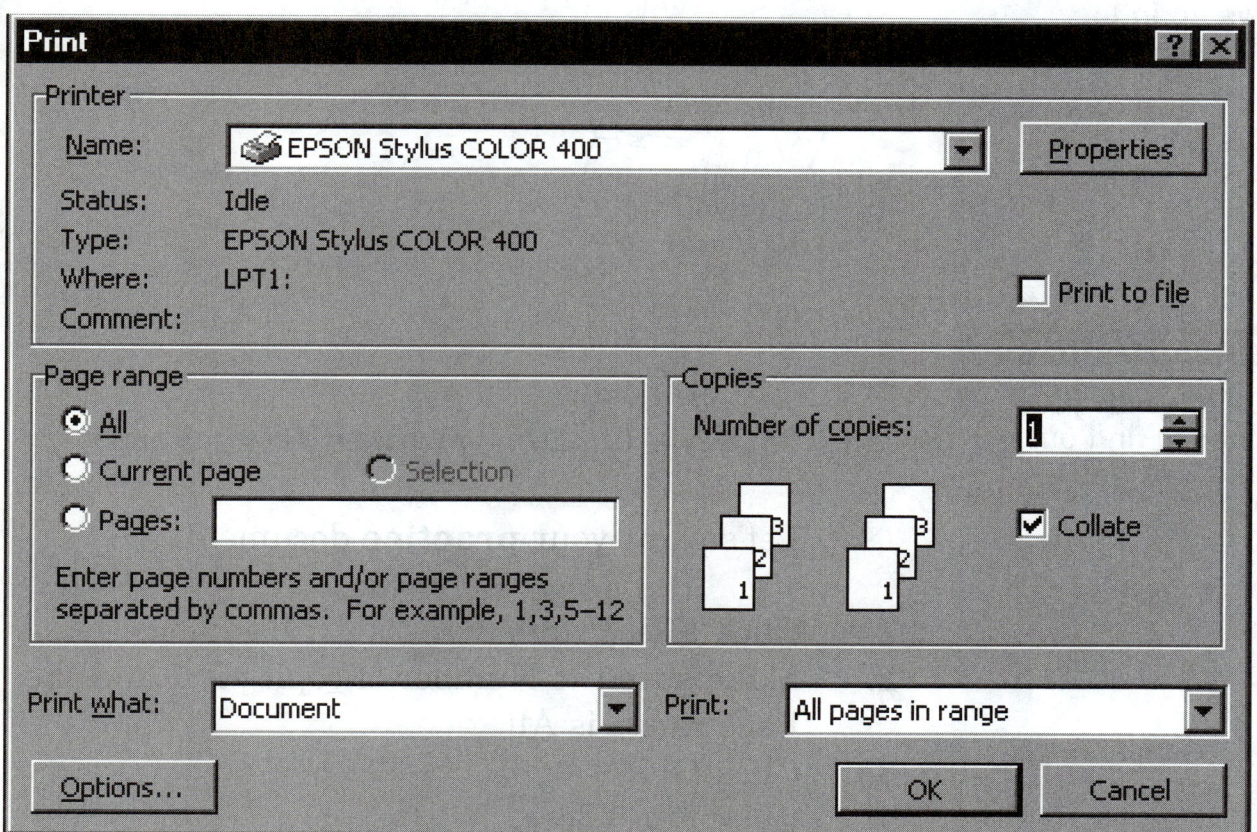

Figure 1-17. The Print dialog box

JEFF THE REF

If you have any trouble with the choices in the dialog box, just click the Cancel button and try again. If you clicked OK and nothing happens at the printer, ask your teacher to make sure the right printer shows up in the Print dialog box.

MASCOT MAX

Check with your teacher to find out how to use the printer.

If you want to make more than one copy, click on the Number of copies box and type in how many you want to make.

You can also click the Print button on the Standard toolbar to print your document. The print dialog box won't appear, but your document will print according to the last settings you made in the print dialog box.

Trainer Terry Says:

Let's print your **practice** document!

1. Click File, Print.
2. Make sure the Number of copies is *1* and the Page range is All.
3. Click OK.
4. Click File, Close.

MEET #5
THE TRIPLE JUMP

The triple jump is a track and field event in which each athlete combines three big leaps in one to see who can jump the farthest. In this meet, you'll learn:

- **Third-Finger Reaches**
- **Third-Finger Key Words**
- **Review First- and Second-Finger Reaches**
- **Review First- and Second-Finger Key Words**
- **Practice First-, Second-, and Third-Finger Key Words**

ON YOUR MARK

Third-Finger Reaches

Coach Carrie Says:

Let's continue to build speed and reach for more keys!

The third, or ring, finger of your left hand hits *s* on the home row. That finger also reaches up slightly left to *w* and slightly right down to the bottom row for *x*.

The third finger on your right hand hits *l* on the home row. That finger also reaches up slightly left to *o* and slightly right down to the bottom row for the period (.).

Use the period at the end of a sentence. You also use periods at the end of an abbreviation and as a decimal point in numbers.

After using a period to end a sentence, press the spacebar once and then go on to the next word or sentence.

Figure 1-18. Third-finger home keys and reaches

GET SET

Third-Finger Key Words

Trainer Terry Says:

Practice the third-finger reaches you just learned. Put your fingers through these motions without tapping the keys.

1. The third finger of your left hand touches *s* on the home row.
2. The third finger of your left hand touches *w*, up and slightly to the left.
3. The third finger of your left hand touches *x*, down and slightly to the right.
4. The third finger of your right hand touches *l* on the home row.
5. The third finger of your right hand touches *o*, up and slightly to the left.
6. The third finger of your right hand touches the period (.), down and slightly to the right.
7. Open a new document in Word.
8. Now build speed by typing the following letters and key words.

swsxs swsxs swsxs swsxs

swsxs swsxs swsxs swsxs

six six six sew sew sew

lol.l lol.l lol.l lol.l

lol.l lol.l lol.l lol.l

low low low old old old ill ill ill

lot lot lot sit sit sit wet wet wet

tex tex tex co. co. co.

9. Close the document without saving it.

Go!

Review First- and Second-Finger Reaches

MASCOT MAX

Don't worry if you make some mistakes. You may not be a track star yet!

Coach Carrie Says:

Okay, let's go back and practice those first- and second-finger reaches. Look at the first group of letters on the next page, *frf*. Close your eyes and mentally make the reaches.

Now get ready to type each of the reaches on the next page five times—with your eyes closed! And no peeking! Do this with each of the three-letter groups.

Trainer Terry Says:

You are better than you think you are right now. Prove it by typing with your eyes closed!

1. Open a new document and type the following list.

frf frf frf frf frf

ftf ftf ftf ftf ftf

fgf fgf fgf fgf fgf

fbf fbf fbf fbf fbf

fvf fvf fvf fvf fvf

juj juj juj juj juj

jyj jyj jyj jyj jyj

jhj jhj jhj jhj jhj

jnj jnj jnj jnj jnj

jmj jmj jmj jmj jmj

ded ded ded ded ded

dcd dcd dcd dcd dcd

kik kik kik kik kik

k,k k,k k,k k,k k,k

2. Leave the document open for the next race.

Review First- and Second-Finger Key Words

Trainer Terry Says:

1. Press the Enter key twice.
2. Now type the following key words for the first and second fingers of each hand. Again, type each word five times with your eyes closed!

JEFF THE REF

After you complete the key words, check what you typed. Retype any portion that you typed incorrectly.

fur fur fur fur fur

fun fun fun fun fun

gun gun gun gun gun

gum gum gum gum gum

guy guy guy guy guy

buy buy buy buy buy

but but but but but

hut hut hut hut hut

jut jut jut jut jut

vug vug vug vug vug

jim jim jim jim jim

dim dim dim dim dim

kid kid kid kid kid

red red red red red

cue cue cue cue cue

my, my, my, my, my

3. Leave your document open for the next race.

Practice First-, Second-, and Third-Finger Key Words

Coach Carrie Says:

Okay, now it's time to win the triple jump! Use the reaches of all three fingers for key words.

You are now beginning to build a memory pathway between your eyes and your fingers. When your eye sees a letter, the correct finger wants to move in the direction of that key.

Trainer Terry Says:

1. Press the Enter key twice.
2. Now type the following key words.

fur fur fur fun fun fun

gun gun gun gum gum gum

guy guy guy buy buy buy

but but but hut hut hut

jut jut jut vug vug vug jim jim jim dim dim dim

kid kid kid red red red cue cue cue my, my, my,

lot lot lot sit sit sit wet wet wet tex tex tex

co. co. co.

---

3. When you're done typing this meet, save the document as **triple**.
4. Close the document after you save it.

MEET #6 REACHING FOR MORE SPEED

In this meet, you'll learn the fourth-finger keys and continue to reach for more speed by practicing the keys for the first three fingers. By the end of this meet, you'll know:

- Fourth-Finger Reaches
- Fourth-Finger Key Words
- Review First- and Second- Finger Reaches
- Review Third-Finger Reaches
- Practice First-, Second-, and Third-Finger Key Words
- Key Words for All Fingers
- A Progress Report on You!

ALMOST THERE.

ON YOUR MARK

Fourth-Finger Reaches

Coach Carrie Says:

The fourth finger, or pinky, of your left hand types *a* on the home row. That finger also reaches up slightly left to type *q* and slightly right down to the bottom row to type *z*.

The fourth finger on your right hand types the semicolon (;) on the home row. That finger also reaches up slightly left to type *p* and slightly right down to the bottom row to type the forward slash (/).

Figure 1-19. Fourth-finger home keys and reaches

GET SET

Fourth-Finger Key Words

Coach Carrie Says:

Practice the fourth-finger reaches you just learned. Put your fingers through these motions without tapping the keys.

1. The fourth finger of your left hand touches *a* on the home row.

2. The fourth finger of your left hand touches *q*, up and slightly to the left.

3. The fourth finger of your left hand touches *z*, down and slightly to the right.

4. The fourth finger of your right hand touches the semicolon (;) on the home row.

5. The fourth finger of your right hand touches *p*, up and slightly to the left.

6. The fourth finger of your right hand touches the forward slash (/), down and slightly to the right.

Trainer Terry Says:

1. Open a new, blank document in Word.
2. Now build speed by typing the following letters and punctuation marks. Say each character to yourself as you type it.

---

aqa aqa aqa aqa aqa

aza aza aza aza aza

;p; ;p; ;p; ;p; ;p;

;/; ;/; ;/; ;/; ;/;

aqa aqa aqa aqa aqa

aza aza aza aza aza

;p; ;p; ;p; ;p; ;p;

;/; ;/; ;/; ;/; ;/;

---

3. Now type the following fourth-finger key words. After typing a new word once, try to speed up the next time you type it.

---

fat fat fat fat fat pat pat pat pat pat

zip zip zip zip zip qt. qt. qt. qt. qt. qt.

---

4. Leave your document open for the next race.

After you complete the race, check what you typed against the book. Retype any portion that you typed incorrectly.

Go!

Review First- and Second-Finger Reaches

Coach Carrie Says:

Get a quick jump off the starting block by practicing your first- and second-finger reaches. These letter combinations should be very familiar to you by now!

Trainer Terry Says:

1. Press Enter twice in your open document.
2. Try building your speed as you go farther in this race!

---

frf ftf fgf fbf fvf juj jyj jhj jnj jmj

frftfgfbfvf jujyjhjnjmj frftfgfbfv jujyjhjnjmj

ded dcd kik k,k ded dcd kik k,k ded dcd kik k,k

ded dcd kik k,k ded dcd kik k,k ded dcd kik k,k

---

3. Leave your document open.

Review Third-Finger Reaches

Trainer Terry Says:

Okay, now let's limber up your third fingers with these reaches. Type each three-letter group five times.

1. Press Enter twice.
2. After you take a look at each new set of letters, see if you can type the letters with your eyes closed!

---

sws sws sws sws sws sxs sxs sxs sxs sxs

lol lol lol lol lol l.l l.l l.l l.l l.l

3. Leave your document open for the next race.

Practice First-, Second-, and Third-Finger Key Words

Coach Carrie Says:

Let's review and practice all of the key words for the first three fingers. In the next race, put your fingers through the motions of typing each new word without actually tapping the keys. Then close your eyes and type the word five times.

Typing with your eyes closed like this helps you focus on the correct fingers and reaches. And it prevents you from looking at the screen or the keyboard.

JEFF THE REF

After you complete the race, check what you typed against the book. How well did you type the words without looking? I'll bet you did a pretty good job!

Trainer Terry Says:

1. Press Enter twice.
2. Type the following key words.

---

fur fur fur fur fur fun fun fun fun fun

gun gun gun gun gun gum gum gum gum gum

guy guy guy guy guy buy buy buy buy buy

but but but but but hut hut hut hut hut

jut jut jut jut jut vug vug vug vug vug

jim jim jim jim jim dim dim dim dim dim

kid kid kid kid kid red red red red red

cue cue cue cue cue my, my, my, my, my,

lot lot lot lot lot sit sit sit sit sit

wet wet wet wet wet tex tex tex tex tex

co. co. co. co. co.

---

3. Leave your document open for the next race.

Key Words for All Fingers

Coach Carrie Says:

Let's head for the finish line in record time! Type the following key words for all four fingers. Say each letter to yourself as you tap the key.

Trainer Terry Says:

1. Press Enter twice.
2. This time, press Enter at the end of each line. Remember to use the fourth finger of your right hand.

---

fur fun gun gum guy buy but hut jut vug

jim dim kid red cue my,

lot sit wet tex co.

fat pat zip qt.

fur fun gun gum guy buy but hut jut vug

jim dim kid red cue my,

lot sit wet tex co.

fat pat zip qt.

fur fun gun gum guy buy but hut jut vug

jim dim kid red cue my,

lot sit wet tex co.

fat pat zip qt.

---

3. Save the document you created for this meet as **keyword**.

 Mascot Max Says:

Congratulations! You have now completed the 25 key words that cover the entire alphabet, plus the comma and the period!

Coach Carrie Says:

 Keep the key-word list with you so that you can memorize the list by fingers:

First Fingers:
fur fun gun gum guy buy but hut jut vug

Second Fingers:
jim dim kid red cue my,

Third Fingers:
lot sit wet tex co.

Fourth Fingers:
fat pat zip qt.

GET UP TO SPEED

Now you can now use the All the Right Type software program on your book's CD for extra practice with the home-row keys. Start the program and then click the Learning Lab building.

In the Learn New Keys menu, click number **1—Home Row**, and then click <u>S</u>elect. Type the exercise as shown.

After you finish with the Learning Lab exercise, a check mark on the menu will show that you have completed it. Next, you can click the Practice Pavilion building to try a fun rowing race against the computer! Again, click number **1—Home Row** from the menu, and then click <u>S</u>elect. Start by clicking 15 WAM and then click OK. See if you can win the race!

If you want more practice on home-row keys, click the Skill Building and select **1—Home Row**.

MASCOT MAX

The secret to building your success is PRACTICE, PRACTICE, PRACTICE! From now on, resist any urge to look at the keyboard or the screen—this will only slow down your typing speed.

GOLD MEDAL

A Progress Report on You!

Coach Carrie Says:

Step up to the podium and accept the Gold Medal! You have now learned how to type the whole alphabet and the two most important punctuation marks, the comma and the period. You now have within your fingers the ability to type any word in the English language!

In your daily practice, you should type the 25 key words that contain the alphabet. In doing so, your fingers will memorize the location of each letter.

Congratulations on winning the Gold Medal with the great progress you are making. Carry the key word list with you and look at it from time to time to help you remember the words. What a way to build typing speed!

MEET #7
SPRINTING AGAINST THE CLOCK

Okay, it's time to see how fast you have become by testing your typing against the clock. In this meet, you'll learn:

- Typing Capital Letters
- Key Word Warm Up
- Typing the Alphabet
- Typing Against the Clock

ON YOUR MARK

Typing Capital Letters

Coach Carrie Says:

Capital letters are used to begin the first word of a new sentence and proper nouns. Proper nouns include names (such as Carrie), places (such as New York), and things (like the title of a book or magazine).

Hold down the Shift key with the fourth finger on your right hand to type a capital letter on the left side of the keyboard. Hold down the Shift key with the fourth finger on your left hand to type a capital letter on the right side of the keyboard.

Figure 1-20. Hold down the Shift keys to type capital letters.

If you are typing several capital letters in a row, such as USA, use the fourth finger of your left hand to press the Caps Lock key. Pressing this key makes all the letters you type capital letters. Press the Caps Lock key again to turn off the Caps Lock.

Fig 1-21. Use the Caps Lock Key to type several Capital letters in a row.

Trainer Terry Says:

Now let's practice typing capital letters.

Remember to press the Shift key with the fourth finger of the hand that isn't typing the letter.

1. Open a new blank document.
2. Type the following key words.

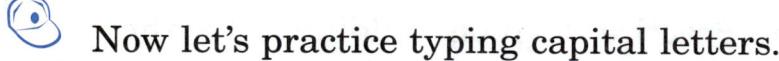

Fur Fun Gun Gum Guy

Buy But Hut Jut Vug Jim Dim

Kid Red Cue My, Lot Sit Wet Tex Co.

Fat Pat Zip Qt.

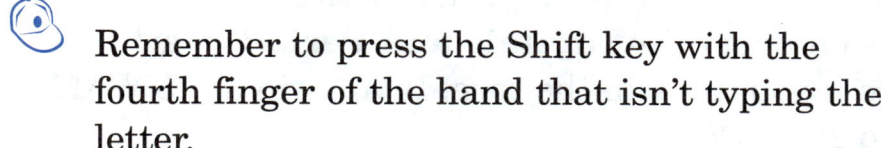

3. Close the document without saving it.

MEG THE MIKE

Some keyboards have a light that goes on when you press the Caps Lock key. When the first letter of each word is capitalized, you are typing in *initial caps*. When all the letters of a word are capitalized, you are typing in *all caps*.

JEFF THE REF

After you finish the race, check what you typed against the book. Did you type all the capital letters correctly?

GET UP TO SPEED

Now you can now use the All the Right Type software program on your book's CD for extra practice with capital letters. Start the program and then click the Learning Lab building.

In the Learn New Keys menu, click number **2—E and U**, and then click <u>S</u>elect. Type the exercise as shown. Also practice the Learning Lab exercise number **3—Capitals and Period**. After you finish with the Learning Lab exercise, a check mark on the menu will show that you have completed it.

Next, you can click the Practice Pavilion building to try the rowing race against the computer. Again, practice number **2—E and U**, as well as number **3—Capitals and Period**. Start with 15 WAM and see if you can win the race! If you win at 15 WAM, try moving up to 20 WAM.

If you want more practice on capitals and home-row keys, click the Skill Building and select **2—E and U**, as well as **3—Capitals and Period**.

GET SET

Key Word Warm Up

Trainer Terry Says:

Let's try a little memory game to warm up for timed typing.

1. Open a new document.
2. Close your eyes and type the 25 key words from memory.
3. After you finish, check your typing against the list below.

Coach Carrie Says:

Don't peek! This drill will give you an idea of how many key words you remember. If you recall even half of them, you are making great progress. Continue to memorize the key words in your spare time.

fur fun gun gum guy buy but hut jut vug jim

dim kid red cue my, lot sit wet tex co. fat pat

zip qt.

JEFF THE REF

How well did you do? I'll bet you remembered quite a few of the key words!

Trainer Terry Says:

1. Make sure your document is still open.
2. Now type the key-word list twice. Say the letters to yourself as you tap the keys.

fur fun gun gum guy buy but hut jut vug jim dim

kid red cue my, lot sit wet tex co. fat pat zip qt.

fur fun gun gum guy buy but hut jut vug jim dim

kid red cue my, lot sit wet tex co. fat pat zip qt.

3. Leave your document open.

 Go!

Typing the Alphabet

Coach Carrie Says:

The following race uses all the letters of the alphabet. You will now be adding the alphabet to your regular warm-up routine.

Trainer Terry Says:

1. Press Enter twice.
2. Say and think each letter as you type it.
   Keep your eyes only on the book as you type.

ab ab ab cde cde cde fg fg fg

abcdefg abcdefg abcdefg

hi hi hi jkl jkl jkl hijkl hijkl hijkl

abcdefghijkl mnop mnop mnop

abcdefghijklmnop qrs qrs qrs tuv tuv tuv

qrstuv qrstuv qrstuv abcdefghijklmnopqrstuv

wxyz wxyz wxyz

abcdefghijklmnopqrstuvwxyz

abcdefghijklmnopqrstuvwxyz

JEFF THE REF

After you finish the race, check what you typed against the book. Retype any portion that you typed incorrectly.

3. Close the document without saving it.

GOLD MEDAL

Typing Against the Clock

Coach Carrie Says:

Let's go for the gold! The only way to find out how much your typing speed is improving is to take a *timed writing*. In a timed writing, you type an exercise for a certain length of time. Timed writings can be for half a minute, a minute, even up to two or three minutes when you gain more speed.

Typing speed is measured in *words a minute* or *WAM*. Because words vary in the number of letters they have, a standard word in typing is five keystrokes. This includes punctuation marks and spaces.

Look at the timed writing on page 71. The number at the end of each line in the timed writing exercise tells you how many standard words are in the line. The scale at the bottom of the exercise tells you how many words you typed in an incomplete line.

In the next race, if you typed all of the first line in a 30-second timing, that means you typed 10 standard words. If you typed all of the first line and also typed through the word *sit* on the second line, that means you typed 14 standard words—10 on the first line plus 4 on the second.

Here's a hint: On the scale below the exercise on the next page, see where the word *sit* falls.

Trainer Terry Says:

Give it a try now by sprinting against the clock! Type the following exercise ten times for 30 seconds each.

1. Open a new document.
2. Press Enter twice between each timing.
3. Write down your timed writing speeds and note the best one. See if you can increase your speed as you go.

---

fur fun gun gum guy buy but hut jut vug jim dim kid   **Words 10**

red cue my, lot sit wet tex co. fat pat zip qt.   **Words 20**

...1 ...2 ...3 ...4 ...5 ...6 ...7 ...8 ...9 ...10

---

4. When you finish, save your work on this meet as **time**.
5. Print one copy of the document, and then close it.

Coach Carrie Says:

To calculate your WAM typing speed for this exercise, multiply the standard words you typed by two, because you only typed for half a minute.

After you finish all ten timings, go back and figure out your WAM speed for each timing.

GET UP TO SPEED

Now you can now use the All the Right Type software program on your book's CD to take a timed writing. Start the program and then click the Testing Center building.

In the Testing Center dialog box, click number **S1M7TIME**, and then click <u>S</u>elect. Click 1 minute as the duration for the timed writing, and then click OK. Read the information about how to take the timed writing on screen, and then click OK again.

You will be timed as you type the 25 key words. At the end of the timed writing, a dialog box will pop up showing you how many words a minute you typed, as well as how many errors you made. Click Campus to return to the software's main menu or click <u>R</u>edo Test to try again.

MEET #8
WHAT'S YOUR SPEED?

In every race, it's important to know what your speed is. How many seconds faster or slower did you run? It's also important to know how to type numbers in your documents. In this Game you will learn how to use the number keys on the top row of the keyboard to type numbers in text. You'll also do some warm-up drills to get ready for your next timed writing by:

- Learning to Type Numbers
- Warm-Up Drills
- Timed Writing

ON YOUR MARK

Learning to Type Numbers

Coach Carrie Says:

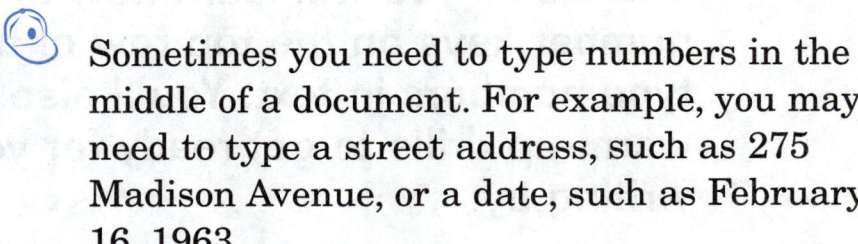
Sometimes you need to type numbers in the middle of a document. For example, you may need to type a street address, such as 275 Madison Avenue, or a date, such as February 16, 1963.

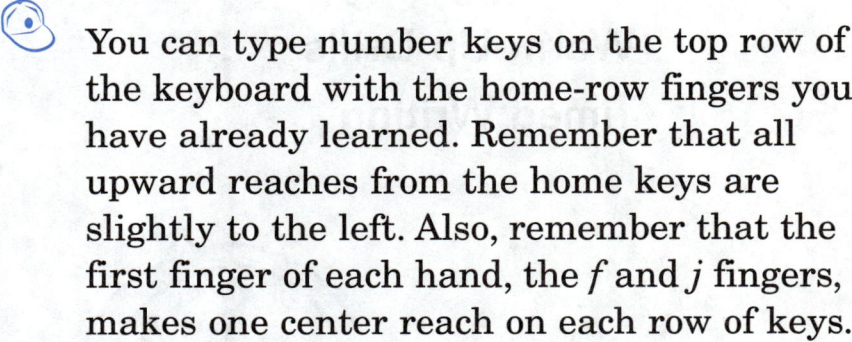
You can type number keys on the top row of the keyboard with the home-row fingers you have already learned. Remember that all upward reaches from the home keys are slightly to the left. Also, remember that the first finger of each hand, the *f* and *j* fingers, makes one center reach on each row of keys.

JEFF THE REF

You can also type numbers using the number keypad at the right of your computer keyboard, which you will learn to use in Season 3.

Look at Figure 1-22 to see the reaches each finger makes to type the number keys:

- The fourth finger on the left hand, the *a* finger, reaches up and to the left to type *1*.
- The third finger on the left hand, the *s* finger, reaches up and to the left to type *2*.
- The second finger on the left hand, the *d* finger, reaches up and to the left to type *3*.
- The first finger on the left hand, the *f* finger, reaches up and to the left to type *4*. This finger also reaches up and slightly to the right to type *5*.
- The first finger on the right hand, the *j* finger, reaches up and to the left to type *6*. This finger also reaches up and to the left to type *7*.
- The second finger on the right hand, the *k* finger, reaches up and to the left to type *8*.
- The third finger on the right hand, the *l* finger, reaches up and to the left to type *9*.
- The fourth finger on the right hand, the *;* finger, reaches up and to the left to type *0*.

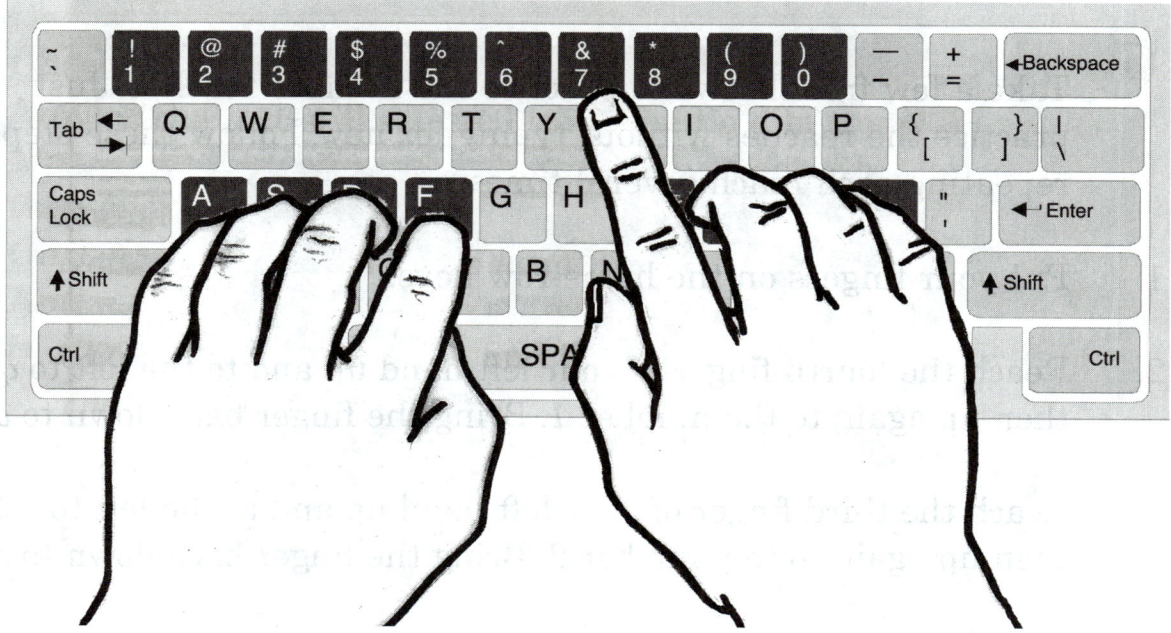

Figure 1-22. Number key reaches from the home-row keys

 Remember, the number *0* (zero) is different than the letter *o*. Also, the number *1* is different than the letter *l*, even though they look much the same.

GET SET

Trainer Terry Says:

 Take a few free throws to practice the number reaches. Just practice the reaches without typing for now. Follow these steps, repeating each reach several times:

1. Put your fingers on the home-row keys.

2. Reach the fourth finger of your left hand up and to the left to *q* and then up again to the number *1*. Bring the finger back down to *a*.

3. Reach the third finger of your left hand up and to the left to *w* and then up again to the number *2*. Bring the finger back down to *s*.

4.   Reach the second finger of your left hand up and to the left to *e* and then up again to the number *3*. Bring the finger back down to *d*.

5.   Reach the first finger of your left hand up and to the left to *r* and then up again to the number *4*. Bring the finger back down to *f*.

6.   Reach the first finger of your left hand up and to the left to *r* and then up again to the number *5*. Bring the finger back down to *f*.

7.   Reach the first finger of your right hand up and to the left to *y* and then up again to the number *6*. Bring the finger back down to *j*.

8.   Reach the first finger of your right hand up and to the left to u and then up again to the number *7*. Bring the finger back down to *j*.

9.   Reach the second finger of your right hand up and to the left to *i* and then up again to the number *8*. Bring the finger back down to *k*.

10.   Reach the third finger of your right hand up and to the left to *o* and then up again to the number *9*. Bring the finger back down to *l*.

11.   Reach the fourth finger of your right hand up and to the left to p and then up again to the number *0*. Bring the finger back down to *;*.

12.   Now repeat the number reaches for each finger by reaching directly from the home-row keys to the numbers with each finger.

Trainer Terry Says:

Now let's try numbers and letters together.

1. Open a new document.
2. Type the following exercise.

a1;0 a1;0 a1;0 a1;0 a1;0

s219 s219 s219 s219 s219

d3k8 d3k8 d3k8 d3k8 d3k8

f4j7 f4j7 f4j7 f4j7 f4j7

f5j6 f5j6 f5j6 f5j6 f5j6

a1;0 a1;0 a1;0 a1;0 a1;0

s219 s219 s219 s219 s219

d3k8 d3k8 d3k8 d3k8 d3k8

f4j7 f4j7 f4j7 f4j7 f4j7

f5j6 f5j6 f5j6 f5j6 f5j6

3. Leave your document open for the following drills.

Warm-Up Drills

 Okay, let's warm up with our key words. Then type the **a;sl** drill, also known as the Expert's Rhythm Drill.

1. Press Enter twice.
2. Type the following drills.

---

fur fun gun gum guy buy but hut jut vug

jim dim kid red cue my, lot sit wet tex co.

fat pat zip qt.

ab cde fg hi jkl mn op qrs tuv wxyz

abcdefg hijklmnop qrstuv wxyz

abcdefghijklmnopqrstuvwxyz

ab cde fg hi jkl mn op qrs tuv wxyz

abcdefg hijklmnop qrstuv wxyz

abcdefghijklmnopqrstuvwxyz

asdf fdsa jkl; ;lkj asdf fdsa

jkl; ;lkj asdf fdsa jkl; ;lkj

asdf fdsa jkl; ;lkj asdf fdsa

jkl; ;lkj asdf fdsa jkl; ;lkj

a; sl dk fj gh gh fj dk sl a; sl dk fj gh

gh fj dk sl a;

a; sl dk fj gh gh fj dk sl a; sl dk fj gh

gh fj dk sl a;

a;sldkfjghghfjdksl a;sldkfjghghfjdksla;

a;sldkfjghghfjdksla;

a;sldkfjghghfjdksl a;sldkfjghghfjdksla;

a;sldkfjghghfjdksla;

---

3. Close your document without saving it.

JEFF THE REF

How well did you do? Check what you typed for errors. Did you get the feel of the rhythm in the Expert's Rhythm Drill?

GET UP TO SPEED

Now you can now use the All the Right Type software program on your book's CD for extra practice with the number keys. Start the program and then click the Learning Lab building.

In the Learn New Keys menu, scroll down and click as many of the number exercises as you want to practice. The number exercises are near the end of the list. Type the exercises as shown. After you finish with the Learning Lab exercise, a check mark on the menu will show that you have completed it.

Next, click the Practice Pavilion building to try the rowing races against the computer. Do as many of the number races as you like. Scroll down the Practice Pavilion menu to select the number races. Start with 15 WAM and see if you can win the race! If you win at 15 WAM, try moving up to 20 WAM.

If you want more practice on the number keys, click the Skill Building and scroll down to select the exercises for the number keys. Good luck and have fun!

Go!

Coach Carrie Says:

Okay, now try to score some points with your next timed writing! Take five 30-second timings on the following exercise. Double space between timings (press the Enter key twice).

Think of the space or punctuation mark after a word as part of the word you just typed. Press the spacebar with the same smooth, rhythmic beat as the letters.

JEFF THE REF

After you complete the race, check what you typed against the book. Retype any words that you typed incorrectly.

If the first letter of your first word automatically changes to a capital letter, don't worry. Microsoft Word's AutoCorrect feature has capitalized it for you automatically. You'll learn how to change features like AutoCorrect later in the book.

Also, don't worry if what you typed is only two lines long when the book shows four. Microsoft Word allows more of the words to fit on a line.

WHAT'S YOUR WAM?

To find out your score, look at the number to the right of the last complete line you typed. Then, if you typed a partial line, look at the number scale on the bottom and see where your line ends. Add that number to your whole line number to find out your WAM.

Don't forget: A standard word in typing is five keystrokes.

MASCOT MAX

Remember, click **File** and then **Save** to save your work.

Trainer Terry Says:

1. Open a new document.
2. If you complete the entire paragraph before the time is up, start at the beginning again and keep typing!

	WORDS
You have come a long way in a very short time. You	10
have learned all the keys and can strike these keys	20
without looking down at your fingers, at a chart, or	30
at your screen. You will get better and better and	40
make fewer and fewer errors.	

...1...2...3...4...5...6...7...8...9...10

---

3. When you finish, save your work on this Game as **score**. Then close it.

GET UP TO SPEED

Now you can now use the All the Right Type software program on your book's CD to take a timed writing. Start the program and then click the Testing Center building.

In the Testing Center dialog box, click number **S2G2TIME**, and then click Select. Click 1 minute as the duration for the timed writing, and then click OK. Read the information about how to take the timed writing on screen, and then click OK again.

You will be timed on the paragraph. At the end of the timed writing, a dialog box will pop up showing you how many words per minute you typed as well as how many errors you made. Click Campus to return to the software's main menu or click Redo Test to try again.

MEET #9
JUMPING HURDLES

In some races, runners need to be able to jump hurdles and still run for speed. This can be difficult, but it can also make the race more exciting!

In typing, you sometimes need to make a difficult reach to type special characters. This Game will teach you how to reach for the special character keys on your computer keyboard. You'll learn:

- Special Character Reaches
- Special Characters on the Top Row
- Warm-Up Drills
- Review Numbers and Letters
- Timed Writings

ON YOUR MARK

Special Character Reaches

Coach Carrie Says:

Special characters can be marks of punctuation or symbols used as abbreviations. Some special character keys are located on or near the home-row keys. Many others are located on the top row of the keyboard.

First, let's learn about the special character keys that are on or near the home row of the keyboard:

- The fourth finger of your right hand reaches up one row next to the letter *p* to type the left bracket (*[*). This same finger also reaches up one row and to the right to type the right bracket (*]*).

- Press and hold down the Shift key while you type the brackets if you want to type the "curly" brackets: *{* or *}*. The "curly" brackets are also called braces.

- Press and hold down the Shift key while you type the semicolon key (;) and you will get the colon (:).

- One key to the right of the semicolon gives you the apostrophe ('). Press and hold down the Shift key while you type the apostrophe key to type quotation marks (" and ").

- Press and hold down the Shift key while you type the forward slash key to get the question mark (?).

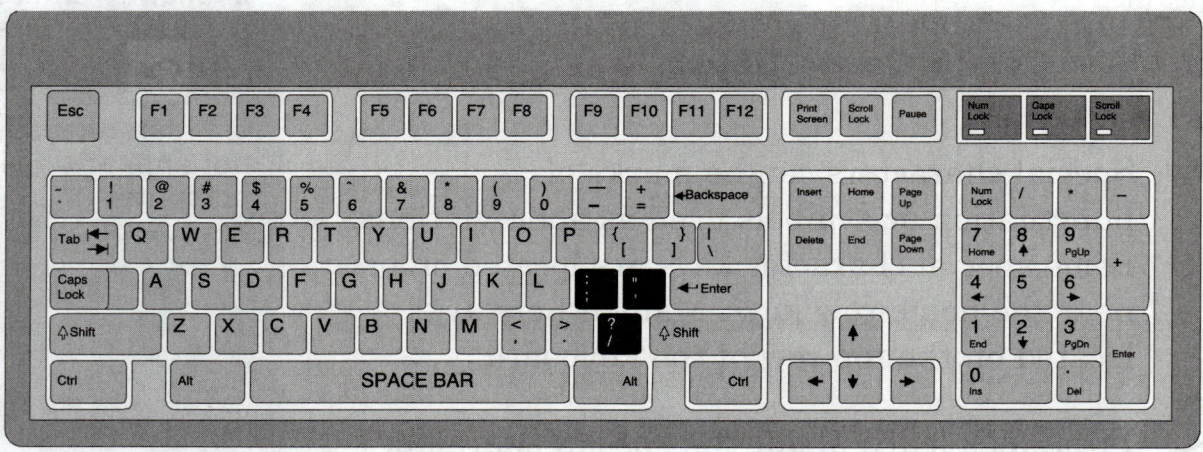

Figure 1-23. Type these special keys with the fourth finger of your right hand.

GET SET

Trainer Terry Says:

JEFF THE REF

Remember to use the Shift key when typing the braces ({ and }), the quotation marks (" and "), the colon (:), and the question mark (?).

Let's practice the special character reaches. Just practice the reaches without typing for now. Follow these steps:

1. Put your fingers on the home-row keys.
2. Reach the fourth finger of your right hand up to the *p*, then over to the left bracket (*[*). Bring the finger back down to *;*.
3. Reach the fourth finger of your right hand up to the *p*, then over to the right bracket (*]*). Bring the finger back down to *;*.
4. Reach the fourth finger of your right hand over to the apostrophe ('). Bring the finger back to *;*.
5. Reach the fourth finger of your right hand down to the forward slash (/). Bring the finger back up to *;*.
6. Open a new document in Word.
7. Now try the special character reaches you just learned by typing the following exercise.

---

p[p] p{ p} p[p] ;:; ;:; ;:; ;'" ;'" ;'" p/? p/? p/?

p[p] p{ p} p[p] ;:; ;:; ;:; ;'" ;'" ;'" p/? p/? p/?

p[p] p{ p} p[p] ;:; ;:; ;:; ;'" ;'" ;'" p/? p/? p/?

---

8. Close the document without saving it.

Special Characters on the Top Row

Coach Carrie Says:

Most special characters on your computer keyboard are found on the top row. They appear on the number keys, above the numerals. You use the same number-key reaches you've already learned, but you press Shift as you tap the number keys to make the special characters.

For example, to type an exclamation point (*!*), you reach up to the top row with your left pinky to *1*, then press the Shift key with your right pinky while you strike the *1*.

Figure 1-24 shows the special character keys on the top row of the keyboard. Refer to the following Training Table to learn about all the special character reaches.

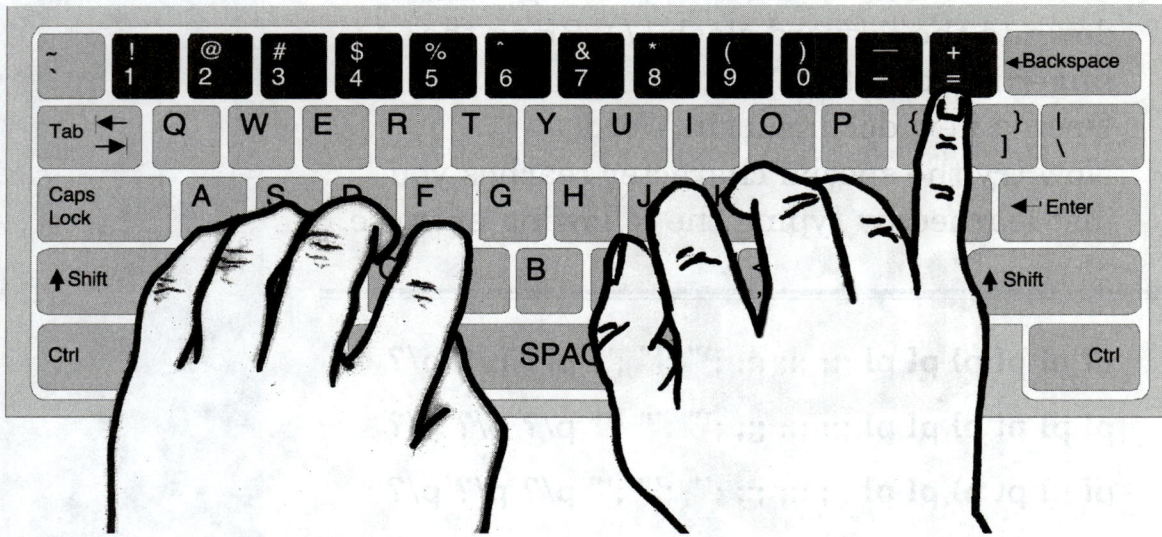

Figure 1-24. Use the Shift key and the top row number reaches to type these special characters.

Training Table: Special Character Keys

Symbol	Finger	Reach
! (exclamation point)	**A** finger	Reach to **1**, press **right Shift** key, strike **1** to get **!**. Return to home row.
@ (at sign)	**S** finger	Reach to **2**, press **right Shift** key, strike **2** to get **@**. Return to home row.
# (number sign)	**D** finger	Reach to **3**, press **right Shift** key, strike **3** to get **#**. Return to home row.
$ (dollar sign)	**F** finger	Reach to **4**, press **right Shift** key, strike **4** to get **$**. Return to home row.
% (percent sign)	**F** finger	Reach to **5**, press **right Shift** key, strike **5** to get **%**. Return to home row.
^ (caret)	**J** finger	Reach to **6**, press **left Shift** key, strike **6** to get **^**. Return to home row.
& (ampersand)	**J** finger	Reach to **7**, press **left Shift** key, strike **7** to get **&**. Return to home row.
* (asterisk)	**K** finger	Reach to **8**, press **left Shift** key, strike **8** to get *****. Return to home row.

Training Table: Special Character Keys

Symbol	Finger	Reach
((left parenthesis)	L finger	Reach to **9**, press **left Shift** key, strike **9** to get **(**. Return to home row.
) (right parenthesis)	; finger	Reach to **0**, press **left Shift** key, strike **0** to get **)**. Return to home row.
- (hyphen)	; finger	Reach to -. Return to home row.
_ (underline)	; finger	Reach to -, press **left Shift** key to get _. Return to home row.
= (equal sign)	; finger	Reach to =. Return to home row.
+ (plus sign)	; finger	Reach to =, press the **left Shift** key to get +. Return to home row.
[(left bracket)	; finger	Reach up and right to get [. Return to the ;.
] (right bracket)	; finger	Reach up and over more to get]. Return to the ;.
{ (left brace)	; finger	Reach to [, press the **left Shift** key to get {. Return to the ;.
} (right brace)	; finger	Reach to], press the **left Shift** key to get }. Return to the ;.

GET SET

Trainer Terry Says:

Now let's practice the special character reaches for the top row.

1. Put your fingers on the home-row keys.

2. Reach the fourth finger of your left hand up to the *1*, which you use to get *!*. Bring the finger back down to *a*.

3. Reach the third finger of your left hand up to *2*, which you use to get *@*. Bring the finger back down to *s*.

4. Reach the second finger of your left hand up to *3*, which you use to get *#*. Bring the finger back down to *d*.

5. Reach the first finger of your left hand up to *4*, which you use to get *$*. Bring the finger back down to *f*.

JEFF THE REF

Remember to touch the Shift key with the hand opposite the one you are using to make your reaches to the top row.

MASCOT MAX

You already know the @ symbol from e-mail addresses!

6.   Reach the first finger of your left hand up to *5*, which you use to get %. Bring the finger back down to *f*.

7.   Reach the first finger of your right hand up to *6*, which you use to get ^. Bring the finger back down to *j*.

8.   Reach the first finger of your right hand up to *7*, which you use to get &. Bring the finger back down to *j*.

9.   Reach the second finger of your right hand up to *8*, which you use to get *. Bring the finger back down to *k*.

10.   Reach the third finger of your right hand up to *9*, which you use to get (. Bring the finger back down to *l*.

11.   Reach the fourth finger of your right hand up to *0*, which you use to get). Bring the finger back down to *;*.

12.   Reach the fourth finger of your right hand up to -, which you use to get _. Bring the finger back down to *;*.

13.   Reach the fourth finger of your right hand up to =, which you use to get +. Bring the finger back down to *;*.

Trainer Terry Says:

1. Open a new document.
2. Now type the top row special character reaches you just learned.

---

a1!a a1!a a1!a s2@s s2@s s2@s d3#d d3#d d3#d f4$f f4$f f4$f f5%f f5%f f5%f j6^j j6^j j6^j j7&j j7&j j7&j k8*k k8*k k8*k l9(l l9(l l9(l ;0); ;0); ;0); ;-_; ;-_; ;-_; ;=+; ;=+; ;=+;

Use the exclamation point to express excitement!

My e-mail address is joef@aol.com.

Use a #2 pencil when taking this exam. You need to score 70% to pass the test.

The price of milk at the A&P once was less than $1 per gallon.

Use the caret (^) to mark where something should be inserted.

The asterisk (*) is used to mark footnotes in text.

Parentheses, 0, are used to set off optional text.

Two hyphens (--) make a dash.

You can find solutions to common math problems such as 2 + 2 = 4 at the http://www.math_masters.com web site.

JEFF THE REF

Remember to use the Shift key as necessary for typing top row special characters.

---

3. Leave the document open for the next drill.

Warm-Up Drills

 Trainer Terry Says:

Okay, let's warm up with our key words.

1. Press Enter twice.
2. Close your eyes and type the 25 key words from memory.
3. After you finish, open your eyes and see how many you remembered.
4. Then type the key words again while looking at the list.

---

fur fun gun gum guy buy but hut jut vug jim dim

kid red cue my, lot sit wet tex co. fat pat zip qt.

5. Now type the following drills:

ab cde fg hi jkl mn op qrs tu vwx yz

abcdefg hijklmnop qrstu vwxyz

abcdefghijklmnopqrstuvwxyz

ab cde fg hi jkl mn op qrs tu vwx yz

abcdefg hijklmnop qrstu vwxyz

abcdefghijklmnopqrstuvwxyz

asdf fdsa jkl; ;lkj asdf fdsa

jkl; ;lkj asdf fdsa jkl; ;lkj

asdf fdsa jkl; ;lkj asdf fdsa

jkl; ;lkj asdf fdsa jkl; ;lkj

a; sl dk fj gh gh fj dk sl

a; sl dk fj gh gh fj dk sl a;

a; sl dk fj gh gh fj dk sl

a; sl dk fj gh gh fj dk sl a;

a;sldkfjghghfjdksla; a;sldkfjghghfjdksla;

a;sldkfjghghfjdksla;

a;sldkfjghghfjdksla; a;sldkfjghghfjdksla;

a;sldkfjghghfjdksla;

MASCOT MAX

Keep your eyes on the book when you type and remember to build speed with rhythm.

ALMOST THERE.

6. Keep your document open for the next drill.

JEFF THE REF

Cool off! You might want to take a break between each drill and shake your fingers out if you're getting tired. But don't take too long of a break, because we're working on building your typing strength!

Review Numbers and Letters

Coach Carrie Says:

Let's take a few moments to review typing numbers and letters together.
1. Press Enter twice.
2. Focus your attention on each letter and number as you type.

a1;0 a1;0 a1;0 a1;0 a1;0

s219 s219 s219 s219 s219

d3k8 d3k8 d3k8 d3k8 d3k8

f4j7 f4j7 f4j7 f4j7 f4j7

f5j6 f5j6 f5j6 f5j6 f5j6

a1;0 a1;0 a1;0 a1;0 a1;0

s219 s219 s219 s219 s219

d3k8 d3k8 d3k8 d3k8 d3k8

f4j7 f4j7 f4j7 f4j7 f4j7

f5j6 f5j6 f5j6 f5j6 f5j6

3. Leave your document open.

Trainer Terry Says:

Now think of the home-key finger you use to reach for each number. For example, think *s* and with that finger reach up to the top row to type *2*; think *l* and reach up to the top row with that finger to type *9*.

1. Press Enter twice.
2. Type the following numbers.

---

10 10 10 10 10 29 29 29 29 29 38 38 38 38 38

47 47 47 47 47 56 56 56 56 56

10 10 10 10 10 29 29 29 29 29 38 38 38 38 38

47 47 47 47 47 56 56 56 56 56

---

3. When you've finished these drills, close the document without saving it.

 GET UP TO SPEED

Now you can now use the All the Right Type software program on your book's CD for extra practice with the some of the special keys. Start the program and then click the Learning Lab building.

In the Learn New Keys menu, scroll down and click number **12— X and Apostrophe**. You can also try number **13—Comma and ?** and as many of the number exercises as you want to practice. The special key and number exercises are near the end of the list. Type the exercises as shown. After you finish with the Learning Lab exercise, a check mark on the menu will show that you have completed it.

Next, you can click the Practice Pavilion building to try the rowing races against the computer. Do as many of the special character and number races as you like. Scroll down the Practice Pavilion menu to select the number races. Start with 15 WAM and see if you can win the race! If you win at 15 WAM, try moving up to 20 WAM.

If you want more practice on the number keys, click the Skill Building and scroll down to select the exercises for the special character keys and number keys. Good luck and have fun!

Go!
Timed Writings

Coach Carrie Says:

Let's take six 30-second timings on the following paragraph starting on the first line each time. Double-space between timings (press the Enter key twice).

Remember to double the number of words typed in the half-minute timing to get the one-minute rate.

Trainer Terry Says:

1. Open up a new document in Word.
2. If you complete the entire paragraph before the time is up, start at the beginning again and keep typing!

JEFF THE REF

Remember not to stop or look up if you feel yourself typing a wrong key. Keep moving ahead, and then go back and check what you typed against the book.

WHAT'S YOUR WAM?

To find out your score, look at the number to the right of the last complete line you typed. Then, if you typed a partial line, look at the number scale on the bottom and see where your line ends. Add that number to your whole line number to find out how many words per minute you typed.

Don't forget: A standard word in typing is five keystrokes.

WORDS

To be sure that you are being fair to yourself, do everything   12

you can to make sure that you are really trying to learn to   24

type by touch--that means that you do not depend on seeing   36

letters on the computer's keys or on a keyboard chart. Also,   48

resist the idea of checking the strokes as they appear on the   60

computer screen. Every step you take to avoid looking will   72

help and will pay you a very big reward.

...1...2...3...4...5...6...7...8...9...10...11...12

3.   When you finish, save your work on this Game as **rim**, then close the document.

GET UP TO SPEED

Now you can now use the All the Right Type software program on your book's CD to take a timed writing. Start the program and then click the Testing Center building.

In the Testing Center dialog box, click number **S2G4TIME**, and then click <u>S</u>elect. Click 1 minute as the duration for the timed writing, and then click OK. Read the information about how to take the timed writing on screen, and then click OK again.

You will be timed on the computer as you type the paragraph. At the end of the timed writing, a dialog box will pop up showing you how many words per minute you typed, as well as how many errors you made. Click <u>C</u>ampus to return to the software's main menu or click <u>R</u>edo Test to try again.

SEASON 2

BASKETBALL
PUTTING IT ALL
TOGETHER—WORD
PROCESSING BASICS

During Basketball Season, you'll build a variety of word processing skills. You'll learn how to edit and format documents in Microsoft Word, and you'll learn about other word processing features such as numbered lists, finding and replacing text, and the spell checker.

If you're ready, lace up your gym shoes and let's hit the court!

GAME #1
TIPPING OFF
WITH THE
FUNDAMENTALS

In this Game, you start with the fundamentals of word processing: inserting, editing, and deleting text. You'll learn to open a document, move the insertion point around, and select text you want to edit.

These are the basics—like passing, dribbling, and shooting in basketball. Using these word processing skills, you can turn a rough draft into a polished document that says exactly what you want to say! So let's get started by:

- **Moving the Insertion Point**
- **Opening a Document**
- **Selecting Text**
- **Proofreading Marks**
- **Inserting, Editing, and Deleting Text**

CHALK TALK

Moving the Insertion Point

Coach Carrie Says:

 To edit in Microsoft Word, just move the insertion point to wherever you want to make a change. Then, you can insert a new word or letter or delete an existing word or letter.

 For example, if you typed *baskettball* and then realized that you had typed too many *ts*, you would first move the insertion point in front of the extra *t* and then make the change.

 To move the insertion point, you can use special keys on your keyboard, as in Figure 2-1, or click the mouse pointer where you want the insertion point to be.

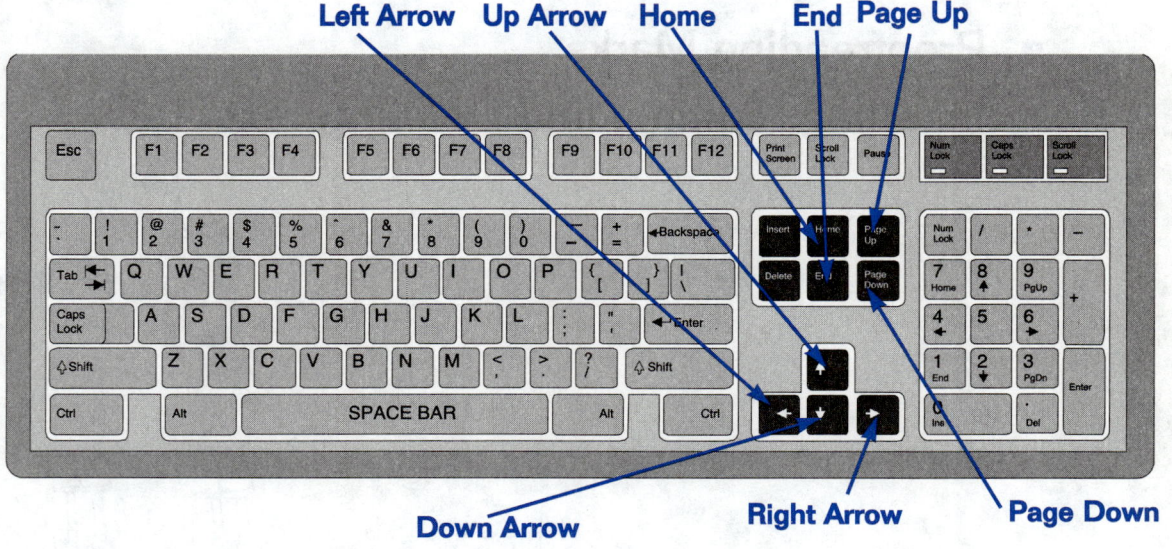

Figure 2-1. Computer keyboard

Take a look at the following Training Table for a summary of the keys that are used to move the insertion point.

Training Table: Move the Insertion Point

Key	What It Does
Up Arrow	Moves insertion point up one line. Press and hold down to scroll up.
Down Arrow	Moves insertion point down one line. Press and hold down to scroll down.
Left Arrow	Moves insertion point left one character. Press and hold down to continue moving Insertion point left.
Right Arrow	Moves insertion point right one character. Press and hold down to continue moving Insertion point right.
Home	Moves insertion point to the beginning of the current line.
End	Moves insertion point to the end of the current line.
Page Up	Moves insertion point up one screen.
Page Down	Moves insertion point down one screen.

 PC users, press and hold down the Ctrl+Home to move the insertion point to the beginning of the document. Press Ctrl+End key to move to the very end of the document.

Mac users, press Command+Home to move the insertion point to the beginning of the document. Press Command+End to move to the end of the document.

JEFF THE REF

You may see a set of number keys on your computer keyboard also labeled with arrows, Home, End, Page Up, and Page Down. These keys have two jobs: When the Num Lock light is on, you use the keys to type numbers; when the light is off, you use them to move the insertion point. You will learn more about using these number keys in Season 3.

Opening a Document

Coach Carrie Says:

 Often, you will make editing changes to an existing document. To open a document that you saved earlier, click the File menu, and then click Open.

 The Open dialog box will appear. Here you can type the file name of the document or use the mouse to select the drive and/or folder where the document has been saved. Click the Look in menu arrow to select a drive or folder, and then click on the document you want to open. You can also type the document name in the File name text box. Once you have selected the right document, click Open.

Click on the document you want to open

Click here to select drive or folder.

Or type the document name here

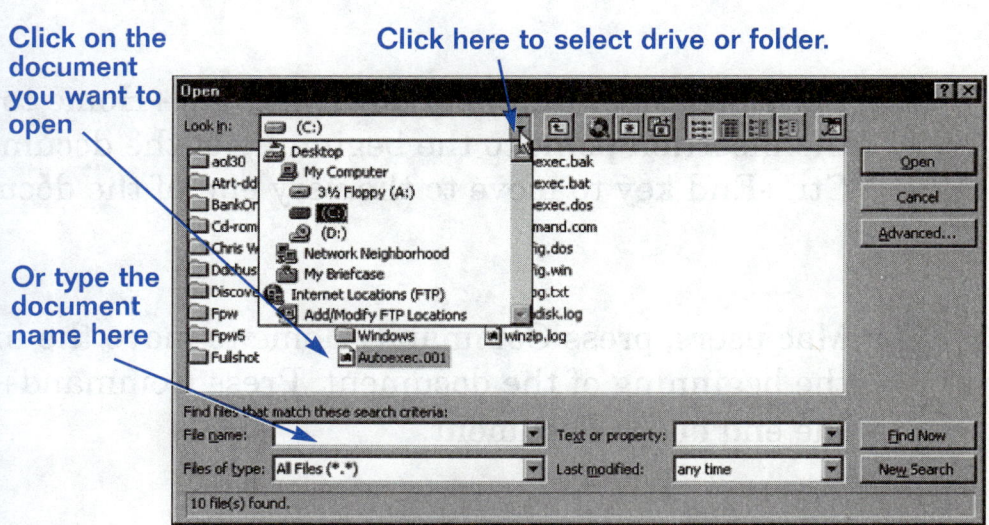

Figure 2-2. The Open dialog box

FREE THROWS

Trainer Terry Says:

Let's try opening a document now.

1. Start Word.
   If you forget how to start Word, check back in Season 1, Meet 1.
2. Insert the CD from the back of this book into your CD-Rom drive.
3. Click File, and then click Open.
   The Open dialog box appears.
4. Click the arrow next to the Look in menu.
   The menu opens.
5. Click the CD drive on the menu.
   A series of folders will appear in the main window of the dialog box.
6. Double-click the student data folder.
   A number of Word documents will appear in the main window.
7. Click **01league**, and then click Open.
8. After the file opens, save it as **league**.

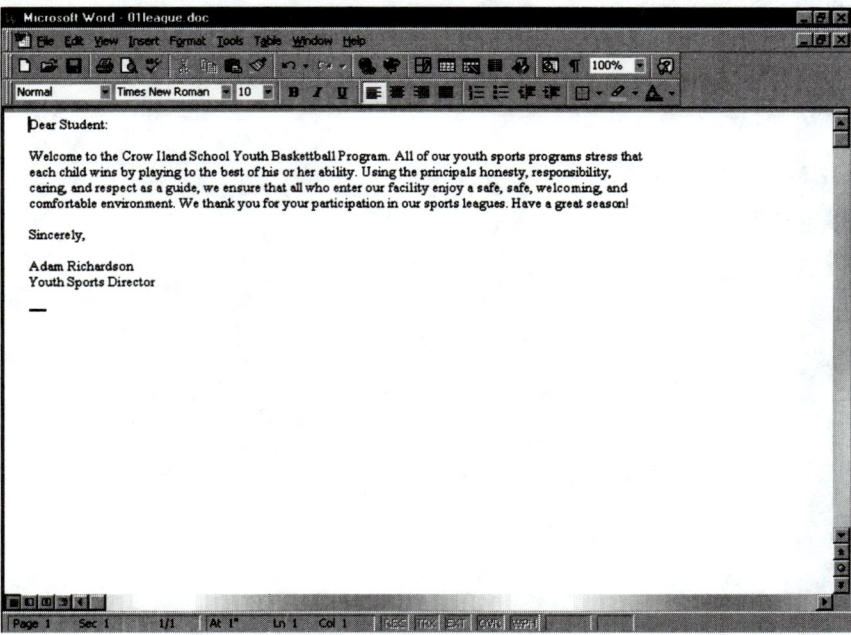

Figure 2-3. This is the document you opened.

JEFF THE REF

If you don't have the CD that comes with your book, check with your teacher about where to locate the data files. Also, check with your teacher about where you should save the new document called **league.**

If you notice spelling errors or other mistakes in this document, don't worry—and don't correct them! We'll fix these later in this game.

9. Press the Page Up key to make sure the insertion point is at the top of the document.

10. Press the Down Arrow key twice.
The insertion point moves to the beginning of the sentence starting with the word Welcome.

11. Press the End key.
The insertion point moves to the end of the line.

12. Use the arrow keys to move the insertion point to the beginning of the word *thank* in the final line of the letter.

13. Use the mouse to move the insertion point to the beginning of the word *Youth* in the first line of the letter.

14. Press Home to move the insertion point to the beginning of the line.

15. Press Page Down.
The insertion point moves down one screen.

Selecting Text

Coach Carrie Says:

To edit a Word document, you should know how to select text. Selected text can be deleted or replaced with new text.

There are several ways to select text. To select an entire word, position the mouse pointer over the word and double-click. The word appears highlighted, as in Figure 2-4.

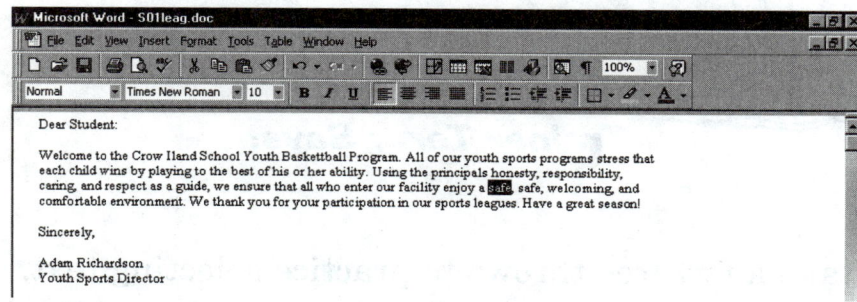

Figure 2-4. The word *safe* has been selected.

You can also select text using the keyboard. Press and hold Shift key and then press either the Left or Right Arrow key.

To select an entire word using the keyboard:

PC users, press Ctrl+Shift, and then the Right or Left Arrow key.

Mac users, press Command+Shift, and then the Right or Left Arrow key.

One other way to select text with the mouse is to click and drag over the text you want to highlight. To do this click in front of the words or letters you want to select. Then, hold down the mouse button and move the mouse pointer over the text.

FREE THROWS

Trainer Terry Says:

Let's take a few free throws to practice selecting text.

1. In the **league** document, double-click the word *School* to select it.
2. Move the insertion point to the beginning of the word *respect* in the third line.
3. Use the Shift and Right Arrow keys to select the word *respect*.
4. Move the insertion point to the beginning of the word *participation* in the last line of the letter.
5. 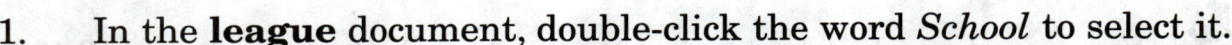 PC users, press Ctrl+Shift and the Right Arrow key to select the word *participation*.

   Mac users, press Command+Shift and the Right Arrow key to select the word *participation*.
6. Use the mouse to select the text *Adam Richardson* by clicking and dragging over it.

Proofreading Marks

Coach Carrie Says:

 At times, you will need to make editing changes that have been marked on a paper copy of the document. Proofreading marks are symbols used to show on paper what changes should be made and where.

 The three most common proofreading marks are the *insertion mark* (^), the *paragraph mark* (¶), and the *delete mark* (ℓ).

 The *insertion mark* tells you where to insert new text.
The *paragraph mark* tells you where to begin a new paragraph.
The *delete mark* tells you which text to delete.

MEG THE MIKE

The editing skills we talk about here occur in what is called *insert mode*. That means that all new typing at the insertion point moves existing text to the right. On some keyboards, you can press the Insert key to switch to *Overtype mode*. In Overtype mode, all new typing *replaces* the existing text to the right of the insertion point.

JEFF THE REF

Sometimes the Backspace key has the word *Backspace* on it and sometimes it has a left-pointing arrow.

Inserting, Editing, and Deleting Text

Coach Carrie Says:

 When you edit text in Word, you can either insert new text, delete existing text, or change existing text.

 To insert text, place the insertion point where you want the new text to go, and then start typing. The existing text moves to the right of the new text.

 To delete text, place the insertion point in front of the text you want to delete, and then press the Delete key. Hold down the Delete key to continue deleting letters to the right of the insertion point.

 You can also delete text with the Backspace key, which is usually found at the upper right of the keyboard. Pressing Backspace deletes text to the left of the insertion point.

 To split a paragraph into two paragraphs, position the insertion point where you want the new paragraph, and then press Enter.

TIP OFF

Trainer Terry Says:

 Okay, you've already learned a lot about selecting and editing text. Now let's get this first game started with the opening tip-off!

 The **league** document has several errors in it. Look at the proofreading marks in Figure 2-5 to see what editing changes you need to make. Then follow the steps on the next page.

Dear Student:

Welcome to the Crow Iland School Youth Basketball Program. All of our youth sports programs stress that each child wins by playing to the best of his or her ability. Using the principals honesty, responsibility, caring, and respect as a guide, we ensure that all who enter our facility enjoy a safe, safe, welcoming, and comfortable environment. We thank you for your participation in our sports leagues. Have a great season!

Sincerely,

Adam Richardson
Youth Sports Director

Figure 2-5. Make the changes shown by the proofreading marks.

JEFF THE REF

If your preferences are set to check spelling as you type, you'll notice a red squiggly line under misspelled words.

1. Move the insertion point after the *I* in *Iland*. Type *s*. The word should be *Island*.
2. Delete the extra *t* in the word *basketball*.
3. Change the word *principals* in the second line to *principles*. You can do this by deleting the *a* and inserting an *e* after the *l*.
4. In the third line, delete the extra word *safe* and the comma that comes after it.
5. Split the paragraph in two. The second paragraph should begin with the word *Using*.
6. Save your changes.
7. Close the document.

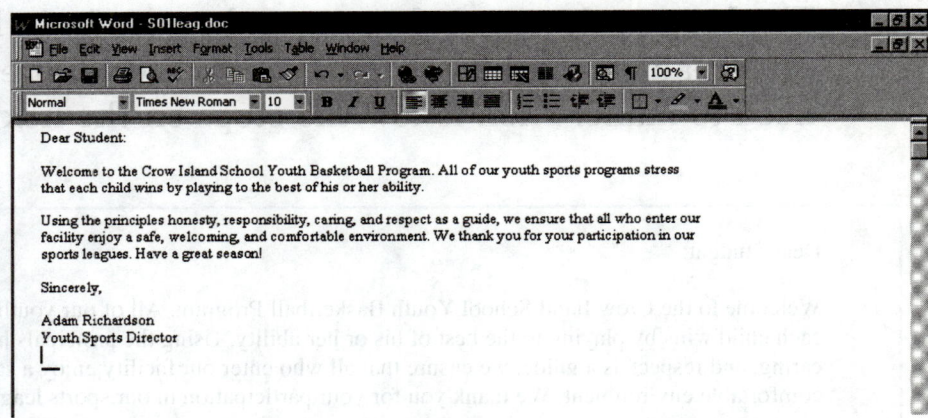

Figure 2-6. This is the edited document.

GAME #2
SCORING WITH THE
PICK-AND-ROLL

The pick-and-roll is a tried and true play for scoring a basket. In the pick-and-roll, one player sets a "pick"—or a screen—in front of his or her teammate, who is dribbling the ball. After the first player sets the pick, he or she suddenly "rolls" or moves away from the person with the ball.

All the moving around in this play mixes up the defense and gives the player with the ball lots of options.

Moving text around in Microsoft Word is as simple as the pick-and-roll, and like the play, you are given lots of options. You'll learn:

- Cutting and Pasting Text
- Dragging and Dropping Text
- Copying Text

Chalk Talk

Cutting and Pasting Text

Coach Carrie Says:

 Okay, all you hoop heroes! It's time to put on a few moves and take the ball to the basket! Moving text in Microsoft Word is easy, and there are plenty of ways you can do it. The easiest way is to *cut and paste* text.

 The first step is to select the text you want to move. Then you cut it. To cut, click the <u>E</u>dit menu and then click C<u>u</u>t. You can also click the Cut button ⌗ on the Standard toolbar.

 Once you cut the text, move the insertion point to where you want the text to appear and then paste in the text. To paste, click the <u>E</u>dit menu and then click <u>P</u>aste. You can also click the Paste button 🗒 on the Standard toolbar.

Here's a cool way to cut and paste text quickly: Select the text you want to move, and then:

 PC users, press Ctrl+X.

 Mac users, press Command+X.

 The text is cut.

 Next, move the insertion point to where you want to place the text, and then:

 PC users, press Ctrl+V.

 Mac users, press Command+V.

 The text is pasted into the new spot. Practice using these keyboard shortcut keys to edit text faster!

 When you cut or copy text in a document, you are actually placing it on the clipboard for temporary storage. The text stays on the *clipboard*, ready for you to paste, until you cut or copy another piece of text. You can paste text from the clipboard over and over again—as many times as you want.

MEG THE MIKE

Cutting text removes it from its current spot in the document so that it can be used somewhere else.
Copying text makes a copy of the text so that it can be used somewhere else, but the original text stays put.
Pasting text means that you insert cut or copied text into a document.

JEFF THE REF

If you see that you have made a mistake by copying the wrong text or by pasting it in the wrong place, here's a quick way to take care of it:

Simply click the Undo button to undo the last thing you did in Word. Click the Undo button more than once to keep undoing previous actions.

If you see that clicking Undo actually undoes something you want to keep, there's no problem. Simply click the Redo button ↷ to change the document back to the way it was before you clicked Undo.

FREE THROWS

Trainer Terry Says:

👟 Take a few free throws to practice cutting and pasting text. Follow these steps.

1. Open a new document in Word.
2. Type the 25 key words. Refer to the following list if you need help remembering:

---

fur fun gun gum guy buy but hut jut vug jim dim

kid red cue my, lot sit wet tex co. fat pat zip qt.

---

3. Move the insertion point to the end of the list and press Enter twice. This creates two new lines.
4. Select the word *buy*. Click the Edit menu and then click Cut.
5. Move the insertion point to the beginning of the second new line. Click the Edit menu and then click Paste.
6. Select the word *jim*. Click the Cut button ✂.
7. Move the insertion point to the right of the word *buy*. Click the Paste button 📋.

Dragging and Dropping Text

Coach Carrie Says:

 There's more than one way to cut to the basket, and there's more than one way to cut and paste text. In Word, you can also move text by *dragging* and *dropping*. With this method, you use the mouse to select and drag text to its new position.

 First, select the text you want to move using the mouse. After the text is selected, move the mouse until the mouse pointer changes from an I-beam ⌶ to an arrow ⬉ . Now hold down the mouse button and drag the mouse pointer to where you want the text to be moved. Release the mouse button and the text you dragged will then be "dropped" in place.

 When you drag the text, the mouse pointer changes to an arrow with a box ⬉ . The box tells you that you are moving selected text.

FREE THROWS

Trainer Terry Says:

 Let's take a few free throws to practice dragging and dropping text.

1. In the key word document you created earlier, drag and drop the word *red* to the new line, positioning it to the right of the word *jim*.
2. Drag and drop the word *gum* to the new line, positioning it to the right of the word *red*.

Copying Text

Coach Carrie Says:

 Sometimes you need to use a piece of text more than once. Rather than type it again, you can copy it.

 Select the text you want to copy. Click the Edit menu, and then click Copy. You can also click the Copy button on the Standard toolbar.

 Once you copy the text, move the insertion point to where you want the text to appear and then paste in the text. To paste, click the Edit menu and then click Paste. You can also click the Paste button on the Standard toolbar.

 The copied text now appears both in its original position and in the spot where you pasted it.

 Another cool way to copy and paste text quickly is to select the text you want to copy, then:

 PC users, press Ctrl+C.

 Mac users, press Command+C.

 The text is copied.

 Next, move the insertion point to where you want to place the text, then:

 PC users, press Ctrl+V.

 Mac users, press Command+V.

 The text is pasted into the new spot.

FREE THROWS

Trainer Terry Says:

Okay, let's take a few more free throws to practice copying text.

1. Move the insertion point to the right of the word *gum*, at the end of the second line.
2. Press Enter five times to add more lines to the document.
3. Select the words *buy jim red gum*.
4. Click <u>E</u>dit and then click <u>C</u>opy. The words are copied to the clipboard.
5. Move the insertion point two lines down.
6. Click <u>E</u>dit and then click <u>P</u>aste. The copied text is inserted.
7. Now select the words *dim kid cue my*, from the first line.
8. Click the Copy button  on the Standard toolbar.
9. Move the insertion point two lines beyond the last line of text.
10. Click the Paste button on the Standard toolbar. The copied text is inserted.
11. Save the practice document as **cutpaste** and then close it.

TIP OFF!

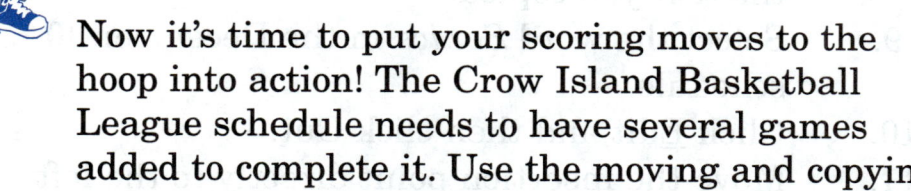

Trainer Terry Says:

Now it's time to put your scoring moves to the hoop into action! The Crow Island Basketball League schedule needs to have several games added to complete it. Use the moving and copying skills you just learned to make the changes.

1. Open the document **02sched** from the student data folder.
2. Save the document as **schedule**.
3. Move the insertion point to the bottom of the document, two lines after the last line of text.
4. Type *December 30* and then press Enter twice. (There are no games scheduled for December 23.)
5. Select the entire schedule of league games for December 16.
   Your document should look like Figure 2-7 below.

MASCOT MAX

If you don't have the CD that comes with your book, check with your teacher about where to locate the data files. Also, check with your teacher about where you should save the new document called **schedule**.

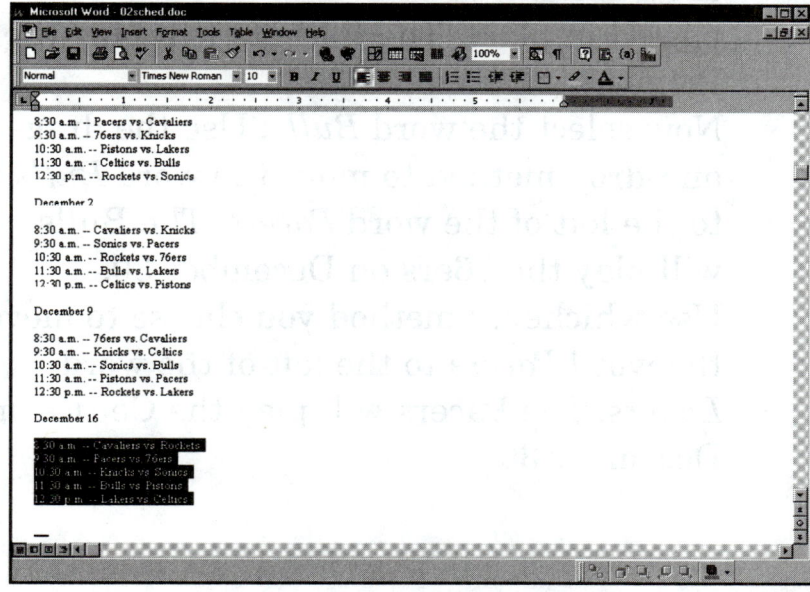

Figure 2-7. Select the schedule of league games for December 16 and then copy it.

JEFF THE REF

Make sure not to select the space after the word *Rockets*. If you do and the next line of the schedule moves up, press Enter to move the line back to where it should be.

6. Click <u>E</u>dit and then click <u>C</u>opy to copy the selected text.

7. Move the insertion point two lines below December 30.

8. Click <u>E</u>dit and then click <u>P</u>aste to paste the text you copied.

9. Select the word *Sonics* in the December 30 schedule.

10. Click <u>E</u>dit and then click Cu<u>t</u>.

11. Move the insertion point directly to the left of the word *Rockets* in the first line of the December 30 schedule.

12. Click <u>E</u>dit and then click <u>P</u>aste. The word *Sonics* is pasted in place. The Cavaliers will play the Sonics on December 30.

13. Now select the word *Rockets*. Click the Cut button ✂ on the Standard toolbar.

14. Move the insertion point to the left of the word *Bulls*. Click the Paste button 📋 on the Standard toolbar. The word *Rockets* is pasted in place. The Rockets will play the Pistons on December 30.

15. Now select the word *Bulls*. Use the drag-and-drop method to move the word *Bulls* to the left of the word *Pacers*. The Bulls will play the 76ers on December 30.

16. Use whichever method you choose to move the word *Pacers* to the left of the word *Lakers*. The Pacers will play the Celtics on December 30.

17. Use whichever method you choose to move the word *Lakers* to the right of the words *Knicks vs.* The Lakers will play the Knicks on December 30.

Your document should now look like Figure 2-8.

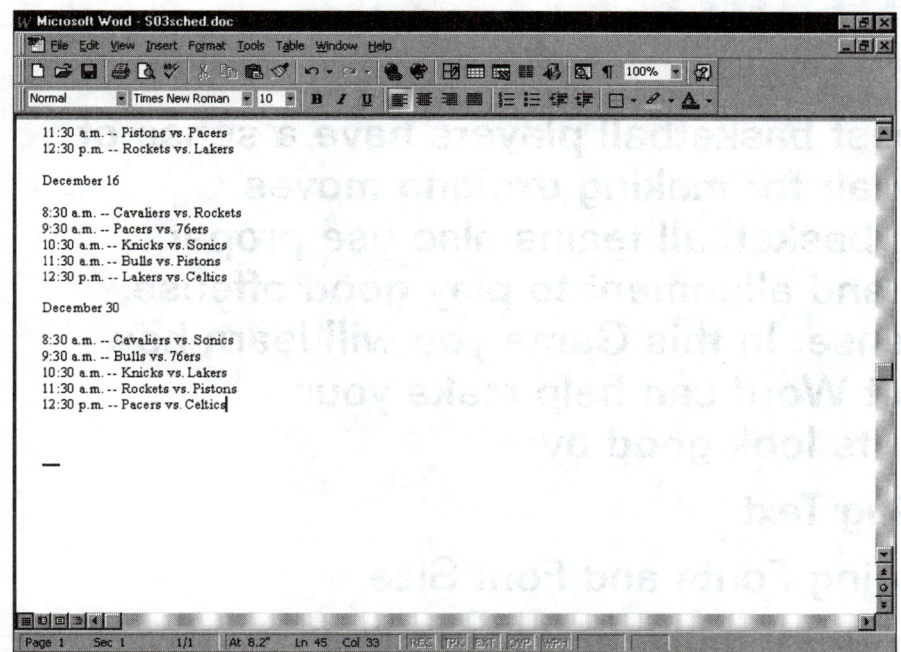

Figure 2-8. The new league schedule now has games added for December 30.

18. Save your changes and then close the document.

GAME #3
LOOKING GOOD ON
THE COURT

The best basketball players have a sense of style, a flair for making exciting moves. Winning basketball teams also use proper spacing and alignment to play good offense and defense. In this Game you will learn how Microsoft Word can help make your documents look good by:

- Aligning Text
- Changing Fonts and Font Size
- Using Bold, Italic, and Underline

CHALK TALK

Aligning Text

Coach Carrie Says:

 Now that you know the basics of editing text in Microsoft Word, let's take a look at basic document formatting. With Word's formatting features, you can make your documents look better and highlight important information.

 The first step in document formatting is to align the text in a way that fits the kind of information you're presenting to your readers. For example, headings or titles in documents are often centered. Body text in most documents is either aligned left or justified.

 You can align text four different ways in Microsoft Word:

- Click the Align Left button on the Formatting toolbar to align all the lines in a paragraph along the left side of the document.

- Click the Center button on the Formatting toolbar to center all the lines in a paragraph between the left and right sides of the document.

- Click the Align Right button on the Formatting toolbar to align all the lines in a paragraph along the right side of the document.

- Click the Justify button 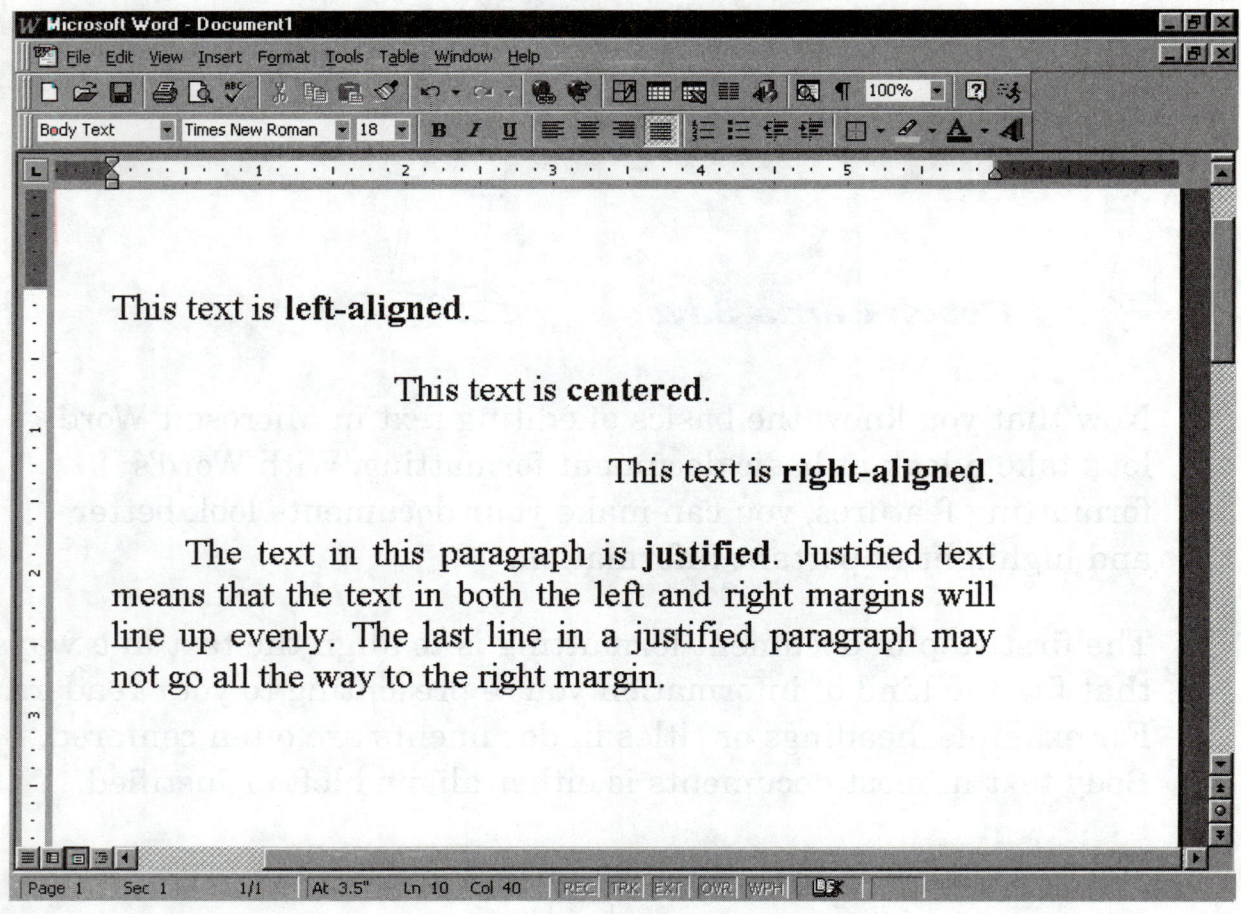 on the Formatting toolbar to align all the lines in a paragraph along both sides of the document.

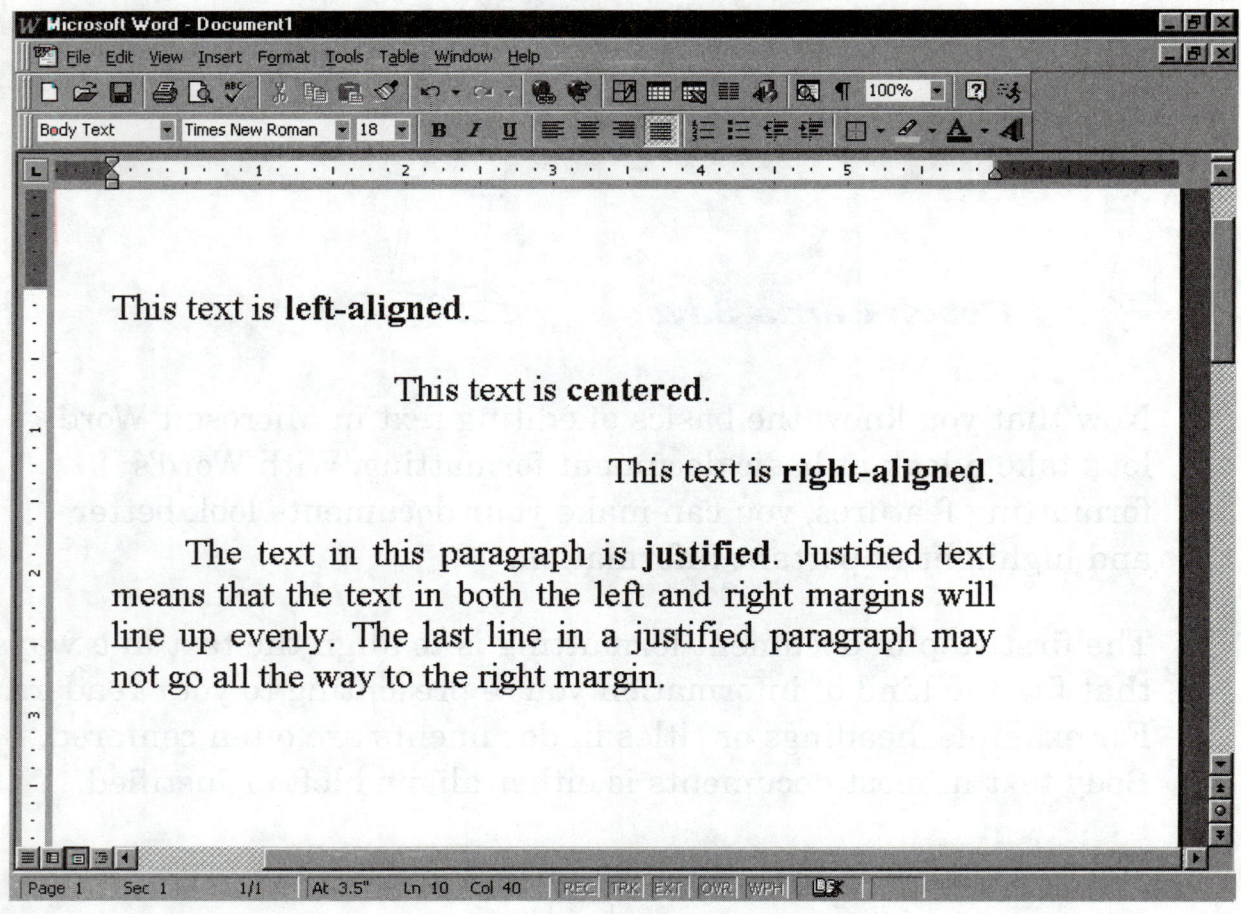

Figure 2-9. You can align text four different ways in Word.

Training Tables: Align Text

Shortcuts	Macintosh
Left align text	Press and hold down Command and then press *l* (Command+L).
Right align text	Press and hold down Command and then press *r* (Command+R).
Center text	Press and hold down Command and then press *e* (Command+E).
Justify text	Press and hold down Command and then press *j* (Command+J).

Shortcuts	PC
Left align text	Press and hold down Ctrl and then press *l* (Ctrl+L).
Right align text	Press and hold down Ctrl and then press *r* (Ctrl+R).
Center text	Press and hold down Ctrl and then press *e* (Ctrl+E).
Justify text	Press and hold down Ctrl and then press *j* (Ctrl+J).

 You can change text alignment either before or after you type text. To change alignment before typing, click the alignment button you want on the Formatting toolbar, and then begin typing. To align text you have already entered, place the insertion point within the line or paragraph that you want to align, and then click the alignment button you want.

FREE THROWS

Trainer Terry Says:

Take a few free throws to practice aligning text.

1. Open the document **03packet** from the student data folder.
2. Save the document as **packet**.
3. Select the first paragraph of text.
4. Click the Center button ▣ on the Formatting toolbar.
5. Select the second paragraph of text.
6. Click the Align Right button ▣ on the Formatting toolbar.
7. Select the third paragraph of text.
8. Click the Justify button ▣ on the Formatting toolbar.
9. Press the Enter button twice to add two lines at the end of the document.
10. Click the Align Left button ▣ and then type *Align Left*. Press Enter twice.
11. Click the Center button ▣ and then type *Center*. Press Enter twice.
12. Click the Align Right button ▣ and then type *Align Right*. Press Enter twice.
13. Click the Align Left button ▣.

Changing Fonts and Font Size

Coach Carrie Says:

 After your text is aligned the way you want it, you can decide whether to use a different *font* and/or font size.

 Choose a *serif* font for the body text of your document because serif fonts are easiest to read. Choose a *sans serif* font for headings because sans serif fonts stand out on the page.

 Font size refers to the size of the letters in your document. Font size is measured in *points*. There are 72 points in an inch. Most body text is typically 10 or 12 points. Point size for headings depends on the type of heading and document you are creating.

 To change font or font size, select the text you want to change and then click the Format menu. Next, click Font. The Font dialog box opens.

 In the Font dialog box, click in the Font list box to select a new font. You can also type a font name in the Font box.

 Click in the Size list box to select a new font size. Again, you can also type a new font size in the Size box.

MEG THE MIKE

A *font* or *typeface* is a specific design for characters of type. A serif font includes curves at the tips of the letters. Example:

Times New Roman

A sans serif font does not include curves at the tips of the letters. Example:

Helvetica

JEFF THE REF

Microsoft Word offers many different fonts from which you can choose. Be careful to use only two or three fonts in a document and to choose fonts that will help strengthen your document's message. Avoid fonts that will distract your readers.

Select font from this list. Type new size here.

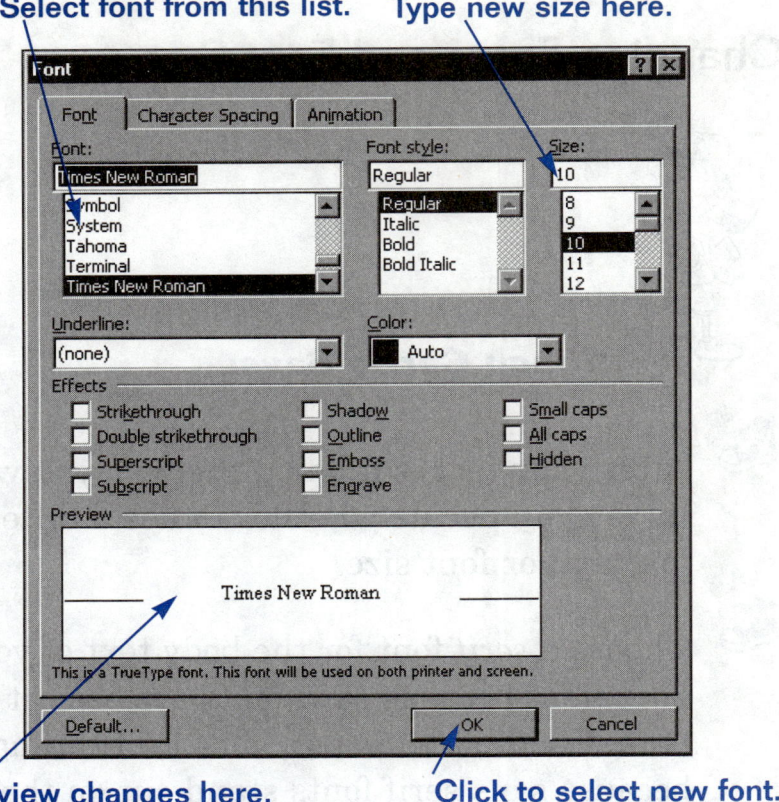

Preview changes here. Click to select new font.

Figure 2-10. Use the Font dialog box to change typeface and font size.

Any change you make to the font or font size will appear in the Preview window at the bottom of the dialog box. After you have made the selections you want, click OK to make the changes in your document text.

Check the Font and Font Size boxes on the Formatting toolbar to see the font settings for the text where the insertion point is currently located.

Font box   Font size   Align left   Justify

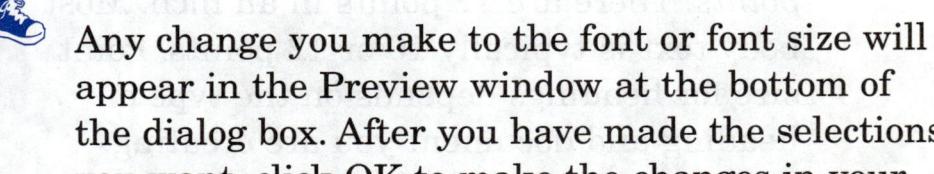

Center   Align right

Figure 2-11. Use the Formatting toolbar to change text alignment, typeface, and font size.

FREE THROWS

Trainer Terry Says:

MASCOT MAX

A cool way to make quick font changes is to click in the Font and Font Size drop-down lists on the Formatting toolbar.

 Take a few free throws to practice changing typeface and font size. Follow these steps:

1. In the **packet** document open on screen, select the first three paragraphs of text.
2. Click the Format menu, and then click Font. *The Font dialog box opens.*
3. Click *12* in the Size list box. *Notice the change to the text shown in the Preview window.*
4. Click OK. The body text changes to 12 points.
5. Select the three headings, *Align Left*, *Center*, and *Align Right*.
6. Click the Font box on the Formatting toolbar, and then click to select Arial from the drop-down menu. *The three headings change to the Arial font.*
7. With the three headings still selected, click the Font Size box on the Formatting toolbar. Click to select *18* from the Font Size drop-down menu. *The headings change to 18 points. Your document should look like the one shown in Figure 2-12.*

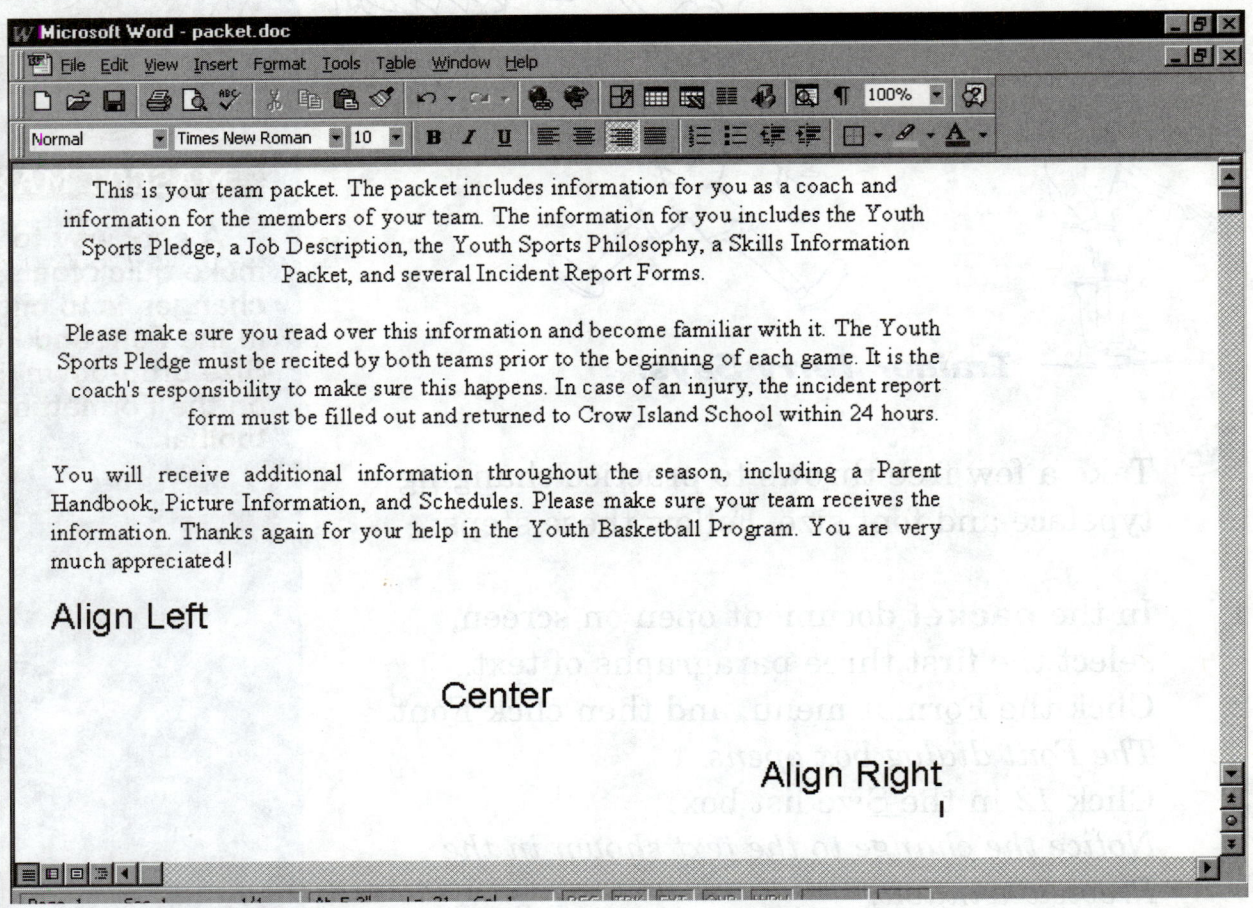

Figure 2-12. Here's how the **packet** document looks with font and font size changes.

Using Bold, Italic, and Underline

Coach Carrie Says:

 Use font styles to add emphasis to certain words in your document, such as titles of books and articles or important phrases you want the reader to notice. Font styles include **bold**, *italic,* and <u>underline</u>.

 Bold is typically used to make an important word or phrase jump out at the reader. *Italic* is normally used for titles of books, magazines, songs, articles, or movies. <u>Underline</u> is usually used to emphasize headings.

 Notice the three font style buttons shown in Figure 2-13. The quickest way to change font style is to click one of the font style buttons on the Formatting toolbar before typing your text. When you've finished typing the emphasized text, click the font style button again to turn off the font style.

Bold   Italic   Underline

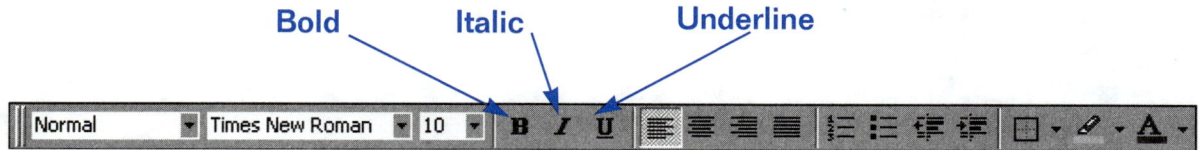

Figure 2-13. Change the font style with these buttons on the Formatting toolbar.

JEFF THE REF

Avoid using too many different font styles in your document. The more text you emphasize, the less the text stands out from the crowd.

 Here's another cool way to make quick font style changes:

Shortcuts	Macintosh
Bold	Press and hold down Command and then press *b* (Command+B).
Italic	Press and hold down Command and then press *i* (Command+I).
Underline	Press and hold down Command and then press *u* (Command+U).

Shortcuts	PC
Bold	Press and hold down Ctrl and then press *b* (Ctrl+B).
Italic	Press and hold down Ctrl and then press *i* (Ctrl+I).
Underline	Press and hold down Ctrl and then press *u* (Ctrl+U).

You can also change font styles by using the Font dialog box (F<u>o</u>rmat, <u>F</u>ont). In the Font dialog box, click to select the font style from the Font style list box. Click *Regular* for no font style and click *Bold Italic* for both bold and italic. For underlining, click to select the type of underlining you want from the <u>U</u>nderline drop-down list box.

 The font style changes you select will appear in the Preview window. Click OK to make the changes in your document text.

Click in the Font style list box to make changes.

Underline drop-down list box

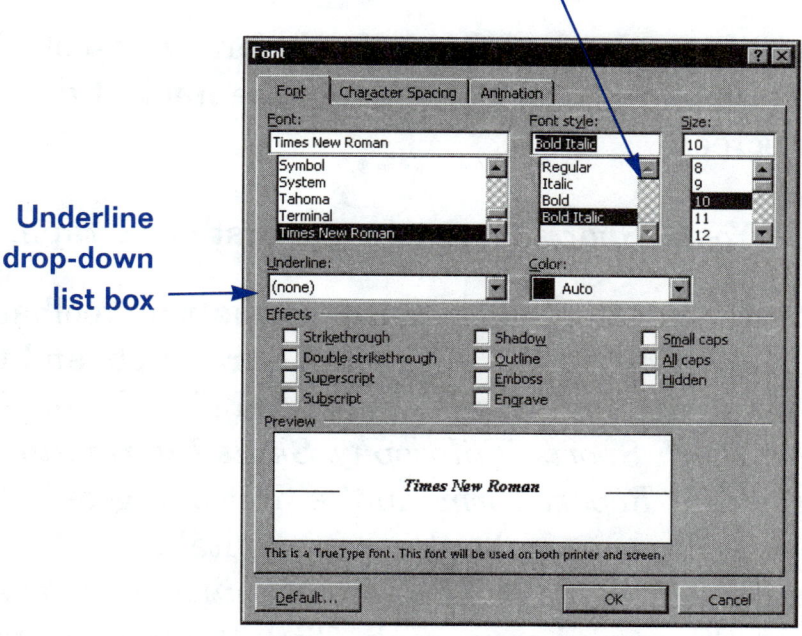

Figure 2-14. You can use the Font dialog box to change font styles.

 You can change the font style of existing text by selecting it and then clicking one of the font style buttons on the toolbar or using the Font dialog box. It's best to use the Font dialog box when you're making more than one change to the text.

 For example, if you want to change the typeface, font size, and font style of a heading, select the heading and use the Font dialog box to make all your changes at once. That way you can preview the changes before you make them.

FREE THROWS

Trainer Terry Says:

Okay, one last trip to the free throw line before we tip off this game. Practice changing font styles using the **packet** document open on your screen.

1. Select the text *Youth Sports Pledge* in the first paragraph, and then click the Italic button [*I*] on the Formatting toolbar.

2. Select the text *Job Description* in the first paragraph, and then press Ctrl+I if you're on a PC, or Command+I if you're on a Mac.

3. Select the text *Youth Sports Philosophy*, *Skills Information Packet*, and *Incident Report Forms* in the first paragraph. Use any method you choose to make these words italic.

4. Select the sentence *It is the coach's responsibility to make sure this happens* in the second paragraph. Click the Bold button on the Formatting toolbar.

5. Select the three headings, *Align Left*, *Center*, and *Align Right*.

6. Click F<u>o</u>rmat and then <u>F</u>ont to open the Font dialog box.

7. Click to select *Single* from the <u>U</u>nderline drop-down list box.

8. Click to select *Arial Black* from the <u>F</u>ont list box, and then click *20* in the <u>S</u>ize list box. Notice the changes in the Preview window.
    You may have to scroll down in the <u>S</u>ize list box to select 20 *points.*

9. Click OK to make the changes in your document.

10. Save your changes to **packet** and close the document.

TIP OFF

Trainer Terry Says:

Get ready for the opening tip! The Crow Island Basketball League needs to send an information flyer to coaches, parents, and students. Use the formatting skills you have learned to make the document more appealing and to emphasize text. Follow these steps:

1. Open the document **03info** from the student data folder.
2. Save the document as **info**.
3. Select the first line of text, *Crow Island School Youth Basketball League*.
4. Click the Font drop-down list on the Formatting toolbar, and then select *Arial*.
5. With the text still selected, click the Font Size drop-down list on the Formatting toolbar, and then select *16* points.
6. With the text still selected, click the Bold button **B** on the Formatting toolbar, and then click the Center button on the Formatting toolbar.
    Notice the changes to the heading.
7. Now select the next line of text, *General Information*.
8. Click the Format menu, and then click Font.
    The Font dialog box opens.
9. Select these options in the Font dialog box:
    *   Font: Arial
    *   Font style: Bold
    *   Size: 14 points
    *   Underline: Single

JEFF THE REF

If you see that you have made a mistake in your formatting changes, remember that you can click the Undo button 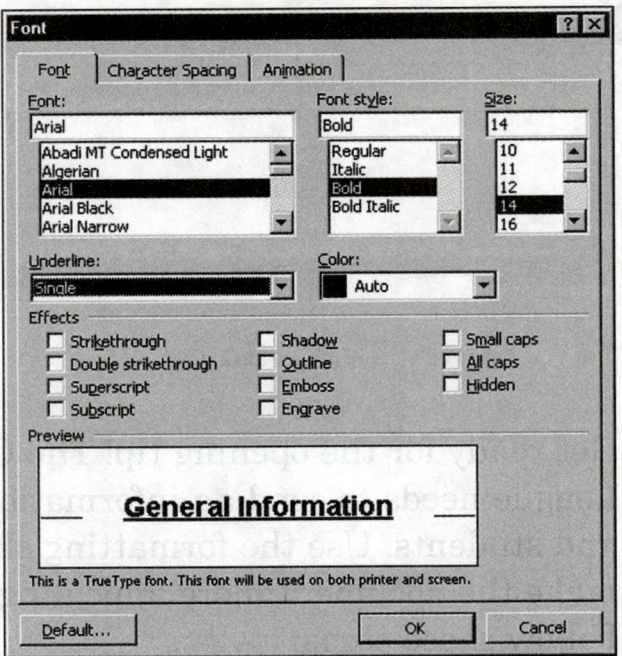 to undo the most recent change you made. Click the Undo button more than once to keep undoing previous actions.

Figure 2-15. Make multiple changes in the Font dialog box.

10. Note the changes in the Preview window, and then click OK.

11. With the heading still selected, click the Center button on the Formatting toolbar.

12. Select all of the body text paragraphs, starting with *All coaches are volunteers* and continuing to the end of the document.

13. Click the Font Size drop-down list on the Formatting toolbar, and then select *12*.

14. Now select the text *All coaches are volunteers. We need your help!*

15. Click the Bold button **B** on the Formatting toolbar.

16. Select the text *Cars parked on Willow Road may be ticketed* at the end of the third paragraph.

17. Click the Italic button 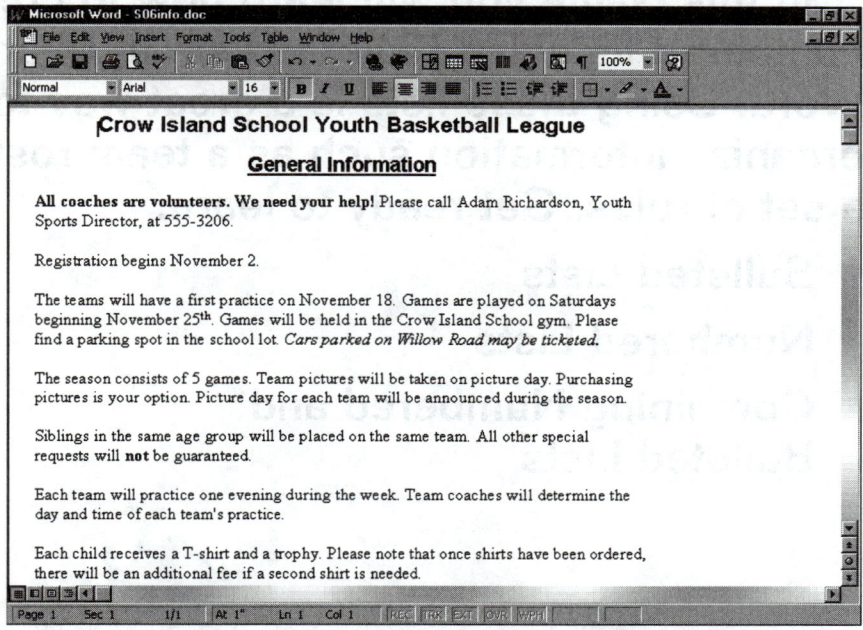 on the Formatting toolbar.

18. Select the word *not* in the paragraph that begins with the word *Siblings*.

19. Click the Bold button **B** on the Formatting toolbar.
    Your document should now look like the one shown in Figure 2-16.

Figure 2-16. Here's the **info** document with formatting and alignment changes.

20. Save your changes, and then close the document.

GAME #4
THE STARTING LINEUP

In this Game you will learn how to create numbered lists and bulleted lists in Microsoft Word. Using these lists is a great way to organize information such as a team roster or a set of rules. Get ready to learn:

- Bulleted Lists
- Numbered Lists
- Combining Numbered and Bulleted Lists

CHALK TALK

Bulleted Lists

Coach Carrie Says:

 Bullets are used to emphasize points in a list of information. Bullets are typically dots or symbols that appear in front of text items.

 To create a bulleted list in Word, click the

Bullets button ⬛ on the Formatting toolbar, and then begin typing text items. At the end of each text item, press Enter to start a new item. Word will automatically place a bullet in front of the new item. When you've finished typing the bulleted list, click

the Bullets button ⬛ again to turn off the bullet list formatting. Another way to end a bulleted list is to press Enter twice.

JEFF THE REF

Keyboard alert! Depending on your keyboard, the key you press to start a new line might be called "Enter" or "Return."

You can also change existing text into a bulleted list. Simply select the text you want to change, and then click the Bullets button . Remove bullets from an existing bulleted list by selecting the list and then clicking the Bullets button .

If you want to jazz up the shape of your bullets, click the Format menu and then click Bullets and Numbering. The Bullets and Numbering dialog box appears as in Figure 2-17. Click the Bulleted tab in the dialog box. A selection of different bullets appears. Click the type of bullet you want, and then click OK.

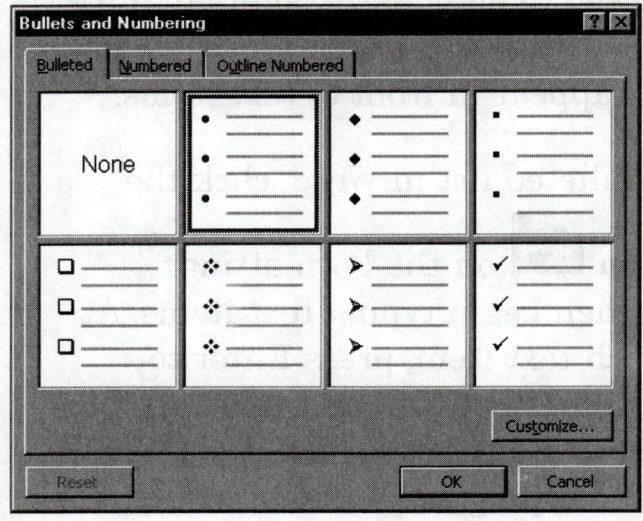

Figure 2-17. Use the Bullets and Numbering dialog box to change the shape of your bullets.

FREE THROWS

Trainer Terry Says:

Okay, let's try a few free throws to practice bulleted lists. Follow these steps:

1. Open the document **04coach** from the student data folder.
2. Save the document as **coach**.
3. Notice how difficult it is to read the list of guidelines for the coaches.
4. Select the list text, starting with *Once the season starts* and continuing to the end of the document.
5. Click the Bullets button on the Formatting toolbar. The text changes to a bulleted list.
6. Click outside the selected text. Save your work.
   Your document should look like the one shown in Figure 2-18.

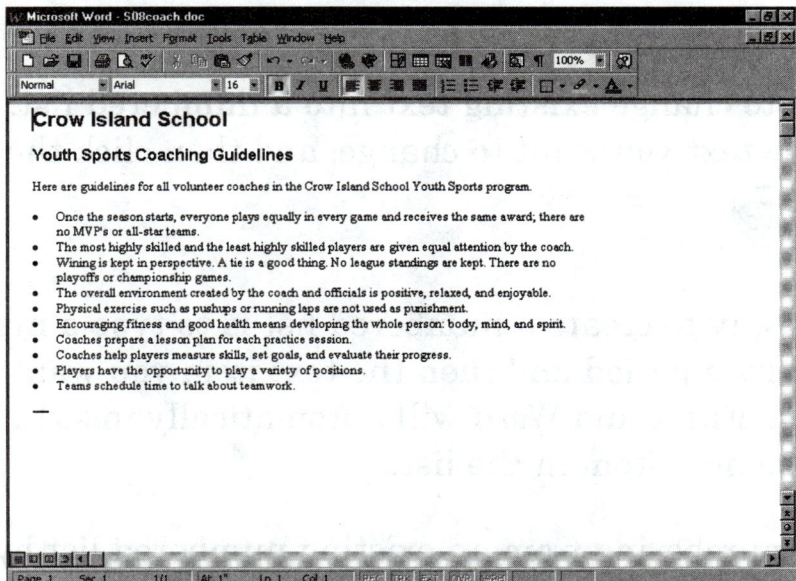

Figure 2-18. Change a list of items to a bulleted list.

7. Print one copy of the document and then close it.

Numbered Lists

Coach Carrie Says:

 Numbered lists are used to assign an order to a list of information. You can create numbered lists in much the same way as you create a bulleted list.

 To create a numbered list in Word, click the Numbering button on the Formatting toolbar, and then begin typing text items. At the end of each text item, press Enter to start a new item. Word will automatically start the new item with the next number in the list. When you've finished typing the numbered list, click the Numbering button again to turn off the numbered list formatting. Another way to end a numbered list is to press Enter twice.

 It's easy to change existing text into a numbered list. Just select the text you want to change, and then click the Numbering button .

 Another way to create a numbered list is to type a number followed by a period and then the text item you want to start the list. Press Enter and Word will automatically insert a number before the next item in the list.

 Remove numbering from an existing numbered list by selecting the list and then clicking the Numbering button .

If you want to change the type of numbers used in your numbered list, click the Format menu and then click Bullets and Numbering. The Bullets and Numbering dialog box appears in Figure 2-19. Click the Numbered tab in the dialog box.

 A selection of different numbering styles appears, including Roman numerals and lettering. Click the style you want, and then click OK.

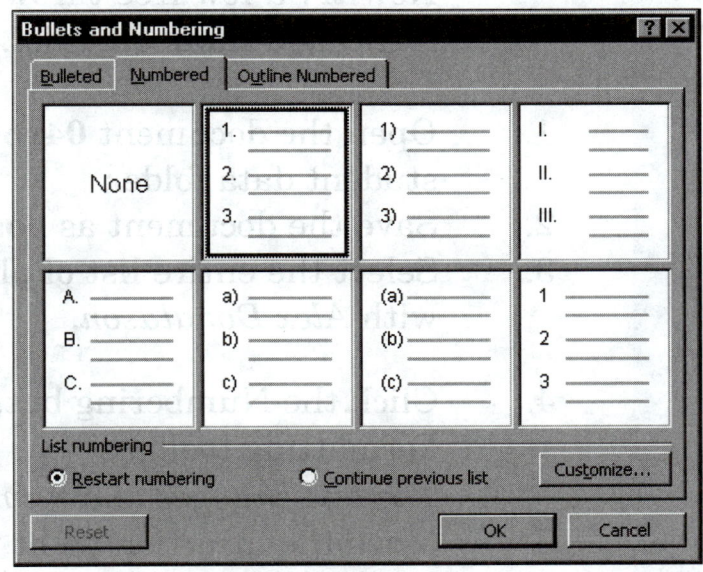

Figure 2-19. Use the Bullets and Numbering dialog box to change numbering style.

JEFF THE REF

The Roman numerals and lettering styles on the Numbering tab of the dialog box are typically used for creating outlines. Try to avoid these styles for normal numbered lists.

FREE THROWS

Trainer Terry Says:

Now try a few free throws to practice creating a numbered list.

1. Open the document **04roster** from the student data folder.
2. Save the document as **roster**.
3. Select the entire list of players, starting with *Alex Donaldson*.
4. Click the Numbering button ▤ on the Formatting toolbar.
   The text changes to a numbered list.
5. Move the insertion point to the right of the last name in the list, *Griffin Reed*.
6. Press Enter.
   The next number in the numbered list sequence appears.
7. Type the next name for the team roster: *Terry Chao*.
8. Press Enter again and then type the last name in the team roster: *Max Fortier*.
9. Select the entire list again, and then click the Numbering button ▤.
   The numbered list is returned to normal text.

10. Click the Numbering button 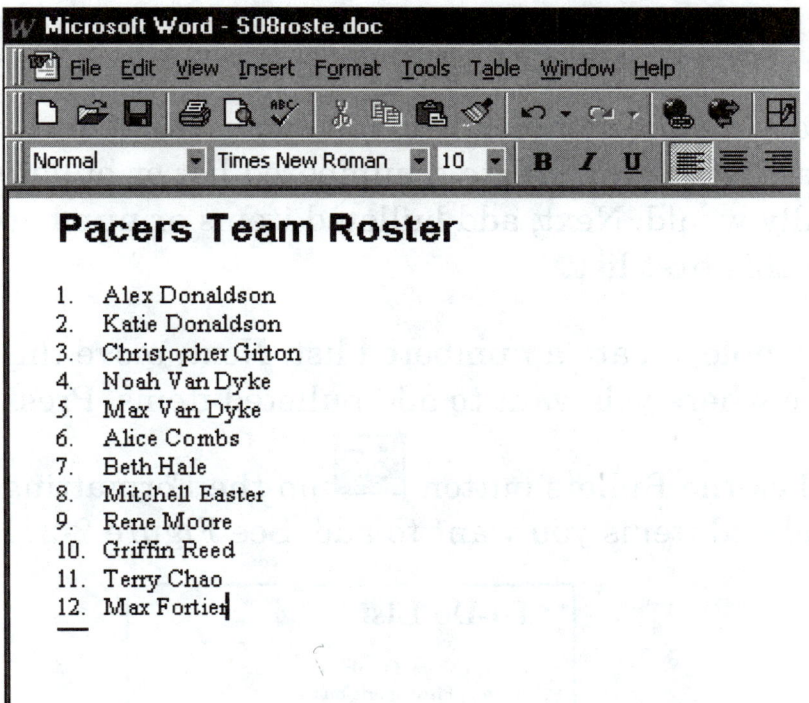 again to change the text back to a numbered list. Click outside the selected text and then save your work.

Your document should look like the one shown in Figure 2-20.

Figure 2-20. Change a list of items to a numbered list.

11. Print one copy of the document and then close it, saving the changes.

Combining Numbered and Bulleted Lists

 ### *Coach Carrie Says:*

To create a more complex list, you can combine numbered and bulleted lists. First, create a numbered list or bulleted list as you normally would. Next, add bulleted items or numbered items within this first list.

 For example, create a numbered list. Next, move the insertion point to where you want to add bulleted items. Press Enter and then click the Bullets button ▦ on the Formatting toolbar. Type the bulleted items you want to add. See Figure 2-21.

To-Do List

1. Finish yard work
   - Plant spring bulbs
   - Cut grass
   - Clear out weeds from flower beds
2. Paint garage doors
3. Paint ceiling in the sun room
4. Clean up basement
5. Move furniture to storage

Figure 2-21. A combined numbered and bulleted list

 You may want to increase the indent for the items you add to an existing bulleted or numbered list. For example, if you add bulleted items to a numbered list, select the bulleted items and then click the Increase Indent button ▦ on the Formatting toolbar. The bulleted items will move to the right by half an inch.

 Increasing the indent helps separate the two types of list and makes the list easier to read. If you want to move the items back to the left, click the Decrease Indent button .

FREE THROWS

Trainer Terry Says:

Okay, take one more trip to the free throw line to get ready for our game. Create the "To-Do List" you saw in Figure 2-21 by following these steps:

1. Create a new document by clicking File and then clicking New.
2. Type *To-Do List* as the first line of the document.
3. Format the To-Do List heading as 18 point, bold.
   Here's a hint: Click the Font Size drop-down list on the Formatting toolbar and select 18. Next, click the Bold button on the Formatting toolbar.
4. Press Enter twice, and then click the Numbering button  on the Formatting toolbar.
5. Type the following text items to create the numbered list:
   Finish yard work
   Paint garage doors
   Paint ceiling in the sun room
   Clean up basement
   Move furniture to storage

JEFF THE REF

Make sure you change the font and point size back to 10 point, Times New Roman, no bold, as in the document shown in Figure 2-21, before you click the Numbering button and start typing the list.

6.   Now move the insertion point to the end of the first item in the numbered list. Press Enter.
Notice that Word automatically adds another number to the list.

7   With the insertion point on the new line, click the Bullets

button  on the Formatting toolbar.

8.   Now type the following text items as a bulleted list within the numbered list:
Plant spring bulbs
Cut grass
Clear out weeds from flower beds

9.   Select the three bulleted items and then click the Increase

Indent button on the Formatting toolbar twice. The bulleted items are indented within the numbered list.

10. Save the document as **todo**. Print one copy and then close the document.

TIP-OFF!

Trainer Terry Says:

Okay, time to tip off another game. This time, you will use numbered and bulleted lists to create a document that tells players, coaches, and parents about important ideas behind having fun in the Crow Island School Basketball League. Follow these steps:

1. Open the document **04list** from the student data folder.
2. Save the document as **list**.
3. Select the first line of text, *Crow Island School*.
4. Format this heading as 16 point, Arial, bold, centered.
   You can use either the Formatting toolbar or the Font dialog box to make the formatting changes.
5. Now select the next line of text, *Youth Sports Philosophy*.
6. Format this heading as 14 point, Arial, bold, centered.
7. Select the list text, beginning with *Participation—Everyone plays* and continuing to the end of the document.
8. Click the Numbering button ▤ on the Formatting toolbar.
   The text is now formatted as a numbered list.
9. Format the first word of each list item as bold.
   Your document should look like the one shown in Figure 2-22.

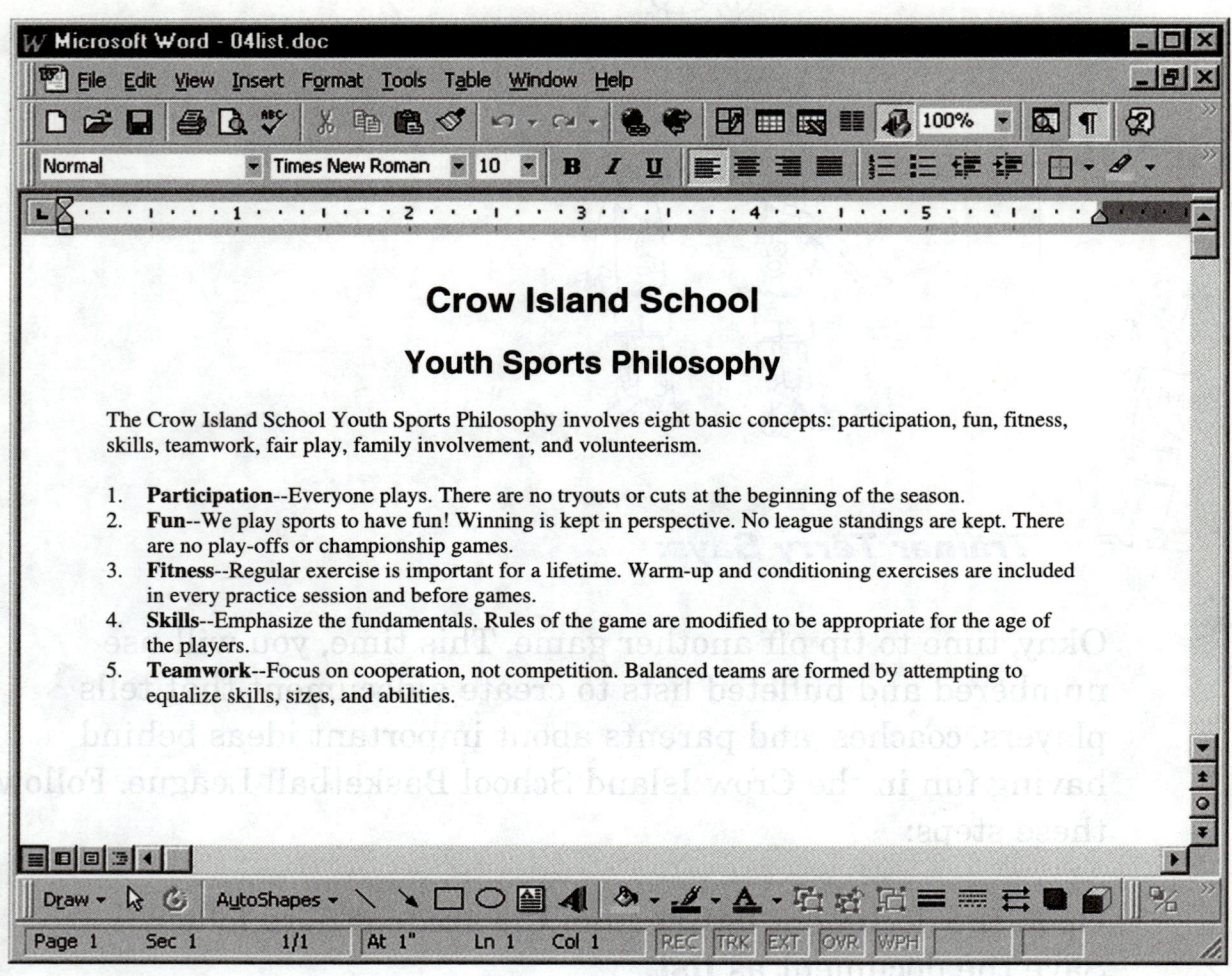

Figure 2-22. The text has been formatted as a numbered list.

Trainer Terry Says:

Great job! You've created a numbered list for the document. Now it's time to complete the document by adding a few more items to the numbered list and then adding some bulleted points to one of the numbered items.

1. Move the insertion point to the end of the last numbered list item, and then press Enter.
2. Add the following three items to the numbered list:

   Fair Play—Fair play involves respect for oneself, for one's teammates, for the other team, as well as for the rules and the officials who uphold them.

   Family—Youth sports is a family program. Parents are kept informed about the program.

   Volunteers—Volunteer coaches are carefully selected on the basis of their knowledge.

3. Format *Fair Play*, *Family*, and *Volunteers* as bold.
4. Move the insertion point to the end of the first item in the numbered list.
5. Press Enter and then add the following two bulleted points:

   Once the season starts, everyone plays equally in every game and receives the same award; there are no MVPs or all-star teams.

   The most highly skilled and the least highly skilled players are given equal attention by the coach.

JEFF THE REF

Make sure the items in the bulleted list are not formatted as bold. If they are, select the text and click the Bold button on the Formatting toolbar.

MEG THE MIKE

Remember: To make a dash (—), just type two hyphens (--). Word will automatically create a dash for you.

6. Use the Bullets and Numbering dialog box to change the bullet style to the arrow style.

7. Select the two bulleted items you just added, and then click the Increase Indent button 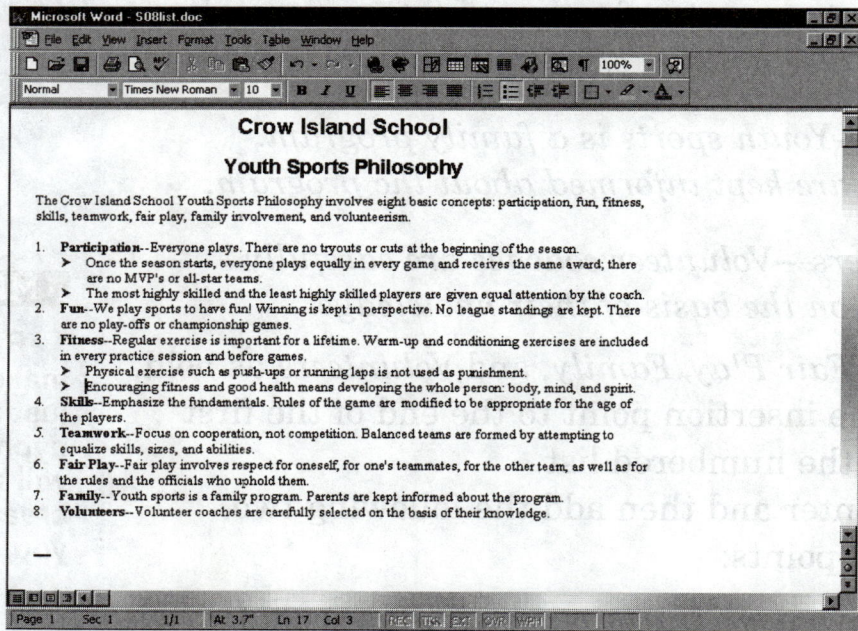.

8. Add the following two bulleted items to the third item in the numbered list:

Physical exercise such as push-ups or running laps is not used as punishment.

Encouraging fitness and good health means developing the whole person: body, mind, and spirit.

9. Select the two bulleted items you just added, and then click the Increase Indent button .

Your document should look like the one shown in Figure 2-23.

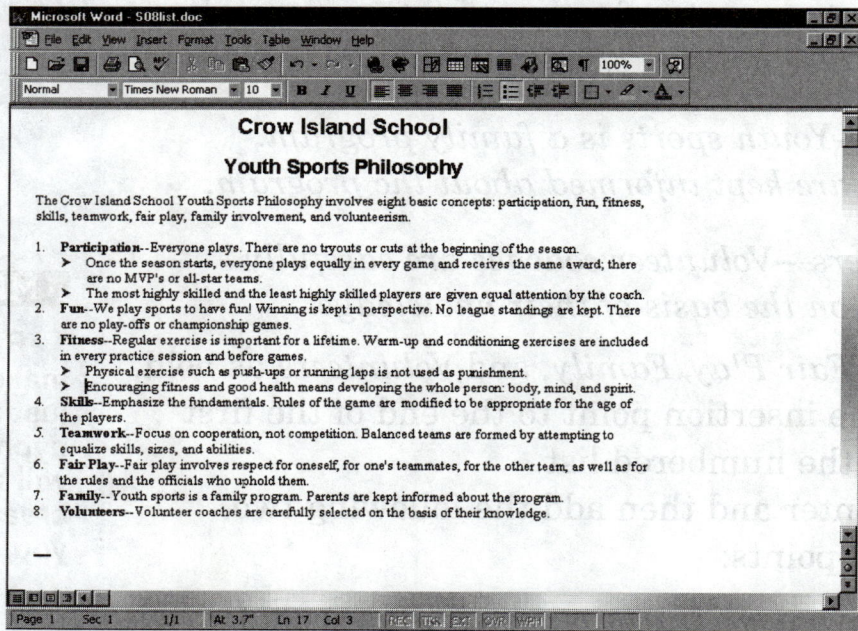

Figure 2-23. Bulleted items have been added to the numbered list.

10. Save your changes and then close the document.

THE FINAL FOUR

 Let's see if you can try out some of the skills you've learned during basketball season. Try creating your own to-do list showing tasks you need to complete. You can include schoolwork, chores at home, and hobbies or projects on which you're working.

 Use your creativity in formatting the list. You can make it either a numbered or a bulleted list—or combine the two if you like!

GAME #5
USING THE PROPER SPACING

Proper spacing is important to playing good offense and defense in basketball. Keeping enough distance between you and the other players on your team will help you cover the court on defense and give you plenty of room to make good passes on offense.

Using the proper spacing is also important in creating your documents in Microsoft Word. In this Game you will learn:

- Line Spacing
- Indenting Text

CHALK TALK

Line Spacing

Coach Carrie Says:

 You can change the line spacing of the text in your document from single spacing to double spacing. Double-spaced text has a line of space between each line of text and may be easier to read than single-spaced text. Single-spaced text has no line of space between each line of text.

 To change line spacing, move the insertion point to the paragraph you want to change. Click the F̲ormat menu, and then click P̲aragraph. The Paragraph dialog box opens, as shown in Figure 2-24.

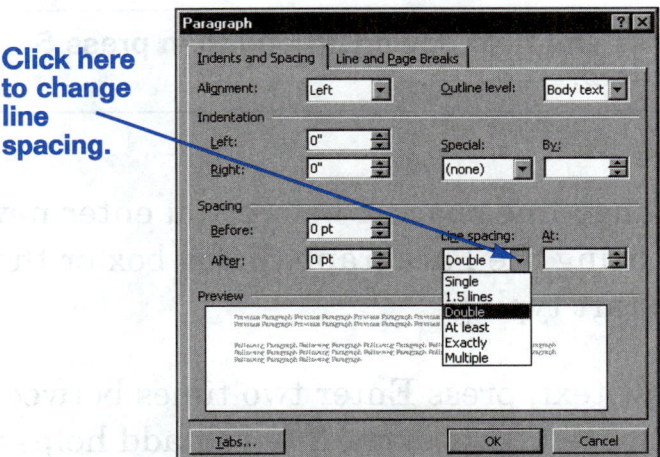

Figure 2-24. Use the Paragraph dialog box to change line spacing.

Click the Line spacing drop-down list to select the spacing you want. Most documents use either single spacing or double spacing, but Word provides other custom spacing options, too.

 Here's a cool way to change line spacing quickly: Put the insertion point in the paragraph you want to change, and then press one of the following key combinations:

Shortcut	Mac
Single spacing	Press and hold down Command and then press 1 (Command+1).
Double spacing	Press and hold down Command and then press 2 (Command+2).
1.5 line spacing	Press and hold down Command and then press 5 (Command+5).

Shortcut	⊞ PC
Single spacing	Press and hold down Ctrl and then press 1 (Ctrl+1).
Double spacing	Press and hold down Ctrl and then press 2 (Ctrl+2).
1.5 line spacing	Press and hold down Ctrl and then press 5 (Ctrl+5).

 You can also change line spacing before you enter new text. Just set the spacing using the Paragraph dialog box or the shortcut keys, and then start typing!

 When typing new text, press Enter two times between paragraphs that are single spaced. This extra line you add helps readers see that a new paragraph is beginning. Press Enter only once between paragraphs that are double-spaced.

FREE THROWS

Trainer Terry Says:

Okay, let's try some free throws to practice changing line spacing. Follow these steps:

1. Open the document **05basket** from the student data folder.
2. Save the document as **basket**.
3. Place the insertion point in the first paragraph of text.
4. Click the F̲ormat menu, and then click P̲aragraph.
5. Click the Li̲ne spacing drop-down menu, and then select *Double*.
6. Click OK to make the change in your document.
7. Delete the extra line between paragraphs, and then move your insertion point to the second paragraph of the document.
8. Double-space the text:

    PC users, press Ctrl+2.

    Mac users, press Command+2.
9. Again, delete the extra space between paragraphs, and then double-space the final paragraph of the document.

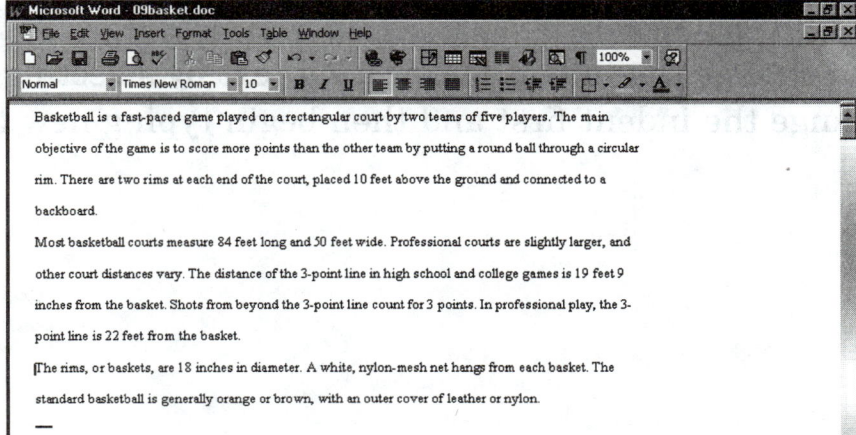

Figure 2-25. The text in the **basket** document has been double-spaced.

Indenting Text

Coach Carrie Says:

 Notice that it's hard to tell where the new paragraphs begin in the double-spaced text of the **basket** document. To help your readers tell where new paragraphs begin in a double-spaced document, you can automatically indent the first line of each new paragraph.

 Use the Paragraph dialog box to change paragraph indents. In the paragraph dialog box, click the Special drop-down list, and then select *First line*. Word automatically suggests a half-inch indent for the first line of new paragraphs. Notice the change in the Preview window and then click OK to make the change in your document text.

 To turn off first line indents, open the Paragraph dialog box again and select *(none)* from the Special drop-down list.

 You can change the indent for existing text by selecting it, or you can change the indent first and then begin typing new text.

FREE THROWS

Trainer Terry Says:

 Now take a couple more free throws to practice changing indents before we tip off this Game.

1. Select all three paragraphs of text in the **basket** document.
2. Click F_ormat, _Paragraph.
3. Select *First line* from the _Special drop-down list.
4. Click OK.

   The paragraphs in the double-spaced text are now much easier to see, as shown in Figure 2-26.

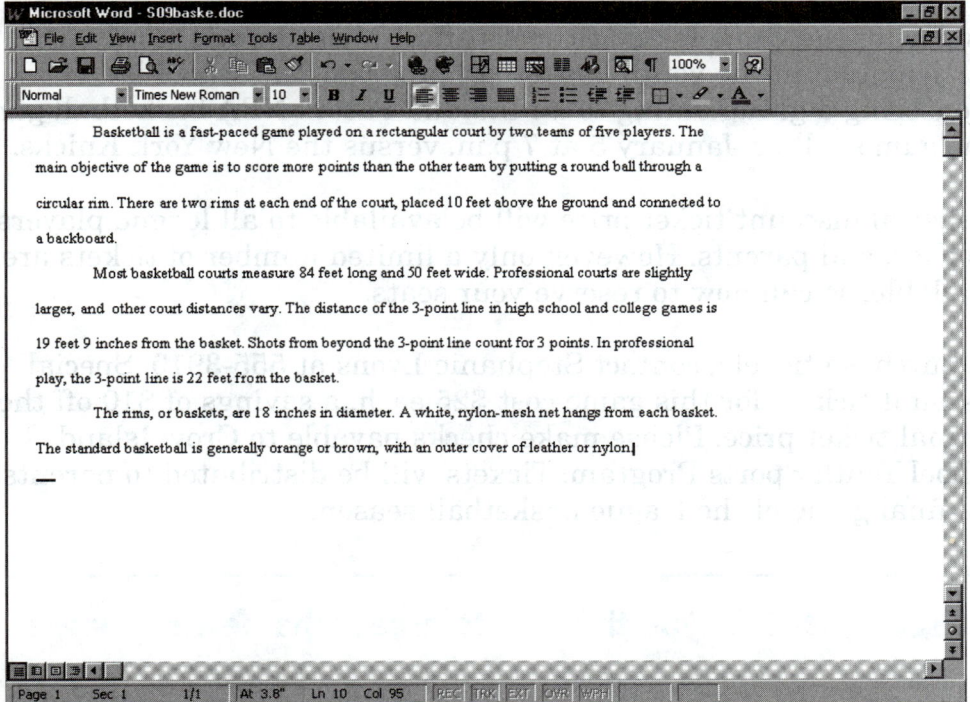

Figure 2-26. Use first line indents for double-spaced paragraphs.

5. Save your work in the **basket** document, and then close the document.

TIP-OFF!

Trainer Terry Says:

Let's get ready for the opening tip! You will create a new document that uses various types of line spacing and indents.

1. Open a new document.
2. Type the text shown in Figure 2-27.

Crow Island School Basketball League

Group Outing to a Pacers Game!

As part of the Crow Island School's effort to encourage family participation in the youth basketball program, the school is sponsoring a group outing to an Indiana Pacers NBA basketball game. The game will be January 5 at 7 p.m. versus the New York Knicks.

A special discount ticket price will be available to all league players, coaches, and parents. However, only a limited number of tickets are available, so call now to reserve your seats.

To purchase tickets, contact Stephanie Lyons at 555-3910. Special discount tickets for this game cost $25 each, a savings of $10 off the normal ticket price. Please make checks payable to Crow Island School Youth Sports Program. Tickets will be distributed to parents at the final game of the league basketball season.

Figure 2-27. Type this text to create the new document.

3. Format the first line of text as a heading, 18 point, Arial, bold, centered.
4. Format the second line of text as a heading, 10 point, Times New Roman, bold and underlined, flush left.

5. Double space the first paragraph of body text and use a first line indent. This paragraph begins with the words *As part of the Crow Island School's.*

6. Single space the next paragraph of body text. Format this paragraph as bold and italic.

7. Double space the last paragraph of body text and use a first line indent.

    When finished, your document should look like the one shown in Figure 2-28.

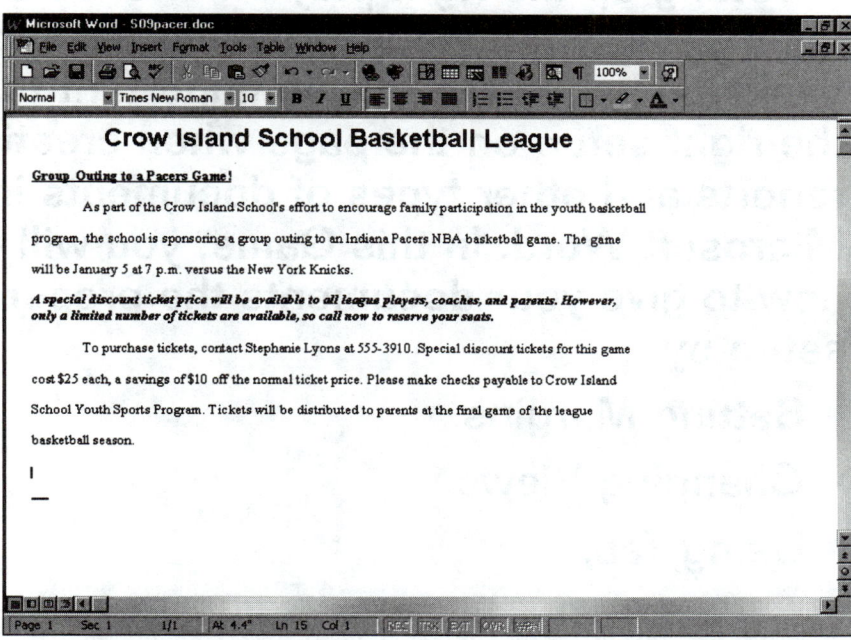

Figure 2-28. Your finished document should look like this.

8. Save the document as **pacers** and then close the document.

GAME #6
SETTING UP
THE RIGHT PLAY

Setting up the right play on offense and defense is critical to successful teamwork on a basketball squad. It is also important to use the right setup on the page when creating reports and other types of documents in Microsoft Word. In this Game, you will learn how to give your documents the proper page setup by:

- **Setting Margins**
- **Changing Views**
- **Using Tabs**

CHALK TALK

Setting Margins

Coach Carrie Says:

 Margins are the white spaces around the four edges of your document—top, bottom, left, and right. Microsoft Word gives each new document you create *default* margins of 1.25 inches on both the left and right sides of the page and 1 inch at both the top and bottom of the page.

 You can change the margins by clicking the File menu and then clicking Page Setup. When you do so, the Page Setup dialog box opens. If it isn't already selected, click the Margins tab and then enter the margin measurements you want to use in the Top, Bottom, Left, and/or Right text boxes. You can also click the small arrows at the right of each of these boxes to increase or decrease the margins.

MEG THE MIKE

Margins are used to provide a border of white space around the edges of your document to help aid the reader. Try to avoid margins that are too narrow or too wide. Margins of between 1 and 2 inches are usually best.

Change margins here.

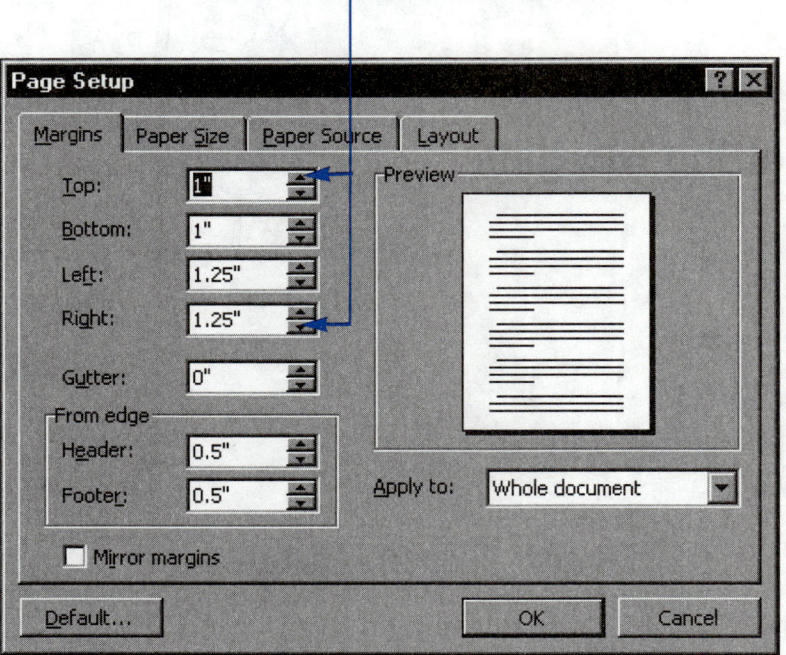

Figure 2-29. Use the Page Setup dialog box to change margins.

 Once you've made the changes to the margin settings, you can check the results in the Preview window. You can then apply the changes to either the entire document or parts of the document by clicking the option you want in the Apply to drop-down list. Click OK when you're ready to make the changes in your document.

Changing Views

Coach Carrie Says:

Microsoft Word has five different views you can use for entering and editing text.

- *Normal view* is the easiest view and is used for most keyboarding and editing.

- *Page Layout view* is the best view for checking the format of an entire document, including margins, line spacing, and graphics. This view is slower to work in than Normal view.

- Use *Outline view* to create document outlines and work with the organization of a document. You will learn more about Outline view and creating an outline in Season 3.

- Use *Online Layout view* to help you work with layouts for documents you create for the Internet or World Wide Web.

- Use *Master Document* view to work with large documents that contain many different types of sections.

JEFF THE REF

We won't work with Online Layout view or Master Document view in this book.

MEG THE MIKE

To help you see where your margins have been set, you can use the Ruler. The horizontal Ruler appears at the top of the Word document window. If you are in Page Layout view, a vertical Ruler will also appear at the left of the Word document window. The Ruler is marked off in inches to help guide you in page layout and formatting.

If you don't see the ruler in your document window and you want to turn it on, click View and then click Ruler. If the Ruler is already on, a check mark will appear next to the Ruler option in the View menu.

To change views, click the View menu and then select from the list the view you want to use, as shown in Figure 2-30.

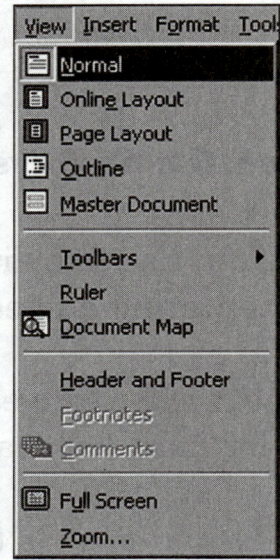

Figure 2-30. Use the View menu to select a different view.

Another way to change views is to click one of the View buttons at the left end of the horizontal scroll bar, as shown in Figure 2-31. The horizontal scroll bar is near the bottom of the Word screen.

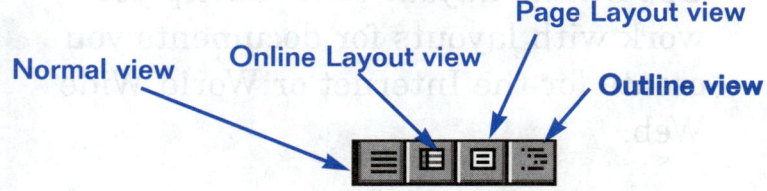

Figure 2-31. Click one of the View buttons to change views.

FREE THROWS

Trainer Terry Says:

Okay, let's try some free throws to practice changing margins.

1. Open the document **06pass** from the student data folder.
2. Save the document as **pass.**
3. Click the <u>V</u>iew menu, and then click <u>P</u>age Layout.
   The document changes to Page Layout view.
4. Click the <u>F</u>ile menu, and then click Page Set<u>u</u>p.
   The Page Setup dialog box opens.
5. Make sure the Margins tab is selected. If not, click <u>M</u>argins.
6. Change the <u>T</u>op margin to 2 inches.
7. Change the Le<u>f</u>t margin to 1.5 inches.
   Notice the changes in the Preview window.
8. Make sure *Whole document* appears in the <u>A</u>pply to list box, and then click OK.
9. Click the <u>V</u>iew menu and then click <u>R</u>uler.
   Notice the changes in the document in Page Layout view, as shown in Figure 2-32.

1.5-inch left margin   2-inch top margin

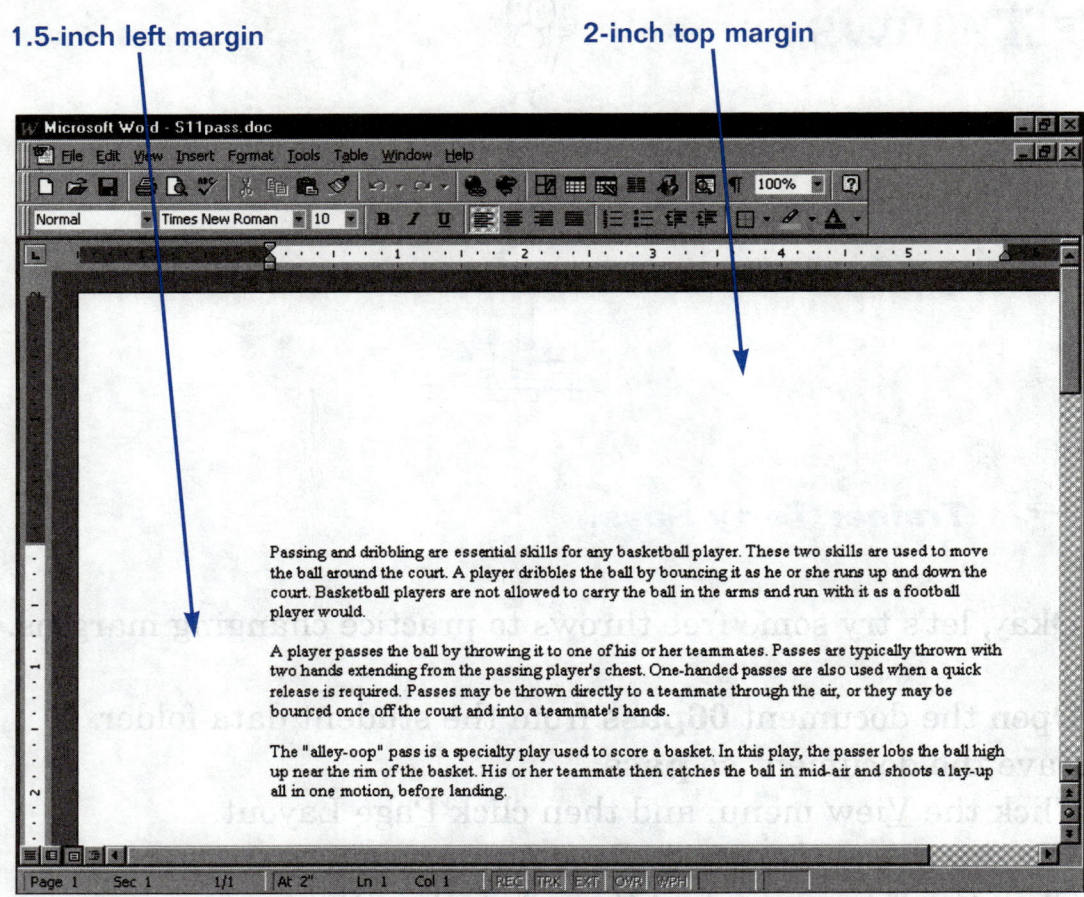

Passing and dribbling are essential skills for any basketball player. These two skills are used to move the ball around the court. A player dribbles the ball by bouncing it as he or she runs up and down the court. Basketball players are not allowed to carry the ball in the arms and run with it as a football player would.

A player passes the ball by throwing it to one of his or her teammates. Passes are typically thrown with two hands extending from the passing player's chest. One-handed passes are also used when a quick release is required. Passes may be thrown directly to a teammate through the air, or they may be bounced once off the court and into a teammate's hands.

The "alley-oop" pass is a specialty play used to score a basket. In this play, the passer lobs the ball high up near the rim of the basket. His or her teammate then catches the ball in mid-air and shoots a lay-up all in one motion, before landing.

Figure 2-32. Use Page Layout view and the Ruler to see the margin changes.

10.   Save your work and leave the **pass** document open on screen.

Using Tabs

Coach Carrie Says:

 Like the first line indent, the Tab key indents a line or paragraph of text. When you press the Tab key, the current line or paragraph moves over to the right.

 Microsoft Word has tabs set to move one half inch every time you press the Tab key. Use the fourth finger of your left hand to press the Tab key. Move the finger up and to the left from the home row to type a Tab. After pressing Tab, return the finger back to the home row.

 Use tabs to indent a new paragraph of text or to move over a line or text item in a list. The Tab key moves text over as far as the small marks shown in the gray area at the bottom of the horizontal ruler. These tab marks are usually set at every half inch, so pressing the Tab key once moves your text over one half inch.

 You can change how far text moves to the right when you press Tab. Click the Format menu and then click Tabs. The Tabs dialog box opens. In the Tabs dialog box, change the distance in the Default tab stops box, and then click OK.

FREE THROWS

Trainer Terry Says:

Try practicing the reach to the Tab key. Practice the reach without pressing the key. Then add some tabs to the **pass** document.

1. Move the fourth finger of your left hand up and to the left to Tab.
2. Move the finger back to *a* on the home row.
3. Repeat the reach to the Tab key and back to the home row several times.
4. Select all text in the **pass** document.
5. Change the line spacing to double space.
6. Delete the extra lines of space between paragraphs.
7. Move the insertion point to the beginning of the first paragraph of the document.
8. Press Tab. The paragraph indents one half inch.
9. Add tabs to the next two paragraphs.
    Your document should look like the one shown in Figure 2-33.

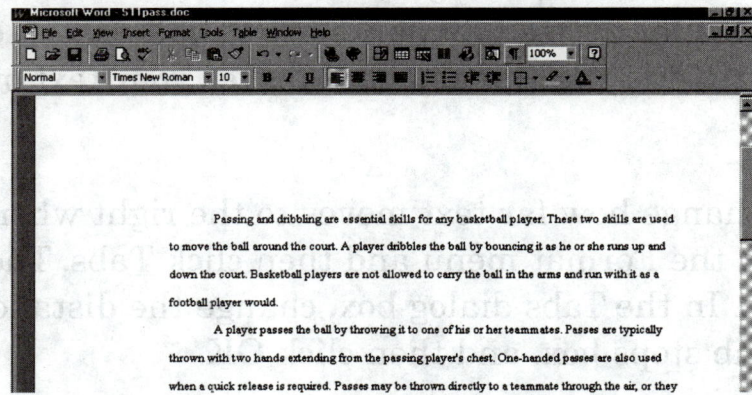

Figure 2-33. Add tabs to indent paragraphs of text.

10. Save your changes to the document and then close it.

TIP-OFF!

Trainer Terry Says:

Okay, basketball stars, let's get ready for the opening tip-off! You will change the page layout of a document, by changing margins and using tabs.

1. Open the document **06defend** from the student data folder.
2. Save the document as **defense.**
3. Click the <u>V</u>iew menu, and then click <u>P</u>age Layout.
   The view changes to Page Layout view.
4. If you can't see the Ruler, click the <u>V</u>iew menu again, and then click <u>R</u>uler.
   Both horizontal and vertical Rulers appear on screen. Your document should look like the one shown in Figure 2-34.

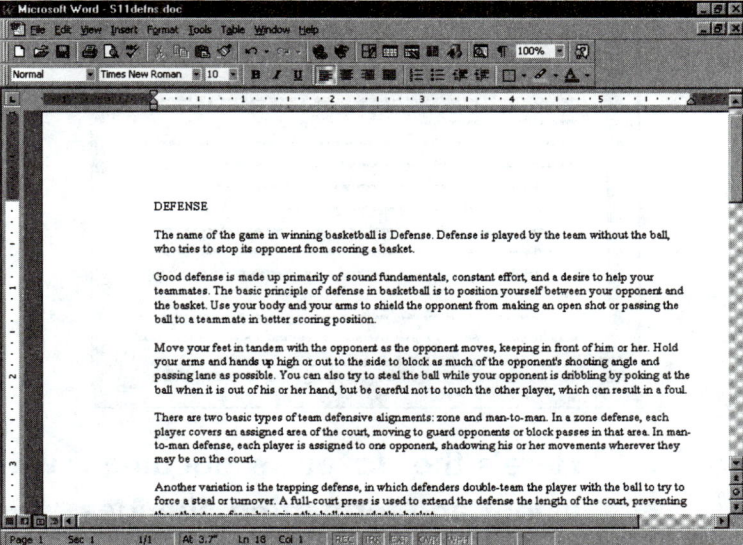

Figure 2-34. Use Page Layout view for the **defense** document.

5. Now make some formatting changes to the document. Change the *DEFENSE* heading to 18 point, Arial, bold, italic. Center the heading.

6. Select all body text and change the line spacing to double spaced. Remove the extra lines between body text paragraphs.

7. Format the following words as italic:

The word *Defense* in the first sentence of the first body text paragraph.

The word *foul* at the end of the third body text paragraph.

The words *zone defense* and *man-to-man defense* in the fourth body text paragraph.

The words *trapping defense*, *turnover*, and *full-court press* in the final body text paragraph.

8. Now add a tab to indent the first line of each body text paragraph. *Do not* add a tab to the very first paragraph of the report.

9. Change the document margins. Click the <u>F</u>ile menu and then click Page Set<u>u</u>p to open the Page Setup dialog box. Change the top margin to 2 inches and change the left and right margins to 1 inch.

10. Note the change in Page Layout view.
Your document should look like the one shown in Figure 2-35.

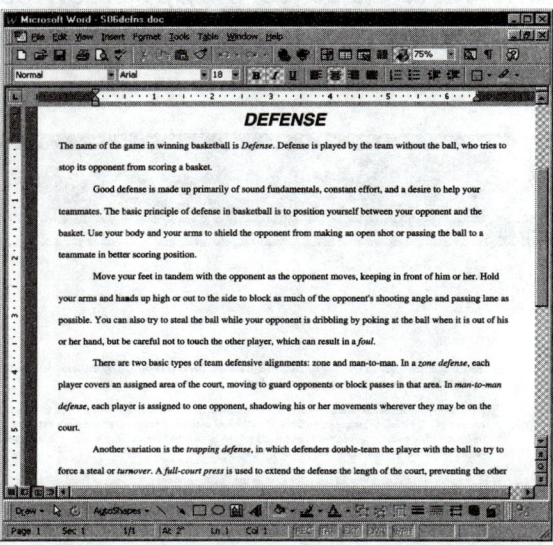

Figure 2-35. Here's the **defense** document with page layout and formatting changes.

11. Save your work on **defense**, then close the document.

THE FINAL FOUR

 Now let's see if you can use some of the page layout skills you've learned on a document of your own. Create your own one-page report that describes the part of basketball, or some other sport, that you like to play most. Do you like to make great passes in basketball? Do you like taking free kicks in soccer? Tell us about your favorite play!

 Use your creativity in formatting the report and setting up the page. Change the margins from the default to a 2-inch top margin and a 1-inch margin on the left and right. Work in Page Layout view to see your changes.

GAME #7
BRINGING IN A
SUBSTITUTION

Sometimes a basketball coach needs to go to the bench for a substitution. Bringing in a new player with fresh legs can help motivate and energize a team. Finding the right player on the bench and replacing the right player on the court are key decisions in winning a game. Likewise, sometimes finding text and replacing it can be essential to creating the document you want.

In this Game you will learn to use the Find and Replace dialog box in Microsoft Word for:

- **Finding Text**
- **Replacing Text**

CHALK TALK

Finding Text

Coach Carrie Says:

 You can use Word's Find and Replace feature to find a specific word or phrase in a document. This is particularly helpful in large documents when you know what you want to find but don't want to spend time scrolling through page after page of text.

 To find a word, phrase, or piece of text (even a series of letters or characters), click the Edit menu and then click Find. The Find and Replace dialog box opens, as shown in Figure 2-36.

Figure 2-36. Use the Find and Replace dialog box to find text.

 Here's a quick way to open the Find and Replace dialog box:

 PC users, press Ctrl+F.

 Mac users, press Command+F.

JEFF THE REF

Take care in typing the word or text you want to search for in the Find and Replace dialog box. Word will match the text exactly as you type it. If you don't find a match, check the text you entered in the Find what box.

 Also, notice that you can click the arrow at the right of the *Find what* box to see a drop-down list showing past text searches.

 To find text, type the word or text you want to find in the Find what box, then click the <u>F</u>ind Next button Find Next . Word moves the insertion point to the next instance of the word or text you entered and highlights it in your document.

 If you want to return to the document, click the Close button ☒ or click Cancel to close the dialog box. If you want to search for the next instance of the word or text, click the <u>F</u>ind Next button Find Next again.

 You can use more complex ways of searching your document by clicking the <u>M</u>ore button More ⯯ in the Find and Replace dialog box. When you click <u>M</u>ore, the dialog box expands to offer you more options, as shown in Figure 2-37.

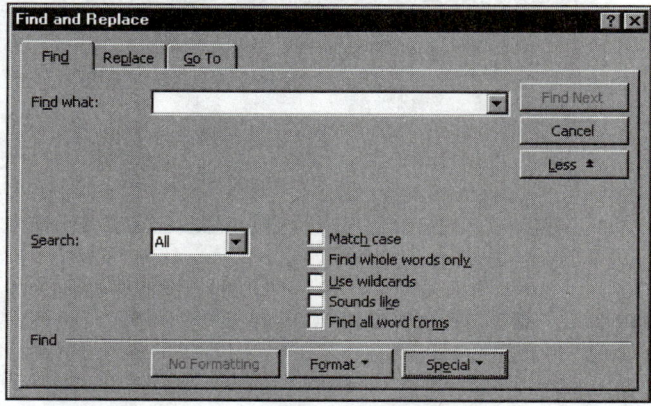

Figure 2-37. The expanded Find and Replace dialog box.

 Check the following Training Table for a quick look at what you can do with each of these options.

Training Table: Find and Replace Dialog Box Options

Option	What It Does
Search	Click the drop-down list to select the portion of the document to search or the direction to search: Up, Down, or All.
Match case	Select this option to find only text that matches the capitalization of the letters of the search text.
Find whole words only	Select this option to find only text that matches the search text as a whole word. For example, if you want to search for the word *and* but do not want Word to find *and* in a word such as **stand**, then select Find whole words only.
Use wildcards	Select this option to use special search characters. For example, you can use an asterisk (*) in place of a letter or group of letters. You can type *h*p* and Word will find all words starting with *h* and ending with *p*, like *hoop* or *help*.
Sounds Like	Select this option to find words that sound alike but are spelled differently, such as *seas* and *sees*.
Find all word forms	Select this option to find all forms of a word, such as *player* and *players*.
Format	Click this button to see a menu of formatting options. Select the formatting options you want to search for and Word will match all instances of text that are formatted that way. For example, you can have Word search for all **bold** formatting or all *italic* formatting.
No Formatting	Click this button to turn off formatting options in the search.
Special	Click this button to search for special codes, such as characters that indicate tabs, the ends of paragraphs, and spaces between words.
Less	Click this button to return the Find and Replace dialog box to the simpler version without the extra options.

FREE THROWS

Trainer Terry Says:

Now step up to the free throw line to practice finding text.

1. Open the document **07offens** from the student data folder.
2. Save the document as **offense**.
3. Move the insertion point to the beginning of the document.
4. Click the Edit menu and then click Find.
    The Find dialog box opens.
5. Type the word *basket* in the Find what text box, and then click Find Next.
    Word finds the first instance of basket *in the document, as shown in Figure 2-38. Notice that this text is part of the word* basketball.

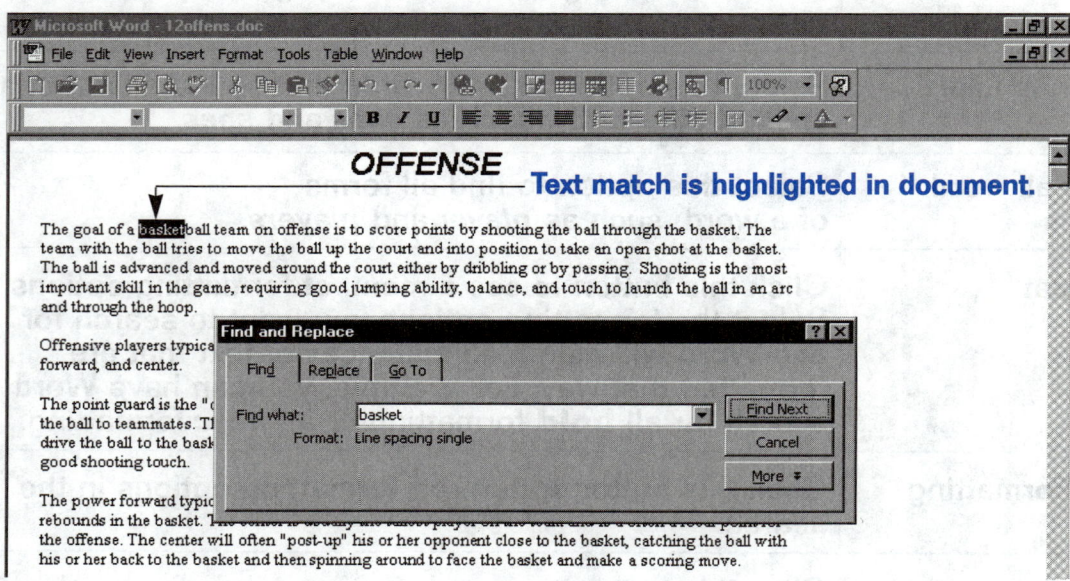

Figure 2-38. Word finds the first instance of *basket*.

6. Click Find Next in the Find and Replace dialog box.
7. Keep clicking Find Next to find all the instances of *basket* in the document.
8. When you reach the end of the document, Word will notify you with a dialog box and ask you if you want to continue searching at the beginning of the document. Click No.

Good job with your first text search! Now try another search using one of the special search options. Follow these steps:

1. Move the insertion point to the beginning of the document.
2. Open the Find and Replace dialog box.
3. Enter the word *basket* in the Fi<u>n</u>d what box, if necessary, and then click <u>M</u>ore.
4. Click to select the Find whole words onl<u>y</u> option, and then click <u>F</u>ind Next.
   Word finds the first whole word match for basket.
5. Keep clicking <u>F</u>ind Next to find all the instances of the whole word *basket* in the document.

Replacing Text

Coach Carrie Says:

 Another way to use Word's Find and Replace feature is to find text in a document and then replace it with other text. This is helpful in large documents when you want to replace text in several places or in all places with new or different text. When you use the replace feature, you can easily make sure you replace all instances of the desired text.

To replace text, click the Edit menu and then click Replace. The Find and Replace dialog box opens to the Replace tab, as shown in Figure 2-39. As with the Find tab, you type the text you want to replace in the Find what text box. You type the new text you want to replace it with in the Replace with text box.

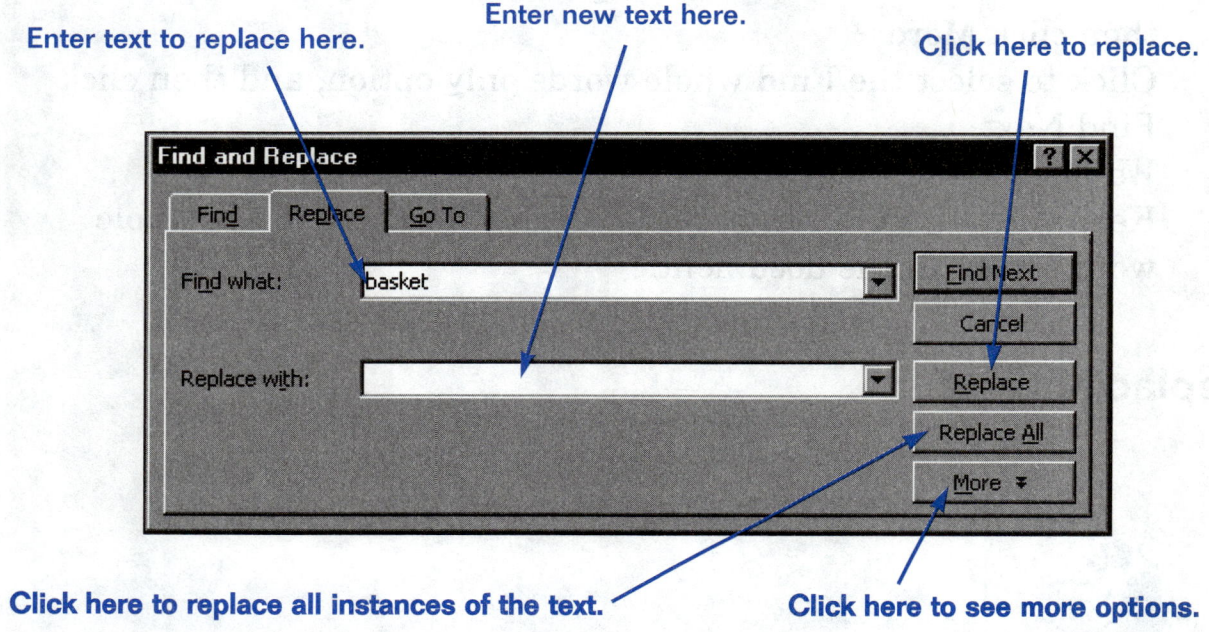

Enter text to replace here.

Enter new text here.

Click here to replace.

Click here to replace all instances of the text.

Click here to see more options.

Figure 2-39. Use the Replace tab of the Find and Replace dialog box to replace text.

 Here's a quick way to open the Replace tab of the Find and Replace dialog box:

 PC users, press Ctrl+H.

 Mac users, press Command+H.

 Also, notice that you can click the arrows at the right of the Find what box and the Replace with box to see a drop-down list showing past text searches and replacements.

Click the <u>F</u>ind Next button to find the first instance of the text you want to replace. Word will highlight the text in your document. Click the <u>R</u>eplace button to replace the text or click <u>F</u>ind Next to move on to the next instance of the text to replace.

 If you want to replace all instances of the desired text in your document, click Replace <u>A</u>ll. Be sure to select the Find whole words onl<u>y</u> option, though. Otherwise, if you are replacing the word *and* with the word *or*, for example, you might end up changing a word such as *stand* to *stor* when you click Replace <u>A</u>ll.

 As in the Find tab, you can click the <u>M</u>ore button  to use more options for finding and replacing text.

 You can also click the <u>G</u>o To tab of the Find and Replace dialog box to move around quickly in large documents. On the <u>G</u>o To tab, you can enter a page number or select another part of the document and enter its number. Then, click Go <u>T</u>o and the insertion point moves to that place in the document.

 Here's a quick way to open the <u>G</u>o To tab of the Find and Replace dialog box:

 PC users, press Ctrl+G.

 Mac users, press Command+G.

JEFF THE REF

If you want to stop replacing text, simply click Cancel to close the Find and Replace dialog box. If you decide you want to change a replacement, close the dialog box and click the Undo button to undo the last replacement you made.

FREE THROWS

Trainer Terry Says:

Okay, more free throw practice now. This time, practice finding and replacing text.

1. In the **offense** document, move the insertion point to the beginning of the document.
2. Click the <u>E</u>dit menu and then click R<u>e</u>place. The Replace tab of the Find and Replace dialog box opens.
3. Type *basket* in the Fi<u>n</u>d what box.
4. Type *hoop* in the Replace wi<u>t</u>h box.
5. Click the <u>F</u>ind Next button. The first instance of *basket* is in the word *basketball*.
6. Click <u>R</u>eplace. The word changes to *hoopball*.
    Don't worry! We'll change this new word back to basketball later!
7. Click <u>F</u>ind Next. Word finds the next instance of *basket*. This time it's the word *basket*.
8. Click <u>R</u>eplace. The word changes to *hoop*.
9. Now click Replace <u>A</u>ll.
    Word goes through the entire document and replaces all instances of basket *with* hoop.
10. Click OK.

Okay, so you realize that replacing *basket* throughout your document might not have been the best idea. Let's go back in and change all the instances of *hoop* back to *basket*.

1.   Move the insertion point to the beginning of the **offense** document.
2.   Open the Replace tab of the Find and Replace dialog box by clicking Edit, Replace.
3.   Type *hoop* in the Find what text box.
4.   Type *basket* in the Replace with text box.
5.   Click Replace All. Word informs you that it made nine replacements.
6.   Click OK.
7.   Save your changes.

TIP-OFF!

Trainer Terry Says:

Now let's jump high for the opening tip! Use the Find and Replace dialog box to make formatting changes to the **offense** document.

1. Move the insertion point to the beginning of the **offense** document.
2. Click <u>E</u>dit, <u>R</u>eplace to open the Replace tab of the Find and Replace dialog box.
3. If necessary, click <u>M</u>ore to expand the dialog box.
4. Make sure the insertion point is in the Fi<u>n</u>d what text box. If there is any text in the Fi<u>n</u>d what text box, select it and then press Delete to remove it.
5. Click the F<u>o</u>rmat button to see a list of options. Click <u>P</u>aragraph. The Find Paragraph dialog box opens, as shown in Figure 2-40.

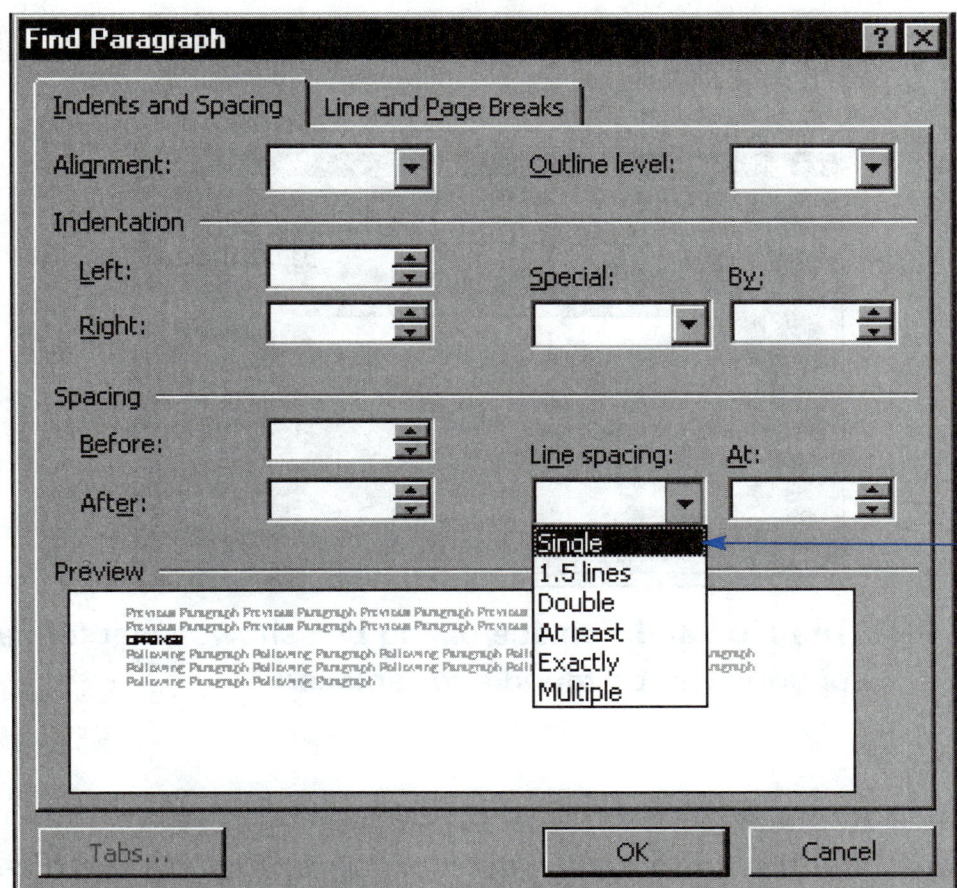

Figure 2-40. Select the formatting you want to find in the Find Paragraph dialog box.

6. Click *Single* from the Line spacing drop-down list, and then click OK. This tells Word to search for single-spaced paragraphs.
7. Move the insertion point to the Replace with text box.
8. Click the Format button again, and select Paragraph.
9. Click *Double* in the Line spacing drop-down list of the Replace Paragraph dialog box. This tells Word to replace single-spaced paragraphs with double-spaced paragraphs.
10. Click OK.
   The Find and Replace dialog box should look like the one shown in Figure 2-41.

Formatting to be found

Formatting that will replace it

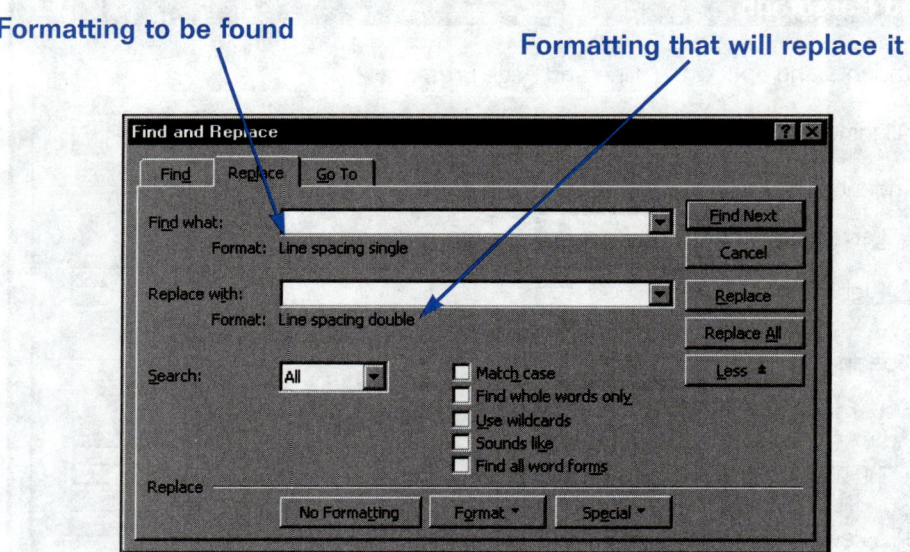

Figure 2-41. The Find and Replace dialog box shows what formatting, options will be found and replaced.

11.   Click Replace All.
       Word replaces all single-spaced paragraphs with double-spaced paragraphs.

12.   Click OK. Delete the extra lines between paragraphs and between the title and body text.

13.   Use the Tab key to indent the second, third, and fourth paragraphs of the report.
       Your document should look like the one shown in Figure 2-42.

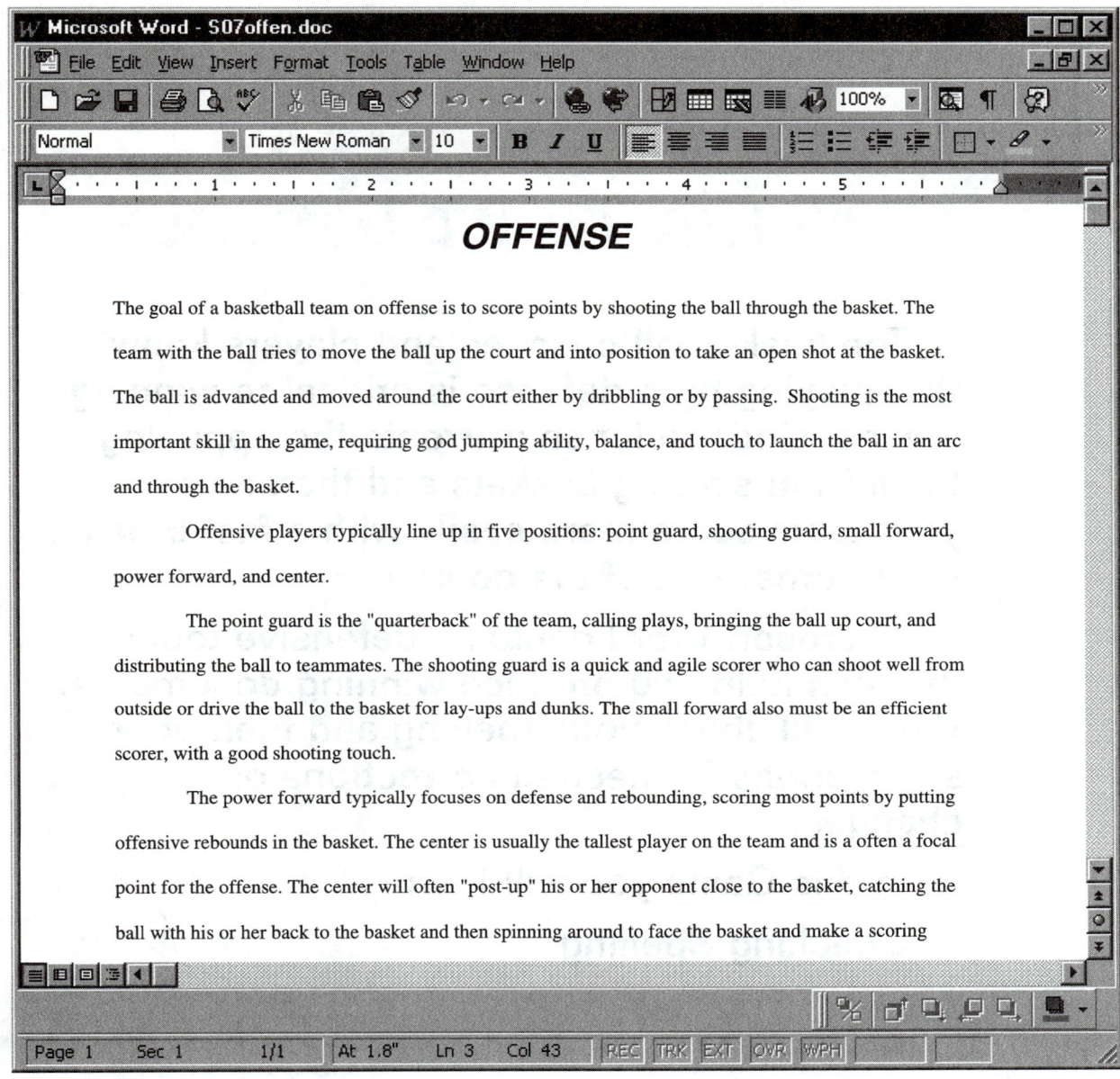

Figure 2-42. The **offense** document with formatting changes.

14. Save your work on **offense** and then close the document.

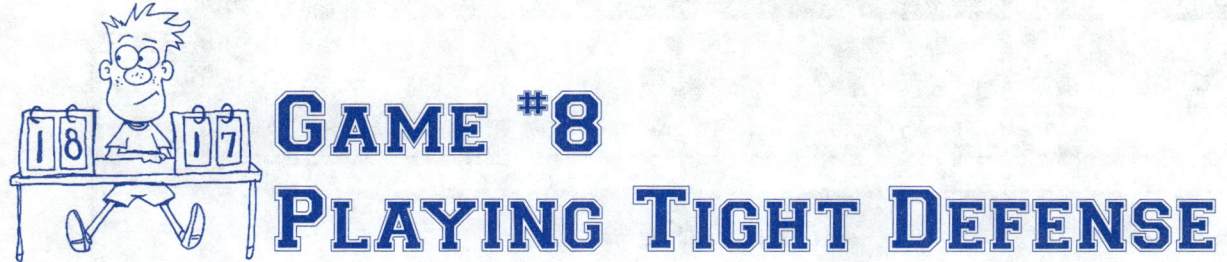

GAME #8
PLAYING TIGHT DEFENSE

Top basketball coaches and players know that playing tight defense is critical to winning games. Good defense prevents the opposing team from scoring baskets and then helps your team score more easily with a fast break to the other end of the court.

Microsoft Word contains defensive tools that can help you produce winning documents. Word will check your spelling and then offer suggestions for needed corrections or changes.

In this Game you will learn:

• Checking Spelling

CHALK TALK

Checking Spelling

Coach Carrie Says:

 Use Word's spell-checking tool to find misspellings, capitalization errors, and repeated words in your documents.

 After you have finished typing your document, check spelling by clicking the Tools menu. Then click Spelling and Grammar. The spell-check tool searches your entire document for spelling errors. If it finds an error, the Spelling and Grammar dialog box opens, as shown in Figure 2-43.

A word that may have a spelling error is highlighted here.

Suggested changes for the highlighted word appear here.

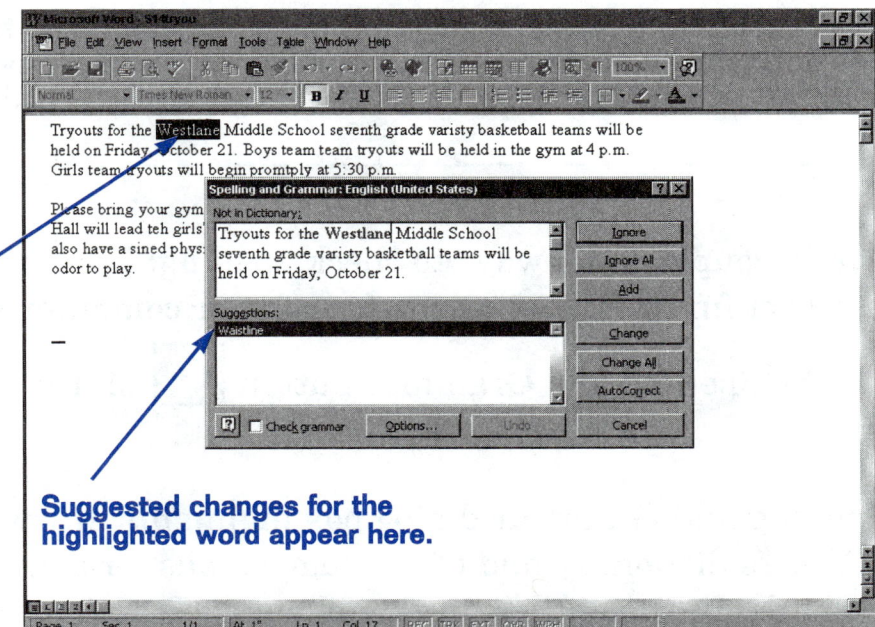

Figure 2-43. The Spelling and Grammar dialog box

You can also check one word or a particular section of your document. Just select the text, then click Tools, Spelling and Grammar.

 Microsoft Word can also check your document for spelling errors as you type. If this option is turned on, you may see wavy red lines (for misspellings) under some of the words in your document.

 Even though some people like to use this option, it can be distracting as you type. To turn off the check spelling and grammar as you type option, see the following table.

 To turn off check spelling and grammar as you type:

MAC	🪟 PC
1. Click the Tools menu and then click Preferences.	1. Click the Tools menu and then click Options.
2. Click the Spelling and Grammar tab of the Preferences dialog box.	2. Click the Spelling and Grammar tab of the Options dialog box.
3. Click to deselect both the Check spelling as you type and Check grammar as you type checkboxes.	3. Click to deselect both the Check spelling as you type and Check grammar as you type checkboxes.

 Here are a couple quick ways to check spelling: Press the F7 key in the row of function keys at the top of your computer keyboard

or click the Spelling and Grammar button ⬜ on the Standard toolbar.

 The Spelling and Grammar dialog box highlights any word that is not in Word's dictionary and offers suggestions for correcting the word. Check out the options in the following Training Table.

Training Table: Spell Checking Options

Option	What It Does
Ignore	Leaves the highlighted word as is.
Ignore All	Leaves all occurrences of the word in the document as is.
Change	Changes the highlighted word to one of the suggested spellings. Click on a suggested spelling to select it.
Change All	Changes all occurrences of the word in the document to one of the suggested spellings.
Add	Adds the highlighted word to the Microsoft Word dictionary. Use this option if the highlighted word does not need to be corrected. Once the word is added to the dictionary, it will no longer show up as a misspelled word in future spell checks.
Delete	Removes the second occurrence of a repeated word.
AutoCorrect	Adds the misspelled word and its correct spelling to the AutoCorrect list.
Close or Cancel	Ends the spelling check and closes the Spelling and Grammar dialog box.

JEFF THE REF

If there are no suggestions or if none of the suggestions make sense, you can click on the highlighted word in the Not in Dictionary window, correct the spelling, and then click Change.

MEG THE MIKE

Microsoft Word's AutoCorrect feature automatically corrects certain common misspellings of words as you type. For example, AutoCorrect automatically changes *teh* to *the* because this is a common typing error.

 When the spelling check is complete, Word notifies you with a dialog box. Click OK. If you have spell-checked only a single word or selection of text, Word will ask you if you want to continue checking the rest of the document. Click Yes to continue or No to close the spell-checking tool.

FREE THROWS

Trainer Terry Says:

Now step up to the free throw line to practice checking spelling.

1. Open the document **08tryout** from the student data folder.
2. Save the document as **tryout**.
3. Click the <u>T</u>ools menu and then click <u>S</u>pelling and Grammar.
   The Spelling and Grammar dialog box opens with the first word that does not match Word's dictionary, Westlane.
4. *Westlane* is a proper name, so click <u>I</u>gnore.
5. Word finds the misspelled word *varisty* and suggests changing it to *varsity*. Click <u>C</u>hange.
6. Word searches for the next error, highlighting the repeated word *team*, as shown in Figure 2-44.
7. Click <u>D</u>elete to delete the extra word. Word deletes it and searches for the next error, highlighting the misspelled word *promtply* and suggesting *promptly* as the first option for correcting the spelling.

JEFF THE REF

If a proper name might occur frequently in your document, you can click Add to add the name to Word's dictionary. After a name is added, Word no longer highlights it as a spelling error.

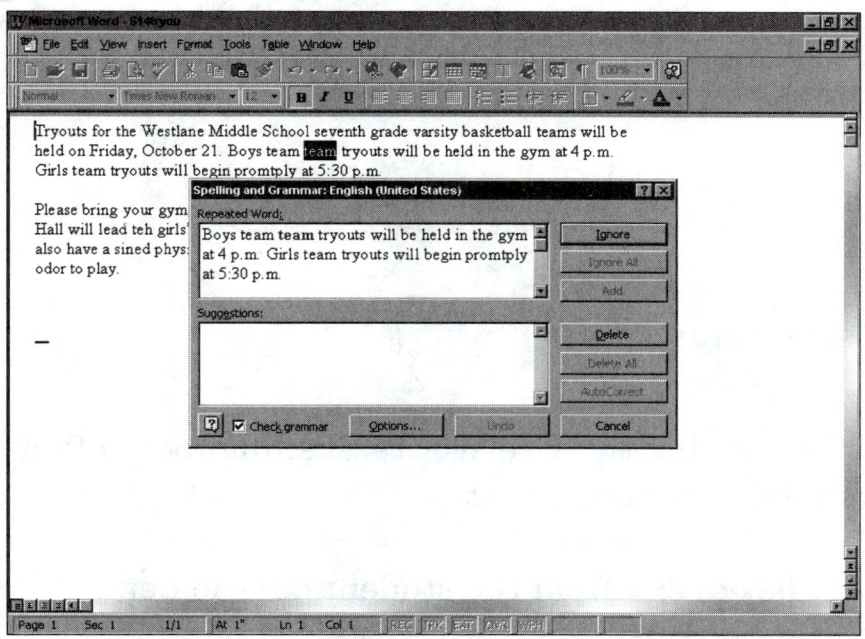

Figure 2-44. Word highlights repeated words.

8.   Click <u>C</u>hange.

9.   Next, the spell checker highlights the misspelled word *teh* and suggests *the* as the first option for correcting the spelling. Because *the* is a frequently used word and you want to correct all instances of this misspelling in the document, click Ch<u>a</u>nge All.

10.   The spell checker highlights the name *Quandt*. Click <u>I</u>gnore.

11.   Word finds the misspelled word *youre*. Change the word to *your*.
Word reaches the end of the document and tells you that the spelling and grammar check is complete.

12.   Click OK.

13.   Now carefully proofread the document. Notice that the word *odor* is used in the final sentence instead of the word *order*.

14.   Change the word *odor* to *order.*

15.   Save your changes and then close the document.

JEFF THE REF

Although Word's spell-checking tool is a great help in finding common errors, it can't tell you when you have used the wrong word. For example, if you use the word *your* when you should have used *you're*, the spell checker will not highlight the error because it doesn't recognize the word as misspelled. Make sure that you proofread your documents carefully in addition to using the spell checker in Word.

TIP-OFF!

Trainer Terry Says:

 Now it's time for the opening tip! Use Word's Spelling tool to find and correct errors in another document.

1. Open the document **08parent** from the student data folder.
2. Save the document as **parent**.
3. Format the line *Volunteers Needed!* as 18 point, Arial, bold, italic. Center the heading.
4. Add the following paragraph to the end of the document.

> If you care to volunteer, please call Donna Northrup in the school's athletic office at 555-4921. Your help is greatly appreciated!

When you have added the text, your document should look like the one shown in Figure 2-45.

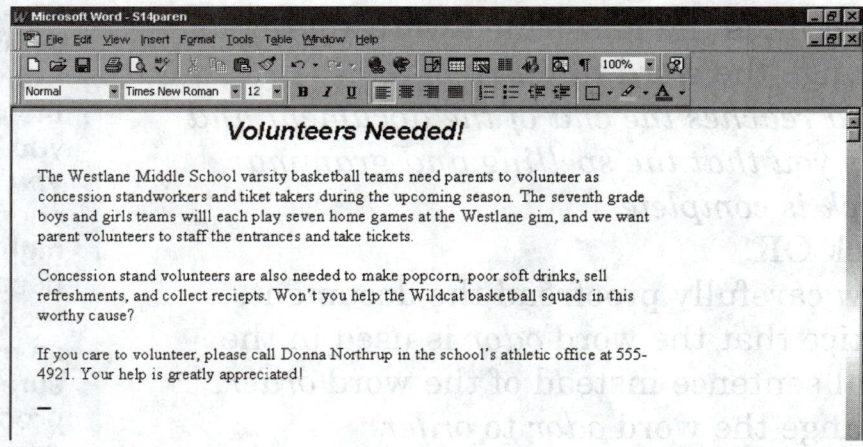

Figure 2-45. The parent document should look like this.

5. Now check the document for spelling errors. Click <u>T</u>ools and then click <u>S</u>pelling and Grammar. The Spelling and Grammar dialog box highlights *Westlane*. Click <u>I</u>gnore.

6. Next, Word highlights *standworkers*. Word suggests *stoneworkers*, but this isn't the right change. Instead, click in the Not in Dictionary window and change *standworkers* to *stand workers*. Click <u>C</u>hange.

7. Continue the spelling check for the rest of the document. Make changes as needed and ignore the suggestion for changing the spelling of *Northrup*.

8. When the spelling check is complete, proofread the document carefully.

9. There is one mistake in word usage that Word didn't catch. Correct the error as needed.

 Here's a hint: soft drinks are neither rich nor poor!

10. Save your changes to **parent** and then close the document.

FINAL FOUR

 Create your own document that asks others for help on a project you need to complete. Perhaps you have a club or school activity with which you need a helping hand, or maybe you want friends in your neighborhood to pitch in on a fun party. Use your imagination to create the document, and then format it and check it for spelling errors.

SEASON 3

BASEBALL

CREATING YOUR OWN SCHOOL REPORT

It's Season Three and time to head out to the old ballpark to get in a few innings of the National Pastime—baseball. You'll play seven Games this Season, in which you'll organize and improve a school report by making use of the drills and skills you've been practicing.

Before the Season's over, you'll get the chance to use an outline, work with more than one document at a time, use the number keypad on your keyboard, use tables to set up info in neat columns and rows, and start new pages exactly where you need them.

To top it off, you'll learn how to add all the stuff to your report that your teachers say you need for full credit—like a *title page*, a *table of contents*, and a *bibliography*. You'll even learn how to put in *footnotes*, *endnotes*, *page numbers*, and *headers* and *footers*.

GAME #1
PLANNING THE BATTING ORDER

In this Game, you'll learn how to create and edit an outline. You can use the outline to organize a report by:

- **Changing to Outline View**
- **Creating an Outline**
- **Editing an Outline**
- **Collapsing and Expanding Outline Topics**

ON DECK

Coach Carrie Says:

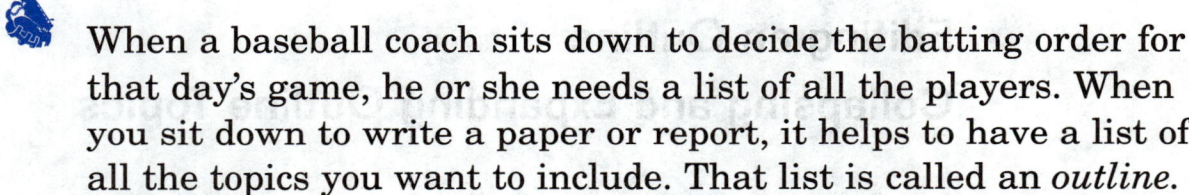

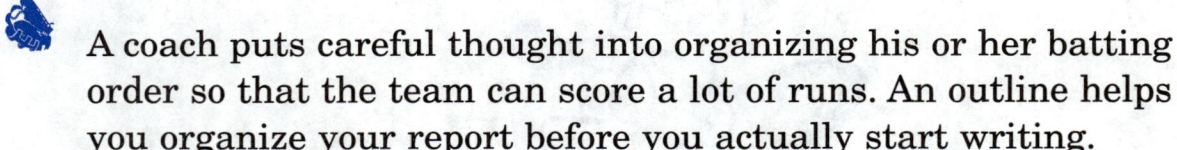

When a baseball coach sits down to decide the batting order for that day's game, he or she needs a list of all the players. When you sit down to write a paper or report, it helps to have a list of all the topics you want to include. That list is called an *outline*.

A coach puts careful thought into organizing his or her batting order so that the team can score a lot of runs. An outline helps you organize your report before you actually start writing.

If the team doesn't get any runs, the coach can change the batting order. Likewise, you can edit your outline by moving the order of topics, or turning a topic into a subtopic.

In this Game, you'll use Word's outline tools to set the batting order for a report. You'll learn how to type topics and subtopics in a document, how to rearrange and edit an outline, and how to hide and show different levels of topics and subtopics.

Changing to Outline View

An outline is a way of organizing the ideas and topics you want to put into your report, speech, or presentation. An outline lets you decide what comes first, what comes last, and how to order everything in between.

Body text is regular text without special formatting.

Toggles is another word for *switches*. Toggle functions are like light switches; they can be turned on or off.

Indented is when a line is moved in away from the margin. You learned about indenting text in Season 2, Game 9.

Coach Carrie Says:

 When you want to create or edit an outline, you use Word's Outline view.

 Outline view displays the Outline toolbar. You can see the Outline toolbar in Figure 3-1. Check out the Training Table on the next page to find out about the Outline toolbar.

Figure 3-1. The Outline toolbar

Training Table: The Outline Toolbar

Button	Button Name	Purpose
←	Promote	Decreases the indent of a topic, and moves the topic up one level
→	Demote	Increases the indent of a topic and moves the topic down one level
⇒	Demote to BodyText	Changes the topic to regular text instead of an outline heading
↑	Move Up	Moves the topic and any subtopics up one line in the outline
↓	Move Down	Moves the topic and any subtopics down one line in the outline
+	Expand	Displays all subtopics under the current topic
−	Collapse	Hides all subtopics under the current topic
1	Show Heading 1	Shows Heading 1 only
2	Show Heading 2	Shows Headings 1 and 2 only
3	Show Heading 3	Shows Headings 1-3 only
4	Show Heading 4	Shows Headings 1-4 only
5	Show Heading 5	Shows Headings 1-5 only
6	Show Heading 6	Shows Headings 1-6 only
7	Show Heading 7	Shows Headings 1-7 only
All	Show All Headings	Shows all heading levels in the outline
=	Show First Line Only	Hides all but the first line of all Body Text paragraphs
A	Show Formatting	Toggles the formatting off or on for all the text in the outline
▣	Master Document View	Toggles back and forth between Outline view and Master Document view

PRACTICE SWINGS

Trainer Terry Says:

 Let's open a new blank document and switch to Outline view:

1. Start Word and open a new, blank document.
2. Click View.
3. Click Outline.
4. Leave your document open. We'll come back to it later.

If you like the mouse better than menu commands, you can click the Outline View button at the left end of the horizontal scroll bar to switch to Outline view.

Mac users can press the shortcut key combination Command+Option+O to switch to Outline View.

MEG THE MIKE

A *style* is a collection of formatting settings that you can apply all at the same time.

In Word, styles have names, like Normal, which is the default style for body text.

Creating an Outline

Coach Carrie Says:

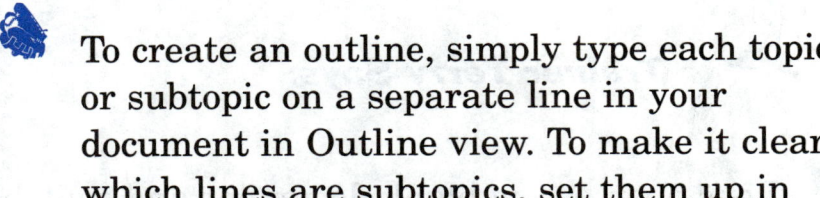 To create an outline, simply type each topic or subtopic on a separate line in your document in Outline view. To make it clear which lines are subtopics, set them up in *indented* levels.

Word automatically changes the formatting *style* for each level so you can see the organization of your outline at a glance. For instance, the top level, Heading 1, is formatted in 14 point, Arial, bold. The next level, Heading 2, is formatted in 12 point, Arial, bold, italic.

When you are ready to write your actual report, use the <u>V</u>iew menu to switch back to <u>N</u>ormal or <u>P</u>age Layout view, and then type in the text under the topic headings.

You can have up to nine levels in an outline. How many levels you use depends on how many topics and subtopics you've got in your report.

The Style box on the Formatting toolbar shows you the name of the formatting style that Word assigns to a topic. Look at Figure 3-2 on the next page to see an example.

PRACTICE SWINGS

Trainer Terry Says:

 To practice creating an outline, let's set up a scouting report for a baseball team. The main topics will be the players' names. Subtopics will include each player's history, positions played, and statistics.

1. Make sure your document is still open in Outline view.
2. On the first line, type *Scouting Report,* and then press Enter.
   Word formats the first line as Heading 1.
3. Press Tab.
   This demotes the new line one level to Heading 2.
4. Type Joe O'Brien and then press Enter.
   Great start! Your outline should look like the one in Figure 3-2.

Style box shows formatting style   Outline Title is Heading 1   Main topic is Heading 2

The minus sign means there are no subtopics under the line

The plus sign means there are subtopics under the line.

Figure 3-2 You can already see the different levels in this outline.

JEFF THE REF

Don't forget that you can use the Promote and Demote buttons on the Outline toolbar instead of Shift+Tab and Tab!

Don't worry if you make a mistake. You can use the same editing tricks you learned about earlier in this book to delete errors, including the Edit, Undo command.

5. Make sure the insertion point is on the blank line under the topic *Joe O'Brien,* and then press Tab.
This demotes the new line one more level to Heading 3.

6. Type *History* and then press Enter.

7. Type *Positions* press Enter.

8. Press Tab.
This demotes the new line one more level to Heading 4.

9. Type *Pitcher* and then press Enter.

10. Type *First Base* and then press Enter.
Whew! Great job! You've now entered the title and the first topic with all of its subtopics. Your outline should look like the one in Figure 3-3.

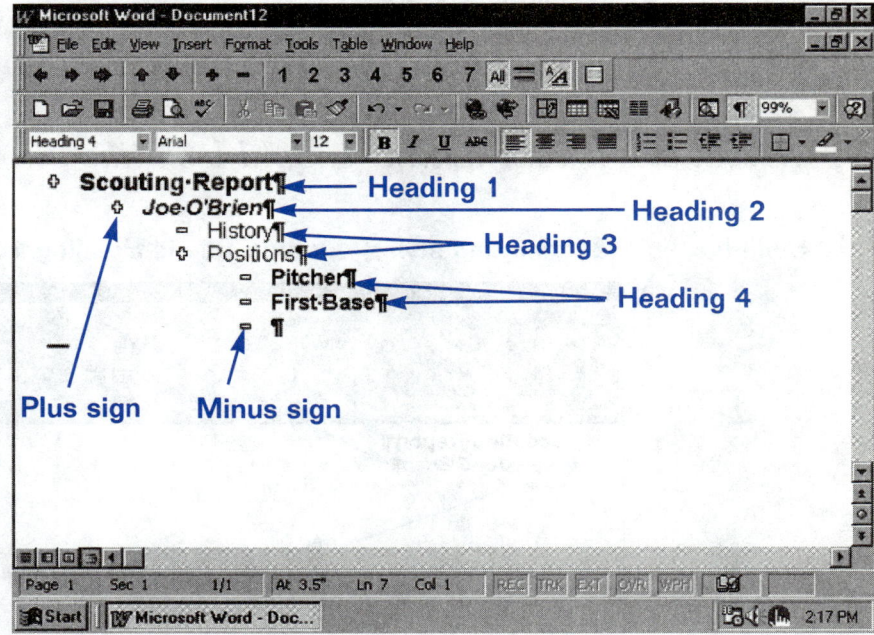

Figure 3-3. The outline now has four levels of topics.

11. Make sure the insertion point is on the blank line under the topic *First Base* and then press the Promote button 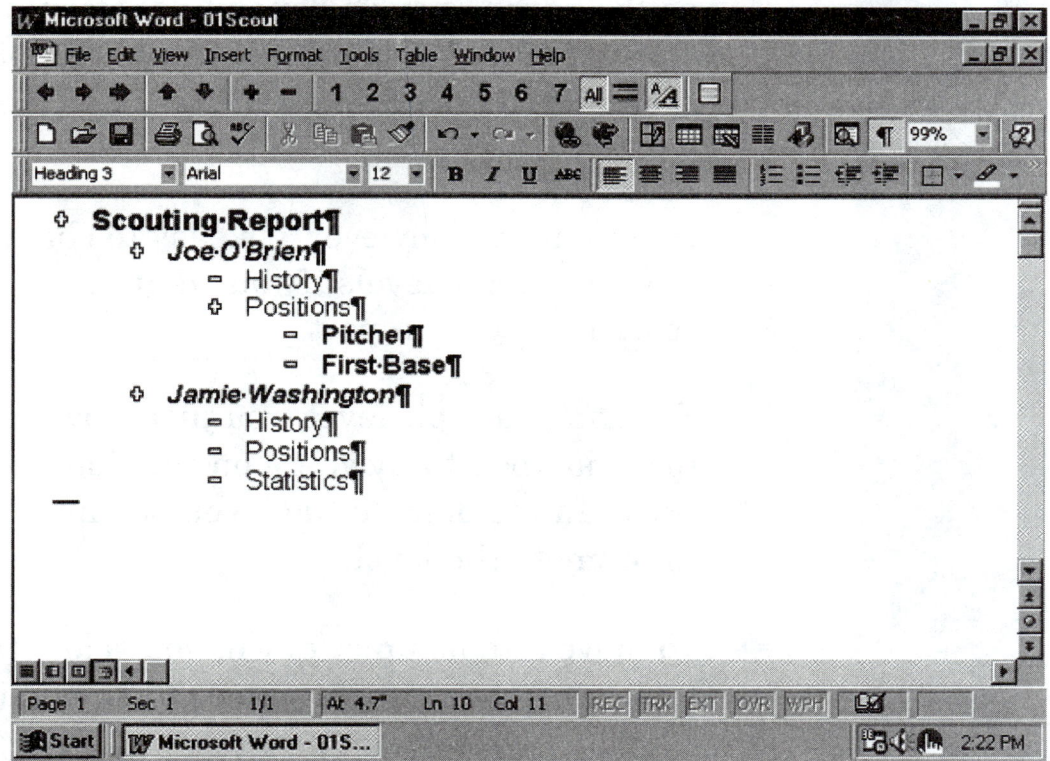 two times.

    This promotes the new line to Heading 2, to match the level of the name of the other player you entered.

12. Type *Jamie Washington* and then press Enter.

13. Press Tab, type *History,* and then press Enter.

14. Type *Positions* and then press Enter.

15. Type *Statistics.*

16. Save the document as **scout.** Leave it open to use again later.

    That's it! The completed outline should look like the one in Figure 3-4.

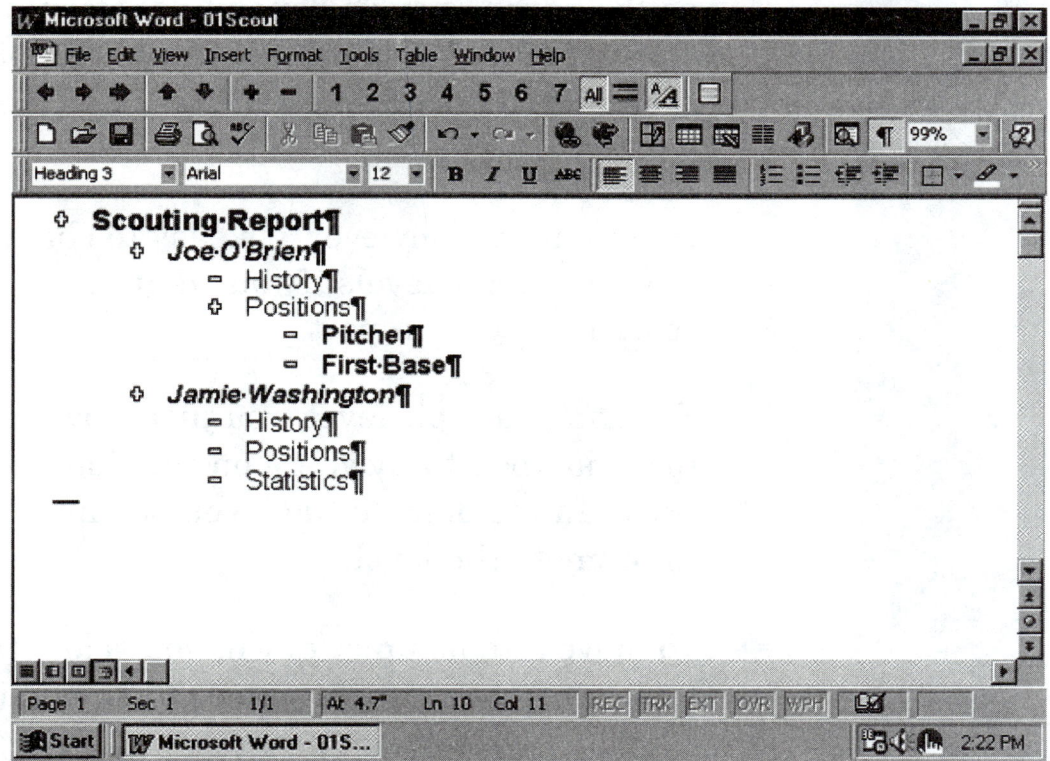

Figure 3-4. The outline is a good way to organize a report.

JEFF THE REF

Don't be tricked into thinking the Move Up and Move Down buttons on the Outline toolbar move the *topic levels* up and down. They don't! They move the selected topic up or down to a new line in the outline document.

Editing an Outline

Coach Carrie Says:

Most editing you do in an outline is the same as the editing you've done in documents in Normal view. You move the insertion point around and insert and delete text wherever you want.

In an outline, however, it's easy to change or move the topic levels if you want to reorganize your report.

To change a topic level, you just move the insertion point anywhere on the line and press Tab to demote the level, or Shift+Tab to promote the level.

To move a topic up or down, you select the topic, and then drag it up or down, or click the Move Up or Move Down button on the Outline toolbar. All of the subtopics move with the main topic, too.

A quick way to select a topic is to click the outline symbol next to it. When you do, all of the subtopics under that topic are selected

PRACTICE SWINGS

Trainer Terry Says:

 To make your Scouting Report outline better, let's add new topics, chang topic levels, and move topics around.

1. Open the **scout** document if it's not already open.
2. Move the insertion point to the end of the line with the topic *First Base,* and press Enter.
    Word inserts a new line at the same level, Heading 4.
3. Type *Outfield* and press Enter.
4. Type *Statistics* and then press Shift+Tab.
    Word promotes the new topic one level to Heading 3.
5. Click the outline symbol next to the topic Outfield.
    This selects the topic.
6. Click the Move Down ⬇ button on the Outline toolbar four times.
    The subtopic Outfield *should be between the subtopics Positions and Statistics, as in Figure 3-5.*

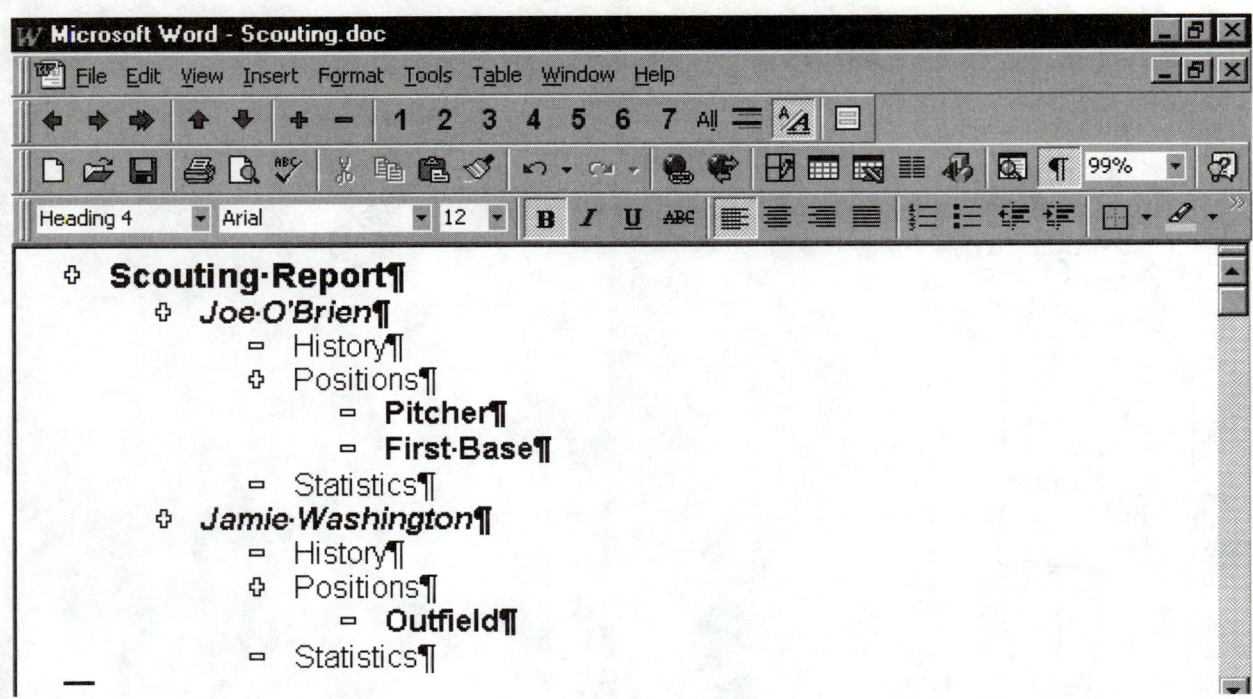

Figure 3-5. The completed outline.

7. Save **scout** document, and keep it open to use later.

Collapsing and Expanding Outline Topics

Coach Carrie Says:

If you don't want to see all the levels of topics in your outline, you can *collapse* some of them. Collapsing topics lets you hide subtopic levels while leaving main topic levels on screen. This is useful when you need to reorganize your main topics but leave subtopics the way they are.

To collapse a topic, just double-click its plus sign outline symbol, or click the Collapse button  on the Outline toolbar.

 When you want to see all the levels again, just *expand* the topic. Double-click the outline symbol again, or click the Expand button on the Outline toolbar.

PRACTICE SWINGS

Trainer Terry Says:

 Let's have some fun collapsing and expanding your outline.

1. Double-click the outline symbol next to the topic *Jamie Washington*.
   The topic is collapsed.
2. Double-click the outline symbol next to the topic *Joe O'Brien*.
   That topic is collapsed, too. See the faint gray lines under the collapsed topics in Figure 3-6? That means that there are hidden subtopics there.

JEFF THE REF

If nothing happens when you try to collapse a topic, there are no subtopics to hide. Likewise, if nothing happens when you try to expand a topic, there are no hidden subtopics. You can tell ahead of time by looking at the outline symbol— if it's a minus sign, there are no subtopics.

Gray line

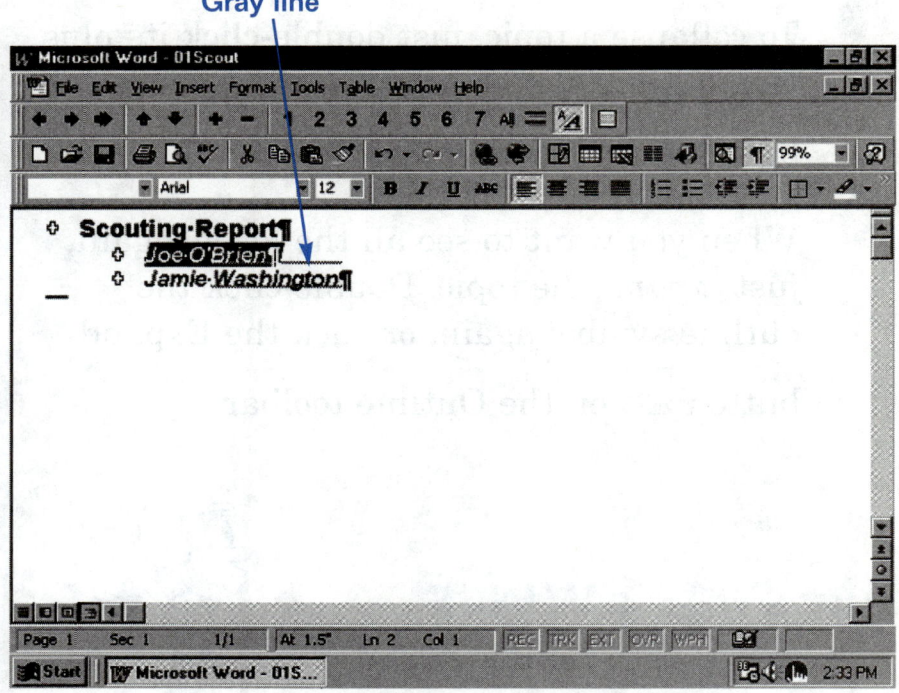

Figure 3-6. A gray line under a topic means that the outline has been collapsed to hide subtopics.

3. Click the Expand button ⊞ on the Outline toolbar.

The selected topic—Joe O'Brien—is expanded, but the subtopic Positions *and the topic* Jamie Washington *are still collapsed. In Figure 3-7, you can see the gray lines that mean there are subtopics still hidden.*

Gray line

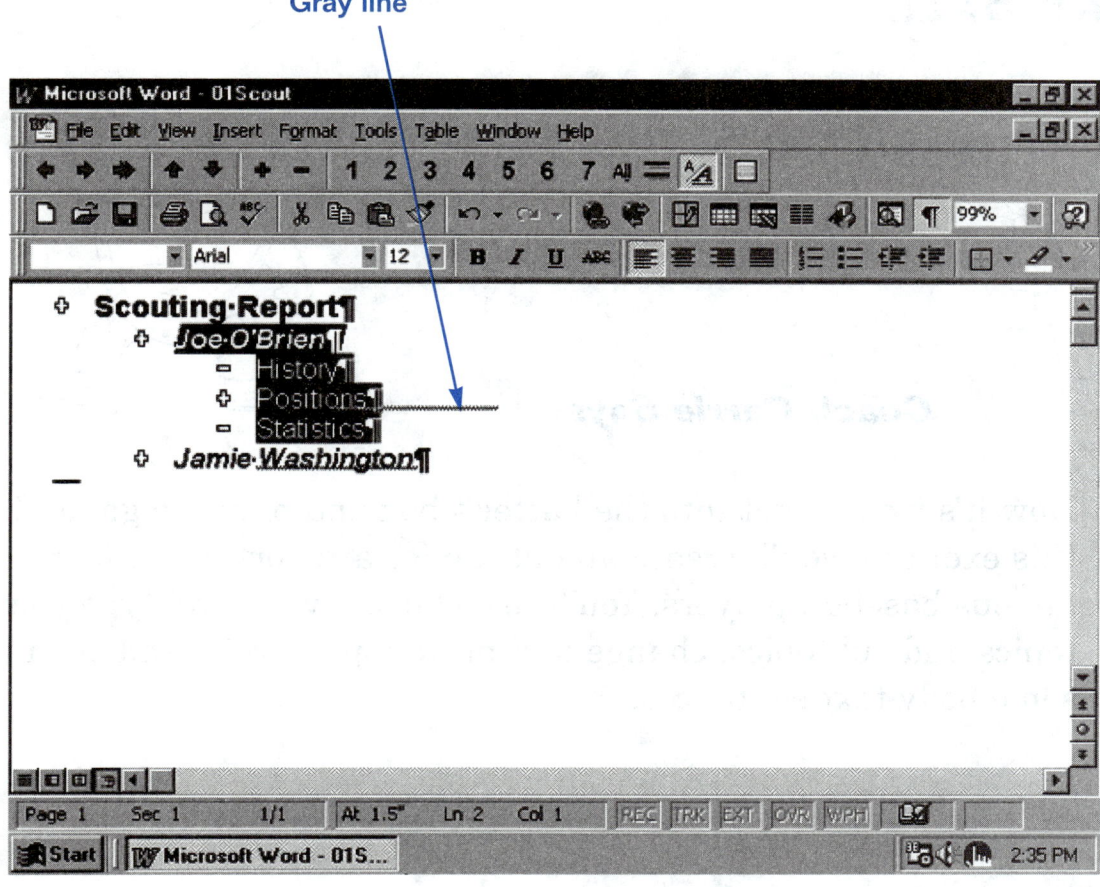

Figure 3-7. Even though the main topic has been expanded, the subtopics are still collapsed.

4. Click the All button 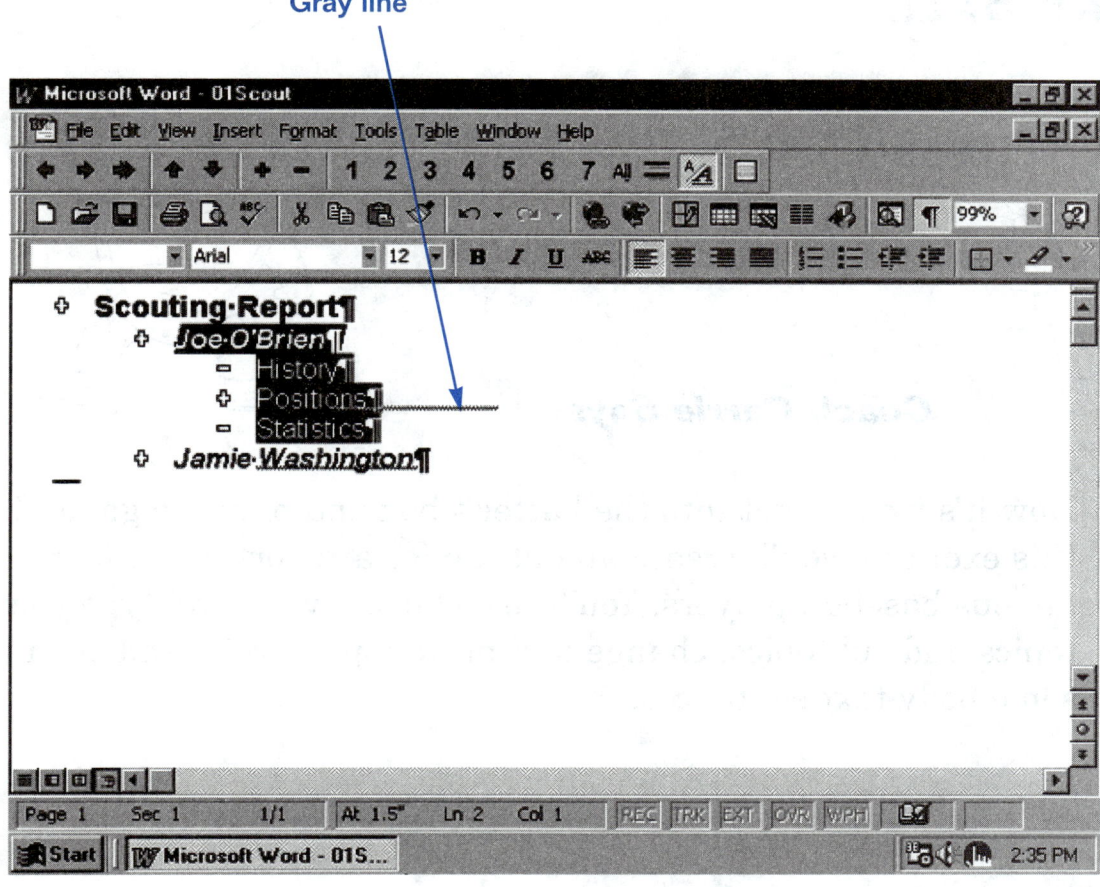 on the Outline toolbar. All topics are displayed.
5. When you are finished, save and close the **scout** document.

PLAY BALL

Coach Carrie Says:

Now it's time to get into the batter's box and play the game. In this exercise, you'll create an outline for a report about four famous baseball players. You'll use Outline view and type your topics and subtopics, change and move topic levels, and even type some body text sentences.

Trainer Terry Says:

When you're ready, get set for the first pitch:

1. Open a new blank document and choose View, <u>O</u>utline to switch to Outline view.
2. Type the report title *Four Baseball Legends,* and then press Enter.
3. Press Tab and type the first main topic, *Mickey Mantle,* and then press Enter.
4. Press Tab and type the first subtopic, *Personal History,* and then press Enter.
5. Type the next subtopic, *Baseball History,* and then press Enter.
6. Type the next subtopic, *Career Highlights,* and then press Enter. *Well done! Step out of the box for a minute and catch your breath. Your outline should look like the one in Figure 3-8.*

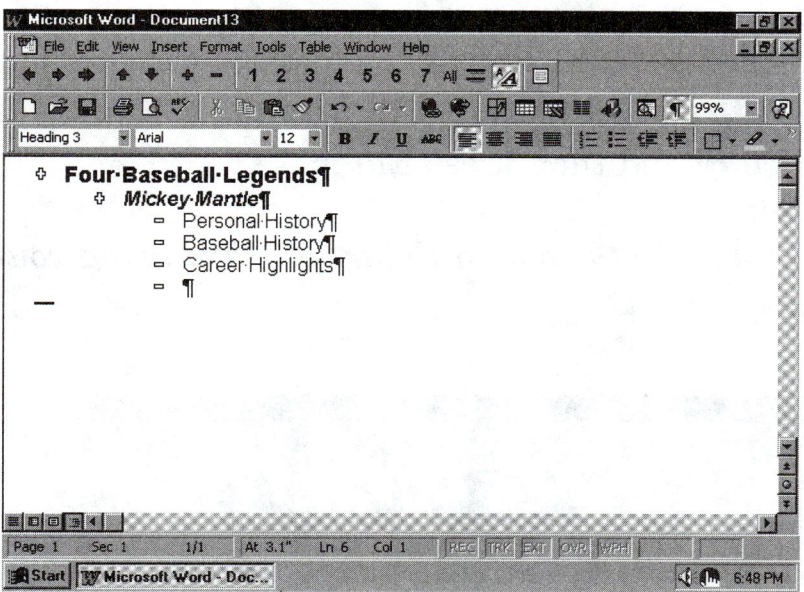

Figure 3-8. The outline begins to take shape.

7. Press Shift+Tab and type *Babe Ruth* and then press Enter.

8. Press Tab and type *Personal History* and then press Enter.

9. Type *Baseball History* and then press Enter.

10. Type *Career Highlights* and then press Enter.
    Notice the pattern? Each main topic— a player—is going to have the same three subtopics.

11. Press Shift+Tab and type *Cy Young* and then press Enter.

12. Press Tab and type, *Personal History* and then press Enter.

13. Type *Baseball History* and then press Enter.

14. Type *Career Highlights* and then press Enter.
    That's three main topics down and one to go. Keep up the good work!

15. Press Shift+Tab and type *Jackie Robinson* and then press Enter.

16. Press Tab and type *Personal History* and then press Enter.

17. Type *Baseball History* and then press Enter.

18. Type *Career Highlights.*

    Now the outline looks like the one in Figure 3-9. Try using your editing skills to improve it.

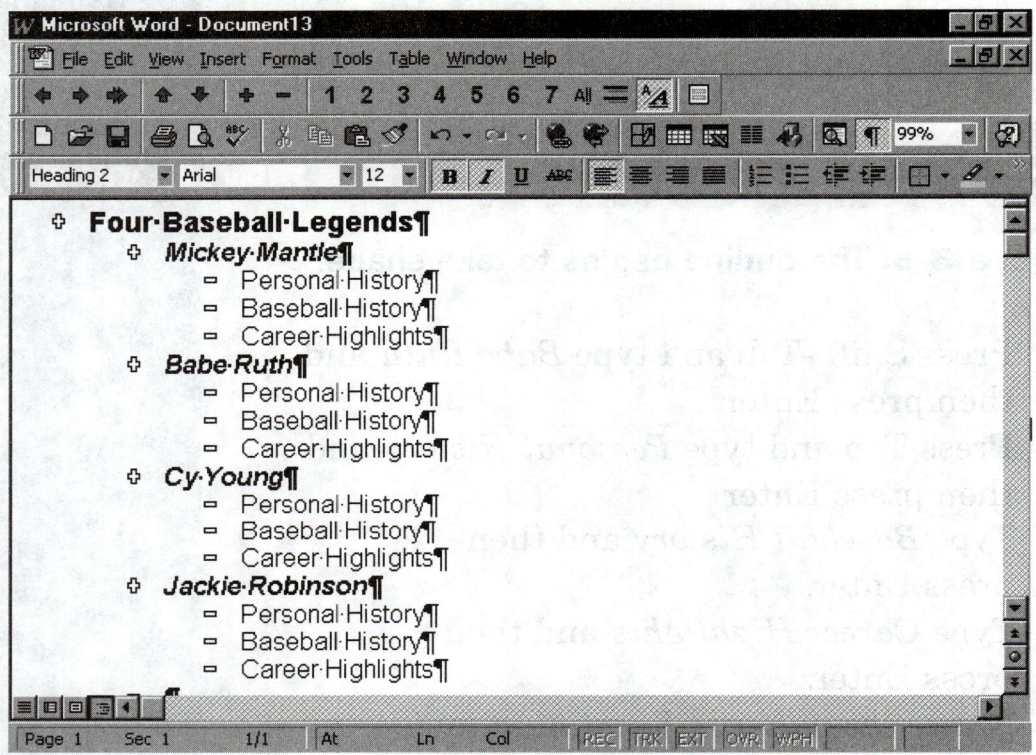

Figure 3-9. The outline now has four main topics with three subtopics each.

19. Click the Show Heading 2 button **2** on the Outline toolbar so that you can see only the main topics in the outline.

20. Click the outline symbol next to the topic *Babe Ruth* to select it, and click the Move Up button so it is listed as the first topic under the title.

21. Click the outline symbol next to the topic *Mickey Mantle* to select it, and click the Move Down button ⬇ twice so it is the last topic listed.

When nothing's selected, your outline should look like the one in Figure 3-10.

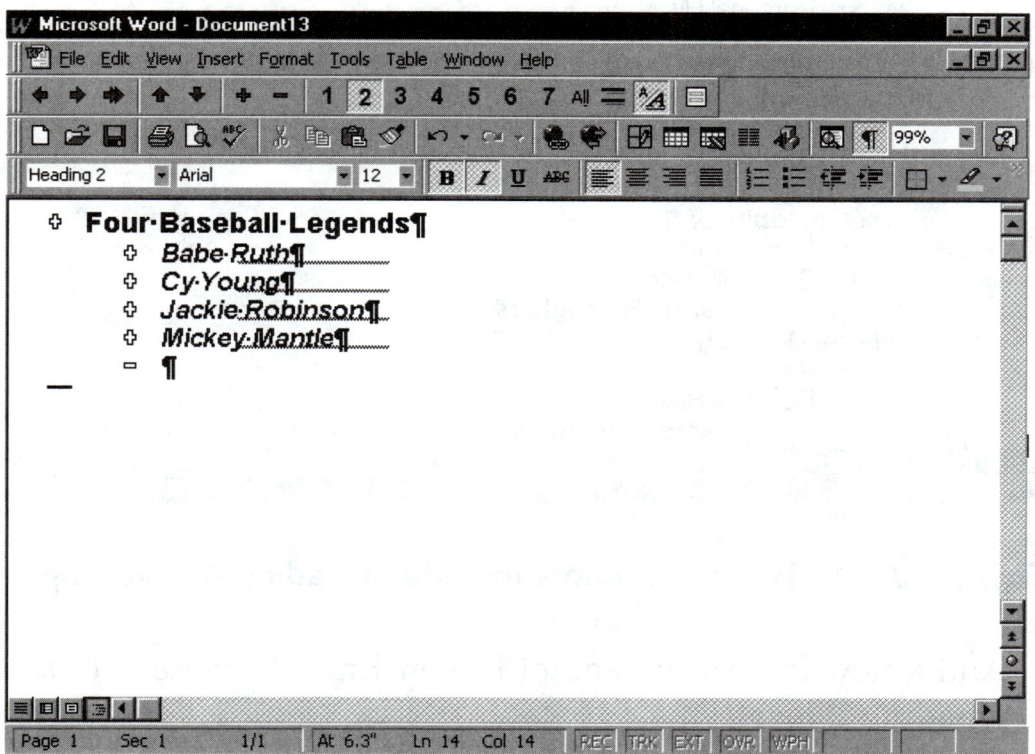

Figure 3-10. The topics are now in order.

22. Click the All button on the Outline toolbar.
23. Move the insertion point to the end of the title line and press Enter.
24. Press Tab and type *Introduction.*
25. Click anywhere in the topic *Career Highlights* in the Babe Ruth section and press Tab. Repeat this step to demote the topic *Career Highlights* for Cy Young, Jackie Robinson, and Mickey Mantle.

Career Highlights will work nicely as a subtopic of Baseball History. The new organization will help make your final report better. It now looks like the one in Figure 3-11.

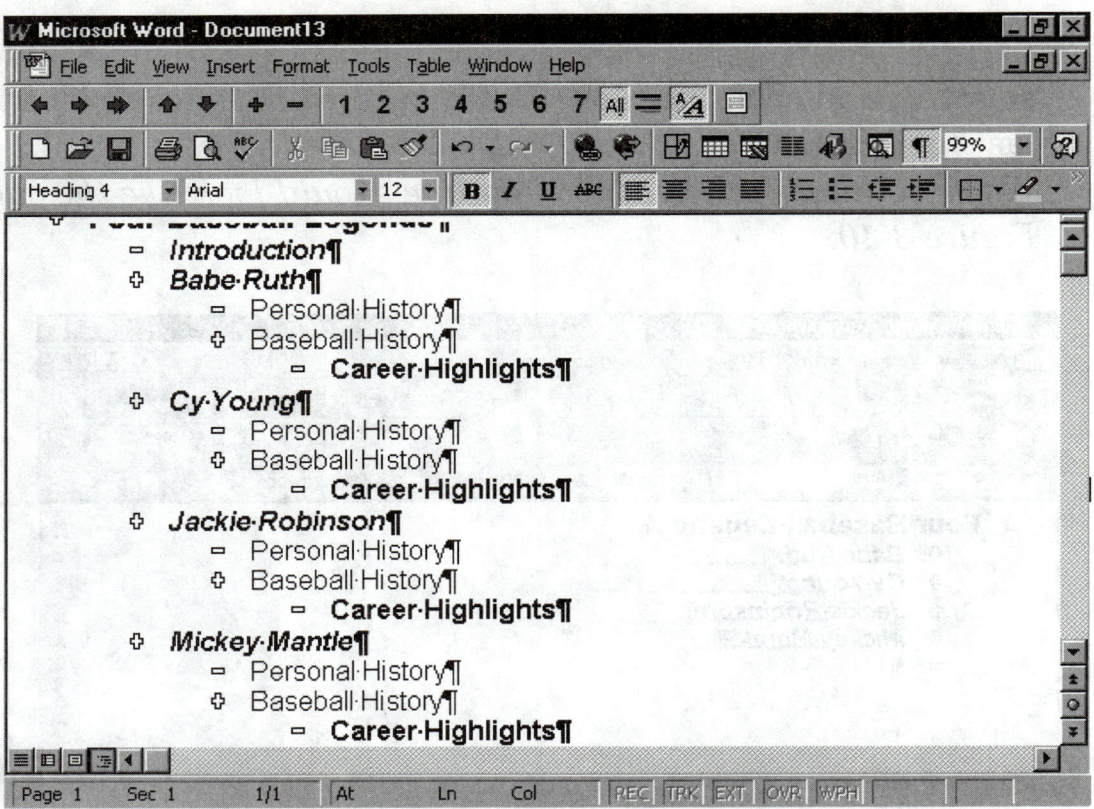

Figure 3-11. The outline now includes Heading 4—level topics.

26.   Add a new line to the end of the outline. Promote it to the Heading 2 level.

27.   On the new line, type the topic *Conclusion,* and then press Enter.

28.   🪟 Press Ctrl+Shift+N to demote the new line to Body Text.
OR

     🍎 Press Command+Shift+N to demote the new line to Body Text.

29.   Type:

If you ask five different baseball fans who they think are the greatest players of all time, you will hear five different answers. Ruth, Young, Robinson, and Mantle may not be the only great baseball legends, but they are four names near the top of every fan's list.

You made it! The end of your winning outline should look like Figure 3-12.

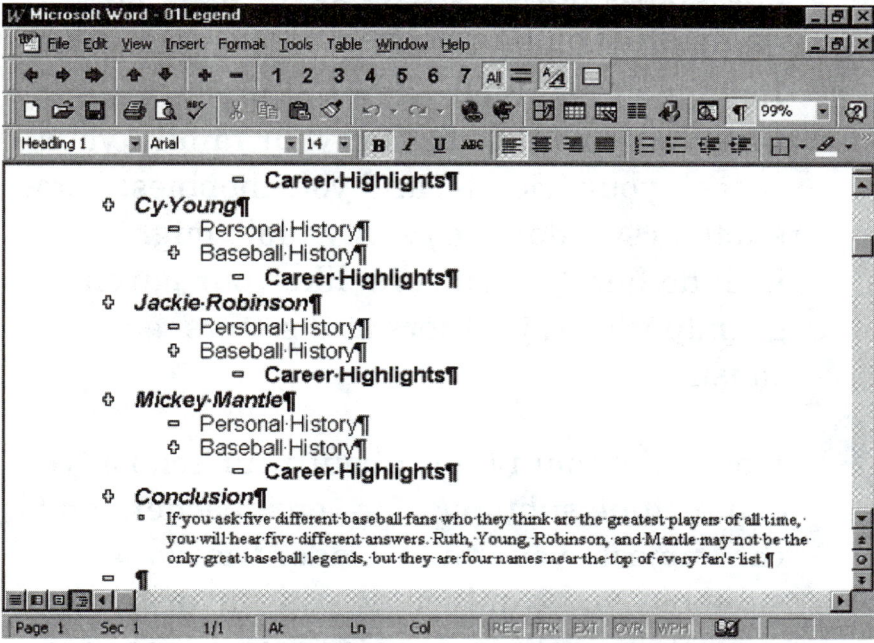

Figure 3-12. You'll use the Body Text paragraph as the conclusion of your report.

30.   Save the document as **legend** and close it.

When you're ready to write your report, switch back to Normal or Page Layout view. The headings all appear aligned left, still formatted, and the Body Text is in place in the document, right where you want it!

MEG THE MIKE

An *autobiography* is a book or report that you write about yourself.

Electives are special courses that you get to pick, like singing in the school chorus or writing for the school newspaper.

Unique means one of a kind, or special.

WORLD SERIES

 Try out the skills you have learned in this Game to create an outline for your own autobiography—a report about yourself.

 Include at least four levels of topics. Be sure to include main topics for your family, your school, your friends, and your hobbies. Some subtopics under the *family* topic might include family members, like your parents, grandparents, brothers and sisters, or cousins.

 Under the main topic about your school, you can include subtopics for your teachers and the subjects you study. Under the *subjects* subtopic, you can include your favorite subject, as well as any electives or specials that you take.

 Try to think up some topics that are unique to you. For instance, are you a scout? Do you have a pet? Do you work to earn money? Do you play sports? Are you good at math? These are all ideas that you can organize into topics and subtopics to write a report about yourself.

GAME #2
USING A LITTLE
TEAMWORK

In this Game, you'll learn how to work with more than one document at a time by:

- **Opening More than One Document**
- **Switching from One Document to Another**
- **Displaying All Documents at the Same Time**
- **Moving Text from One Document to Another**
- **Copying Text from One Document to Another**

ON DECK

Coach Carrie Says:

Although only nine baseball players are in the lineup for each game, a baseball team has extra players in case the coach needs to call in a back-up player.

Usually, you use one document at a time in Word. Sometimes, though, you might need to look at another document while you work. Luckily, with Word it's easy to work with more than one document at a time.

In this Game, you're going to call reinforcements off the bench to help you plug some holes in the report you started in Game 1. You'll learn how to open more than one document at a time, switch back and forth between them, and display all open documents on your screen at the same time. Then, you'll learn how to move and copy text from one document to another.

Opening More than One Document

Coach Carrie Says:

 Opening more than one document in Word is a breeze. You use the same commands to open new documents that you use to open a first document.

PRACTICE SWINGS

Trainer Terry Says:

1. Open the document **02scout** from the student data folder.
2. Save the document as **scout2**.
   *The **scout2** document is a scouting report based on the practice outline you created in the previous Game. You can see it's already got some information in it, but you'll want to add in some details.*

JEFF THE REF

The second time you choose the Open dialog box, the student data folder should already be selected in the Look in drop-down list box. If it's not, click the Look in drop-down arrow and select it.

MASCOT MAX

Do you see that nonprinting characters are displayed in the documents in the figures? It's usually easier to work in Word with nonprinting characters like tabs and paragraph marks displayed. If you don't have your computer set to display them, just click the Show/Hide button ¶ on the Standard toolbar. To turn them off, click it again.

3. Without closing the **scout2** file, choose File, Open again.

4. In the student data folder, double-click the file called **02stats**.

5. Save the document as **stats**.
That's it! Even though it looks like only the stats2 document is open really both scout2 and stats are open at the same time.

Switching from One Document to Another

Coach Carrie Says:

 By default, Word is set up so that only one document window fits on screen at a time. Even if more than one document is open, you can only see one. That's because the other open documents are hidden behind the *active* document.

 If you want to work in a different document, you've got to switch to it, to make it active.

To switch back and forth from one document to another, just open the <u>W</u>indow menu and choose the document you want to make active.

 On the PC, use the shortcut key combination Ctrl+F6 to cycle through all the open documents.

 Mac users can press Command+F6 to cycle through the open documents.

 You can also choose to arrange your documents so that you can simply click inside a document to activate it.

 Here are some tips for figuring out which document is active:
(1) It's on top of the other documents; (2) It's where the insertion point is; (3) Its title bar is brighter than the title bars of the other documents.

MEG THE MIKE

The *active document* is the document that contains the insertion point. No matter how many documents you have open, only one can be active at a time.

PRACTICE SWINGS

Trainer Terry Says:

Try switching back and forth between the **stats** document and the **scout2** document:

1. With the **stats** document displayed in the document window, click the <u>W</u>indow menu command.
   The <u>W</u>indow menu drops down, as in Figure 3-13.

On a PC, there's a number in front of each name and that the number is underlined, like a hot key (because it *is* a hot key).

On a Mac, you'll see a checkmark next to the active document.

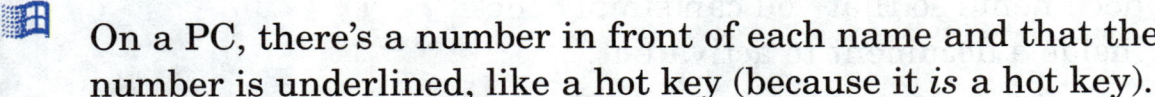

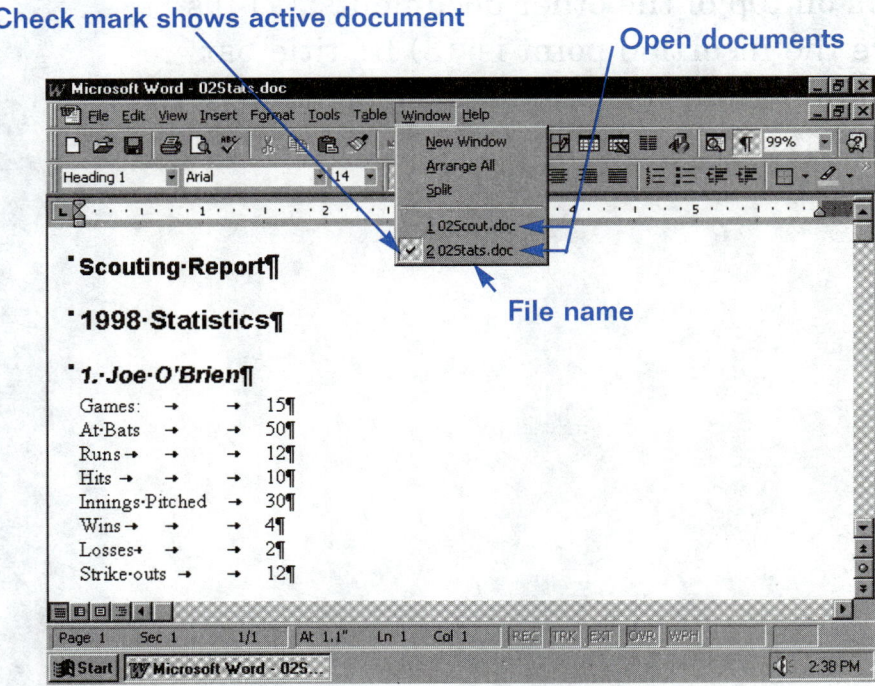

Figure 3-13. Use the Window menu to switch from one open document to another.

2. Click **1 scout2** on the <u>W</u>indow menu.
scout2 is now the active window!

3. Open the <u>W</u>indow menu and click on **2 stats**.
*Now **stats** is active again.*

4.  Press Ctrl+F6.

   Press Command+F6.

   *Word switches to the next open document—in this case, **scout2**.*

5. Still holding down Ctrl or Command, press F6 again.
*Word switches to the next open document—in this case, back to **stats**!*

6. Leave both documents open.

Displaying All Open Documents at the Same Time

RUN HOME!

Coach Carrie Says:

When you need to see all of your open documents at the same time, you can use the <u>A</u>rrange All command on the <u>W</u>indow menu. <u>A</u>rrange All divides the Word window so that each open document takes up a portion of the screen.

In Figure 3-14, three open documents are arranged on screen. The active document is in the middle. Notice that each window has not only a title bar, but a scroll bar, too.

When you're ready to display only one document on screen, simply maximize the window of the document you want to be active.

Word Taskbar button

Active title bar

Scroll bar

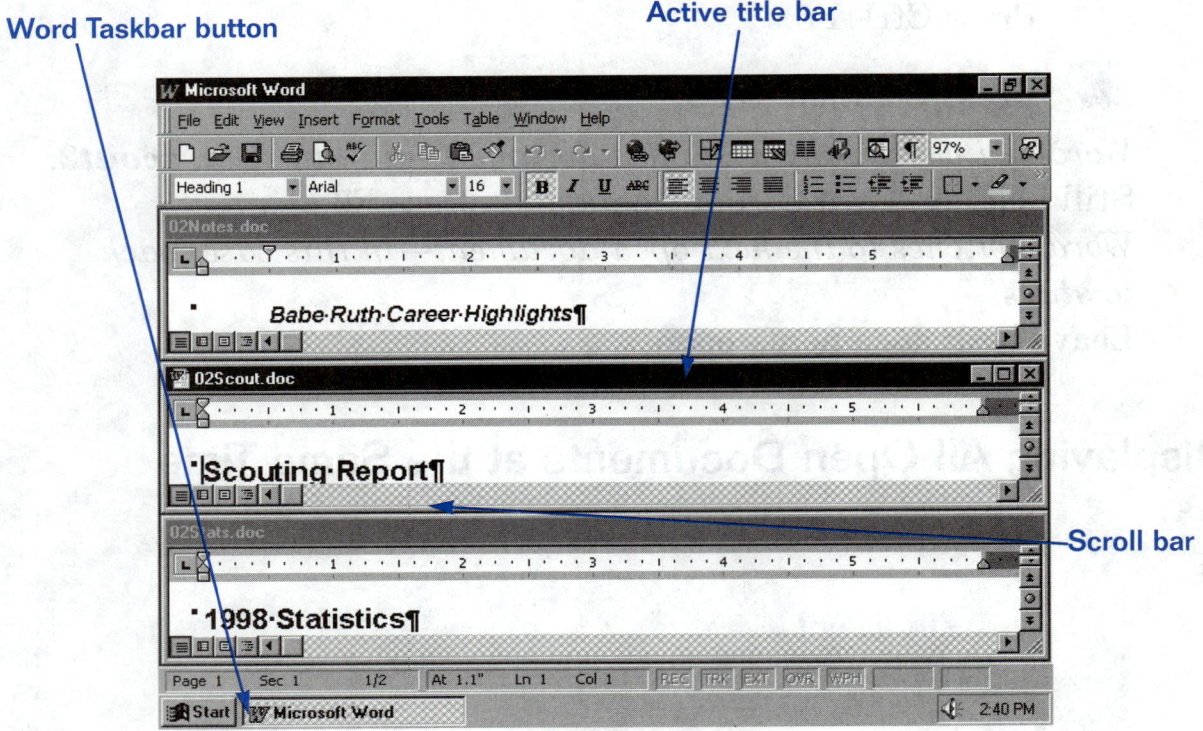

Figure 3-14. Here, three documents are arranged on screen; the active one is in the middle.

Arranging all open windows has some good points and some bad points. On the good side, you can see all the documents you have open. On the bad side, you only see a fraction of each document.

PRACTICE SWINGS

Trainer Terry Says:

 Let's try arranging the **stats** document and the **scout2** document so that you can see them both on screen at the same time.

1. Open the <u>W</u>indow menu and choose <u>A</u>rrange All.
    Word stacks the two documents one above the other, as in Figure 3-15.

Active document has bright title bar and insertion point.

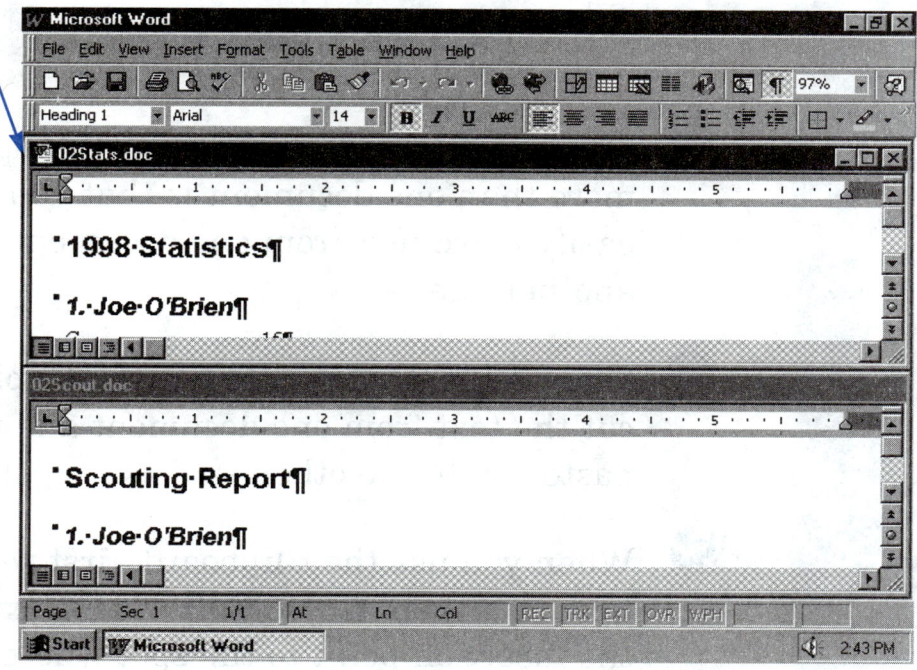

Figure 3-15. You can see both documents on screen at the same time.

MEG THE MIKE

Remember that the *Clipboard* is a temporary storage area. You can cut or copy one selection to the Clipboard at a time. While the selection is on the Clipboard, you can paste it anywhere in the same document or a different document.

2. Open the <u>W</u>indow menu and choose <u>1</u> scout2. Now, the **scout2** document is active.
You can also just click in the document you want to make active.

3. Click the Maximize button on the **scout2** title bar.
*Now, the **scout2** document is the only one you can see. The **stats** document is still open, but it's hidden.*

Moving Text from One Document to Another

Coach Carrie Says:

 One of the best things about working with more than one document is that you can easily move text from one document to another one.

 One way to do this is to use the Clipboard to cut the text from one document and then paste it into the other.

When you use the Clipboard, first select the text, and then choose <u>E</u>dit, Cu<u>t</u>. Next, move the insertion point to the spot where you want to paste the selection. Finally, choose <u>E</u>dit, <u>P</u>aste. Word pastes the selection into the document where the insertion point is.

There are lots of ways to use the Cut, Copy, and Paste commands. The following Training Table lists the menu commands, toolbar buttons, and shortcut keystrokes for each. Use the method you like best.

Training Table: Editing Shortcut Keystrokes

Menu Command	PC Shortcut keys	Mac Shortcut keys	Toolbar button
Edit, Copy	Ctrl+C	Command+C	
Edit, Cut	Ctrl+X	Command+X	
Edit, Paste	Ctrl+V	Command+V	

 Another way of moving text from one document to the other is *drag-and-drop*.

 When you use drag-and-drop, first arrange the documents on screen so that you can see both the text you want to move from one document and the spot where you want to move it to in the other document. Then, select the desired text and release the mouse button. Place the mouse pointer anywhere inside the selected text and then click to drag it into the other document. When you release the mouse button, Word moves the selection to where the insertion point is.

PRACTICE SWINGS

Trainer Terry Says:

 Ok, batters, let's see your moves!

1.  Press Ctrl+F6 to make the **stats** document active.

   Press Command+F6 to make the **stats** document active.

2. Scroll down to the bottom of the **stats** document and select the four lines of statistics under *Chris Alemeda* (see Figure 3-16).

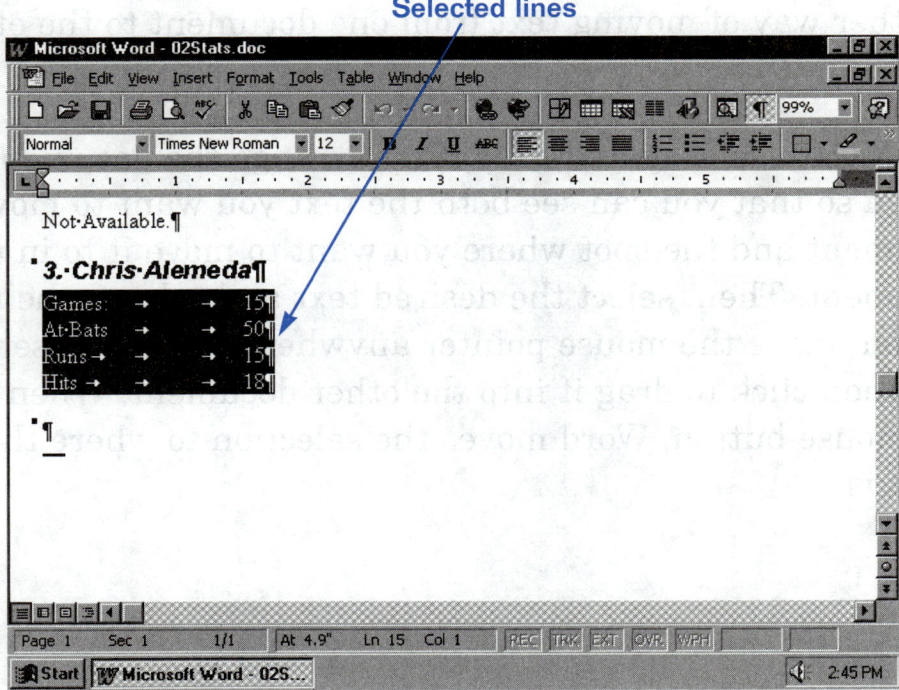

Figure 3-16. Selected text in the **stats** document

3. Click the Cut button 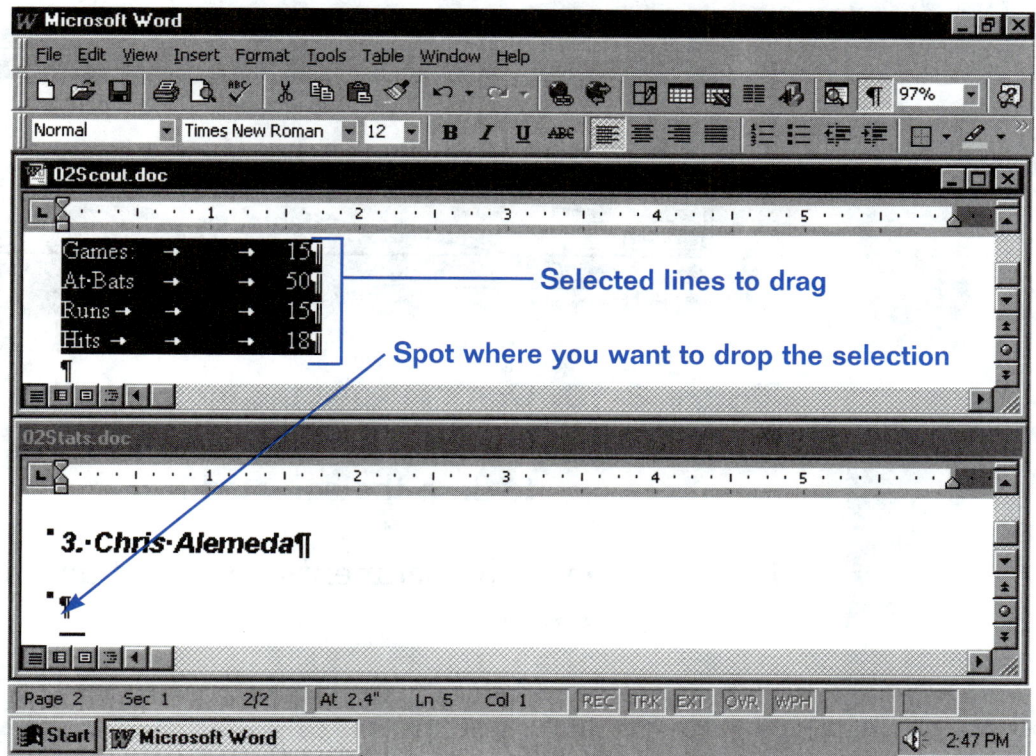 on the Standard toolbar.

4. Open the <u>W</u>indow menu and click <u>**1**</u> **scout**.

5. Move the insertion point to the beginning of the blank line at the end of the document, under the subheading *Statistics*. *This is where you want to paste the selection.*

6. Click the Paste button on the Standard toolbar. *Word inserts the four lines into the **scout2** document.*

7. Open the <u>W</u>indow menu and choose <u>A</u>rrange All.

8. Scroll down in the **stats** document until you can see the end of the document. *Now, let's move the lines back under Chris Alemeda.*

9. Click in the **scout2** document to make it active.

10. Select the four lines of statistics at the end of the **scout2** document. This is the information you are going to move. *OK, if you've set everything up correctly, your screen looks like Figure 3-17. Now, get ready to drag the selection into the **stats** document.*

Figure 3-17. Before you drag-and-drop, make sure the documents are arranged correctly on screen.

JEFF THE REF

If you drop the text in the wrong location, you can use <u>E</u>dit, <u>U</u>ndo and try again.

11. Move the mouse pointer so that it is touching any part of the selection in **scout2**.

12. Press and hold down the left mouse button and drag it into the **stats** document window.

13. When the insertion point that moves with the mouse pointer is on the blank line under *Chris Alameda* (as in Figure 3-18), let go of the mouse button.
Word moves the selection.

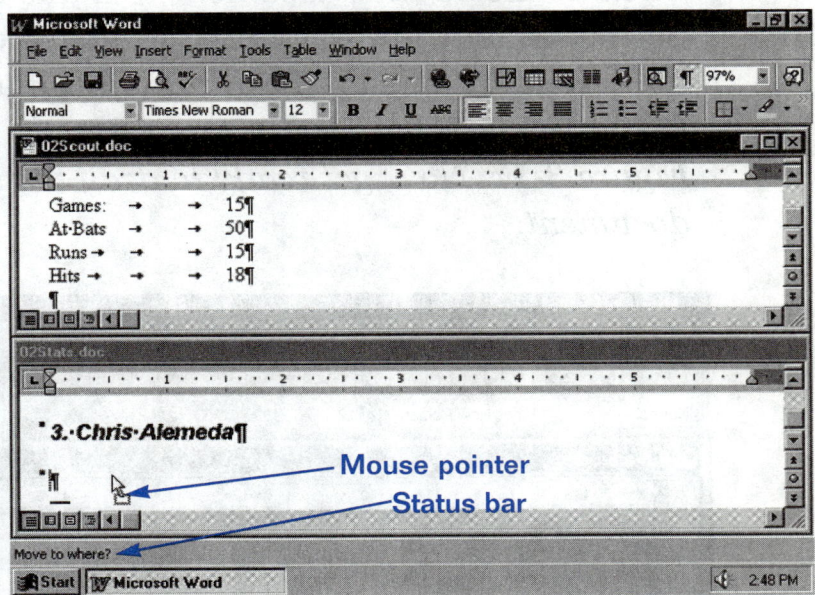

Figure 3-18. Don't release the mouse button until the mouse pointer is where you want to drop the selected text.

14. Keep both documents open and arranged on screen.

Copying Text from One Document to Another

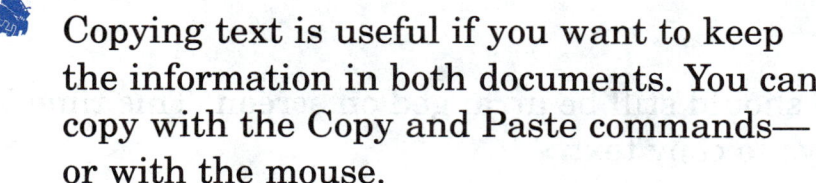

Coach Carrie Says:

Copying text is useful if you want to keep the information in both documents. You can copy with the Copy and Paste commands— or with the mouse.

> On a PC, when you copy with the mouse, hold down the Ctrl key while you drag.

> On a Mac, hold down the Option key while you drag in order to copy a selection with the mouse.

Check back to the Training Table on page 233 for the different ways of using the Copy and Paste commands.

One way to be sure you're copying instead of moving is to look at the mouse pointer— when you copy, the mouse pointer has a little plus sign attached to it (as in Figure 3-19 on page 239); when you move, it doesn't (as in Figure 3-18 on page 236).

Another way is to check out the Status bar. When you are copying, it asks, *Copy to Where?* When you are moving, it asks, *Move to Where?*

JEFF THE REF

If you forget to hold down Ctrl (on a PC) or Option (on a Mac) while you drag a selection, you'll move it instead of copying it. Just choose Edit, Undo and try again.

PRACTICE SWINGS

Trainer Terry Says:

 Your documents should still be arranged on screen. This time let's try different ways to copy text

1. Make **scout2** the active document. Then, scroll down to the last line.
2. Click in the **stats** document to make it active.
3. Select the four lines of statistics for Chris Alemeda if they're not already selected.
4. Move the mouse pointer so that it is touching any part of the selection.

5.   On the PC, press and hold down the mouse button, then press and hold down the Ctrl key.
    OR

    On the Mac, press and hold down the mouse button, then press and hold down the Option key.
    A little plus sign is added to the mouse pointer.

6. Drag the mouse pointer to the last line in the **scout2** document. *Look at Figure 3-19 to see how the mouse pointer should look and where it should be.*

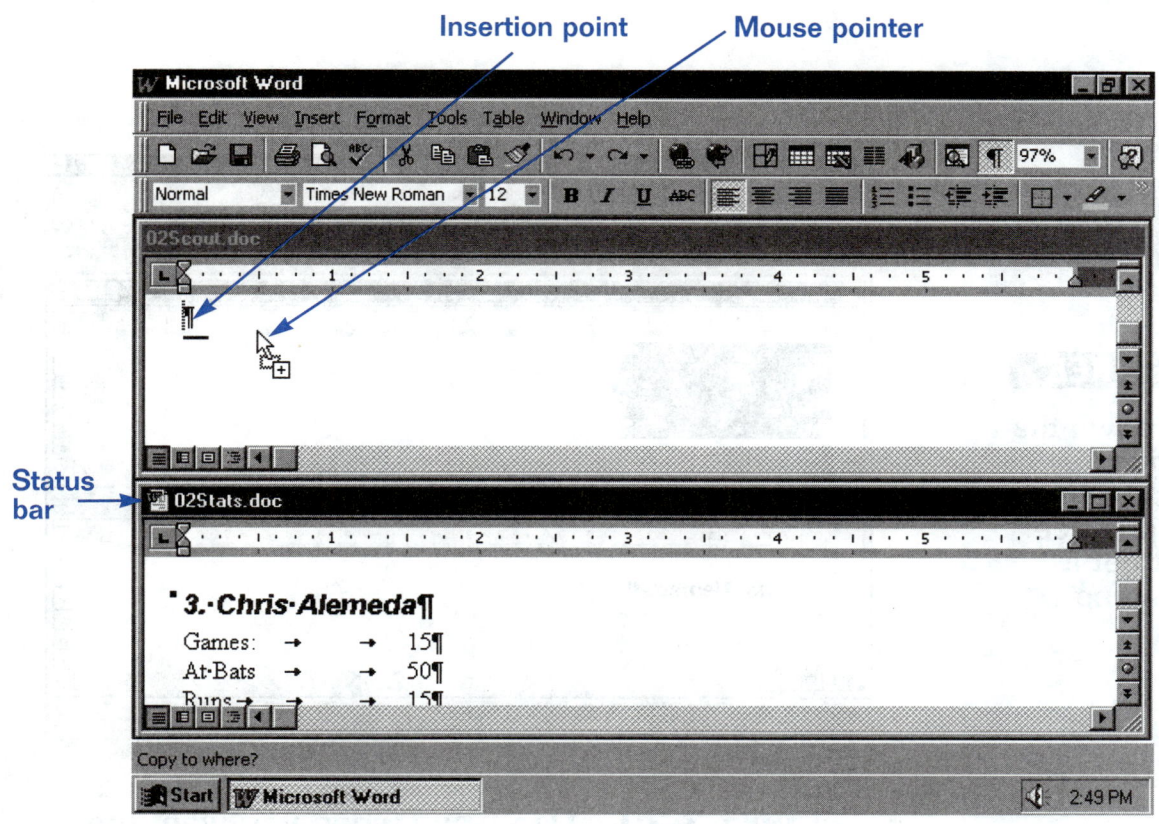

Figure 3-19. When you copy with the mouse, a plus sign is attached to the pointer.

7. ▣ On the PC, let go of the mouse button and the Ctrl key.

OR

 On the Mac, let go of the mouse button and the Option key.
Word copies the selection. Now, the statistics for Alemeda are in both documents (see Figure 3-20).

JEFF THE REF

Holding down the Ctrl or Option key while you drag may take some practice. If you don't get it right away, keep trying.

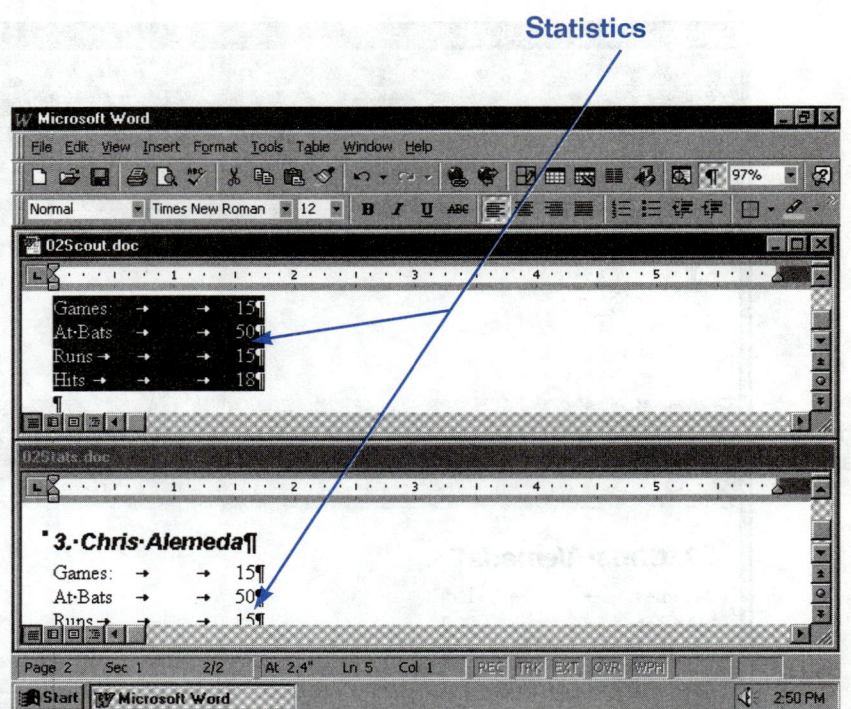

Figure 3-20. Use Copy when you want the information in both documents.

8. Click in the **stats** document to make it active.

9. Click the Maximize button on the **stats** document title bar.

10. In the **stats** document, select the eight lines of statistics under *Joe O'Brien*. *Make sure to include the last paragraph mark in your selection.*

11. Click the Copy button on the Standard toolbar.
Word copies the selection to the Clipboard.

12. Open the <u>W</u>indow menu and click **1** scout2. *Now, the scout2 document is displayed.*

13. Move the insertion point to the beginning of the line *2. Jamie Washington*. *This is where you want to paste the statistics information. Because you've copied the paragraph mark, you'll get a new line when you paste the selection.*

14. Click the Paste  button on the Standard toolbar. *Word pastes the selection into the **scout2** document. Your document should look like Figure 3-21.*

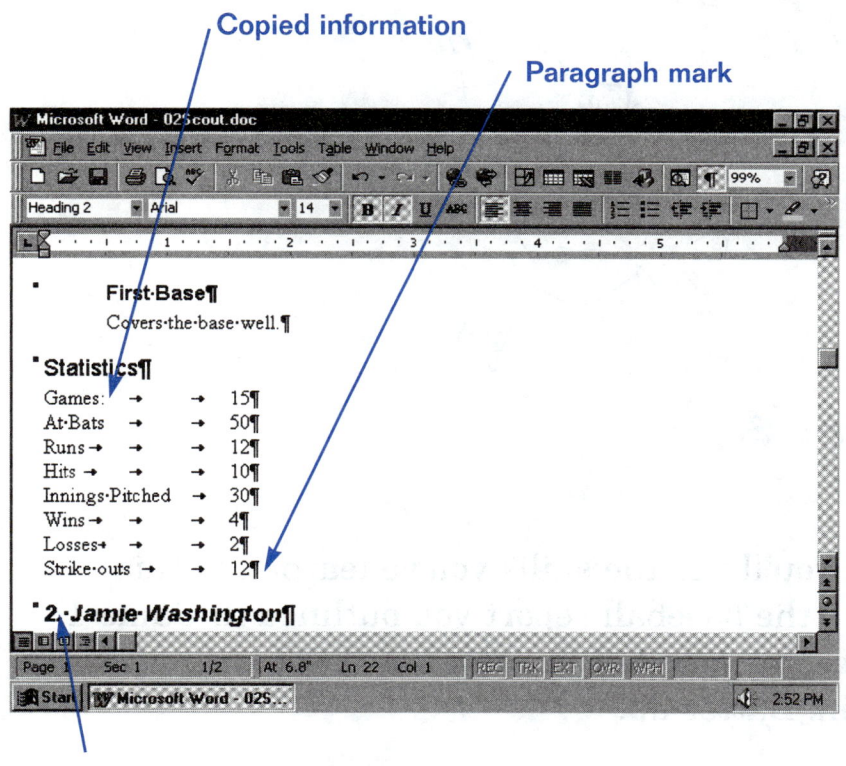

Copied information

Paragraph mark

Heading is on a new line

Figure 3-21. The information is copied into the document.

JEFF THE REF

If you don't include the paragraph mark with the copied selection, you might end up with the last line of the copied statistics on the same line as the heading *Jamie Washington*. It will be formatted like the heading *Jamie Washington*, too.

Use Edit, Undo if you make a mistake and try again.

15.   Click the Save button  on the Standard toolbar, then choose <u>F</u>ile, <u>C</u>lose.
*The **stats2** document is still open.*

16.   Click the Save button on the Standard toolbar, then choose <u>F</u>ile, <u>C</u>lose.
If you try to exit Word when there are documents open, Word will prompt you to save the changes in each one before closing.

PLAY BALL:

Trainer Terry Says:

In this exercise, you'll use the skills you've learned in this Game to improve the baseball report you outlined in Game 1. The report has been expanded already, but there are some facts you need to fill in. Batter up!

1.   Open the file named **02notes** from the student data folder.
This document has notes about the career highlights of the four baseball players in the report.

2.   Save the file as **notes**.

3. Without closing the **notes** file, open the file named **02legend** from the student data folder.

   This report is based on the outline you created in Game 1. The career highlights information has already been added for Jackie Robinson and Mickey Mantle, but it is missing for Babe Ruth and Cy Young.

4. Save the file as **legend**.

5. Choose <u>2</u> **notes** from the <u>W</u>indow menu to make the **notes** document active.

6. Select the five lines under the heading *Babe Ruth Career Highlights*, as in Figure 3-22.

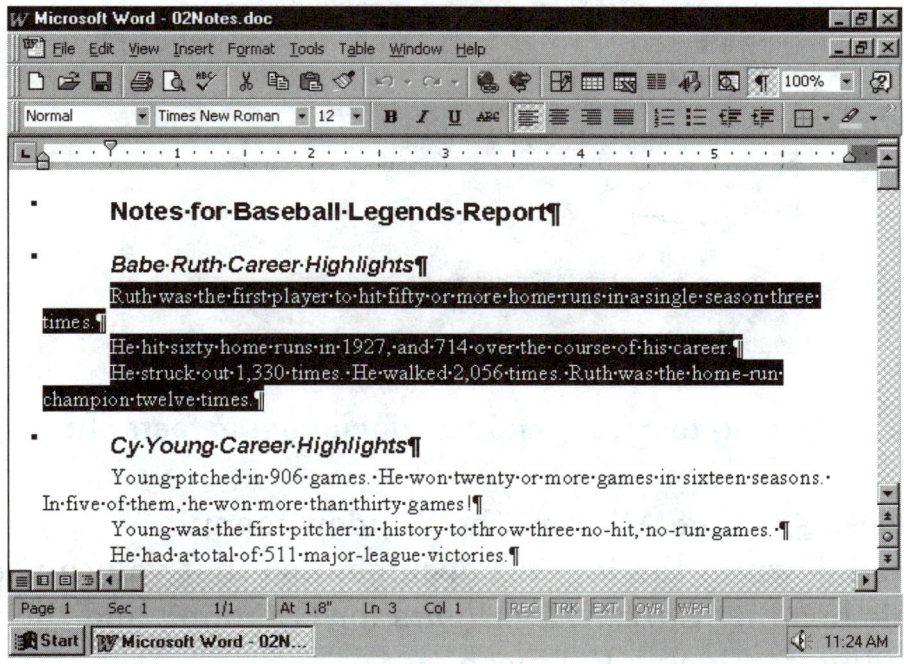

Figure 3-22. You are going to move the selected lines into the **legend** document.

7. Click the Cut button on the Standard toolbar.

8. Choose <u>1</u> **legend** from the <u>W</u>indow menu to make the **legend** document active.

   Remember, if you cut or copy the paragraph mark along with the text, you'll get a new blank line when you paste the selection.

9. Scroll down and place the insertion point at the beginning of the line *Cy Young*.
    This is where you want to insert the career highlight information for Babe Ruth.

10. Click the Paste button 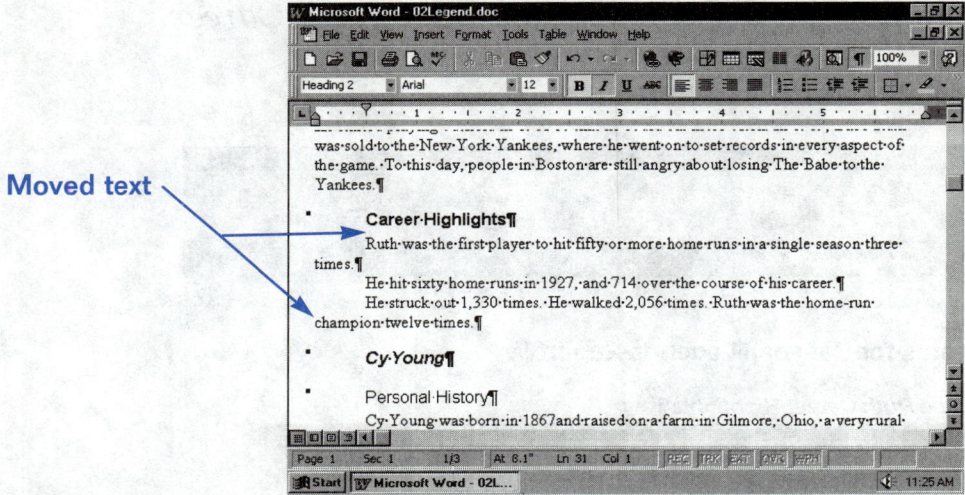 on the Standard toolbar.
    *All right! With the new text in it, the **legend** document should look like the one in Figure 3-23.*

Moved text

Figure 3-23. Moving text from another document is faster then retyping it.

11. Choose Arrange All from the Window menu.
12. Scroll down in the **legend** document so that you can see the topic heading *Career Highlights* for Cy Young and the main heading for Jackie Robinson.
13. Click in the **notes** document to make it active.
14. Select the five lines under the heading *Cy Young Career Highlights*.
    When the documents looks like Figure 3-24, you're ready to drag the selection to its new position.

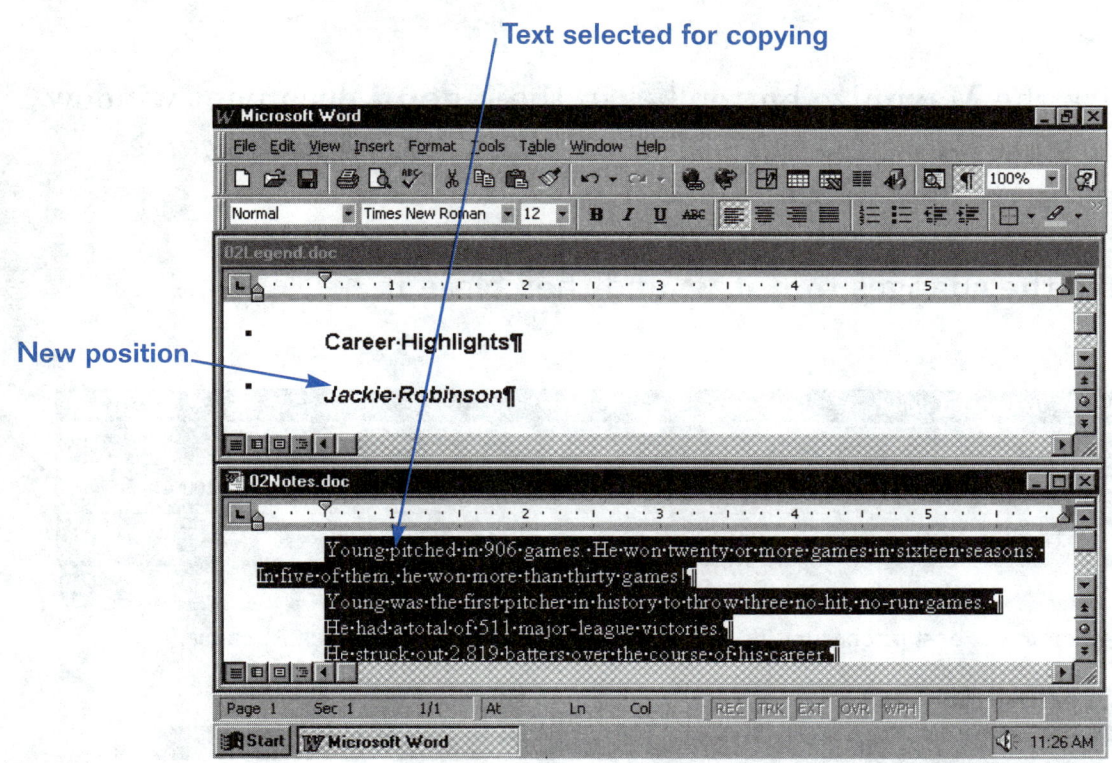

Figure 3-24. When you can see the selected text and the new position on the screen, you're ready to drag-and-drop.

15. On the PC, move the mouse pointer over the selection, and then press and hold down the mouse button and the Ctrl key.

    OR

    On the Mac, move the mouse pointer over the selection, and then press and hold down the mouse button and the Option key.

16. Drag the mouse pointer into the **legend** window.

17. On the PC, when the mouse pointer is at the beginning of the line with the heading *Jackie Robinson*, let go of the mouse button and the Ctrl key.

    OR

    On the Mac, when the mouse pointer is at the beginning of the line with the heading *Jackie Robinson*, let go of the mouse button and the Option key.

18.   Click the Maximize button 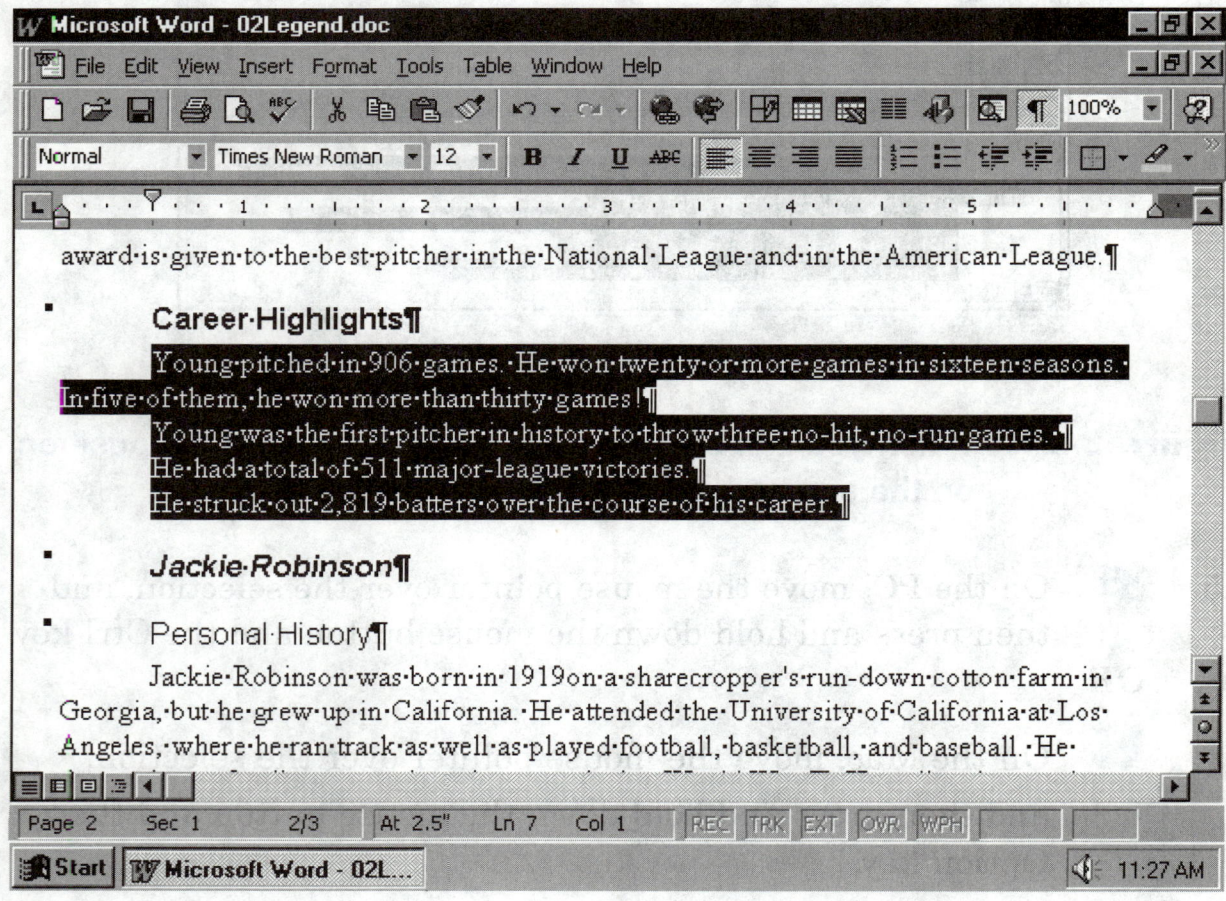 in the **legend** document window. *In Figure 3-25, you can see the addition of Cy Young's career highlights in the **legend** document.*

19.   Save the changes to **legend**, and then close it.

20.   Save the changes to **notes**, and then close it.

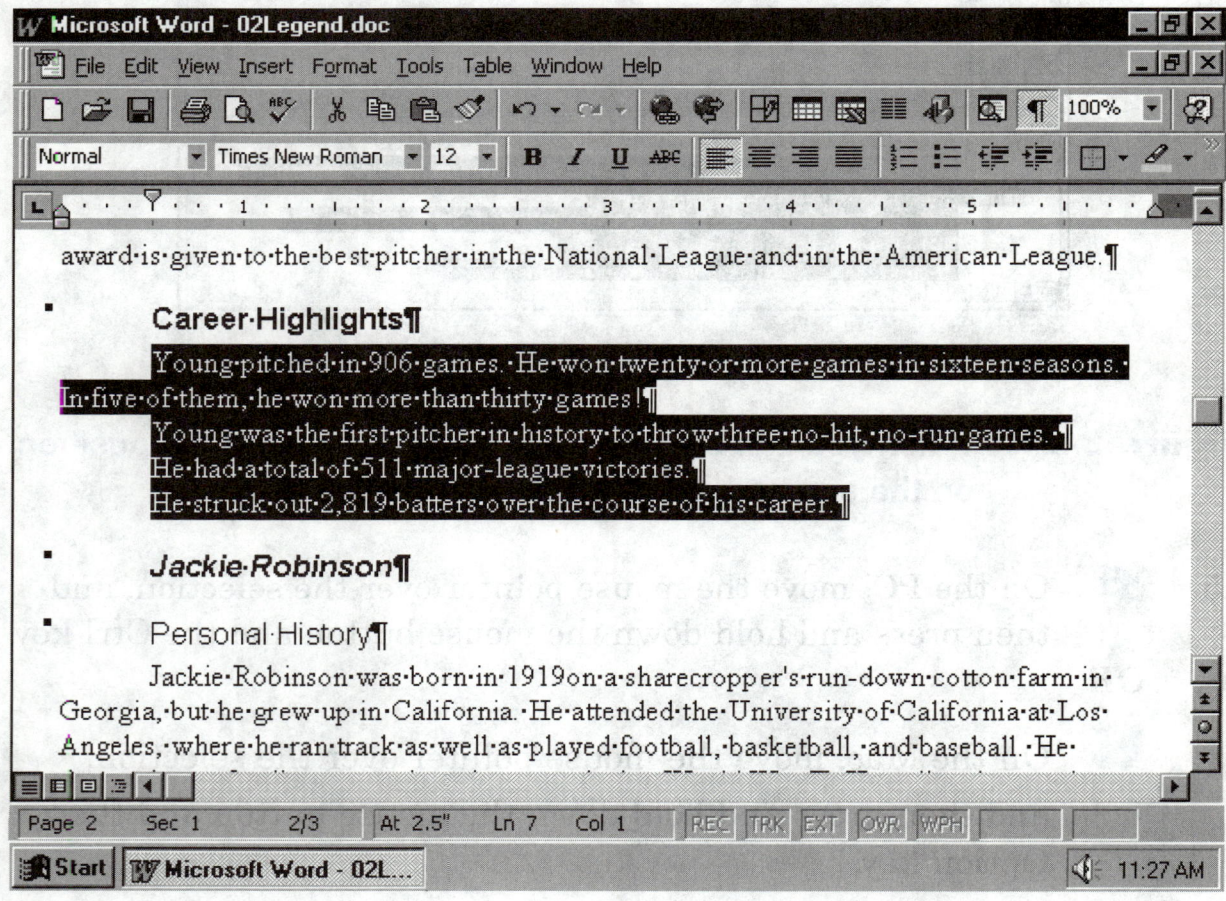

Figure 3-25. You have expanded the report without retyping any text.

THE WORLD SERIES:

To practice the skills you've learned in this Game, create a simple document that includes factoids about yourself, such as how old you are, your favorite food, your favorite color, and so on. You can create the document in Outline view, and set it up with headings and subheadings, if you want. Save the document as **factoids.**

Open both the **factoids** document and the autobiography outline document you created in Game 1. Use the information in the **factoids** document to enhance the autobiography outline. You can move and copy information from the **factoids** document to flesh out existing topics in the autobiography outline or to create new topics in the outline.

If you want, try opening a third document at the same time, and practice moving text among all three.

GAME #3
KEEPING SCORE

In this Game, you'll learn how to use the number keypad by:

- **Positioning Your Fingers on the Number Keypad**
- **Finger Reaches on the Number Keypad**
- **Typing on the Number Keypad**

On Deck

Coach Carrie Says:

 In baseball's American League, the designated hitter bats for the pitcher so that the pitcher can concentrate on pitching only. In word processing, when you need to type numbers without any text, the *number keypad* on the right side of the keyboard makes it possible for you to concentrate on numbers only.

 In this Game, you get to get to focus on typing numbers only. You'll learn how to position your fingers on the number keypad and how to type numbers on the keypad.

Positioning Your Fingers on the Number Keypad

 The number keypad looks a bit like a calculator, because it has both the number keys and keys for entering the symbols for mathematical equations, like a plus sign, and a minus sign. It also has its own Enter key, a Delete key, and the *Num Lock* key.

 Look at Figure 3-26 to see how the number keypad is set up.

MEG THE MIKE

The *number keypad* is a group of keys located on the right side of your keyboard. You use it to type numbers when you don't need to type letters, too. It's great for typing a list of phone numbers, for example, or a column of baseball statistics.

Num Lock is an abbreviation for *Number Lock* (the word Number wouldn't fit on the key). You use Num Lock to toggle back and forth between using the keypad to type numbers and using it to move the insertion point.

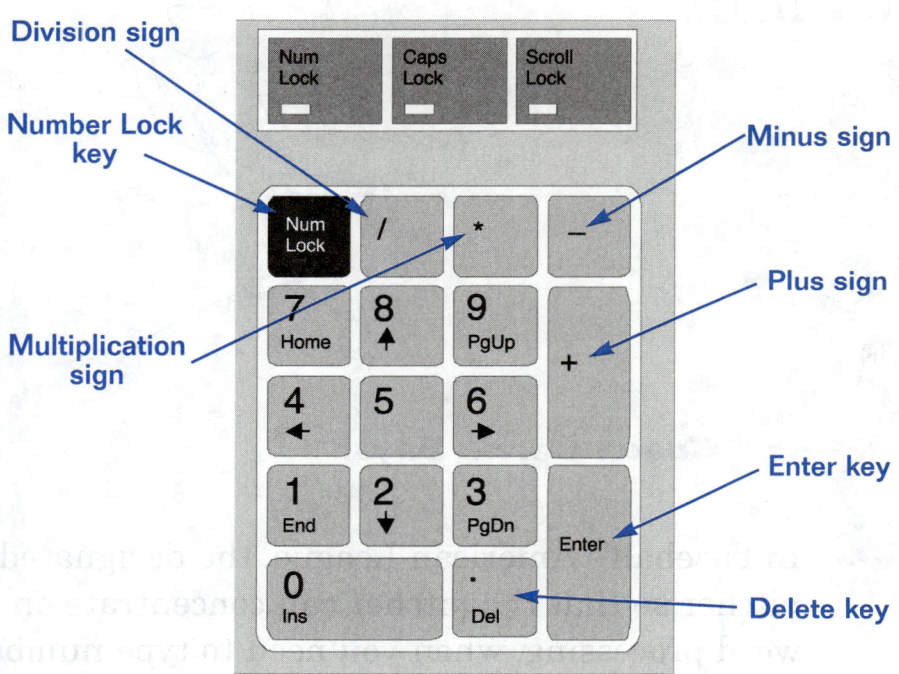

Figure 3-26. The number keypad

 On a Mac extended keyboard, the keypad may look a little different than the one in Figure 3-26. On a Mac keypad, there's a Clear key that shares the Num Lock key.

Just like the alphabetic keyboard has a home row, the number keypad also has a home row. The keypad home row is in the middle, so you can easily move your fingers up and down to reach all the keys.

When you use the number keypad, set up the fingers of your right hand on the home row like this:

Your right index finger goes on the 4.
Your right middle finger goes on the 5.
Your right ring finger goes on the 6.
Your right thumb goes on the 0.
Your right pinky finger goes on the Enter key.

Take a look at Figure 3-27 to see how to place your fingers.

JEFF THE REF

Just because the number keypad looks like a calculator doesn't mean it is a calculator. You can type the numbers and math symbols with the keypad, but it won't do the math for you!

There is usually a raised dot or dash on the 5 key of the number keypad so you can feel that your fingers are in the right place on the home row.

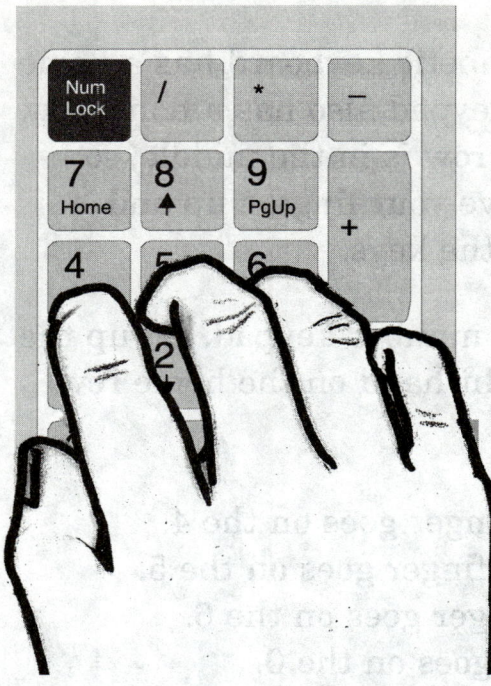

Figure 3-27. The home row on the keypad is the middle row, with the keys for 4, 5, and 6.

PRACTICE SWINGS

Trainer Terry Says:

Let's get comfortable positioning your fingers on the number keypad.

1. Place your right index finger on the 4.
2. Place your right middle finger on the 5.
3. Place your right ring finger on the 6.
   That's the home-row placement.

4. Place your right thumb on the 0.

5. Place your right pinky finger on the Enter key.

6. Use your right middle finger to feel the raised dot or dash on the 5 key.

7. Take your hand off the keypad.

8. Look at the keypad and go through steps 1 through 8 two more times.

 Now, try it without looking.

9. Without looking, position your right hand on the number keypad.

10. Feel the dot or dash on the 5 key to make sure you're in the right place.

11. Look at the keypad to see if you've got it right.

12. Repeat steps 10 through 12 two more times.

13. Keep practicing your finger placement until you feel comfortable with it.

Finger Reaches on the Number Keypad

Coach Carrie Says:

 Once you're comfortable with your home-row finger placement on the number keypad, you can move your fingers around to reach the other keypad keys.

To reach the other number keys, just move the fingers from the home row up or down:

> Your right index finger moves up to touch the 7 and down to touch the 1.

> Your right middle finger moves up to touch the 8 and down to touch the 2.

> Your right ring finger moves up to touch the 9 and down to touch the 3.

 You also have to reach for the special keys on the keypad:

> Your right middle finger moves up to touch the division sign (/).

> Your right ring finger moves down to touch the decimal point (.).

> Your right ring finger moves up to touch the multiplication sign (*).

> Your right ring finger moves diagonally up and right to touch the minus sign (-).

> Your right ring finger moves to the right to touch the plus sign (+).

PRACTICE SWINGS

Trainer Terry Says:

 Let's try some finger reaches on the number keypad:

1.   Position your fingers on the home row.
2.   Move your index finger up to touch the 7 and then back to the 4.
3.   Move your index finger down to touch the 1 and then back to the 4.
4.   Move your middle finger up to touch the 8 and then back to the 5.
5.   Move your middle finger down to touch the 2 and then back to the 5.
6.   Move your ring finger up to touch the 9 and then back to the 6.
7.   Move your ring finger down to touch the 3 and then back to the 6.
8.   Repeat steps 2 though 7 until you feel comfortable reaching for the number keys without looking at the keypad.
9.   Move your ring finger down to touch the decimal point (.) and then back to the 6.
10. Touch the 0 with your thumb.
11. Touch the Enter key with your pinky.
12. Move your middle finger up to touch the division sign (/) and then back to the 5.
13. Move your ring finger up to touch the multiplication sign (*) and then back to the 6.

14. Move your ring finger up and to the right to touch the minus sign (-) and then back to the 6.

15. Move your ring finger to the right to touch the plus sign (+) and then back to the 6.

16. Repeat steps 9 through 15 until you are comfortable reaching for the special keys without looking at the keypad.

Typing on the Number Keypad

Coach Carrie Says:

 Before you type anything on the number keypad, you have to toggle Num Lock on. The keys on the number keypad double as directional keys, and Num Lock lets you switch back and forth between typing numbers and moving the insertion point.

 On a PC, to toggle Num Lock on, press the Num Lock key so that the Num Lock status light is lit.

 To toggle Num Lock on a Mac, you press Shift+Num Lock.

PRACTICE SWINGS

Trainer Terry Says:

Try typing on the number keypad. Relax, and press down firmly on each keystroke. Try not to look at your fingers. Also, be sure to press the spacebar with your left thumb whenever you see a blank space between two numbers. Batter up!

1. Start Word, open a blank document, and make sure that the Num Lock status light is on.
2. Position your fingers on the home row.
3. Type 444 555 666, and then press Enter.
4. Type 456 456 456, and then press Enter.
5. Type 474 474 474, and then press Enter.
6. Type 414 414 414, and then press Enter.
7. Repeat steps 3 through 6, trying not to look at your fingers.
8. Type 444 555 666, and then press Enter.
9. Type 456 456 456, and then press Enter.
10. Type 585 585 585, and then press Enter.
11. Type 525 525 525, and then press Enter.
12. Repeat steps 8 through 11, trying not to look at your fingers.

JEFF THE REFF

If numbers don"t appear in the document, and the insertion point starts moving around, you don't have the Num Lock toggle on!

13.   Type 666 555 444, and then press Enter.

14.   Type 696 696 696, and then press Enter.

15.   Type 636 636 636, and then press Enter.

16.   Type 63.6 63.6 63.6, and then press Enter.

17.   Repeat steps 13 through 16, trying not to look at your fingers.

18.   Type 456 789 456 123 410 410 410 6.36 6.36 6.36, and then press Enter.

19.   Repeat step 18, trying not to look at your fingers.

 Finally, practice using the math symbol keys.

20.   Type 5/5/5 6*6*6 6-6-6 6+6+6, and then press Enter.

21.   Repeat step 20, trying not to look at your fingers.

22.   That's the last set! Save the document as **keypad** and close it.

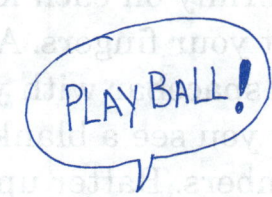

PLAY BALL

Trainer Terry Says:

 In this exercise, you will type lists of important dates and statistics into the report you've been working on. Since you are going to type numbers with no letters, you should use the number keypad. Get ready to score!

1. Open the file named **03legend** from the student data folder.
2. Save the file as **legend3**.
3. Scroll down until you come to the heading *Statistics*, under the topic of *Babe Ruth*.
4. Position the insertion point on the second blank line under the *Statistics* paragraph as shown in Figure 3-28.
   This is where you are going to start typing the numbers.

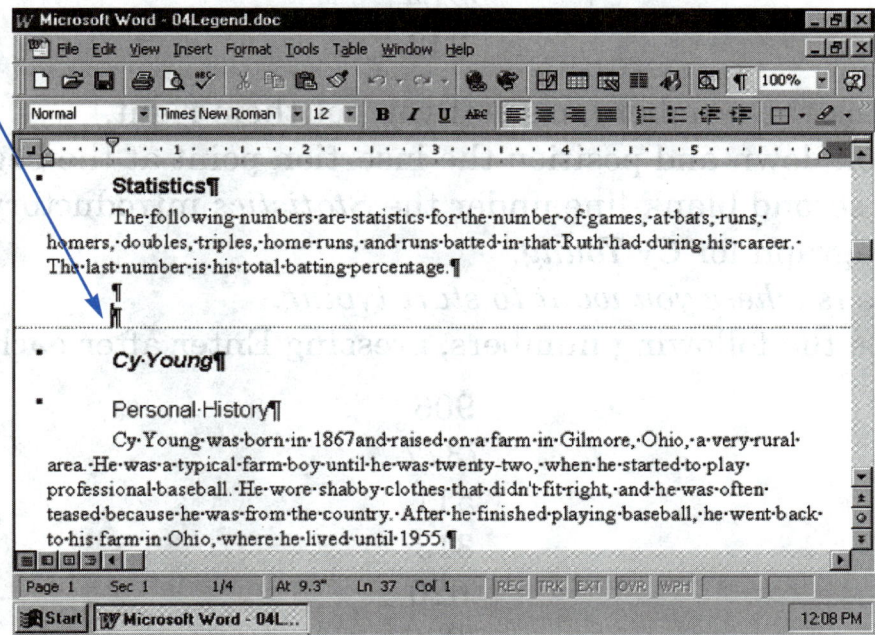

Figure 3-28. Make sure the insertion point is in the right spot before you begin typing.

5. Make sure the Num Lock status indicator is lit.
6. Position your fingers on the keypad.

7. Type the following numbers, pressing Enter after each line:

    2503
    8397
    2174
    2873
    506
    136
    714
    2204
    .342

8. Check the numbers to see if you got them right.

9. Scroll down and position the insertion point at the beginning of the second blank line under the *Statistics* introductory paragraph for *Cy Young*.
    This is where you want to start typing.

10. Type the following numbers, pressing Enter after each line:

    906
    7377
    511
    313
    .620
    7078
    2819
    1209

11. Check the numbers to see if you got them right.

12. Scroll down and position the insertion point at the beginning of the second blank line under the *Statistics* introductory paragraph for *Jackie Robinson*.
    This is where you want to start typing.

13.   Type the following numbers, pressing Enter after each line:

1382
4877
947
1518
273
54
137
734
.311

14.   Check your work. If you've made mistakes, go back and correct them.

15.   Scroll down and position the insertion point at the beginning of the second blank line under the *Statistics* introductory paragraph for *Mickey Mantle*.
This is where you want to start typing.

16.   Type the following numbers, pressing Enter after each line:

2401
8102
1677
2415
344
72
536
1509
.298

17.   That's all the statistics. Compare your document to Figure 3-29. If you've made mistakes, go back and correct them.

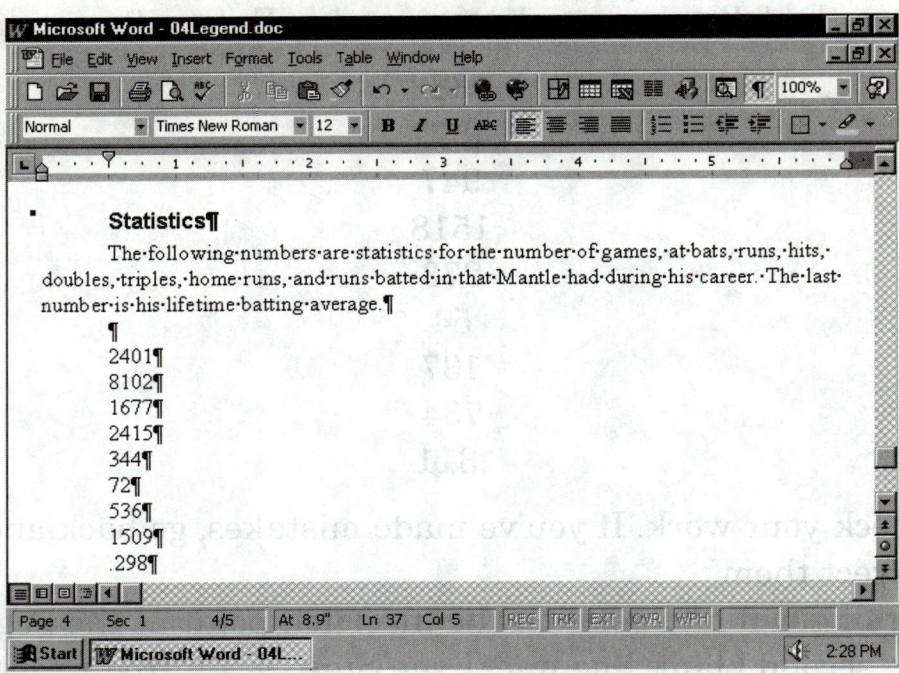

Figure 3-29. Mickey Mantle's statistics typed in the document

18.   Save the document and close it.

THE WORLD SERIES

 To practice the skills you learned in this Game, make a list of some important numbers in your life—for example:

- your birthday using the mm/dd/yy format
  (that means typing the month, then a slash, the day, then a slash, then the last two digits of the year you were born)

- your phone number

- how many sit-ups you can do in a minute

- how long it takes you to get to school

- how much money a school lunch costs

 Try to think of numbers that use all the keys on the number keypad. When you have your list complete, add these statistics into the autobiography you have been working on. Add a heading called *Important Statistics*, and type an introductory paragraph. Then, type in the numbers.

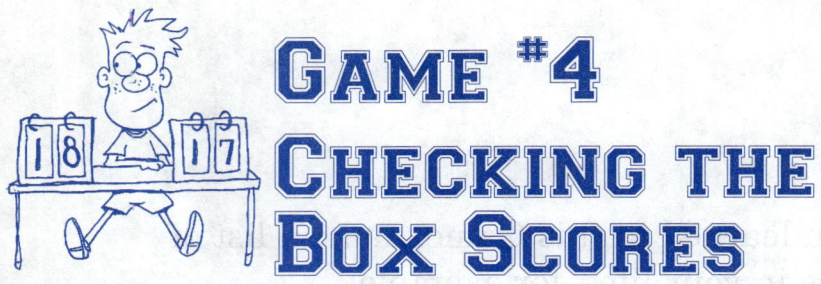

GAME #4
CHECKING THE
BOX SCORES

In this Game, you'll learn how to create and format tables by:

- Creating a Table
- Typing in a Table
- Selecting Parts of a Table
- Adding and Deleting Columns and Rows
- Formatting a Table

ON DECK

Creating a Table

Coach Carrie Says:

 Every day in the newspaper during baseball season, there are lists of statistics called box scores, and serious baseball fans wouldn't think of starting the day without reading them.

 Luckily, it's easy to read the box scores because they are set up in nice, neat *columns* and *rows*—in other words, in a *table*.

 You can use tables in Word to organize information that will be easier to read in columns and rows.

 In this game, you'll find out how to create a table in a Word document. You'll learn the different parts of a table, how to move the insertion point around in it, how to type data into a table, how to add and delete columns and rows, and, how to format a table so that it looks good.

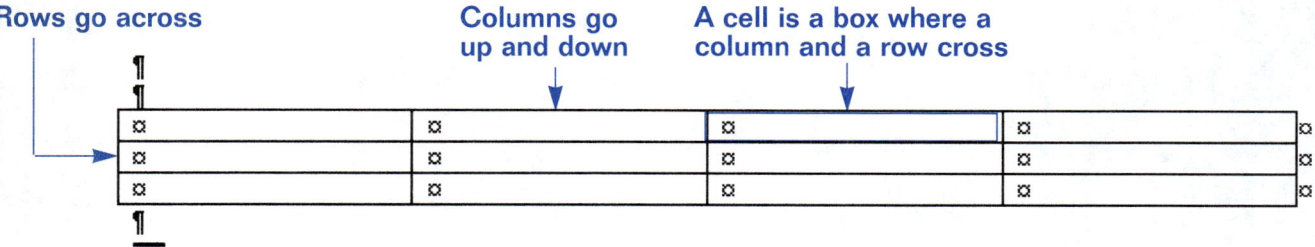

Figure 3-30. This blank table has four columns and three rows.

MEG THE MIKE

A *column* is a list that goes up and down. A *row* is a list that goes across. A *table* is a group of attached columns and rows. The boxes in a table made by the criss-crossing columns and rows are called *cells*.

Gridlines are the nonprinting borders in a table. They are displayed so that you can see the table on screen while you work.

 There are a few different ways to create a table with Word, but the easiest way is with the Insert Table button on the Standard toolbar.

When you click the Insert Table button , a grid drops down representing columns and rows. To select the number of columns and the number of rows you want, click and drag your mouse pointer across the grid. When you release the mouse, Word creates the table in the document, at the insertion point.

 When you create a table on a PC, it is automatically formatted with border lines around every cell. The borders show up on screen, and they print in documents.

 Tables have nonprinting lines around every cell called *gridlines*. Even if you change the formatting so that there are no printing borders, the gridlines help you see the table cells on screen.

PRACTICE SWINGS

Trainer Terry Says:

 In this exercise, you'll open a new document and create a table that you can use as a baseball roster.

1. Open a new blank document in Word, and save it as **roster**.
2. Type *Team Roster* on the first line, centered, in 14 point, Times New Roman.
3. Press Enter three times to leave two blank lines.
4. Switch back to left justification and change the font size to 12 points.
5. Click the Insert Table button ▦ on the Standard toolbar.
   A grid drops down from the button, as in Figure 3-31.

JEFF THE REFF

If you insert a table and nothing seems to have happened, it's probably because the gridlines are turned off. To turn them on, open the Table menu and choose Show Gridlines. You should immediately be able to see the table in the document. To hide the gridlines, open the Table menu and choose Hide Gridlines.

 If you use a Mac, choose Gridlines from the Table menu to toggle on the gridline display. Choose it again to toggle off the gridlines.

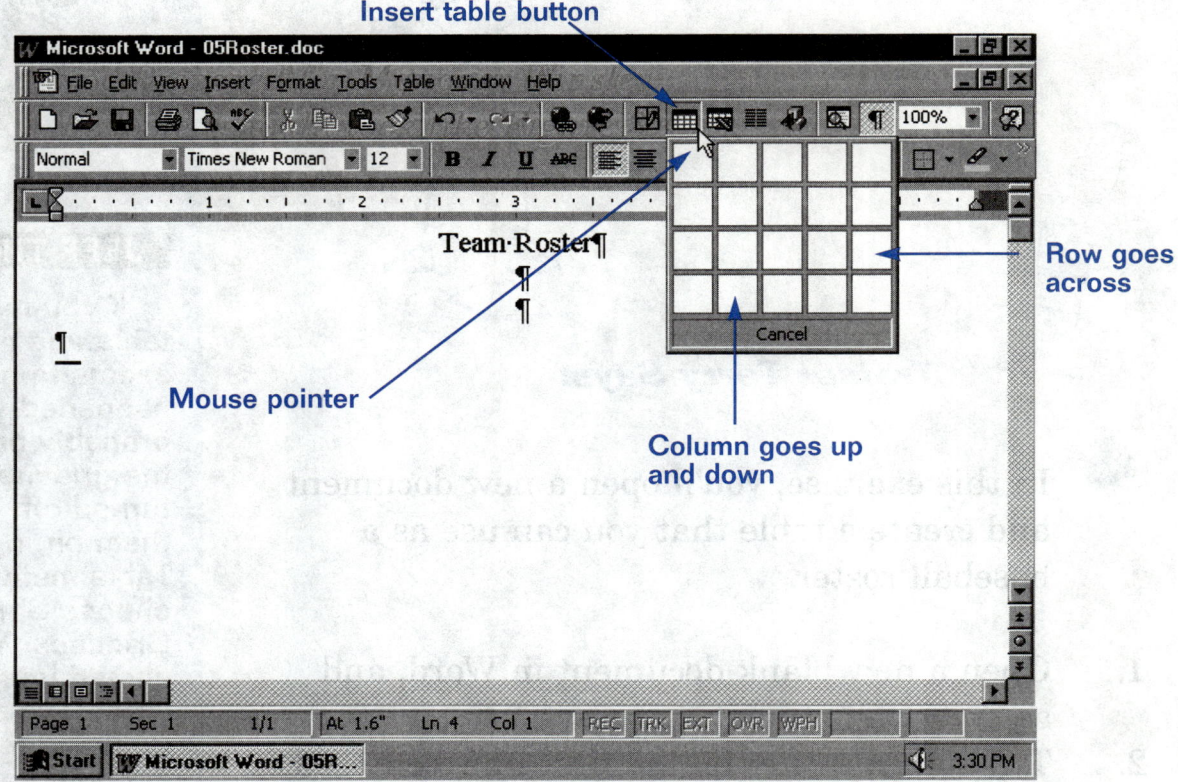

Figure 3-31. Use the Insert Table button to select how many columns and rows you want in your table.

6.   Click and drag your mouse pointer across the grid to select four rows and three columns.
     Word highlights the boxes on the grid as you select them.

7.   Release the mouse button on the highlighted box in the lower right corner.
     Word inserts the table at the insertion point as in Figure 3-32.

Gridlines   End-of-cell marker

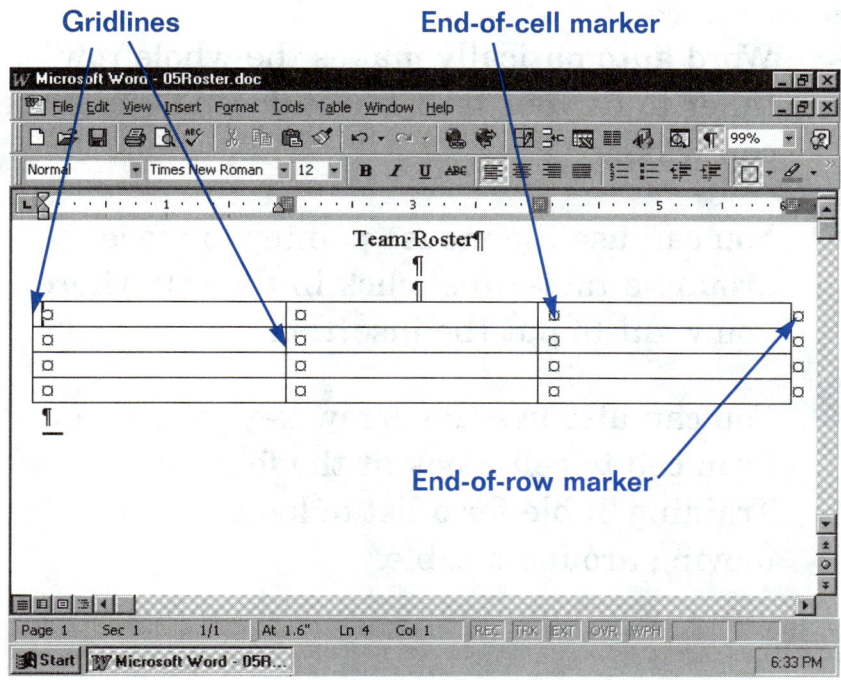

End-of-row marker

Figure 3-32. The table in the document

Typing in a Table

 Coach Carrie Says:

When you create a table, Word puts the insertion point in the top left cell. When you type, the text shows up in that cell. When you reach the right edge of the cell, Word wraps the text to the next line in the cell.

MEG THE MIKE

If you have nonprinting characters turned on, you'll see funny symbols in each cell and outside the right border of the table. The symbols in each cell are called the *end-of-cell markers.* They mark where the last typed space is in a cell. The symbols outside the right border of the table are called the *end-of-row markers.* They mark where the row ends.

JEFF THE REF

If you create a table that's the wrong size, use <u>E</u>dit, <u>U</u>ndo or the Undo button to delete it, and then try again.

 Word automatically makes the whole row taller to fit your text, but it doesn't make the cell wider.

 You can use the mouse pointer to move around a table. Just click in the cell where you want to put the insertion point.

 You can also use the arrow keys to move from cell to cell. Look at the following Training Table for a list of keys used for moving around a table.

Training Table: Typing in a Table

Key Combination	Result
Tab	Moves the insertion point one cell to the right. If the insertion point is in the last cell in a row, pressing Tab moves it to the first cell in the next row. If the insertion point is in the last cell in the last row, pressing tab creates a new row.
Shift+Tab	Moves the insertion point one cell to the left. If the insertion point is in the first cell in a row, pressing Shift+Tab moves it to the last cell in the previous row.
Up arrow	Moves the insertion point one line up in a cell. If the insertion point is in the top line in a cell, pressing the Up arrow moves it to the last line one cell above.
Down arrow	Moves the insertion point one line down in a cell. If the insertion point is in the bottom line in a cell, pressing the Down arrow moves it to the first line one cell below.
Left arrow	Moves the insertion point one space to the left in a cell. If the insertion point is in the first space in a cell, pressing the Left arrow moves it to the last space in the cell to the left.
Right arrow	Moves the insertion point one space to the right in a cell. If the insertion is in the last space in a cell, pressing the Right arrow moves it to the first space in the cell to the right.
Enter	Starts a new paragraph within a cell.

PRACTICE SWINGS

Trainer Terry Says:

You're going to use the table you created in the **roster** document to type in a list of players, their positions, and their batting averages. Try it!

1.   Type *Jamie Washington*.
2.   Press Tab, and then type *Outfield*.
3.   Press Tab and then type *.241*.
      Remember, you can use the number keypad to type the averages!
4.   Press Tab.
      The insertion point moves to the first cell in the next row.
5.   Type *Cam Hudson*.
6.   Press Tab and then type *First Base*.
7.   Press Tab and then type *.199*.
8.   Press Tab and then type *Steven Thompson*.
9.   Press Tab and then type *Catcher*.
10.   Press Tab and then type *.302*.
11.   Press Tab and then type *Christopher Michael Alemeda*.
      The text wraps to the next line when it reaches the right edge of the cell. The whole row gets taller so that the new line fits in the cell.
12.   Press Tab and then type *Shortstop*.
13.   Press Tab and then type *.275*.
      The table is complete. It should look like the one in Figure 3-33.

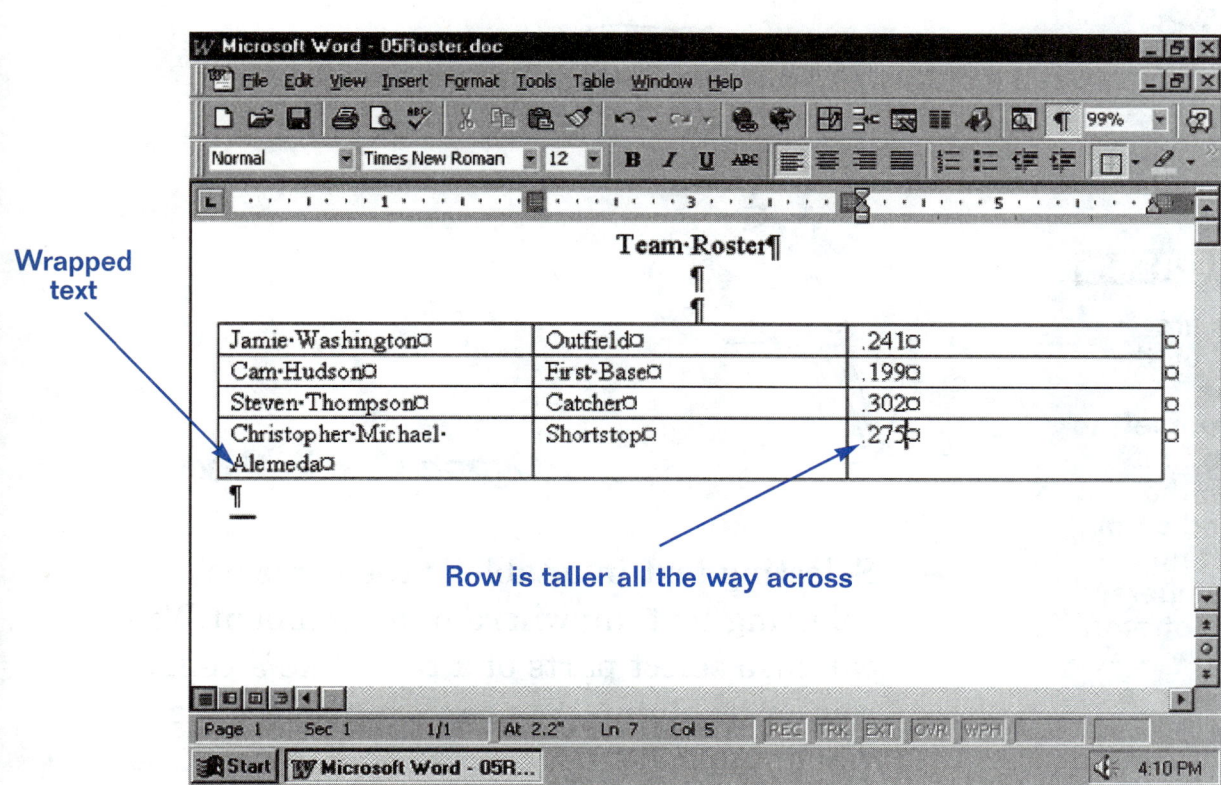

Wrapped text

Row is taller all the way across

Figure 3-33. Every cell in the table is filled.

14.	Save your work and leave the **roster** document open.

JEFF THE REF

Columns are often called by the letters of the alphabet, from left to right. So the first column is A, the next is B, and so on. Rows are often called by numbers, from top to bottom, so the top row is 1, the second row is 2, and so on.

The cell in the top left corner of a table, where column A and row 1 cross, is cell A1. The second cell from the left in the third row from the top is cell B3.

Selecting Parts of a Table

Coach Carrie Says:

 Selecting text in a table is the same as selecting text anywhere in a document. You can also select parts of a table like a cell, a row, or a column. You can even select the whole table.

 The Table menu has commands for selecting a row, a column, or the whole table. Just place the insertion point in the row, column, or table, then open the Table menu and choose the right command.

 To select more than one row, column, or cell, you can drag the mouse pointer across whatever you want to select.

 Once you have part of the table selected, you can select more just by holding down the Shift key and clicking with the mouse pointer.

On a PC, you can easily select an empty cell with the mouse pointer just by double-clicking in the cell. If there's text in the cell, you can select the text by triple-clicking!

 On the Mac, one click will insert the insertion point, two clicks will select a single word, and three clicks will select the complete cell.

PRACTICE SWINGS

Trainer Terry Says:

 Let's practice selecting parts of the table in the **roster** document.

1. Move the insertion point into any cell in row 1—the top row.
2. Open the Table menu and choose Select Row.
   Word highlights the first row.
3. Press and hold down the Shift key, and then click in the third row. Word highlights the second and third rows, too, as in Figure 3-34.

Selected rows

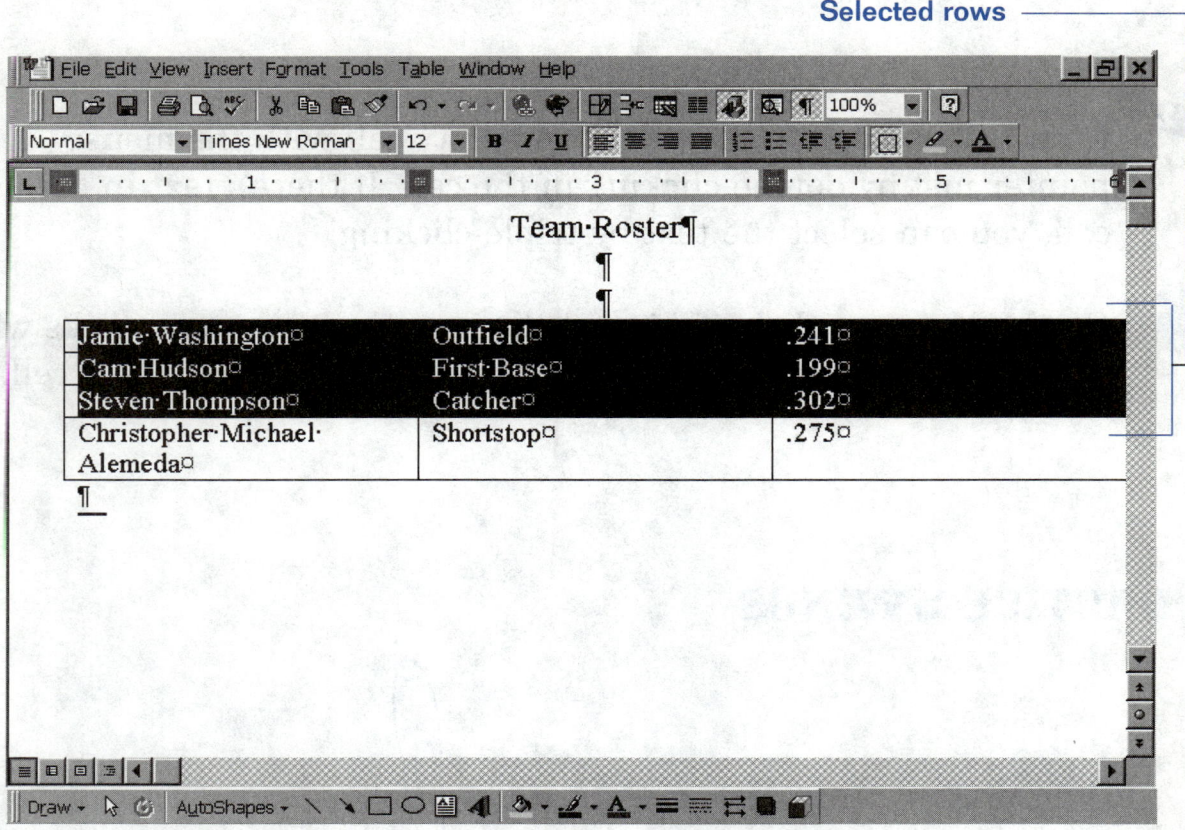

Figure 3-34. You can select more than one row at a time.

4. Keep the **roster** document open.

Adding and Deleting Columns and Rows

Coach Carrie Says:

If you discover that you need more columns or rows in your table, you can insert them. On the other hand, if you have too many, you can delete them.

To add a row in the middle of a table, place the insertion point in the row that will be *below* the new row you are adding, and then choose T<u>a</u>ble, <u>I</u>nsert Row. Word inserts the new row *above* the selected row.

To add a row to the bottom of a table, just put the insertion point in the last cell and press Tab.

To add a column to a table, you have to select the column that will be to the *right* of the new column you are adding, and then choose T<u>a</u>ble, <u>I</u>nsert Column. Word puts the new column to the *left* of the selected column.

To add a column to the right side of a table, you have to first select the end-of-row markers outside the right border of the table. Just click on one of them, and then choose T<u>a</u>ble, Select <u>C</u>olumn. Once you've selected them as in Figure 3-35, choose T<u>a</u>ble, <u>I</u>nsert Columns. Word adds a new column to the right side of the table.

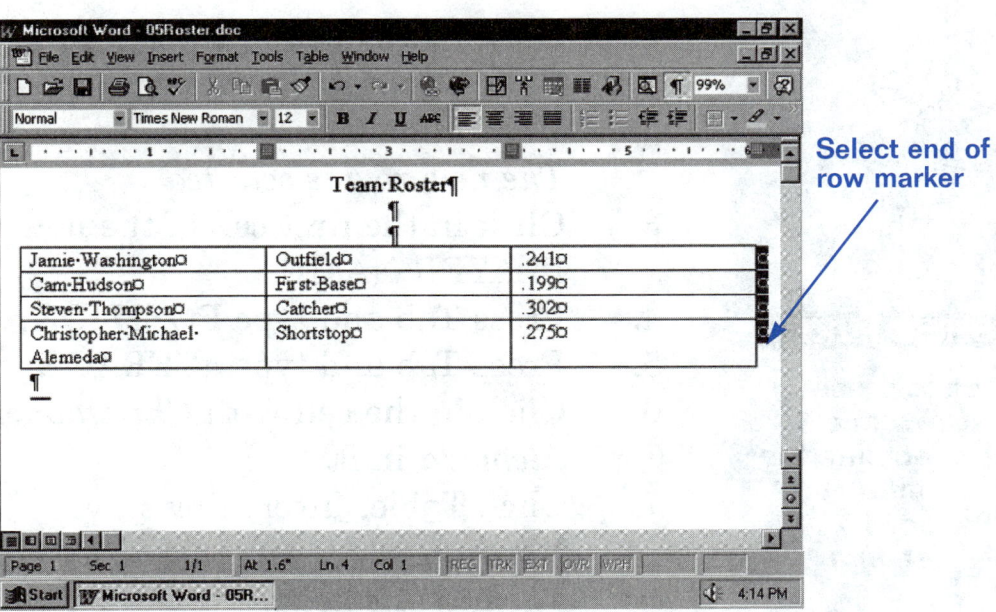

Figure 3-35. You can select the end-of-row markers to add a column to the right side of the table.

JEFF THE REF

If the Insert Columns command or the Delete Columns command isn't on the Table menu, you don't have a column selected! The Insert and Delete commands on the Table menu change depending on what's going on in the table.

MEG THE MIKE

When you use the first row in a table for labeling the table columns, it gets a special name—*Heading Row.*

 To add more than one row, select the number of rows you want to add, and then choose Table, Insert Row. To add more than one column, select more than one column.

PRACTICE SWINGS

Trainer Terry Says:

 Now let's try adding and deleting rows and columns in the table in the **roster** document.

1. Click in any cell in the top row of the table.
2. Click Table, Insert Rows.
    Word adds the new row to the top of the table. The new row is selected.
3. Click in the first cell of the new row and type PLAYER NAME.
4. Press Tab and type POSITION.
5. Press Tab and type AVERAGE.
6. Click in the cell with *Christopher Michael Alemeda* in it.
7. Click Table, Insert Rows.
    Word inserts a new row above Christopher Michael Alemeda.
8. Click Table, Delete Rows.
    Word deletes the row.

9.   Click in any cell in the middle column.
10.   Click T<u>a</u>ble, Select <u>C</u>olumn.
11.   Click T<u>a</u>ble, <u>I</u>nsert Columns.
      Word inserts a new column between the
      PLAYER NAME column and the
      POSITION column as in Figure 3-36.

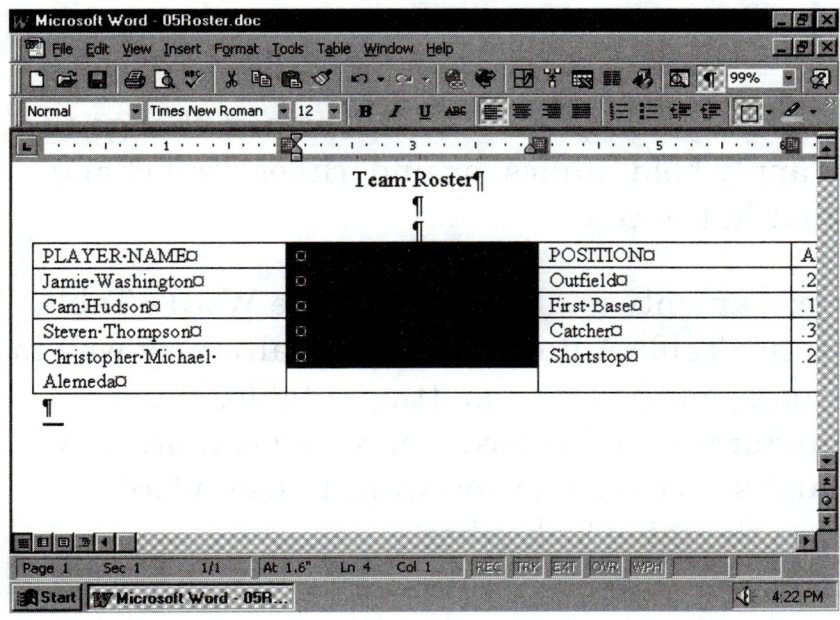

Figure 3-36. Here's a new column in the middle of the table.

12.   Choose T<u>a</u>ble, <u>D</u>elete Columns.
13.   Save the changes and keep the **roster** document open.

Formatting a Table

Coach Carrie Says:

You can also format text you type in a table. You can change the font and font size, apply bold, italics, or underlines, and change the alignment of text in the cells.

If you want to format an entire table, you can use Word's Table *AutoFormat* command. Table AutoFormat is a really easy way to make it look like you spent hours formatting a table. You just open the Table AutoFormat dialog box, where you can preview the AutoFormats and select the one you want to use. Word automatically makes the table look great!

PRACTICE SWINGS

Trainer Terry Says:

Try out a few of the Table AutoFormat styles to see which one makes the table in the **roster** document look the best.

1. Click in any cell in the table in the **roster** document.
2. Click T<u>a</u>ble, Table Auto<u>F</u>ormat.
   The Table AutoFormat dialog box opens as in Figure 3-37.

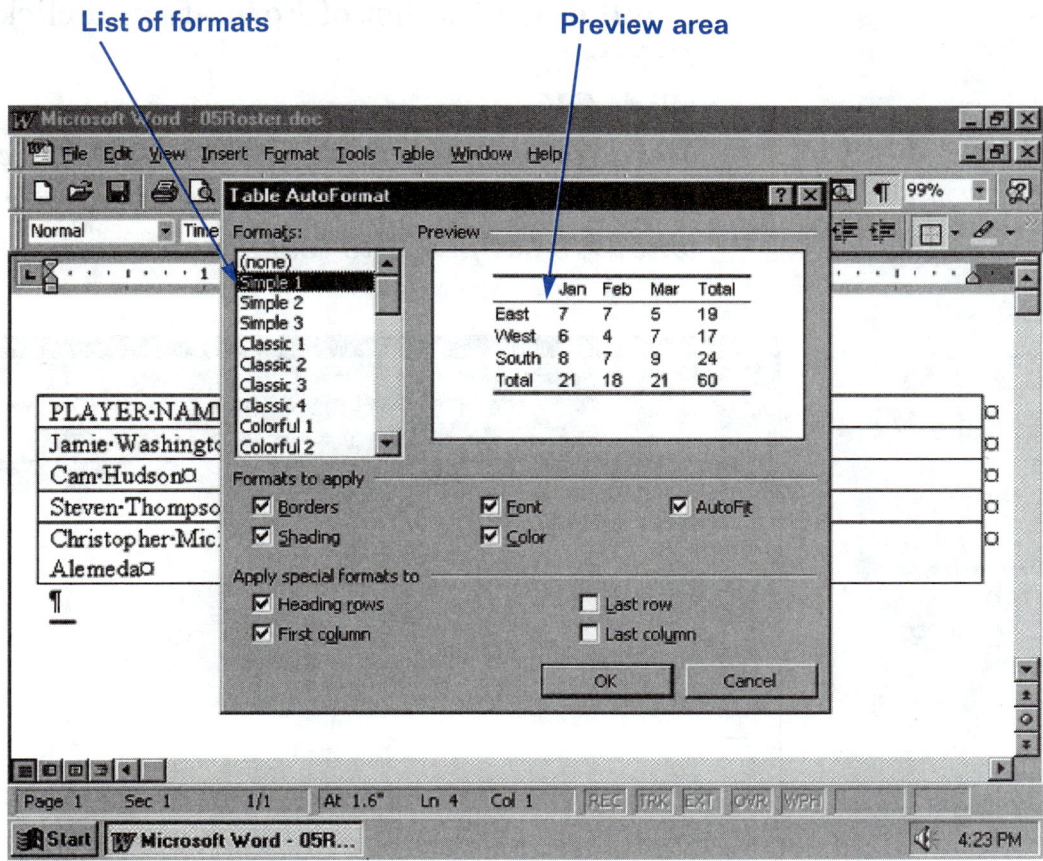

Figure 3-37. You can preview and select a format in the Table AutoFormat dialog box.

3.   Click *Classic* 3 in the list of Forma_t_s.
     Each time you click a name in the list of Forma_t_s, the preview changes so that you can see what the format looks like.

4.   Click *Colorful* 2 in the list of Forma_t_s.

 If the colors don't show up on screen on your Mac, the Color check box in the Table AutoFormat dialog box may not be selected. To display the color, locate the Color checkbox in the AutoFormats dialog and click it to select it.

JEFF THE REF

If you don't like the way the AutoFormat looks, you can use <u>E</u>dit, <u>U</u>ndo to remove it, or just use Table AutoFormat again to pick a different format.

5. Scroll down the list of Forma<u>t</u>s and click *3D Effects 3*.

6. Click OK.

Word formats the table with the 3D Effects 3 AutoFormat. In Figure 3-38, you can see what it's supposed to look like.

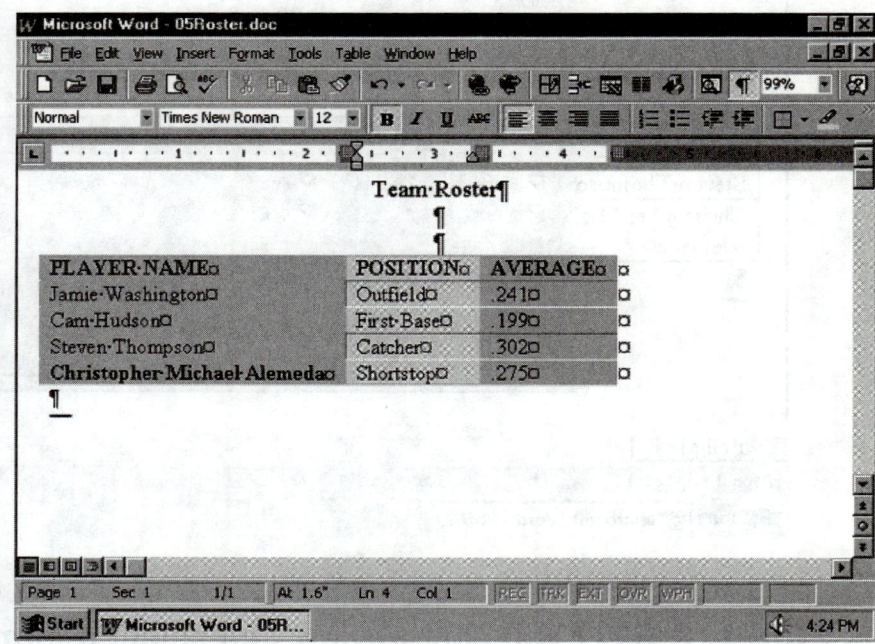

Figure 3-38. The table looks great formatted in the 3D Effects 3 style.

7. Save the **roster** document and close it.

Play Ball

First Base

Trainer Terry Says:

In this exercise, you will create a table where you can type some batting statistics for Babe Ruth, Jackie Robinson, and Mickey Mantle. Ready? Batter up!

1. Open the document **04legend** from the student data folder.
2. Save the document as **legend4**.
3. Scroll to the end of the document, then place the insertion point on the second blank line under the heading *Statistical Comparison.* *This is where you want to insert the table.*
4. Click the Insert Table button 🔲 on the Standard toolbar.
5. Click and drag the mouse across the grid to select three rows and five columns. Release the mouse button to create the table. *Word inserts a 3x5 table into the document.*

JEFF THE REF

If the table is the wrong size, use <u>E</u>dit, <u>U</u>ndo to remove it, then try again.

6. In cell A1 (the first cell), type *Babe Ruth*.

7. Press Tab and type *2503*.

8. Press Tab and type *714*.

9. Press Tab and type *2204*.

10. Press Tab and type *.342*.

11. Press Tab to move the insertion point to the second row, and type *Jackie Robinson*. *The text will wrap in the cell.*

12. Press Tab and type *1382*.

13. Press Tab and type *137*.

14. Press Tab and type *734*.

15. Press Tab and type *.311*.

16. Press Tab and type *Mickey Mantle*.

17. Press Tab and type *2401*.

18. Press Tab and type *536*.

19. Press Tab and type *1509*.

20. Press Tab and type *.298*.

Now the table is full, as in Figure 3-39.

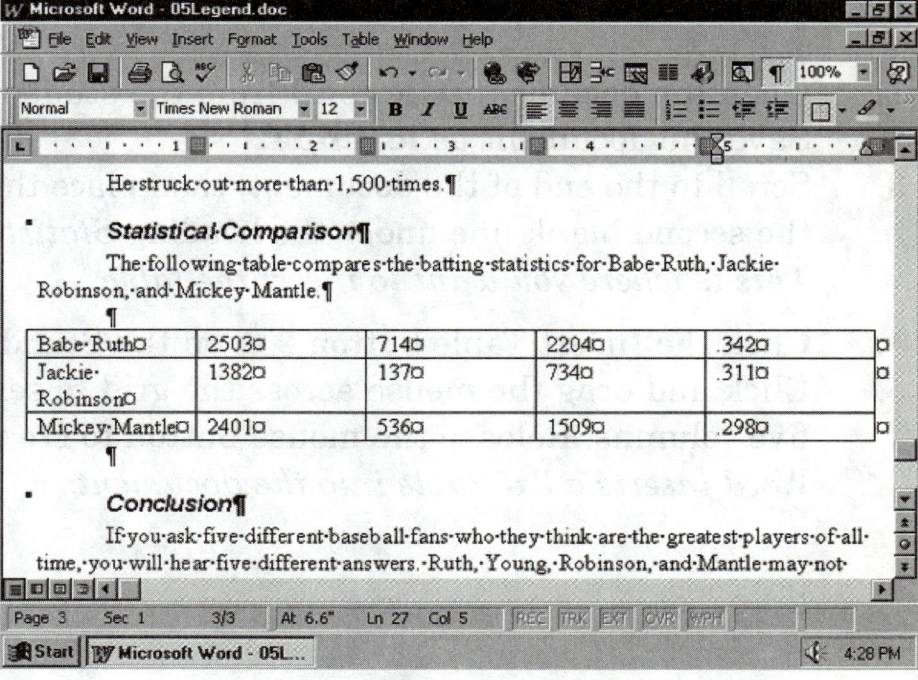

Figure 3-39. All of the statistics are now typed into the table.

Second Base

1. Click in any cell in the first row, then click T<u>a</u>ble, <u>I</u>nsert Rows.
2. Move the insertion point into the new cell A1, and then type *Player*.
3. Press Tab and type *Games*.
4. Press Tab and type *Home Runs*.
5. Press Tab and type *Runs Batted In*.
6. Press Tab and type Percentage.
   The table is easier to read with a Heading Row (see Figure 3-40).

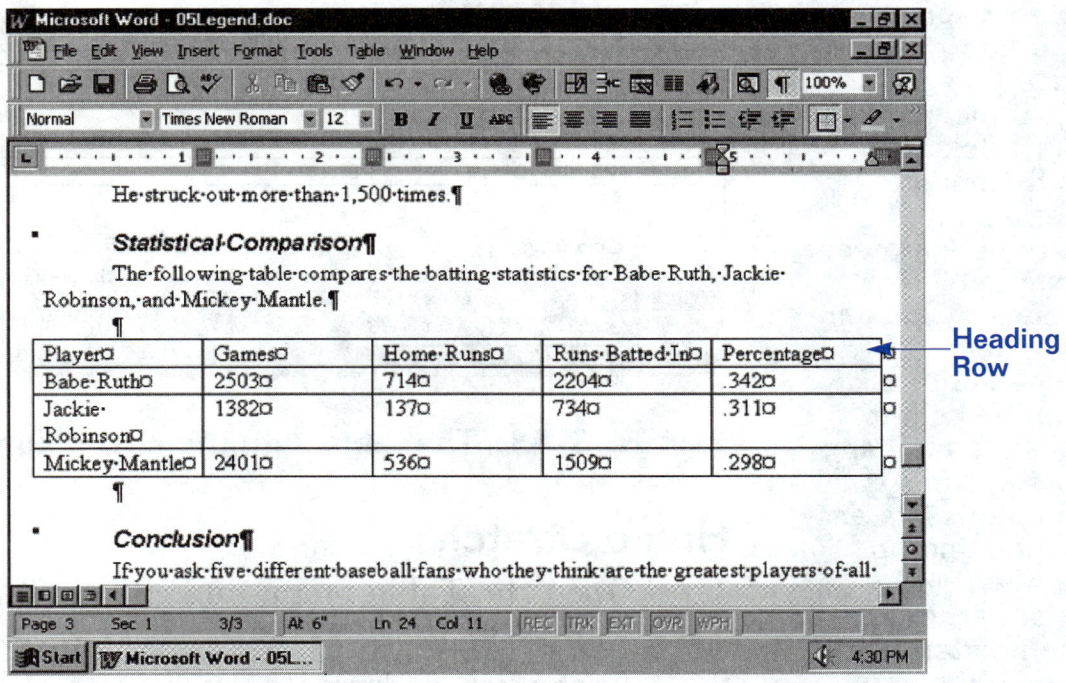

Figure 3-40. The table is easier to read with a Heading Row across the top.

Third Base

1. Click in any cell in the Home Runs column, then click T<u>a</u>ble, Select <u>C</u>olumn.
2. Click T<u>a</u>ble, <u>I</u>nsert Columns.
3. Click in the top cell in the new column and type *At Bats*.
4. Press the Down Arrow key to move the insertion point into the second cell in the column, and type *8397*.

JEFF THE REF

Sometimes, a cell might become selected when you click in it to position the insertion point. This just means that you are clicking when the mouse pointer is in the cell's selection area. You can tell the difference by looking at the mouse pointer—in the text area of the cell, it looks like an I-beam; in the selection area, it looks like an arrow pointing up and to the right. Make sure the mouse pointer is an I-beam before you click in the cell.

5. Press the Down Arrow key again and type *4877.*
6. Press the Down Arrow key again and type *8102.*
   You have all the information you need in your table. It should look like Figure 3-41.

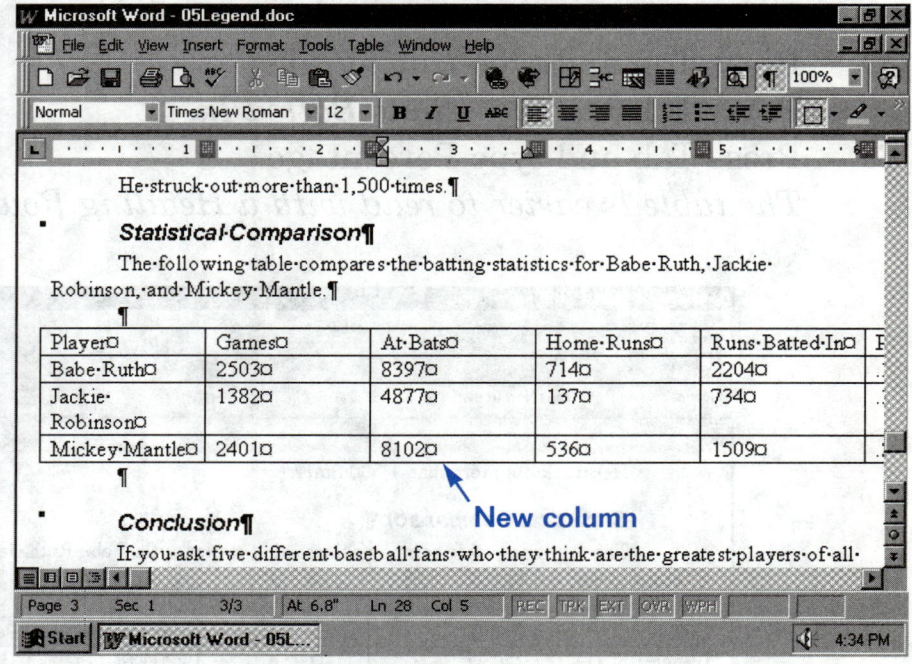

Figure 3-41. The table with the new column filled in.

Home Stretch

1. Open the T̲able menu and choose Table AutoF̲ormat.
2. In the list of Forma̲ts, click *List 1.*
3. Click OK.
   Word formats the table. It should look like Figure 3-42.

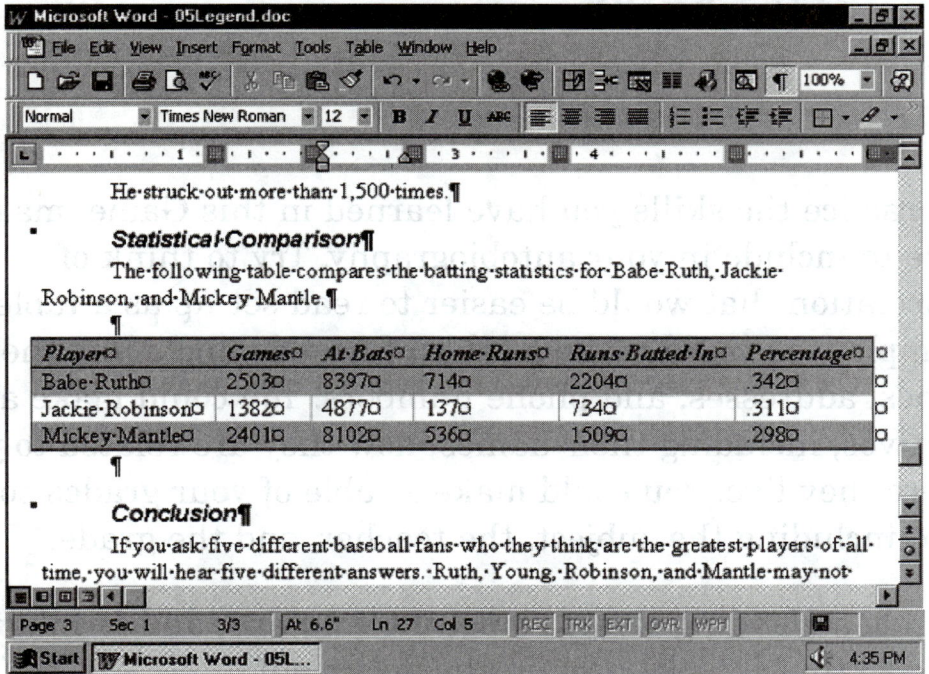

He·struck·out·more·than·1,500·times.¶

Statistical·Comparison¶

The·following·table·compares·the·batting·statistics·for·Babe·Ruth,·Jackie·Robinson,·and·Mickey·Mantle.¶

¶

Player	*Games*	*At·Bats*	*Home·Runs*	*Runs·Batted·In*	*Percentage*
Babe·Ruth	2503	8397	714	2204	.342
Jackie·Robinson	1382	4877	137	734	.311
Mickey·Mantle	2401	8102	536	1509	.298

¶

Conclusion¶

If·you·ask·five·different·baseball·fans·who·they·think·are·the·greatest·players·of·all·time,·you·will·hear·five·different·answers.·Ruth,·Young,·Robinson,·and·Mantle·may·not·

Figure 3-42. The completed table looks great in the document.

4. Save the changes you have made to the **legend4** document, and then close it.

RUN HOME!

THE WORLD SERIES

To practice the skills you have learned in this Game, make a table to include in your autobiography. Try to think of information that would be easier to read set up as a table. For example, you could make a table of friends, including their names, addresses, and phone numbers. You could make a table of relatives, including their names, how they are related to you, and where they live. You could make a table of your grades so far this year, including the subject, the teacher, and the grade.

Include a Heading Row to label the columns, and format the table so that it looks good in the document.

GAME #5
THROWING A CURVE BALL

In this Game, you'll learn how to organize a report with headers and footers, page numbers, and page breaks by:

- Adding Page Numbers to a Document
- Removing Page Numbers
- Creating a Header and a Footer
- Adding Page Numbers and Dates in a Header or a Footer
- Using Page Breaks

MEG THE MIKE

A *header* is text that prints across the top of every page in a document. A *footer* is text that prints across the bottom of every page in a document. A *page break* is a code that tells Word to start a new page.

A *field* is a code for information that might change, like page numbers or dates. When Word finds a field in a document, it automatically replaces the code with the correct information.

ON DECK

Coach Carrie Says:

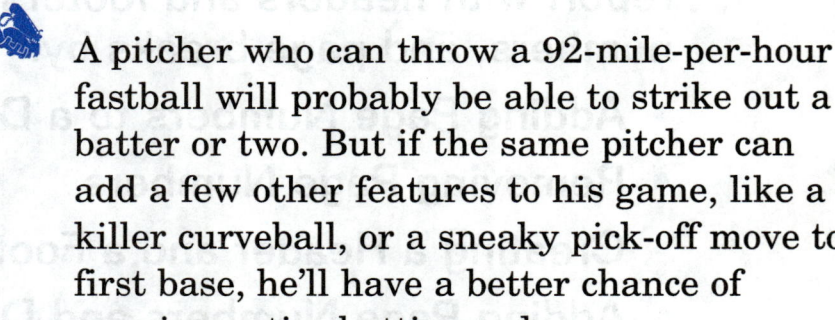

A pitcher who can throw a 92-mile-per-hour fastball will probably be able to strike out a batter or two. But if the same pitcher can add a few other features to his game, like a killer curveball, or a sneaky pick-off move to first base, he'll have a better chance of running entire batting order.

Likewise, there are a ton of features you can add to a document. In this Game, you'll learn a few that can make your report easier to read when it's printed.

First, you'll learn how to add and remove page numbers to your document. Next, you'll learn how to create a *header* and a *footer* in a report, so that you can have useful information like the date printed at the top or bottom of every page.

Finally, you'll learn how to create *page breaks* in your document, so you can make sure that new pages start where you want.

Adding Page Numbers to a Document

Coach Carrie Says:

 You might be tempted to type a page number on every page of your report, but think about this: If you move things around, or add or delete information after you've already typed the page numbers, you'd have to go back and retype them all!

 Luckily, Word can keep track of page numbers for you. Word puts the page numbers in a *field,* so that the numbers can change if necessary. This means that you can change the report as much as you want and Word will take care of making sure the page numbering is correct.

 To add page numbers, you use the Insert, Page Numbers command.

 Usually, Word puts the page number at the bottom of the page, on the right. You can, however, use the options in the Page Numbers dialog box to place the page numbers where you prefer.

 For example, you can put the page numbers at the top of the page and align them left, right, centered or outside.

MEG THE MIKE

Outside alignment means Word will put the numbers on the right side of all right-hand pages and on the left side of all left-hand pages

PRACTICE SWINGS

Trainer Terry Says:

In this exercise, you'll open a version of the Scouting Report document you worked with in Game 2 and add page numbers.

1. Open the file **05scout** from the student data folder.
2. Save the file as **scout5**.
3. Click <u>I</u>nsert, click Page N<u>u</u>mbers.
   The Page Numbers dialog box opens, as in Figure 3-43.

Page number in sample area

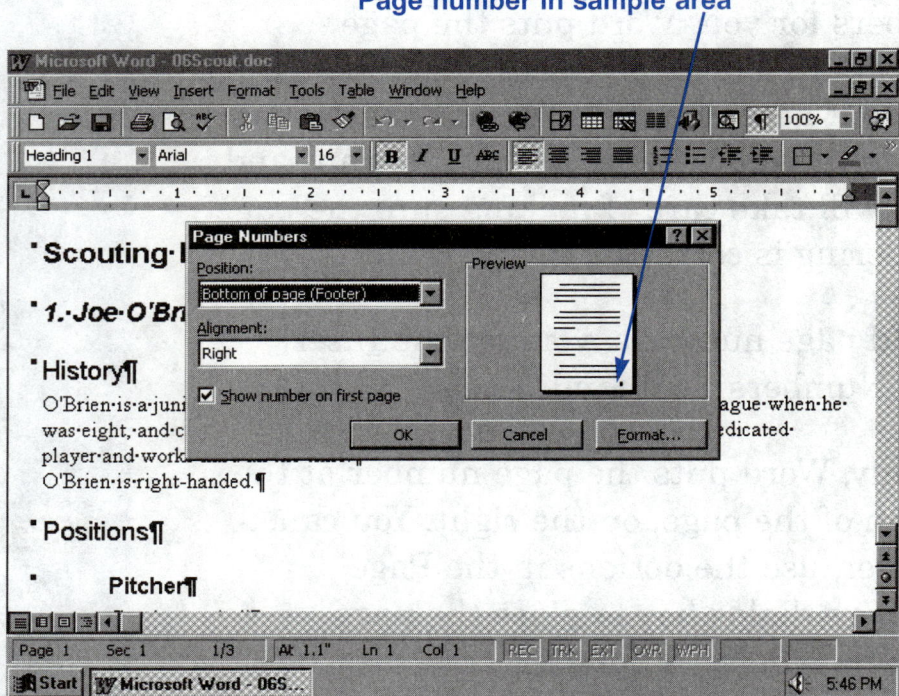

Figure 3-43. You use the Page Numbers dialog box to insert page numbers into a Word document.

4. Click OK.
5. Scroll to the bottom of the page.
   In Page Layout view, Word displays in a light gray color, as in Figure 3-44.

Page number

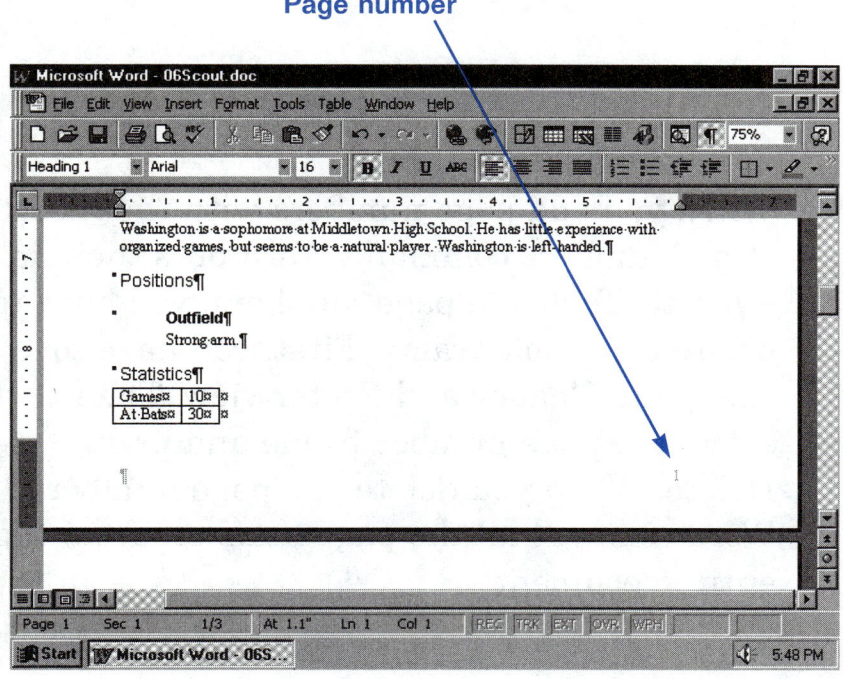

Figure 3-44. In Page Layout view, you can see where the page numbers will print.

6. Scroll through the document to see the page numbers on the other pages.
7. Save the document and keep it open.

JEFF THE REF

You can't see page numbers in Normal view. Click on the Print Preview or Page Layout button. Then, Word will show the page numbers on your screen.

MEG THE MIKE

A *frame* is an invisible box that can be placed around objects like text, fields, and pictures. You can use the frame to help position the object on the page, or to format the object. You'll learn more about frames and boxes in Season 4.

Removing Page Numbers

Coach Carrie Says:

When you add page numbers with the Insert, Page Numbers command Word puts them in a *frame*. To delete page numbers, you have to delete the whole frame. First, you have to change to Header and Footer view. Then select the page number frame and press Delete. When you delete one page number, Word removes all the page numbers from the entire document.

PRACTICE SWINGS

Trainer Terry Says:

Let's try deleting the frame and the page numbers from the **scout5** document.

1. If you're not already in Page Layout view, choose View, Page Layout.

    To change views quickly, click the Page Layout View button 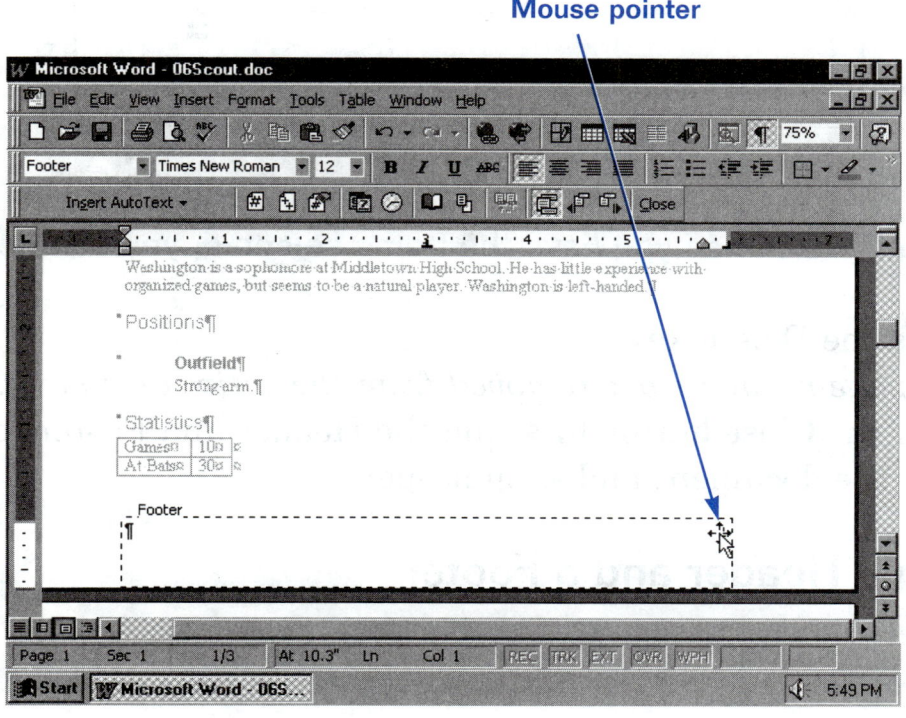 *on the View toolbar at the left end of the Horizontal scroll bar.*

2. Scroll down so you can see any page number.
3. Double-click the page number.
    Word opens the Header and Footer view.
4. Move the mouse pointer over the page number so that the mouse pointer changes to a four-headed arrow (see Figure 3-45).

Figure 3-45. When the mouse pointer moves over a frame, the mouse pointer changes to a four-headed arrow.

5. Click the mouse button.
    Word selects the frame. The selected frame shows up around the page number, as in Figure 3-46.

Frame

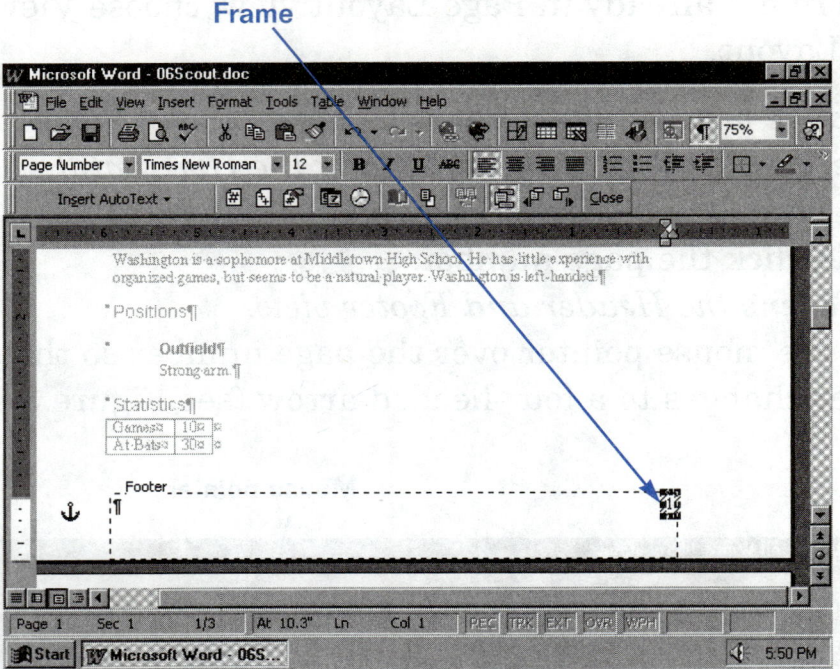

Figure 3-46. Once you have the frame selected, you can delete it.

6. Press the Delete key.
   The page numbers are removed from the entire document.
7. Click the Close button Close on the Header and Footer toolbar.
8. Save the document and keep it open.

Creating a Header and a Footer

Coach Carrie Says:

A header is text that appears across the top of every page in a document. A footer is text that appears across the bottom of every page in a document. You can have a header, a footer, or both in any document you create with Word.

A header can include the name of the person who wrote the report, the title of the report, page numbers, and the date. You can even include pictures. Your teachers might want you to include your room number or the subject.

 To create a header or a footer with Word, click View, Header and Footer, then type the text. When you are done, close the Header and Footer view by clicking the Close button Close . The header or footer will be printed on every page of the document.

When you choose View, Header and Footer, Word switches to Page Layout view, shows the *Header area*, and displays the Header and Footer toolbar see Figure 3-47.

MEG THE MIKE

The *Header area* is the top margin where you type the header text. When you create a header, Word shows the Header area on screen with a dotted line around it.

The *Footer area* is the bottom margin where you type the footer text. When you create a footer, Word shows the Footer area on screen with a dotted line around it.

Insert page number   Insert date   Switch between header and footer

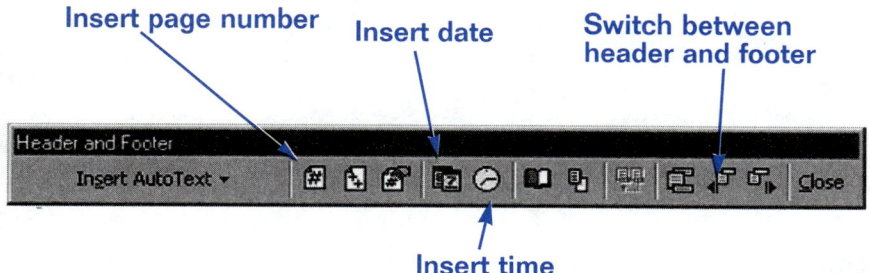

Insert time

Figure 3-47. The Header and Footer toolbar

JEFF THE REF

You can't see your headers or footers on screen in Normal view. To see them the way they will look when the document is printed, you have to switch to Print Preview or Page Layout view.

 You can click the Switch Between Header and Footer button on the Header and Footer toolbar to jump down to the bottom of the page and see the *Footer area*.

Using the buttons on the Header and Footer toolbar you can have Word automatically put page numbers or the date into a header or a footer.

PRACTICE SWINGS

Trainer Terry Says:

 In this exercise, you'll create headers and footers in the **scout5** document.

1. **Scout5** should be open. If not, open it now.
2. Click <u>V</u>iew, click <u>H</u>eader and Footer.
   Word switches to Header and Footer view and shows the Header area on screen.

3. Type *Scouting Report*, then press the Tab key twice.

   The Header and Footer areas have some preset formatting to make entering the header and footer text easier. For example, there are three tab stops: left-aligned, centered, and right-aligned.

4. Type *Coach Taylor*.

   The Header area should look like the one in Figure 3-48.

Report title

Coach's name

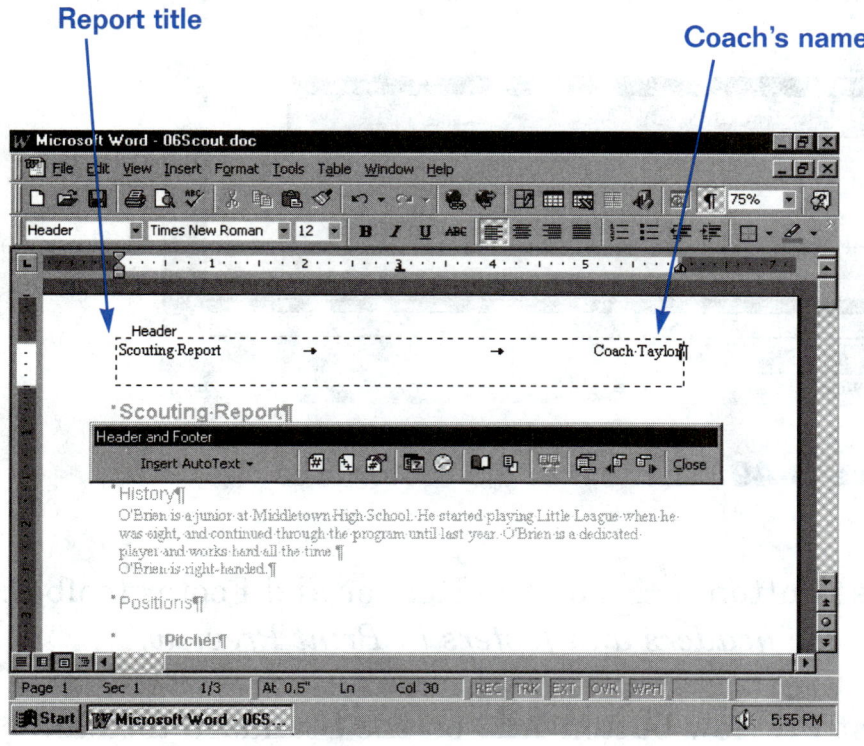

Figure 3-48. The text in the Header area

JEFF THE REF

If the Header and Footer toolbar is covering parts of the screen that you need, you can drag it out of the way. Just move the mouse pointer so it's touching the toolbar, hold down the mouse button, and drag it wherever you want.

5. Click the Switch Between Header and Footer button 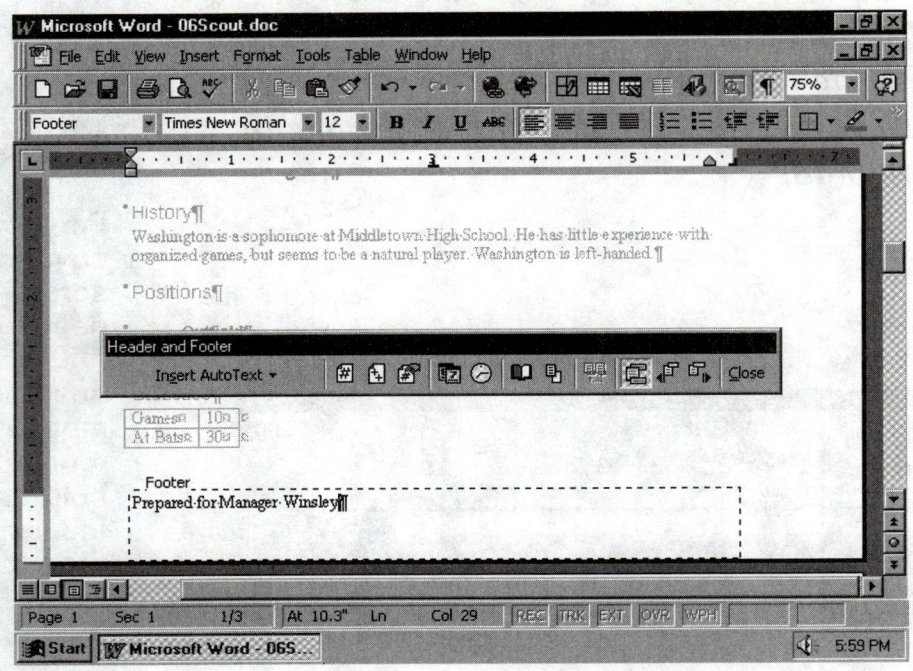 on the Header and Footer toolbar.

6. Type *Prepared for Manager Winsley.*
    The footer should look like Figure 3-49

Figure 3-49. The text in the footer area.

7. Click the <u>C</u>lose button Close on the Header and Footer toolbar.
    Now let's view the headers and footers in Print Preview.

8. Click the Print Preview button on the Standard toolbar.
    In Print Preview, it's tough to read the text, but you can see the header across the top of the page and the footer across the bottom.

9. Click in the vertical scroll bar to see all the pages of your document.

10. Click the <u>C</u>lose button Close on the Print Preview toolbar.

11. Save the document and keep it open.

Adding Page Numbers and Dates in a Header or a Footer

RUN HOME!

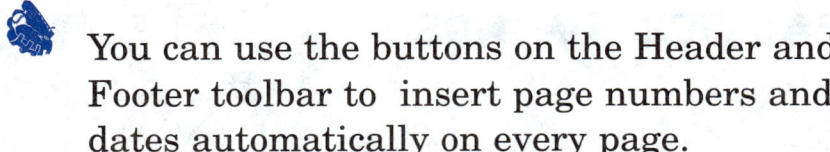

Coach Carrie Says:

⚾ You can use the buttons on the Header and Footer toolbar to insert page numbers and dates automatically on every page.

⚾ To add page numbers or the current date to a header or a footer, just put the insertion point where you want it and click the correct toolbar button.

⚾ There are two other buttons on the Header and Footer toolbar that you might find useful for quickly inserting information into a header or footer:

- Click the Insert Time button 🕐 to insert the current time. The time will update whenever you print the document.
- Click the Insert Number of Pages button 📄 to insert the total number of pages in a document.

JEFF THE REF

Sometimes you don't want the date to change when you print the document. You might want it to show the day you created the document or the day you handed it in to the teacher. In that case, you should just type in the date.

A nice touch to make your report look good is to type the word *Page* in front of the space where you are going to insert the page numbers. Likewise, you can type something like *Printed on:* in front of the space where you are going to insert the current date. Just remember to leave a space after the text you type, so that the space will be included in the printed document.

PRACTICE SWINGS

Trainer Terry Says:

In this exercise, you'll add page numbers and the date to the footer in the **scout5** document.

1.   In the **scout5** document, click <u>V</u>iew, click <u>H</u>eader and Footer.

2.   Click the Switch Between Header and Footer button on the Header and Footer toolbar.
Now you can see the footer text in the Footer area on screen.

3. Move the insertion point to the end of the text, *Prepared for Manager Winsley*, and press the Tab key.

4. Click the Insert Page Number button 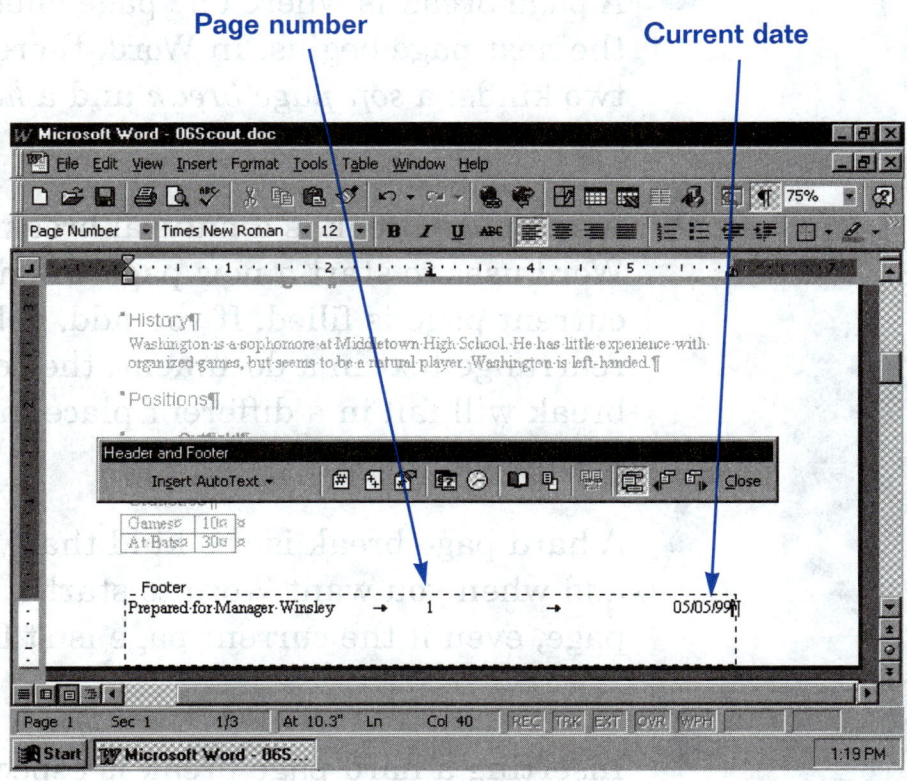 on the Header and Footer toolbar.

    It's as simple as that! Word inserts the page numbers into the Footer area (you can see it in Figure 3-51).

5. Press Tab.

6. Click the Insert Date button on the Header and Footer toolbar.

    Now you've got the date in the footer, too! The Footer area should look like the one in Figure 3-50.

Page number   Current date

Figure 3-50. The page numbers are centered in the footer and the date is flush right.

JEFF THE REF

Don't expect the date on your computer to match the date in the figures. Word inserts the current date, based on your computer's clock/calendar.

7.   Click the <u>C</u>lose button  on the Header and Footer toolbar.

8.   Save the document and keep it open.

Using Page Breaks

Coach Carrie Says:

 A page break is where one page ends and the next page begins. In Word, there are two kinds: a *soft page break* and a *hard page break*.

 A soft page break is a natural break that Word uses to start a new page when the current page is filled. If you add, delete, or rearrange text in a document, the soft page break will fall in a different place in the document.

 A hard page break is the kind that you can add when you want Word to start a new page, even if the current page isn't filled.

 Inserting a hard page break is especially useful when a heading or title in the middle of a document shows up right at the bottom of the page. You can put a hard page break in front of the heading, and it moves to the top of the next page.

The easiest way to put in a hard page break on a PC is to use the shortcut key combination Ctrl+Enter.

The easiest way to put in a hard page break on the Mac is to press Shift+Enter.

 You can also use the menu commands to start a new page. Just click Insert, Break, and then click OK in the Break dialog box to insert the default hard page break.

PRACTICE SWINGS

Trainer Terry Says:

 In this exercise, you'll insert some hard breaks in the **scout5** documet. Here comes the pitch!

1. Make sure you have **scout5** displayed in Page Layout view, then scroll down so that you can see the bottom of the first page and the top of the second page, as in Figure 3-51.
    Notice that the table showing Jamie Washington's statistics is split in the middle by a soft page break.

SEASON 3, GAME 5

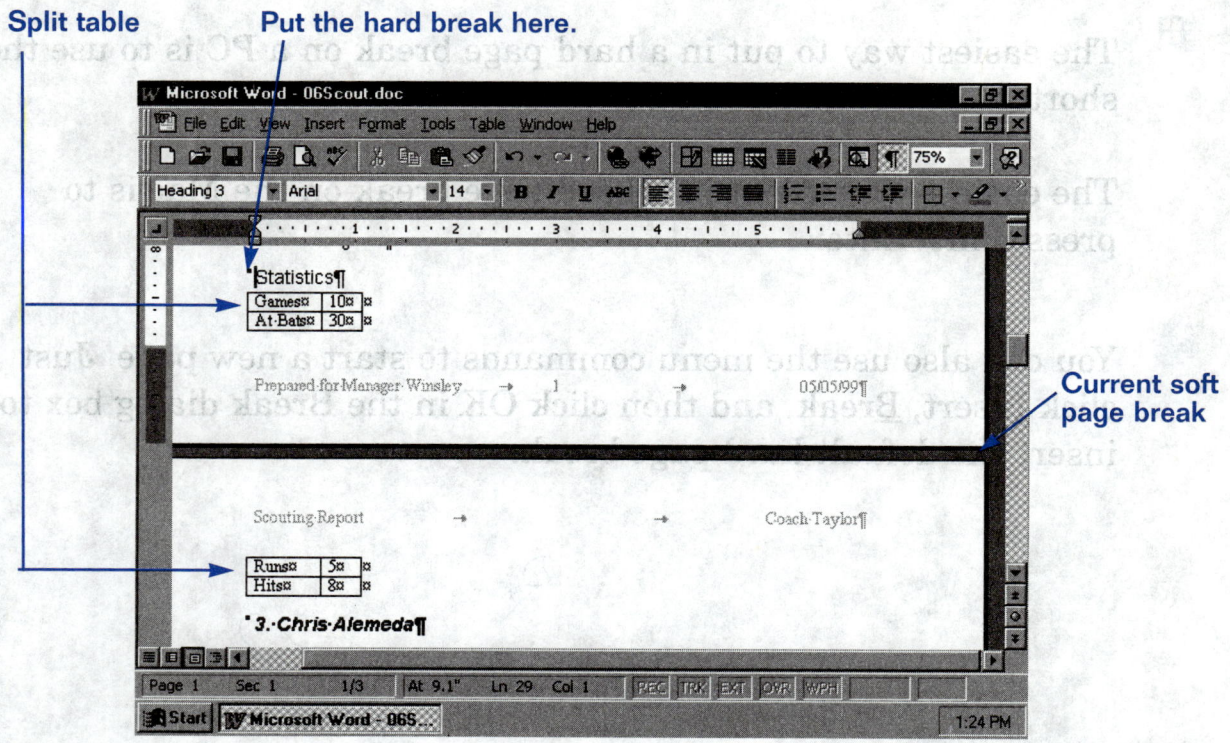

Figure 3-51. A soft page break splits the table of statistics, making it difficult to read.

2.   Move the insertion point to the beginning of the line with the heading *Statistics*.

3.   Press Ctrl+Enter.

OR

Press Shift+Enter.

Word inserts a hard page break and moves the heading Statistics to the top of Page 2.

Another way to use hard page breaks in this document is to put each player on a separate page. First, you have to delete the hard page break you just put in.

4. Press Backspace.
Word deletes the hard page break, and the table is split again.

5. Scroll up and place the insertion point at the beginning of the heading line *2. Jamie Washington* on page 1.

6.  Press Ctrl+Enter.

   OR

    Press Shift+Enter.

7. Scroll down on page 2 and place the insertion point at the beginning of the heading line *3. Chris Alemeda.*

8.  Press Ctrl+Enter.

   OR

    Press Shift+Enter.

9. Scroll down on page 3 and place the insertion point at the beginning of the heading line *4. Cam Hudson.*

10.  Press Ctrl+Enter.

    OR

     Press Shift+Enter.

11. Scroll down on page 4 and place the insertion point at the beginning of the heading line *5. Steven Thompson.*

JEFF THE REF

You can delete a hard page break the way you delete any character in Word, with Backspace or Delete. Press Backspace if the hard page break line is before the insertion point; press Delete if the insertion point is on the hard page break line.

JEFF THE REF

Remember, hard page breaks don't move the way soft page breaks do. If you insert a hard page break, it stays where you put it, whether you add, delete, or rearrange text. For that reason, it's a good idea not to insert hard page breaks until you have finished editing a document. Then, you can use the hard page breaks to help make the finished document look better.

12. ⊞ Press Ctrl+Enter.
OR
 Press Shift+Enter.

Now each player is listed on a separate page. as in Figure 3-52

Top of page 3   Bottom of page 2

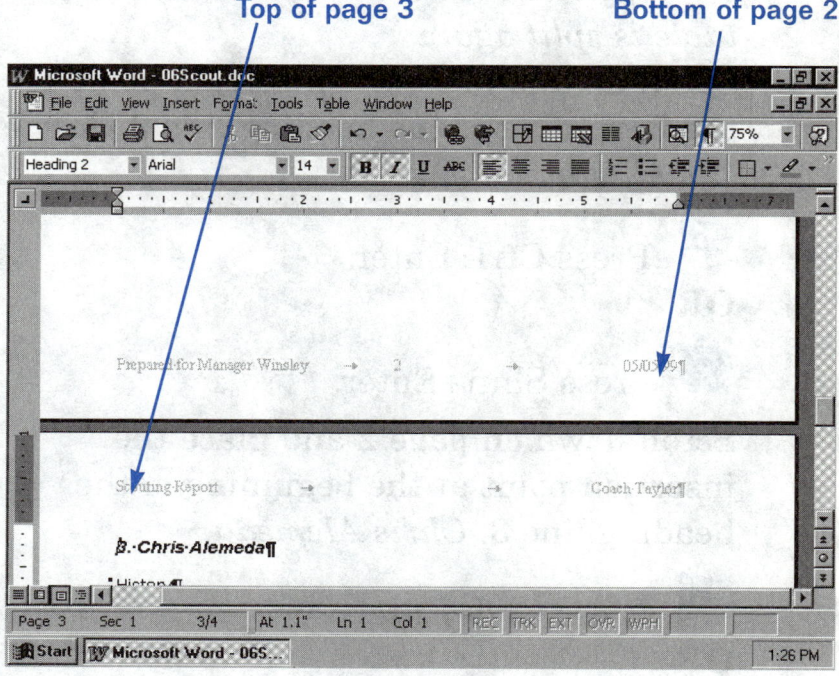

Figure 3-52. The hard page breaks force each player's information to a new page.

13. Scroll through in Page Layout view or Print Preview to see how the page breaks divide the document.

14. Save the **scout5** document and close it.

PLAY BALL!

PLAY BALL

Trainer Terry Says:

 Once you finish writing the report about the four baseball legends, you can add the details to make sure it's a winner!

1. Open the document **05legend** from the student folder.
2. Save the document as **legend5**.
3. Click <u>V</u>iew, <u>H</u>eader and Footer to display the Header area.
4. Type *Four Baseball Legends*.
5. Press Tab twice.
6. Type your name.

7. Click the Switch Between Header and Footer button 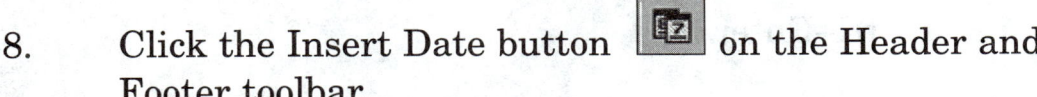 on the Header and Footer toolbar.

8. Click the Insert Date button ⊞ on the Header and Footer toolbar.
9. Press Tab.
10. Type *Page,* then press the spacebar once.

11. Click the Insert Page Number button ⊞ on the Header and Footer toolbar.
    Now the page number is centered with the word Page in front of it.
12. Click the <u>C</u>lose button on the Header and Footer toolbar.
13. Scroll down to the bottom of page 1.
    In Figure 3-53, you can see that the section on Babe Ruth's Baseball History starts near the bottom of page 1. Let's insert a hard page break so that it starts at the top of page 2.

Footer on page 1

Insert a hard page break here

Header on page 2

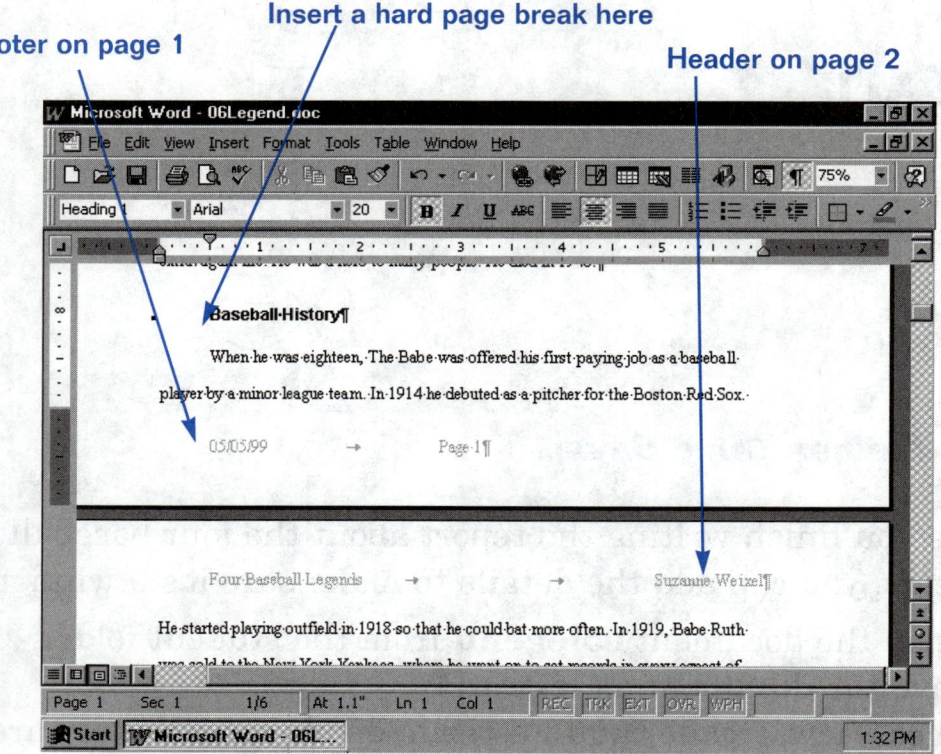

Figure 3-53. You can use a hard page break to move the Baseball History section to the next page.

14. Move the insertion point to the beginning of the heading line Baseball History for Babe Ruth, near the bottom of page 1.

15. Press Ctrl+Enter.
OR
Press Shift+Enter.
The new hard page break forces the section to the top of page 2.

16. Move the insertion point to the beginning of the section heading line *Statistical Comparison* at the bottom of page 5.

17. Press Ctrl+Enter.
OR
Press Shift+Enter.
*Word inserts the last hard page break, as in Figure 3-54. You have finished adding the details to the **legend5** document!*

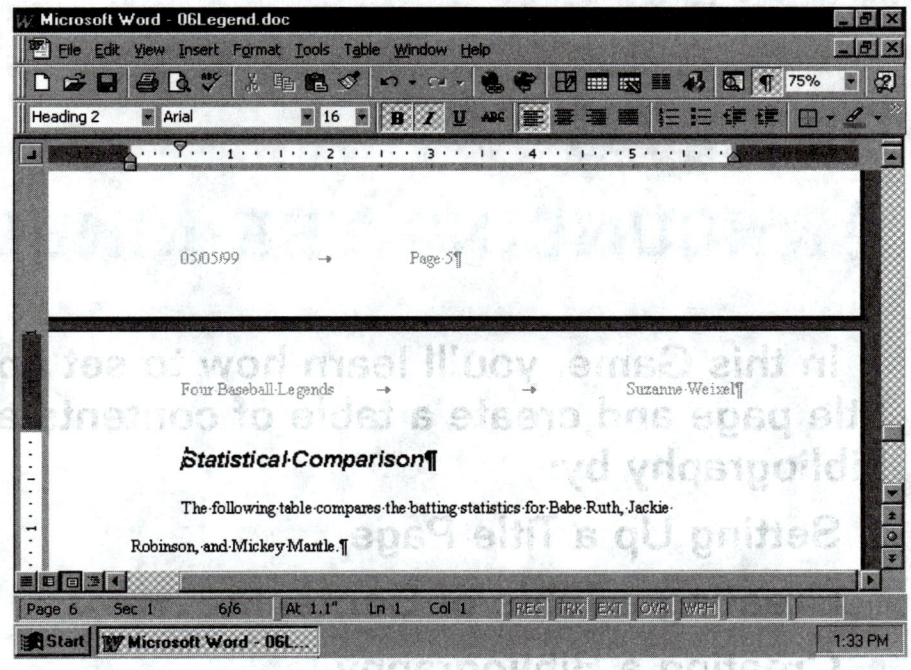

Figure 3-54. The top of the last page of the **legend** document

18.   Save the **legend5** document and close it.

THE WORLD SERIES

To practice the skills you learned in this Game, add a header and a footer to your autobiography. Include page numbers and the current date. Finally, look for places where hard page breaks will make the document look better and be easier to read, then go ahead and put those page breaks in the document.

PLAY BALL!

GAME #6
ANNOUNCING THE LINEUP

In this Game, you'll learn how to set up a title page and create a table of contents and a bibliography by:

- **Setting Up a Title Page**
- **Creating a Table of Contents**
- **Creating a Bibliography**

YOU'RE IN!

ME?

ON DECK

Coach Carrie Says:

 When a baseball game is broadcast, the announcer starts off by telling the audience the names and positions of the players on both teams. After the game, the announcer usually thanks the people who helped produce the broadcast. You can tell the reader what's in your report by including a *title page* and a *table of contents* up front. At the end of the report, you can include a *bibliography* that lists all your references.

Setting Up a Title Page

 Most teachers want you to include a title page or cover on a report. The title usually includes the report title, your name, and the date. You can also add the class or subject, the teacher's name, and your room number.

MEG THE MIKE

The *title page* is the first page in a report. It usually has the report title and the author's name on it, as well as anything the teacher asks for, like the date and the class.

A *table of contents* is a list of the sections in the report and the pages where each section starts.

A *bibliography* is a list of all the sources the author used to learn about the report topic. Each entry in a bibliography usually includes the title, the author, and the publication date of the source.

A title page introduces your report to the reader, so it is important that it looks good.

 You can easily use a page break to make sure the title page is separate from the rest of the report document.

 If you have a header, a footer, or both in the document, you can use a page setup option so that they don't print on the title page.

PRACTICE SWINGS

Trainer Terry Says:

 In this exercise, you'll open a version of the Scouting Report you've been working with in this Season and set up a title page.

 Start by opening the document and inserting a page break to create a new blank page at the beginning of the report.

First Base

1. Open the file **06scout** from the student data folder.
2. Save the file as **scout6**.
3. Click <u>I</u>nsert, <u>B</u>reak. Then click OK to insert a hard page break. *The hard page break forces the beginning of the report onto page 2, leaving a blank page as page 1. This page will be your title page.*

4.   Press Ctrl+Home, press Enter, and then press the Up
      Arrow key.

OR

   Press Command+Home, press Enter, and then press the Up
   Arrow key.

*Now the insertion point is on page 1, on a blank line above
the hard page break, as in Figure 3-55.*

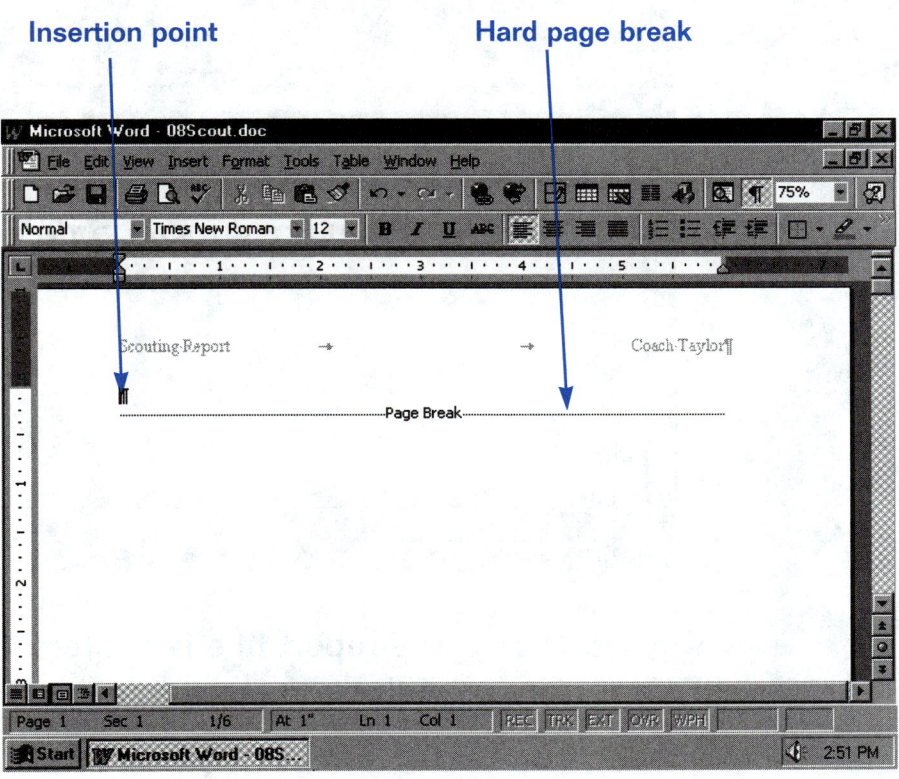

Figure 3-55. The hard page break creates a new page that you can
use for your title page.

JEFF THE REF

When you create a title page using a hard page break, the first line on the new page has the same formatting as the line where you created the hard page break.

5. Type *SCOUTING REPORT* in all capital letters.

6. Select the text and change the font to Arial, 36 point.

7. Click the Center Align button  on the Formatting toolbar.
The report title is now in your document, formatted and aligned (see Figure 3-56).

Figure 3-56. The report title is centered at the top of the title page.

Second Base

1. Make sure the insertion point is at the end of the line with the report title, and then click Format, Paragraph.
In the Format Paragraph dialog box as in Figure 3-57, you can set paragraph spacing options to control how much white space Word leaves before and after a paragraph.

Set paragraph spacing options here.

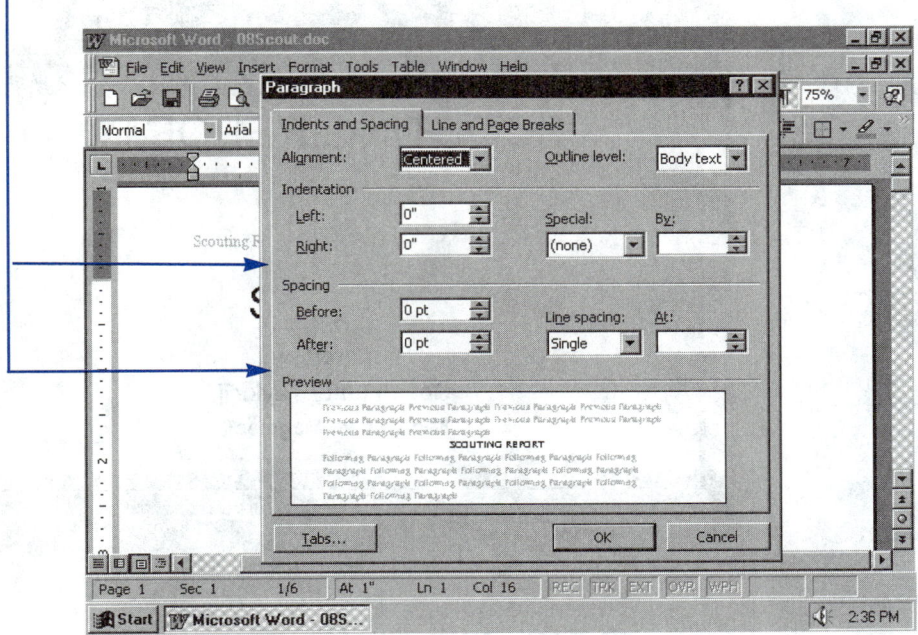

Figure 3-57. Use the Paragraph dialog box to set the paragraph spacing for the title page.

2. In the Spacing <u>B</u>efore text box, enter *72 pt*.
3. Press Tab to move to the Spacing After t<u>e</u>xt box and enter *144 pt*.
4. Click OK.
   Word adjusts the paragraph spacing for the report title, leaving one inch of space before the paragraph and two inches of space after the paragraph.
5. Press Enter to move the insertion point to the next line.
6. Change the font size to 20.
7. Choose F<u>o</u>rmat, <u>P</u>aragraph and enter *0* in the Spacing <u>B</u>efore box and *6 pt* in the Spacing Aft<u>e</u>r box. Then click OK.
8. Type *Prepared by* and press Enter.
9. Type *Coach Lefty Taylor* and press Enter.
10. Change the font size to 18 and type *Middletown Magpies*.
    Now your title page should look like the one in Figure 3-58.

JEFF THE REFF

There are 72 points in an inch. You do the math!

If the spacing of the lines on your screen doesn't seem to match the spacing of the lines in the figures, here are some things to check:

Make sure the Zoom magnification is the same. Do this by clicking in the Zoom box on the Standard toolbar, typing 75, and then pressing Enter.

Make sure you are using the correct font and font size, as described in the steps.

If the spacing still doesn't match exactly, don't worry about it. Your screen might display the text differently. Just make sure your title page looks good.

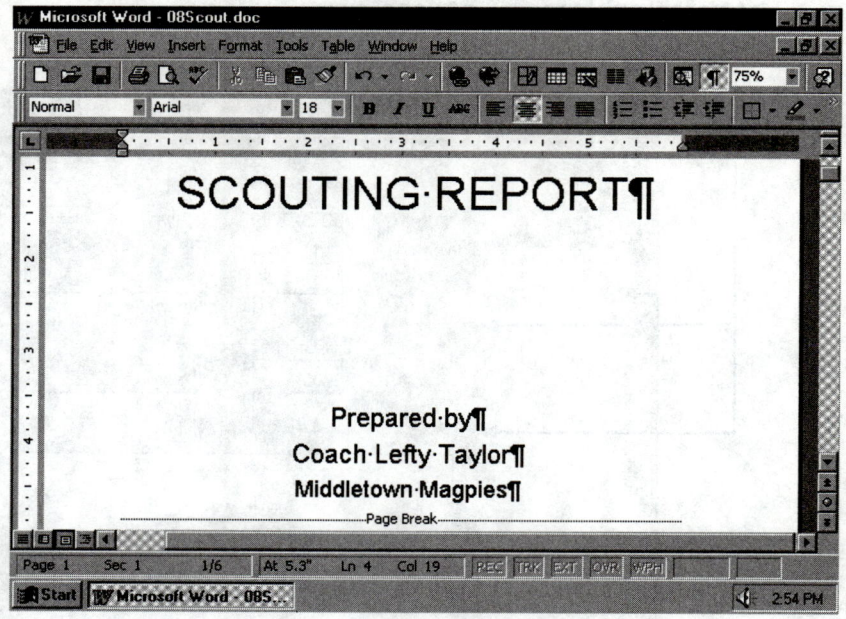

Figure 3-58. Different font sizes and spacing help make the title page interesting.

Third Base

1. Click Format, Paragraph.
2. Leave the Spacing Before setting at 0 and change the Spacing After setting to *144 pt*. Then click OK.
3. Press Enter.
   Now, let's add the date.
4. Open the Insert menu and choose Date and Time.
   The Date and Time dialog box looks like the one in Figure 3-59.

Select this format

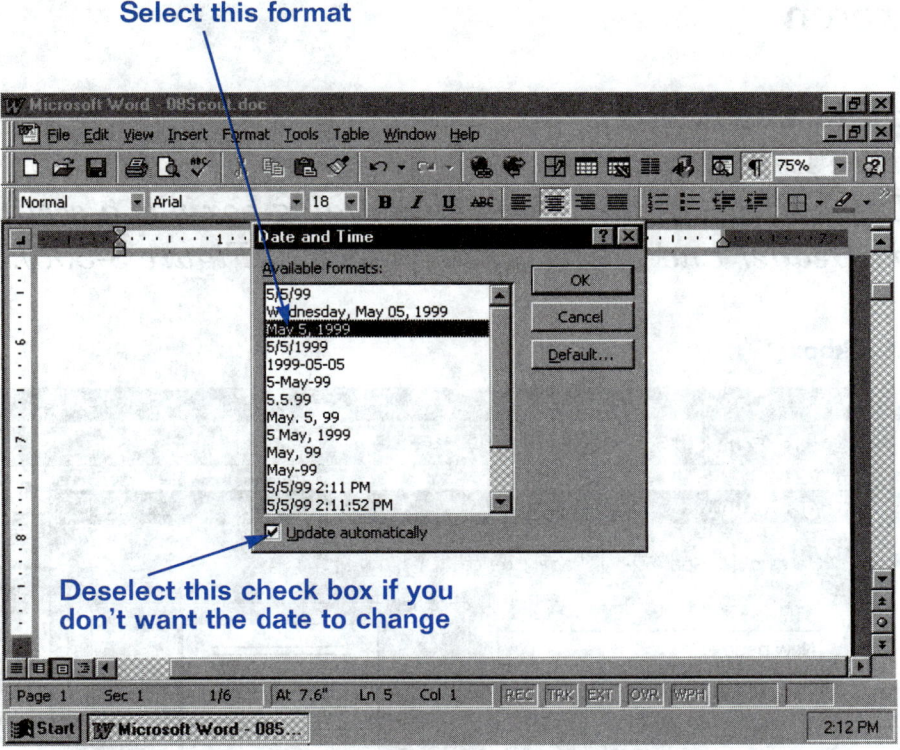

**Deselect this check box if you
don't want the date to change**

Figure 3-59. You can select a date and Word will insert it in the
document.

5. On a PC, click the third format in the list and then click OK.

OR

🍎 On a Mac, click the fourth format in the list, and then
click OK.

*Now the date is in the document and the title page text is
complete. Word will insert the current date every time you
print your document.*

Home Stretch

1. Click File, Page Setup.
2. Click the Layout page tab.
   The Layout page of the Page Setup dialog box has a section for setting Header and Footer options (look at Figure 3-59b).

Select this checkbox

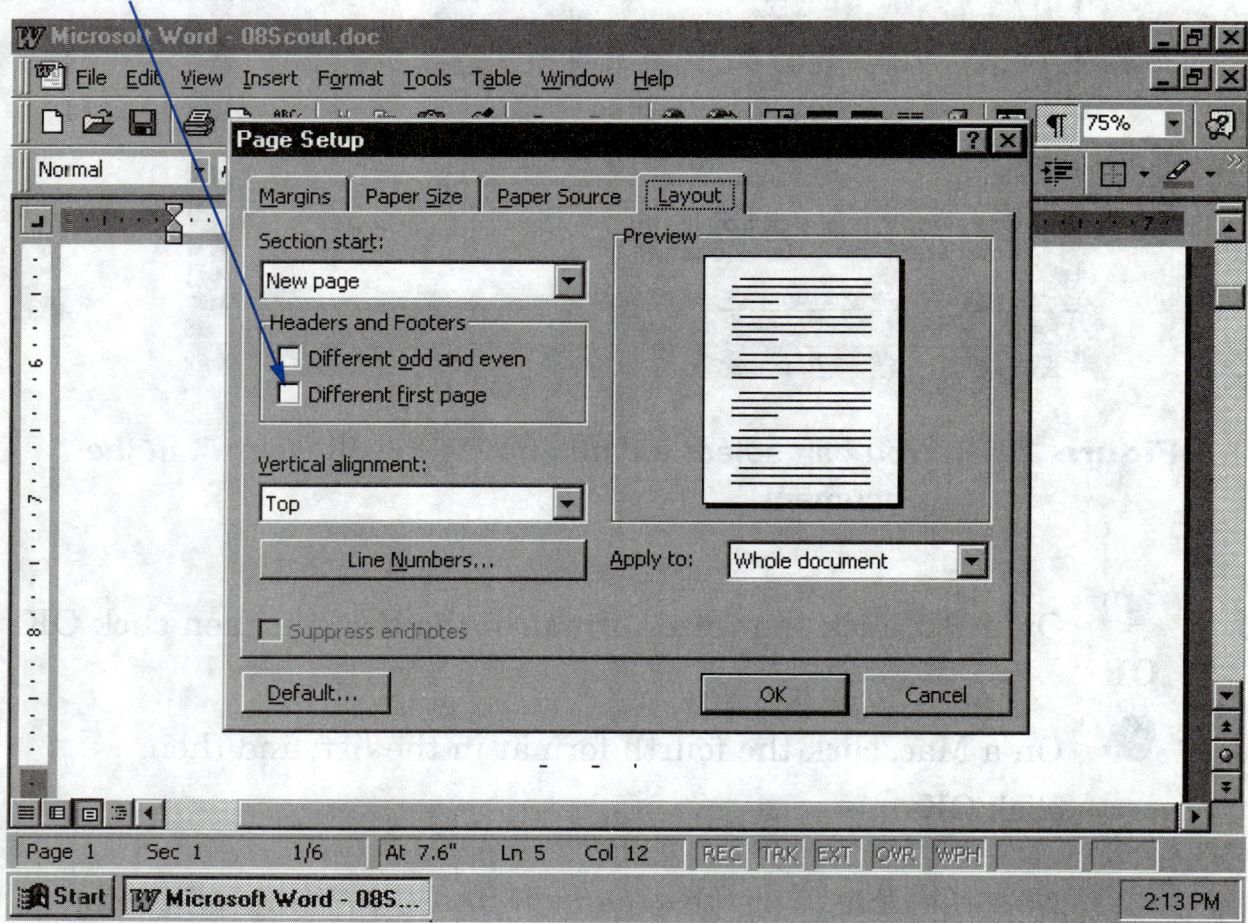

Figure 3-59b. The Layout page of the Page Setup dialog box

3. Click the Different first page check box, and then click OK.

4. Click the Print Preview button 🖨 on the Standard toolbar.
   Now, the title page is complete! In Figure 3-60 you can see how it should look in Print Preview.

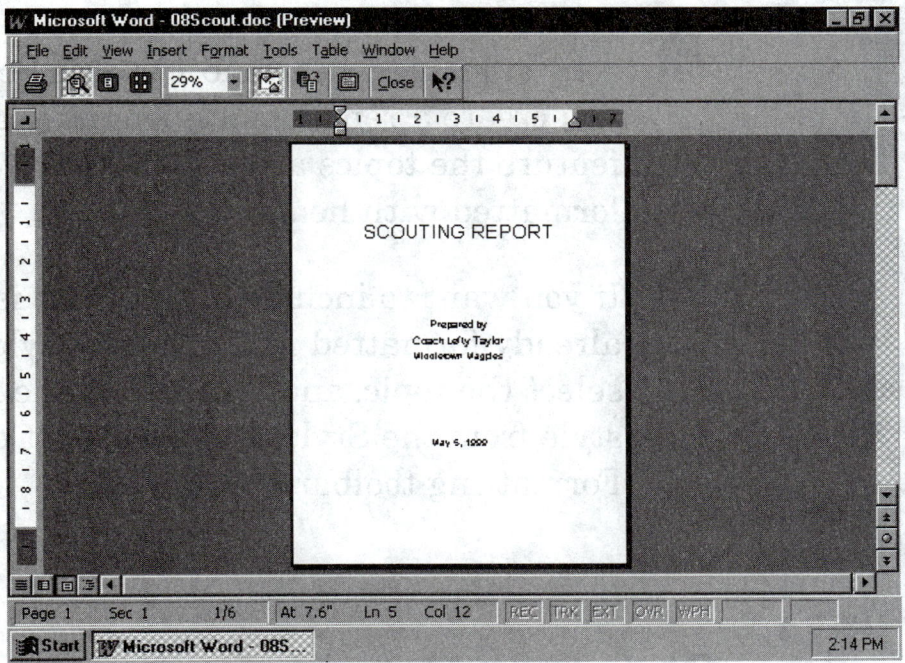

Figure 3-60. The completed title page in Print Preview.

5. Close Print Preview and save the **scout6** document. Keep it open, because you'll learn how to create a table of contents.

Creating a Table of Contents

Coach Carrie Says:

 A table of contents is like a roster of all the topics in a report. It lists the main topics, and maybe some subtopics, too, and it tells you what page each topic starts on. The easiest way to create a table of contents is to let Word do it for you. Then, if the topics or page numbers change, Word can quickly update it.

 To create a table of contents, you use the Insert, Index and Tables command. Word organizes your report based on topics that have been formatted with Word's built-in heading styles.

JEFF THE REFF

Remember, page 1 is now the title page, so the report really starts on page 2.

 As you learned in Game 1 of this Season, if you create a report using Word's Outline feature the topics are automatically formatted with heading styles.

 If you want to include a topic that isn't already formatted in a heading style, you select the topic, and then select the heading style from the Style drop-down list on the Formatting toolbar.

PRACTICE SWINGS

Trainer Terry Says:

 In this exercise, you'll create a table of contents for the Scouting Report.

 Let's start by scrolling through the document to see if all the topics have heading styles.

1. Scroll down to the top of page 2 and click on the line with the text *1. Joe O'Brien.*

   This line is formatted with the Heading 1 style. You can tell by looking in the Style box on the Formatting toolbar, as in Figure 3-61.

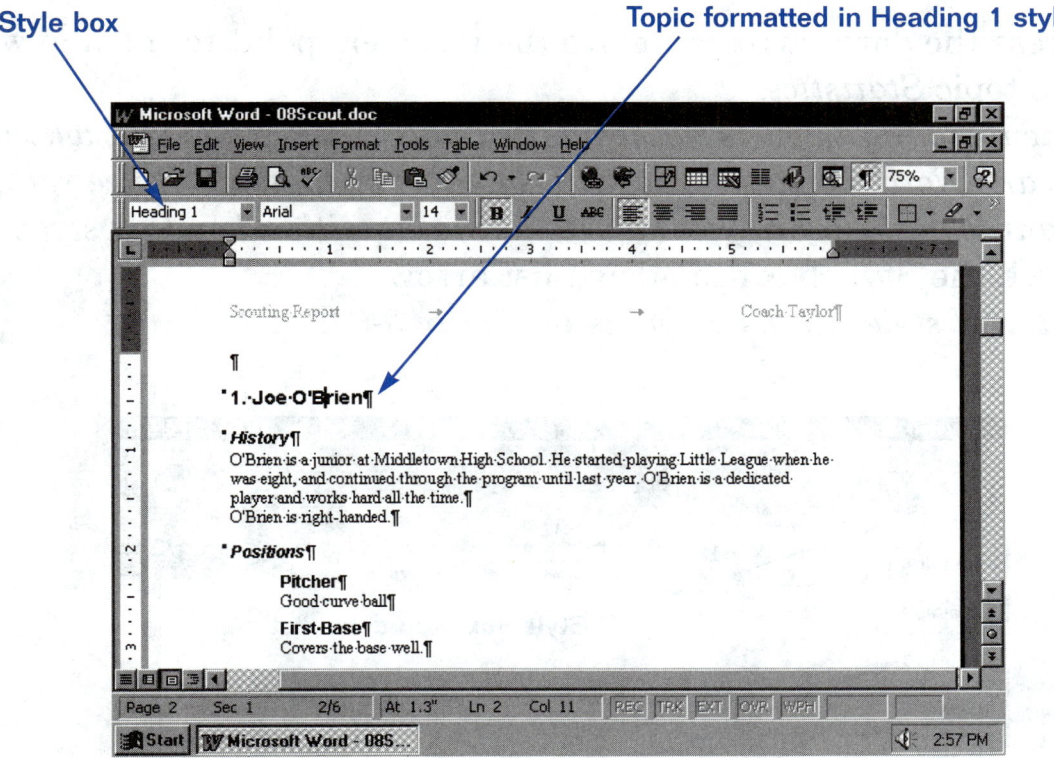

Figure 3-61. Look in the Style box to see if a heading style is in use.

2.   Press the down arrow to move the insertion point to the line with the topic *History,* and look at the Style box.
It is formatted as Heading 2.

3.   Press the down arrow to move the insertion point to the line with the topic *Positions.*
In the style box you can see that it is also formatted as Heading 2. Topics formatted with the same heading style will be listed at the same level in the table of contents. This means that Joe O'Brien, *formatted as Heading 1, will be a major heading, and that* History *and* Positions—*both formatted as Heading 2—will be at the next level in the table of contents.*

4. Press the down arrow to move the insertion point to the line with the topic *Statistics*.
    The topic Statistics is not formatted with a heading style, which means Word won't include it in the table of contents. Since you want it in the table, you have to format it with a heading style.

5. Click the Style box drop-down list arrow.
    A list of styles drops down as in Figure 3-64.

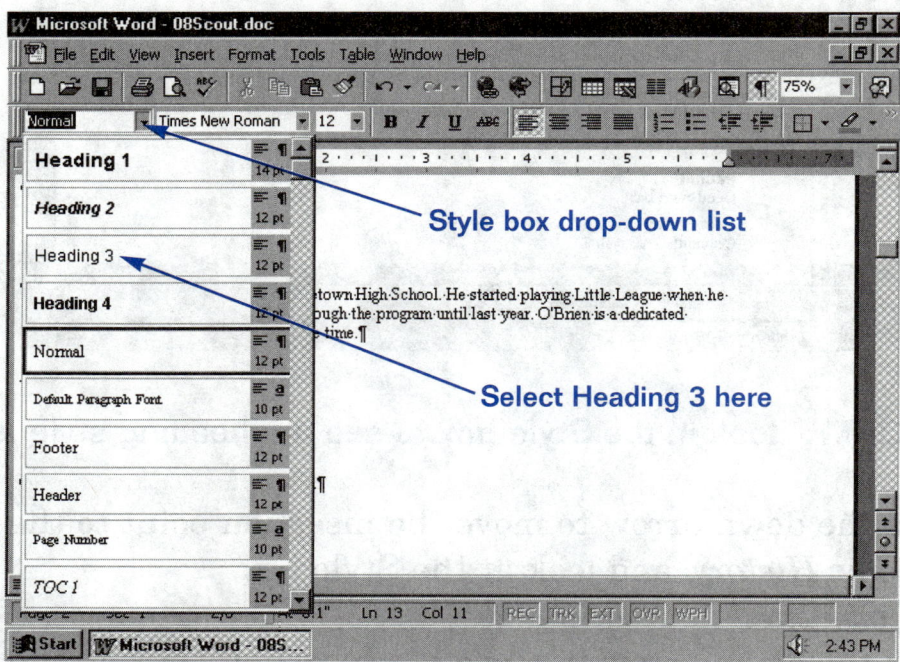

Figure 3-62. Choose a heading style from the Style drop-down list.

6. Click the Heading 3 style on the Style list.
7. Move the insertion point to the blank line at the top of page 2, where you want the table of contents to be inserted.
8. Change the font to Arial and the font size to 24, and then click the Center Align button [icon] on the Formatting toolbar.
9. Type *Table of Contents* and then press Enter twice.
    Now, the insertion point is where you want it to be to create the table of contents.

10. Click <u>I</u>nsert and then click In<u>d</u>ex and Tables.
11. Click the Table of <u>C</u>ontents page tab.
The Table of <u>C</u>ontents page of the Index and Tables dialog box open (see Figure 3-63).

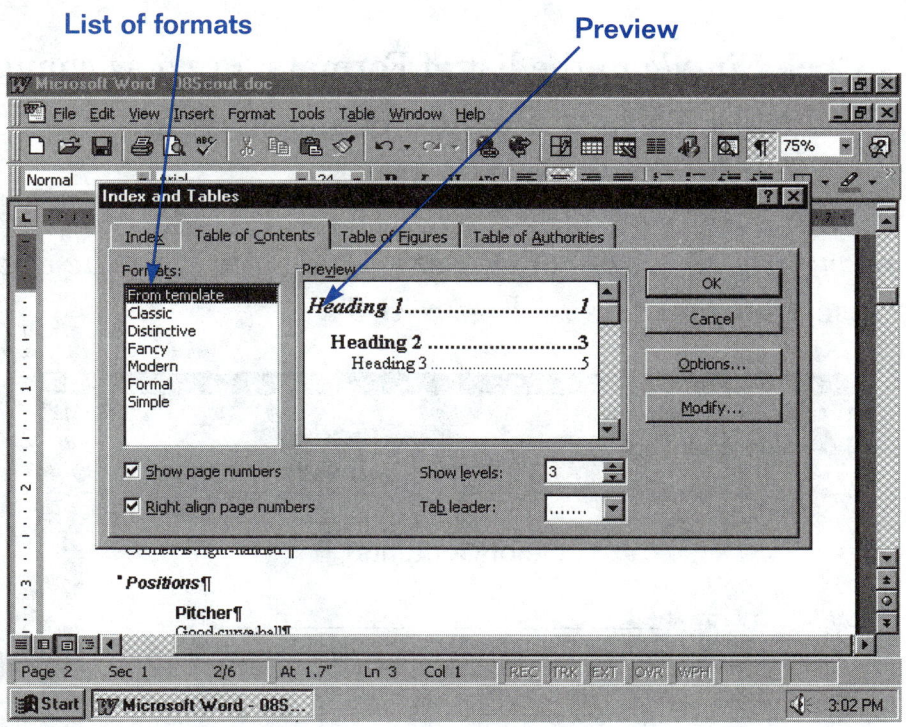

Figure 3-63. You select the table of contents format in the Index and Tables dialog box.

12.   Click *Classic* in the list of Formats. Preview changes.

- Click *Distinctive.* Preview changes again.
- Click OK.

OR

Click *Simple* in the list of Formats. Preview changes.

- Click *Elegant.* Preview changes again.
- Click OK.

Word creates the table of contents and puts it in the document at the insertion point as in Figure 3-64.

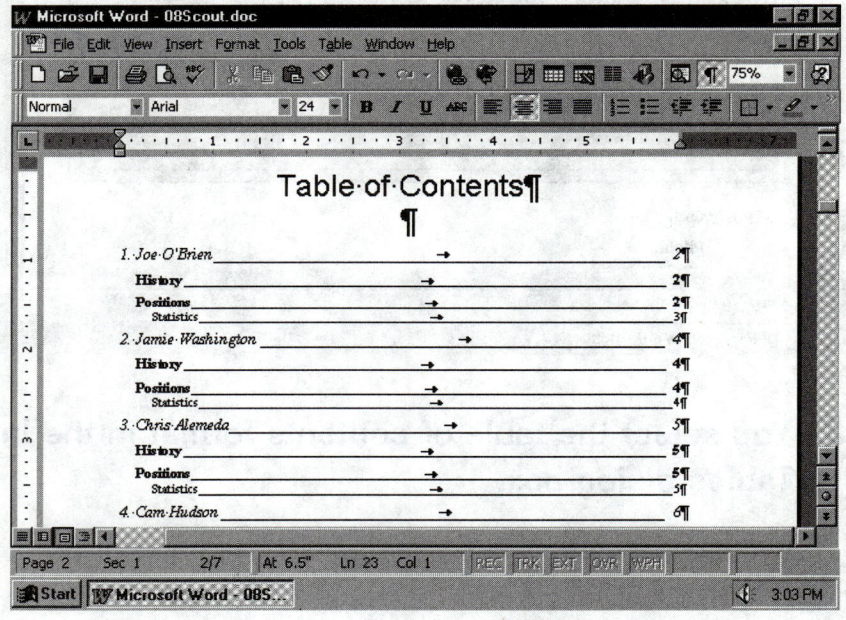

Figure 3-64. The table of contents in the document

When you create a table of contents on a PC, you need to insert a hard page break between the table and the beginning of the report. The page break will change the page numbers for all of the topics.

 When you create a table of contents on the Mac, Word automatically inserts a hard page break after the table. To learn how to update a table of contents, you will insert another hard page break to create a blank page.

13.   Move the insertion point beyond the table of contents, to the beginning of the line with the heading *1. Joe O'Brien* on it.

14.   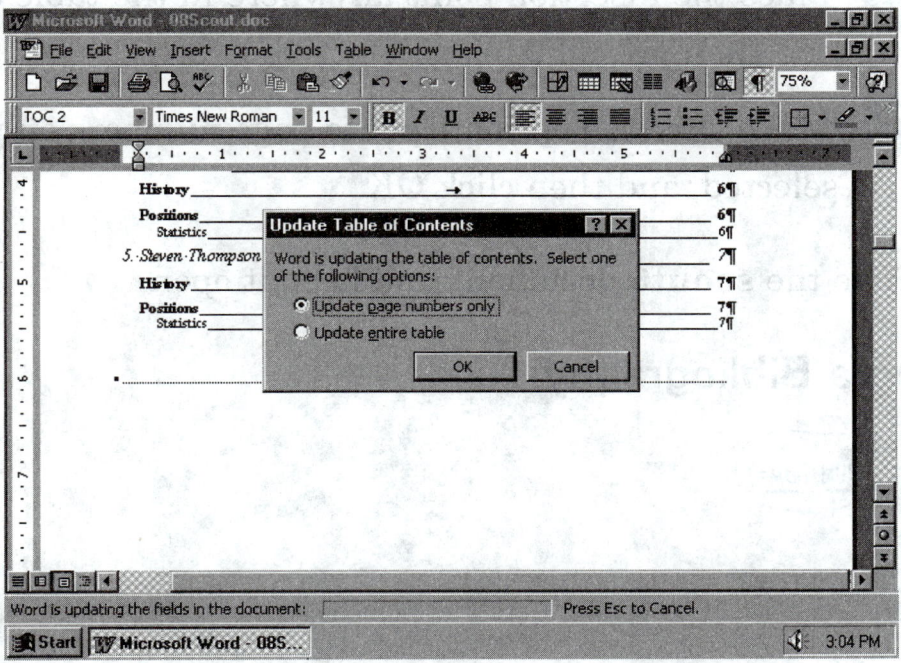 Press Ctrl+Enter.
       OR
       Press Shift+Enter.

15.   Move the insertion point up so that it is on any line in the table of contents, and press F9.
       Word displays the dialog box shown in Figure 3-65.

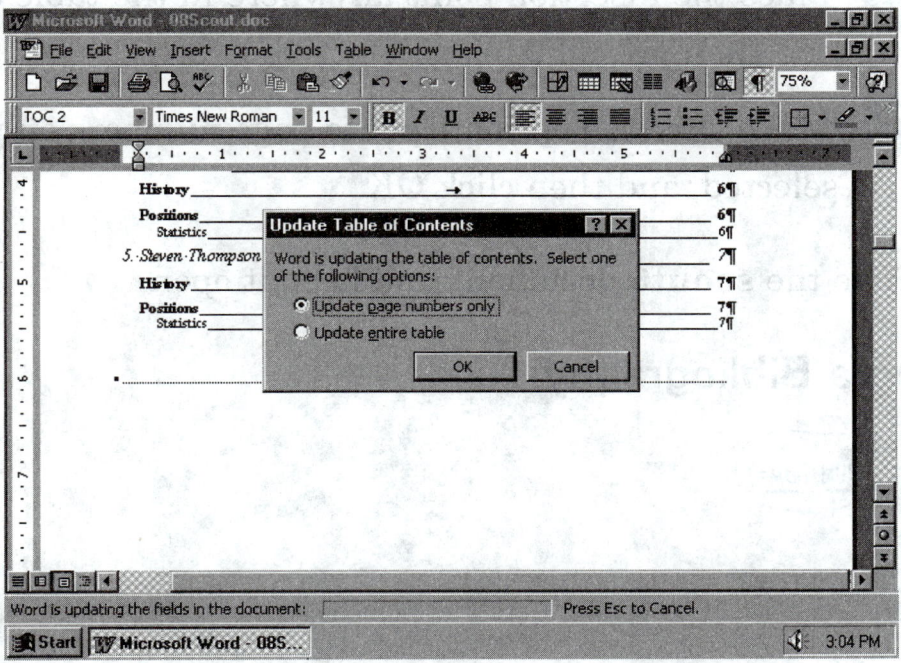

Figure 3-65. You can update the entire table or just the page numbers.

16.   Make sure the option Update page numbers only is selected, and then click OK.
       Word updates the page numbers for the table of contents.

17.   PC users go to step 22.
       OR
       Mac users do steps 18 through 21.

18.  Move the insertion point back up to the top of the blank page 3, where you inserted the extra hard page break.

19. Place the insertion point on the hard page break line and press Delete.
Word deletes the extra page break. Now, update the table of contents again.

20. Place the insertion point anywhere in the table of contents, and then press F9.

21. Make sure the option Update page numbers only is selected, and then click OK.

22. Save the **scout6** document and keep it open.

Creating a Bibliography

RUN HOME!

Coach Carrie Says:

When you write a research report, you read books and articles to find out everything you can about your topic. These books and articles, and anything else you use, are called *resources*.

Before you hand in your report, you must list all of these resources so that the teacher knows where you got your information. The list of resources is called a bibliography. Resources can be telephone interviews and Internet sites, too.

Bibliographies have a standard format. First, for each book you list, you include the author's name, the title of the book, the city where the book was published, the state where the book was published, the name of the publishing company, and the date of publication.

If a bibliography listing takes more than one line, the lines that follow are indented. This kind of indent is called a hanging indent.

Finally, bibliographies should be listed in alphabetical order.

Here's a sample listing:

Vega, Denise, <u>Learning the Internet for Kids:</u>
<u>A Voyage to Internet Treasures</u>. New York,
NY: DDC Publishing, Inc., 1998.

When you list magazine or newspaper articles in a bibliography, you also have to include the magazine or newspaper name, volume, and page number. For Internet sites, you should include the *URL* address.

MEG THE MIKE

URL stands for Uniform Resource Locator, which is the address of a page on the Internet. It's the long string of letters and symbols that usually starts with *WWW* and ends with *.com*, *.org*, or *.edu*.

PRACTICE SWINGS

Trainer Terry Says:

 In this exercise, you'll add a bibliography to the end of the Scouting Report.

1. Make sure **scout6** is open.

2.  Press Ctrl+End, and then press Ctrl+Enter.
   OR
   Press Command+End, and then press Shift+Enter.

3. Click the Style drop-down arrow and select Heading 1, then type *Bibliography* and press Enter twice.
   The title of the bibliography is now on the last page of the document. Because you used the Heading 1 style to format it, you can update the table of contents to include it as a main topic.

4. Open the Format menu and choose Paragraph.
   The Paragraph dialog box opens as in Figure 3-66.

5. Click the Special drop-down list arrow and choose *Hanging*.
   This option will automatically create hanging indents for your bibliography entries.

6. Enter *6 pt* in the Spacing After text box, and then click OK.

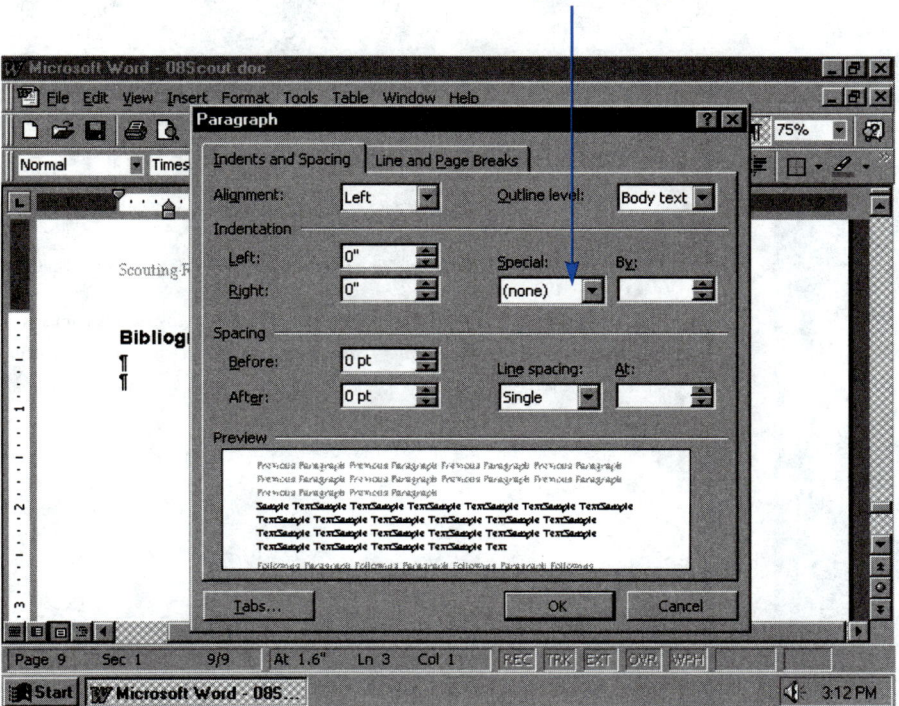

The Special drop-down list

Figure 3-66. Use the Format Paragraph dialog box to set the hanging indent for the bibliography.

7. Type the following four listings. Be sure to use italic for book and newspaper titles.

Lister, Nancy, *Middletown School Athletes*. Middletown, CA: School District Press, 1998.

Preston, James, *Middletown Nine Wins Again.* Middletown, CA: Middletown Crier, May 20, 1998, pg. 10.

Roux, Cathy, *Baseball Player Directory*. Middletown, CA: Sports Publishing, Inc., 1998.

Whitman, Samuel, *Follow the Team.* www.middletown_sports.org: Middletown Sports Web Site, 1998.

JEFF THE REF

If the Web address you type in the document all of a sudden is blue and has a blue underline, Word has automatically formatted it as a *hyperlink*. Just choose Edit, Undo to remove the formatting, and then continue typing.

MEG THE MIKE

A *hyperlink* is text or a picture that connects to another document or another place in the same document. When you click on a hyperlink, Word automatically jumps to the hyperlink destination. Word assumes that when you type a Web address into a document, you want to be able to click the address to jump to it, so Word formats it as a hyperlink.

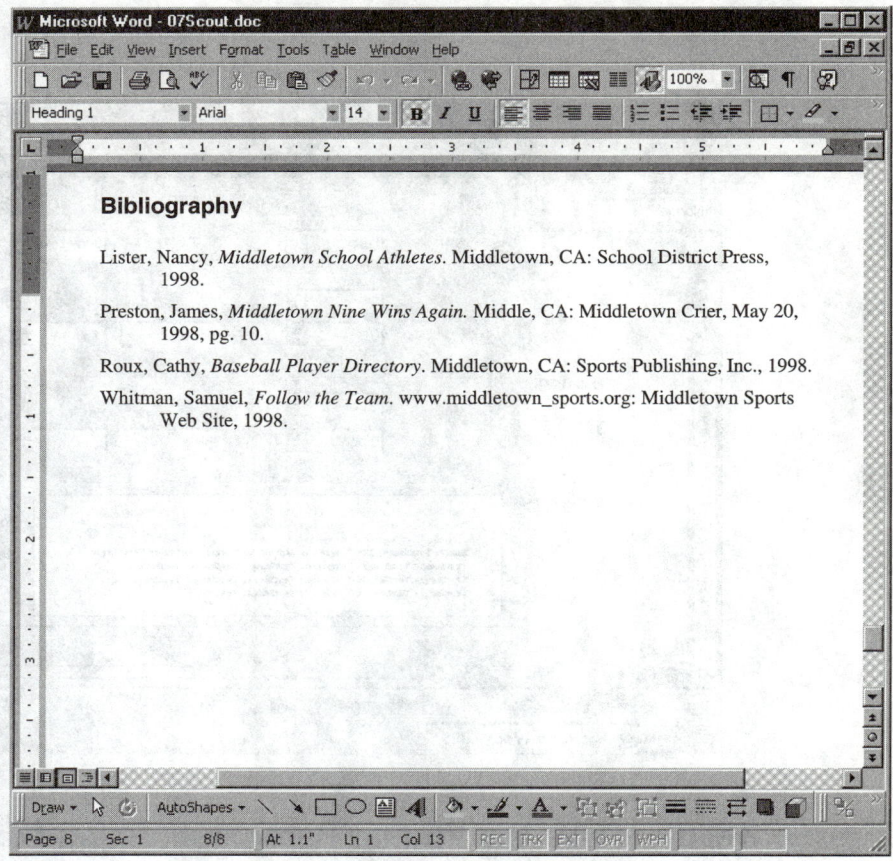

Figure 3-67. The bibliography has four entries.

8. Scroll up and position the insertion point anywhere within the table of contents.

9. Press F9.
Now your bibliography should look like the one in Figure 3-67.

10. Click the Update entire table option button, and then click OK.

11. Click Print Preview button to see the changes in your document.

12. Save the **scout6** document and close it.

PLAY BALL:

Trainer Terry Says:

 In this exercise, you'll spruce up the Four Baseball Legends report by adding a title page, a table of contents, and a bibliography.

First Base

1. Open the document **06legend** from the student data folder.
2. Save the file as **legend6.**

3.   Press Ctrl+Enter.

    OR

     Press Shift+Enter.

4.   Press Ctrl+Home.

    OR

     Press Command+Home.

    The insertion point is now placed in the correct position to start typing the text for your title page.

5. Set the font to 36 point, Times New Roman, bold.

6. Click the Center Align button .

7. Open the F*o*rmat menu and choose *P*aragraph.
8. Enter *108 pt* in the Spacing *B*efore text box.
9. Enter *108 pt* in the Spacing Aft*e*r text box.
10. Click OK.
11. Type *Four Baseball Legends* and press Enter.

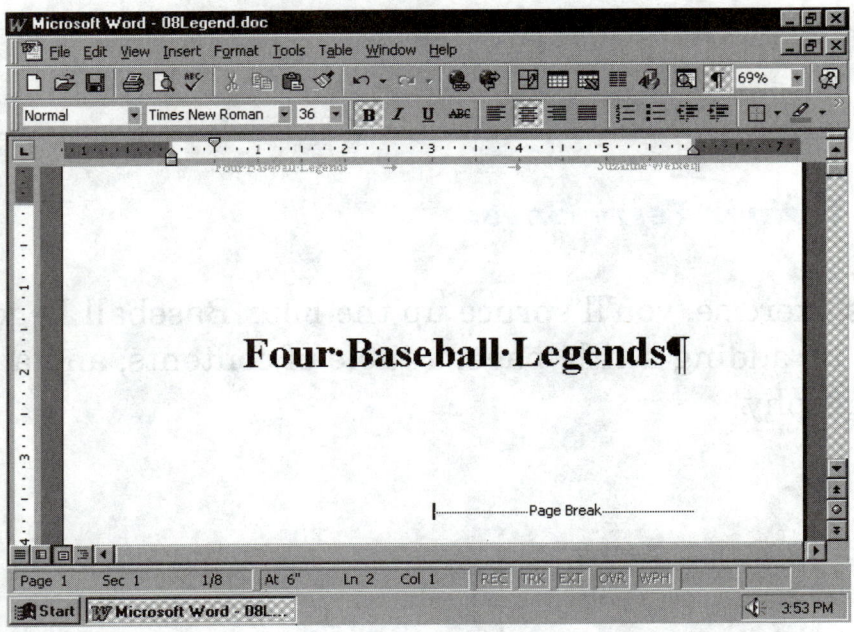

Figure 3-68. The report title is centered on the title page.

Second Base

1. Change the font size to 20 points and turn off the bold.
2. Type *By*, followed by your own name, and then press Enter.
3. Click the Align Right button [image] on the Formatting toolbar.
4. Change the font size to 18 points.
5. Change the paragraph spacing to *0 pt* before and *0 pt* after.
6. Type *American History* and then press Enter.
7. Type *Room 311* and then press Enter.
8. Choose *I*nsert, Date and *T*ime, select a date format, then click OK.
9. Press Enter.

10. Click <u>F</u>ile, Page Set<u>u</u>p, and then click the Layout tab.

11. Select the Different <u>f</u>irst page check box, and then click OK.

12. Click the Print Preview button 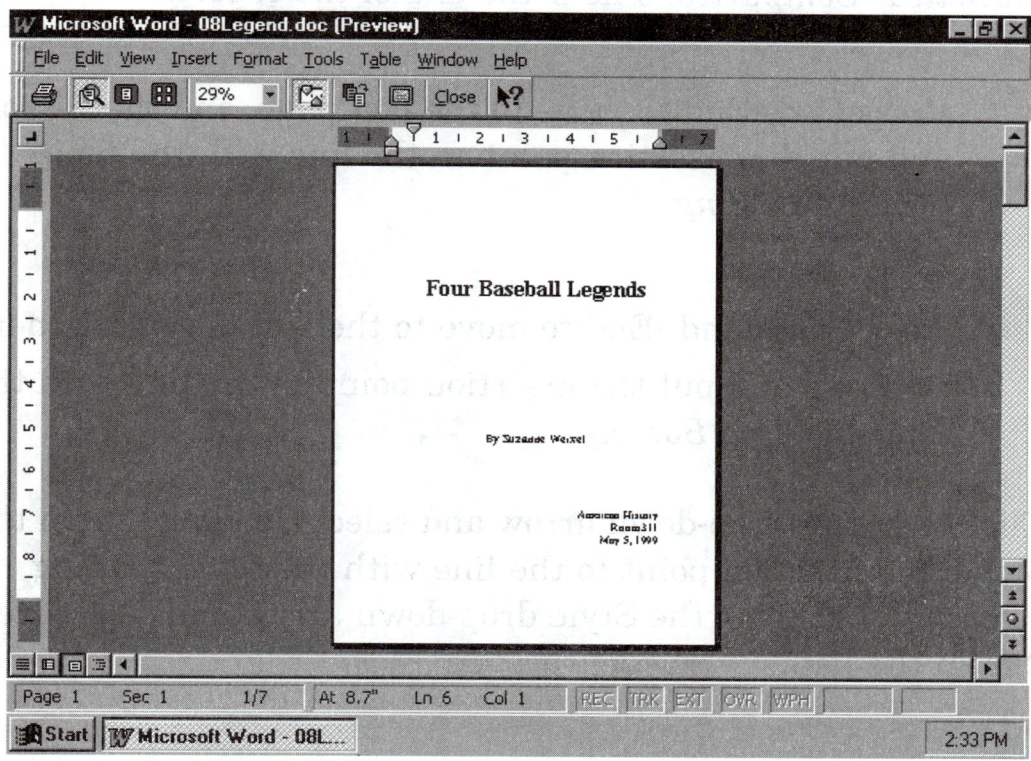 to view your work.
    You've completed the title page! It should look like the title page in Figure 3-69.

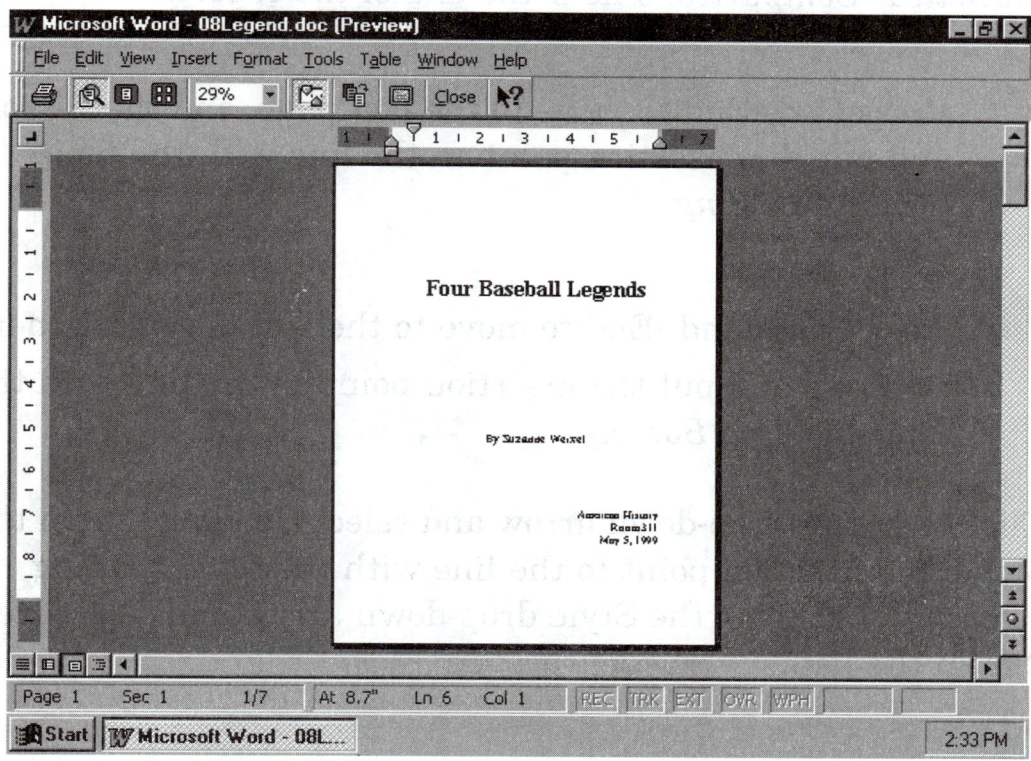

Figure 3-69. The title page in Print Preview

13. Save the **legend6** document and leave it open.

Third Base

 Before you create the table of contents, you have to make sure all the topics you want to include are formatted in the heading styles. All you need to add are the subtopics under the topic *Statistical Comparisons* near the end of the report.

1. Press Ctrl+End to move to the last page, and then scroll up and put the insertion point on the line with the topic heading *Batting*.
   OR

    Press Command+End to move to the last page, and then scroll up and put the insertion point on the line with the topic heading *Batting*.

2. Click the Style drop-down arrow and select Heading 2 from the list.
3. Move the insertion point to the line with the topic heading *Pitching,* then click the Style drop-down arrow and select Heading 2 from the list.

4. Move the insertion point to the blank line at the beginning of page 2 and press Ctrl+Enter.
   OR

    Move the insertion point to the blank line at the beginning of page 2, then skip to step 6.
   If you use a Mac, you do not have to insert a page break because Word for the Mac automatically inserts one when you create the table of contents.

5.   Press the Up arrow to move the insertion point to the new page where you want to put the table of contents.

6.   Set the font to Arial and the font size to 24.

7.   Click the Center Align button 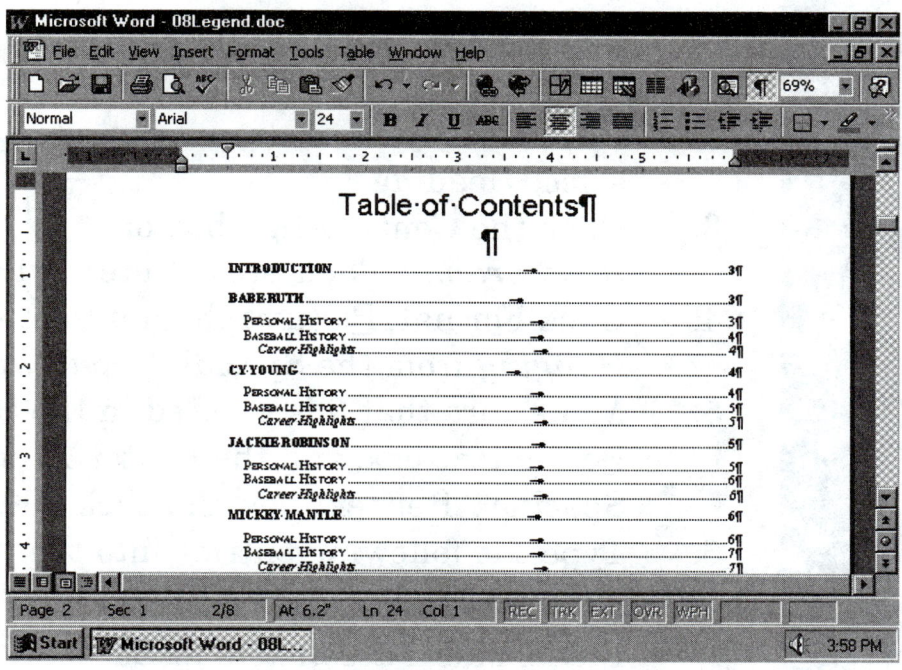 on the Formatting toolbar and type *Table of Contents*. Then press Enter twice.

8.   Click Insert, Index and Tables.

9.   Click the Table of Contents page tab if it's not already in front.

10.   Select the Formal format, and then click OK.
Word inserts the table of contents onto the new page, as in Figure 3-70.

Figure 3-70. The table of contents is in the report.

JEFF THE REF

Remember, if Word automatically formats the web address as a hyperlink, just choose Edit, Undo, and then continue typing.

Home Stretch

 Now let's finish up the report by adding a bibliography.

1. ⊞ Press Ctrl+End, and then press Ctrl+Enter.
   OR

    Press Command+End, then press Shift+Enter.

2. Click the Style box drop-down arrow and select Heading 1.

3. Click the Center Align button , and type *Bibliography*. Then press Enter twice.

4. Click F<u>o</u>rmat, <u>P</u>aragraph, and then select *Hanging* from the <u>S</u>pecial drop-down list.

5. Make sure that *0* is entered in the Spacing <u>B</u>efore text box, and then enter *12 pt* in the Spacing Aft<u>e</u>r text box and click OK.

6. Type the following entries into the bibliography:

   Davis, Mac, *Pacemakers in Baseball*. Cleveland, OH: The World Publishing Company, 1968.

   National Baseball Hall of Fame Web Site, *Members Gallery*. www.baseballhalloffame.org: 1998.

   Shapiro, Milton J., *Champions of the Bat: Baseball's Greatest Sluggers*. New York, NY: Simon & Schuster, Inc., 1967.

   Your bibliography should look like the one in Figure 3-71.

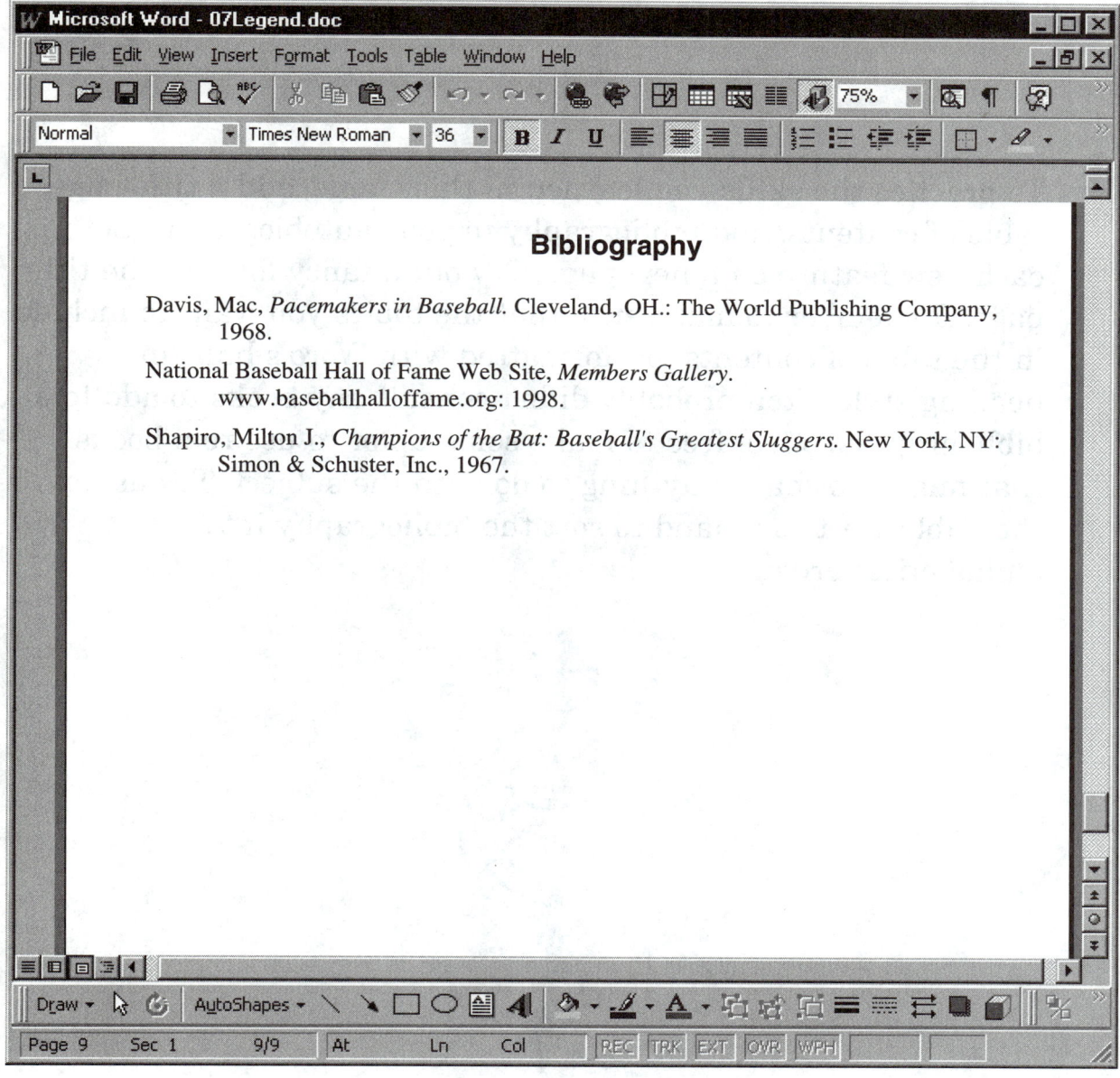

Figure 3-71. The bibliography is in the report.

7.   Move the insertion point to anywhere in the table of contents and press F9.

8.   Select the Update entire table option button, then click OK.

9.   Click the Print Preview button 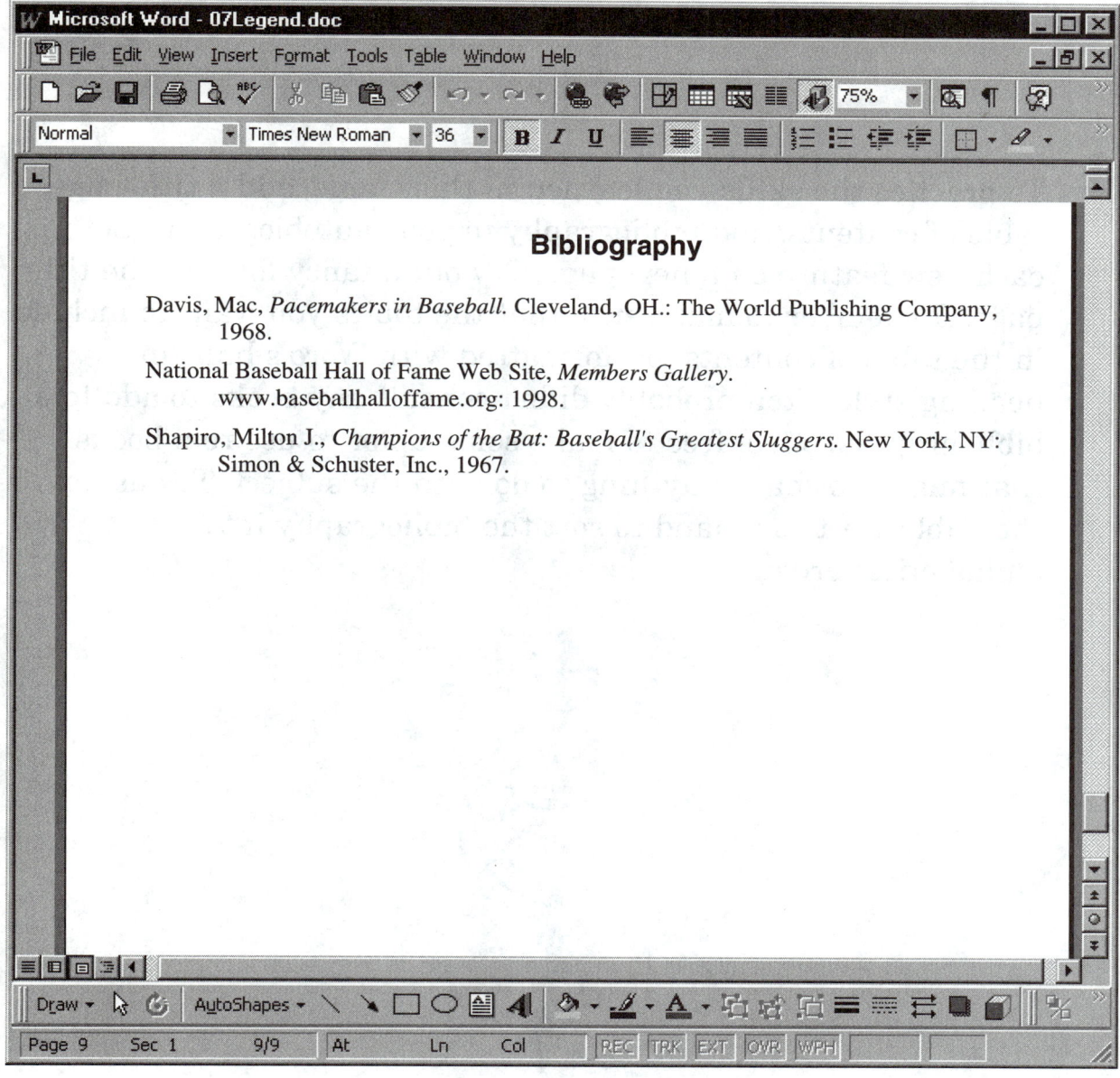 to see the changes you've made to your document.

10.   Save the **legend6** document and close it.

THE WORLD SERIES

 To practice the skills you learned in this Game, add a title page, table of contents, and bibliography to your autobiography. Set up each new feature on a new page. Try out a fancy font for the title page. Remember to make sure that the topics you want to include in the table of contents are formatted with Word's built-in heading styles. You probably didn't consult any books to add to a bibliography, so feel free to make some up or to use real books that might not have anything to do with the subject. Try using the Table, Sort command to sort the bibliography into alphabetical order.

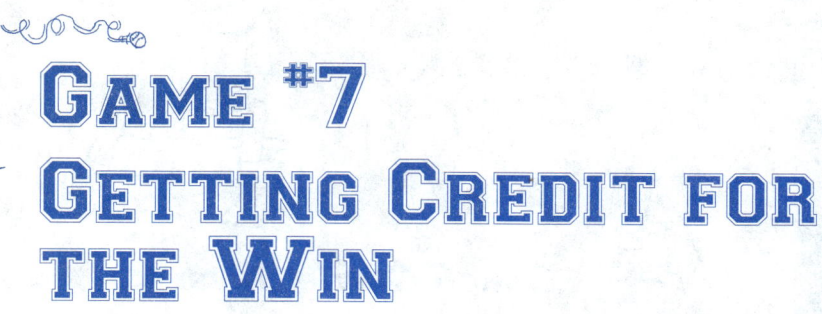

GAME #7
GETTING CREDIT FOR THE WIN

In this Game, you'll learn how to use footnotes and endnotes by:

- Inserting Footnotes
- Inserting Endnotes
- Adding and Deleting Footnotes and Endnotes

MEG THE MIKE

A *footnote* explains or cites information on a page in a report. It is listed at the bottom of the same page.

An *endnote* is a footnote that is listed at the end of a report instead of at the bottom of the page.

A *source* is the book, article, web site, interview, or other place where you learned the information.

A *citation* is a reference to the source that you type in a footnote or endnote.

ON DECK

Coach Carrie Says:

 In baseball, as long as a team keeps a lead and wins the game, the player who was pitching when they took the lead gets credit for the win—even if he leaves the game before the end. The pitcher who comes in and finishes the game gets credit for a save, but not for the win.

 When you're writing a report, if you use ideas or facts that someone else said or wrote, you have to give credit to that person. You can get credit for using the facts in a smart, useful way, but you can't take credit for being the first person to think of them.

 It's against the law to use information that someone else wrote or said without giving that person credit. Using someone else's idea is called *plagiarism*.

 Typically, you give credit in a *footnote* or an *endnote*—a few lines of text, called a *citation,* that explain who or what the *source* was for the information you used in your report.

The only difference between the two types of notes is that a footnote is listed at the bottom of the page on which the information is typed and an endnote is listed at the end of the document.

 In this Game, you'll learn how to insert footnotes and endnotes in your reports to give credit where credit is due.

Insert Footnotes

Coach Carrie Says:

 A footnote has two basic parts:

1. The *footnote mark* is a number, letter, or symbol that is inserted as a *field* right after the information in the report and at the bottom of the page. It lets the reader know that there is extra information that he or she should read at the bottom of the page.
2. The *footnote text* is the citation or explanation that you type. It is printed at the bottom of the page, after the footnote mark, but it does not show up in the main body of the report.

MEG THE MIKE

Remember, in Game 6 you learned that a *field* is a code for information that might change, like a page number, or date.

When you switch to normal view, you can see the footnote text in the footnote pane as in Figure 3-72.

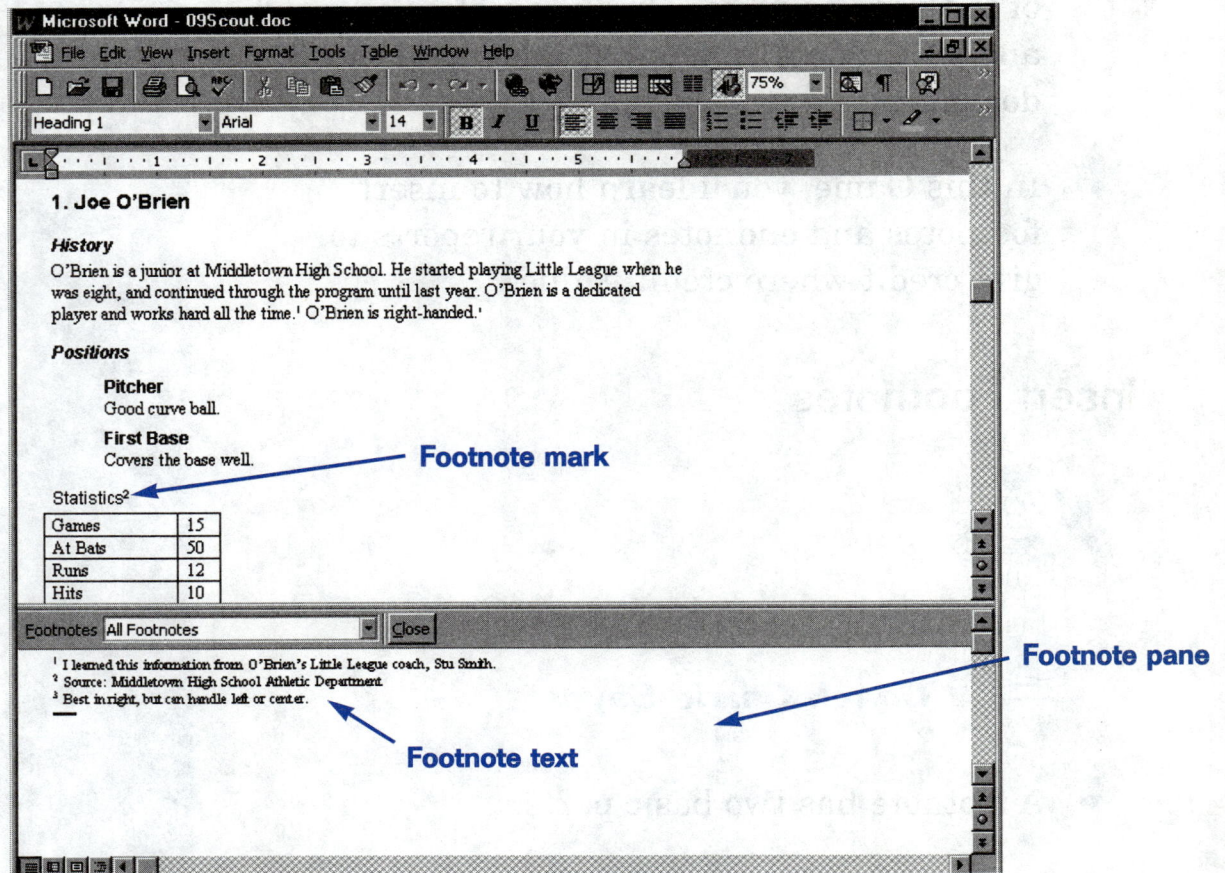

Figure 3-72. You can see footnote marks and text in Normal View.

The easiest way to create footnotes is in Page Layout view. To create a footnote, open the Insert menu, choose Footnote, and then click OK. Word puts the footnote mark into the document and at the bottom of the page. The insertion point moves to the bottom of the page so that you can type the note.

Word automatically uses a numbering scheme that differentiates between endnotes and footnotes so that you can tell them apart. By default, it uses lowercase roman numerals (i, ii, iii, iv, and so on) for endnotes and arabic numerals (1, 2, 3, 4, and so on) for footnotes.

PRACTICE SWINGS

Trainer Terry Says:

Let's open a version of the Scouting Report you've been working with in this Season and insert three footnotes.

1. Open the file **07scout** from the student data folder.
2. Save the file as **scout7**.
3. Scroll down to page 3 and place the insertion point at the end of the third sentence in the paragraph about Joe O'Brien's history.
4. Open the <u>I</u>nsert menu and choose Foot<u>n</u>ote.
    The Footnote and Endnote dialog box opens.
5. Click OK.
    Word inserts the footnote mark and moves the insertion point to the end of the document.
6. Type the following sentence:

> I learned this information from O'Brien's Little League coach, Stu Smith.

In Figure 3-73, you can see the footnote mark at the bottom of the document, along with the note text.

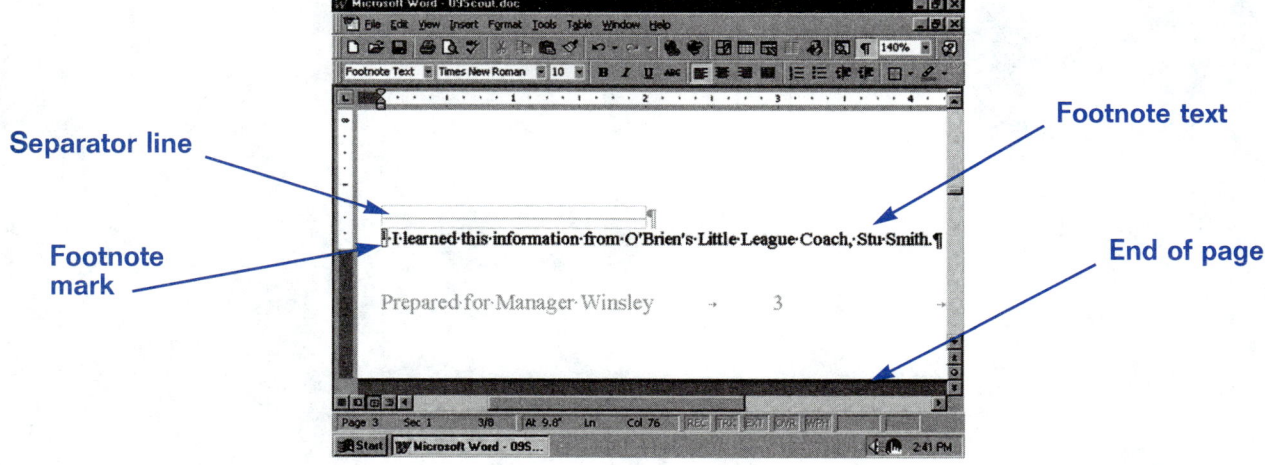

Figure 3-73. Footnotes are printed at the bottom of the page.

MEG THE MIKE

Here are two tricks you can do with footnotes or endnotes:

- Double-click the footnote mark in the report text to jump down to the footnote text; double-click the mark at the bottom of the page to jump up to the mark in the report text.

- Place the mouse pointer over the footnote mark in the report text. When the mouse pointer is near the mark, a ScreenTip shows the note text.

7. Scroll up on page 3 and place the insertion point at the end of the line with the heading *Statistics* on it.

8. Click <u>I</u>nsert, Foot<u>n</u>ote, and then click OK in the Footnote and Endnote dialog box.

9. Type the following:

> Source: Middletown High School Athletic Department.

Now you've got two footnotes on the page.

10. Scroll down to page 4 and place the insertion point after the word *Outfield* under Jamie Washington's *Positions* heading.

11. Click <u>I</u>nsert, Foot<u>n</u>ote, and then click OK in the Footnote and Endnote dialog box.

12. Type *Best in right field, but can handle left or center.*

The text of the third footnote appears at the bottom of page 4.

13. Save the **scout7** document and keep it open.

Inserting Endnotes

Coach Carrie Says:

Inserting endnotes is the same as inserting footnotes, except that you select Endnote in the Footnote and Endnote dialog box. The endnote text appears at the end of the report, instead of at the bottom of the page.

PRACTICE SWINGS

Trainer Terry Says:

Try adding three endnotes to the **scout7** report.

1. Scroll up to the beginning of page 3 and place the insertion point at the end of the first sentence in O'Brien's history.
2. Click Insert, and then click Footnote.
3. Select the Endnote option button.
4. Click OK.
5. Type *All grades are for the 1999-2000 school year.*
    This is your first endnote. Notice that the endnote text is displayed after the bibliography on the last page of the document.
6. Move the insertion point to the end of the second sentence on page 5, in Chris Alemeda's history.
7. Choose Insert, Footnote, make sure the Endnote option button is selected, and then click OK.

8.   Type *Source: Middletown High School Athletic Department*.

9.   Scroll down to page 7 and place the insertion point after the phrase *Can switch-hit* in the history paragraph for Steven Thompson.

10. Choose <u>I</u>nsert, Foot<u>n</u>ote, make sure the <u>E</u>ndnote option button is selected, and then click OK.

11. Type *Stronger batting righty*.
     There are now three endnotes in your document, as you can see in Figure 3-75.

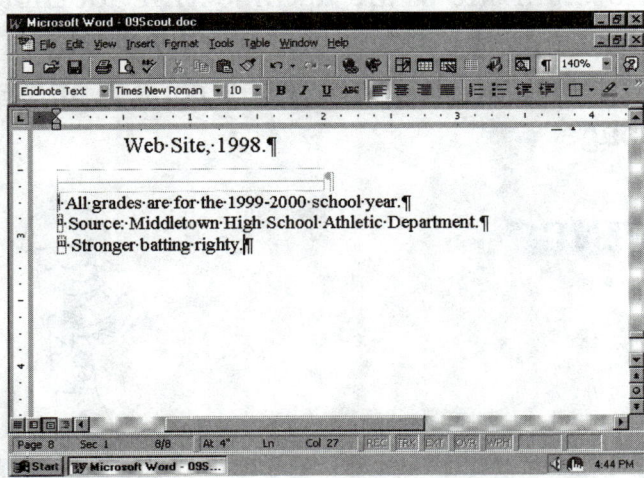

Figure 3-75. All three endnotes are listed together.

12. Save the **scout7** document and keep it open.

Adding and Deleting Footnotes and Endnotes

RUN HOME!

Coach Carrie Says:

The really great thing about creating footnotes and endnotes with Word is that if you add or delete a note or two, or if you rearrange the report, Word automatically renumbers the footnotes and endnotes so that they stay in order.

To add a footnote or an endnote, you just insert it where you want it. If necessary, Word renumbers the marks that are already in the document.

 To delete a footnote or an endnote, you have to delete the note mark from the report text. Since the mark is inserted as a field, to be sure to select the mark correctly, then press Delete. When you delete the mark, the note text is deleted, too, and all the remaining marks are renumbered.

PRACTICE SWINGS

Trainer Terry Says:

 Now let's insert a new footnote and delete an endnote. You'll get to see how Word automatically renumbers the notes already in the report.

1. In the **scout7** document, move the insertion point to the end of the second sentence in the *History* paragraph for Jamie Washington on page 4.
2. Click Insert, Footnote.
3. Select the Footnote option button, and then click OK.
   Word creates a new footnote 3 and renumbers the footnote that was number 3 so that it is now number 4.
4. Type *May need extra coaching.*
5. Scroll to page 5, where the second endnote—*ii*—is displayed in the *History* paragraph.
6. Place the insertion point to the immediate right of the endnote mark.

JEFF THE REF

If the mark isn't selected when you press Backspace, try pressing Backspace again. Or, move the insertion point to the immediate left of the mark, press and hold down the Shift key, and then press the Right Arrow key.

7. Press the Backspace key.
Word selects the endnote mark, as shown in Figure 3-76.

Selected mark

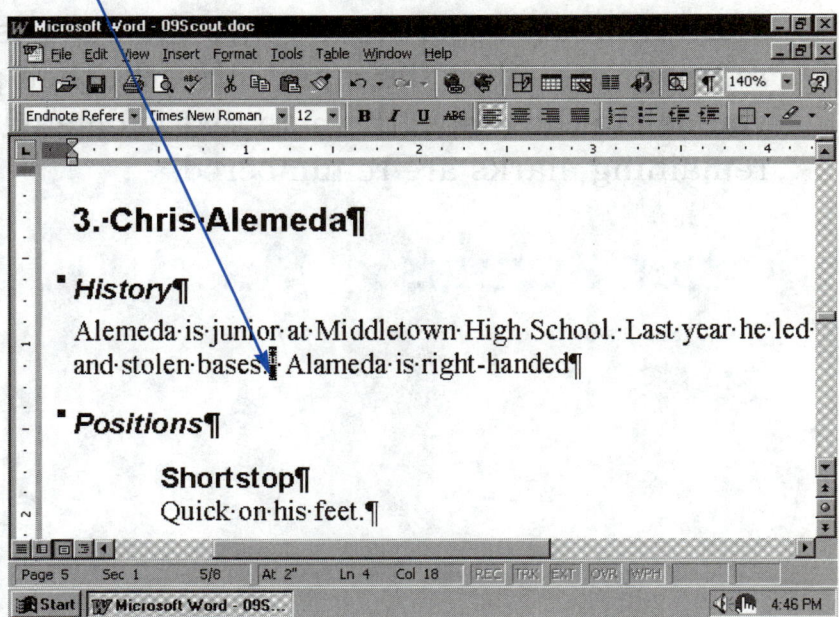

Figure 3-76. You have to select the mark in order to delete it.

8. Press Delete.

9. Press Ctrl+End.
OR
 Press Command+End.
Now there are only two endnotes in the document.

10. Save the **scout7** report document and close it.

PLAY BALL

Trainer Terry Says:

 In this exercise, you'll complete the Baseball Legends report by adding footnotes and endnotes.

1. Open the document **07legend** from the student data folder.
2. Save the file as **legend7**.
3. Place the insertion point at the end of the first sentence of the Introduction, on page 3.
4. Choose <u>I</u>nsert, Foot<u>n</u>ote.
5. Make sure the <u>F</u>ootnote option button is selected, and then click OK.
6. Type *Not everyone will agree that these are the four greatest baseball players ever, but in my opinion they are.*
7. Scroll to the top of page 4 and place the insertion poin after the last sentence in the section about Babe Ruth's baseball history.
8. Choose <u>I</u>nsert, Foot<u>n</u>ote, and then click OK.
9. Type the following sentence:

> Fans still insist the Red Sox have not won the World Series since 1918 because Ruth was traded.

10. Scroll to page 6 and place the insertion point after the last sentence in the paragraph about Jackie Robinson's baseball history.
11. Choose <u>I</u>nsert, Foot<u>n</u>ote, and then click OK.

JEFF THE REF

If there isn't room at the bottom of the page for a footnote, Word automatically puts the note text on the next page where there is room.

12. Type the following sentence:

> Robinson was physically attacked and verbally abused by fans, by players on other teams, and even by players on his own team.

Now you have three footnotes in the document. In Figure 3-77, you can see the third one at the bottom of page 6.

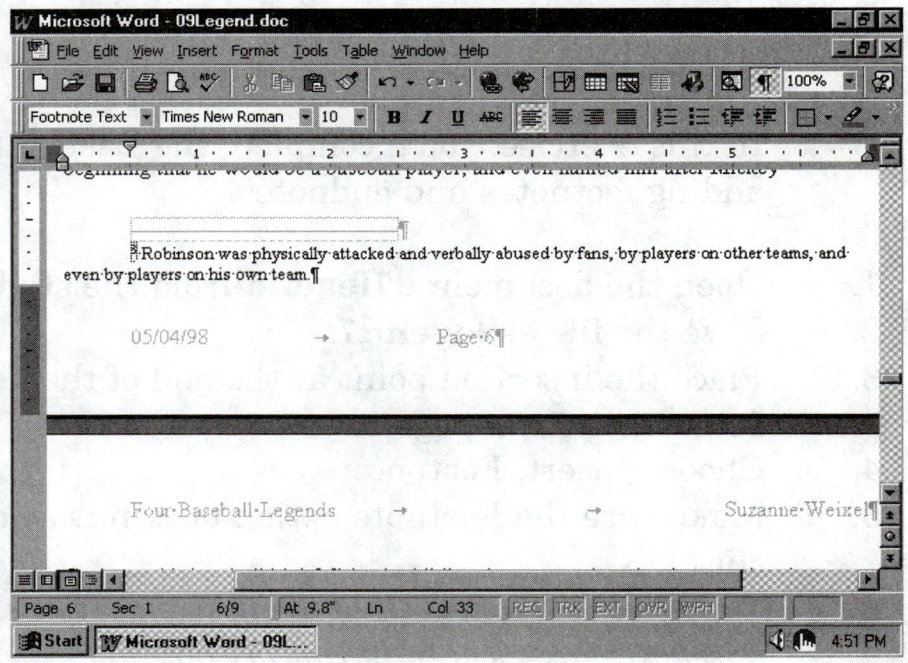

Figure 3-77. Footnote 3 at the bottom of page 6

13. Scroll to page 4 and place the insertion point after the line stating how many times Ruth struck out and how many times he walked.

14. Choose Insert, Footnote.

15. Click the Endnote option button, and then click OK.

16. Type:

> Mac Davis, *Pacemakers in Baseball* (Cleveland, OH: The World Publishing Company, 1968), pg. 89.

17. Scroll to page 7 and place the insertion point after the line stating that Mickey Mantle won the Most Valuable Player award three times.
18. Choose Insert, Footnote, and then click OK.
19. Type:

> Milton J. Shapiro, *Champions of the Bat: Baseball's Greatest Sluggers* (New York, NY: Simon & Schuster, 1967), pg. 131.

20. Scroll to page 8 and place the insertion point after the heading *Statistical Comparisons*.
21. Choose Insert, Footnote, and then click OK.
22. Type:

> National Baseball Hall of Fame Web Site—Members Gallery.

The three endnotes are listed on the last page of the report, as shown in Figure 3-78.

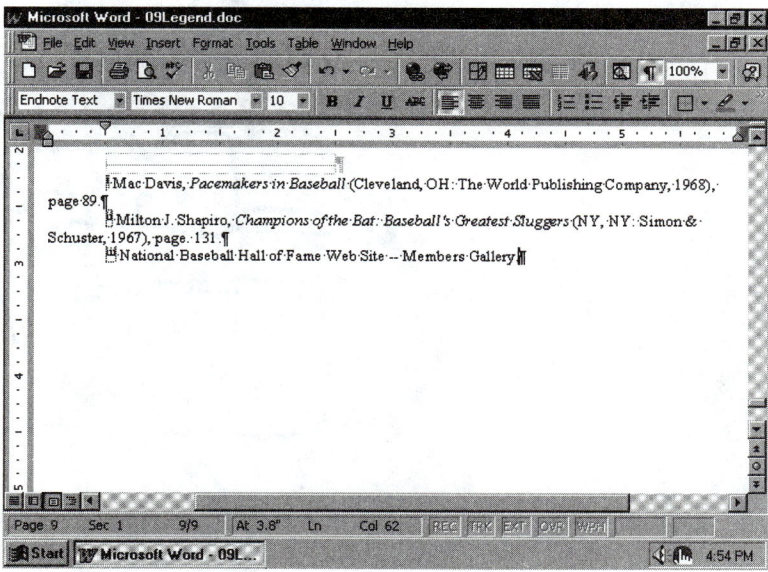

Figure 3-78. The three endnotes on the last page of the report

23. Scroll up to page 3 and place the insertion point to the immediate right of the number 1 footnote mark.

24. Press Backspace to highlight the mark.

25. Press Delete.
    Now there are only two footnotes in the report.

26. Save the **legend7** document and close it.

THE WORLD SERIES

 To practice the skills you learned in this Game, you're going to add footnotes and endnotes to your autobiography. Add explanations for some of the facts you've written about, and thank some of the sources who have helped you. Try to include at least five of each type of note.

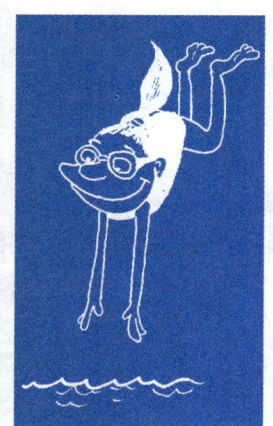

SEASON 4

SWIMMING

DESIGNING GOLD-MEDAL PROJECTS!

Now it's time for the last Season—Swimming! In this Season you'll follow the adventures of the Cyber Swim Team while you learn how to make interesting and useful projects that you can use for your own classroom, club, or team.

You'll learn how to make a splash with creative projects—and the best part is that you can easily use all the skills you'll learn in this Season in real life. You'll make posters, brochures, fancy letters, your own personal Web page, and more!

One Special Note:

You'll need to use the skills you've learned in the first three Seasons. If you get to a concept you have forgotten as you go along, just return to that place in the book and refresh your memory.

Ready? Let's dive in!

EVENT #1
THE TEAM ROSTER:
FIND THE FAMOUS FISH!

Welcome to Season 4! In this Event you'll learn all of the skills you need to produce your own class or team roster with Word's Mail Merge feature.

Before you get started on your own project, you'll help the Cyber Swim Team make a team roster with the following Word Skills:

- **Mail Merge Helper Basics**
- **Making a Data Source Document**
- **Making a Main Document (Catalog)**
- **Merging Documents**

SUIT UP

Coach Carrie Says:

Why would anyone need a roster? Lots of reasons! A roster gives you information about a list, or a catalog, of people. The list can be a list of members of a team, a club, or an organization. Usually, a roster includes a list of names, addresses, and phone numbers—and any other information that relates to the members of a group.

In this Event, the Cyber Swimmers make a roster for their team. In it, they include the names, addresses, and phone numbers of every team member, and also the names of the team members' parents.

Word's Mail Merge Helper will help the swimmers do exactly what they want. Mail Merge helps create form letters, mailing labels, envelopes, and catalogs. In the first Event of the Season, you'll just concentrate on one area—creating a catalog. Or, in this case a roster.

MEG THE MIKE

What does merge mean? To *merge* is to bring two or more things together to form a whole unit.

GETTING YOUR FEET WET
Mail Merge Helper Basics

Trainer Terry Says:

👓 Let's use the first Workout to learn some basics about the Mail Merge Helper.

LAP 1

1.   Open a new blank document in Word.
2.   Click <u>T</u>ools and then click Mail Merge. *The Mail Merge Helper dialog box opens, as in Figure 4-1.*

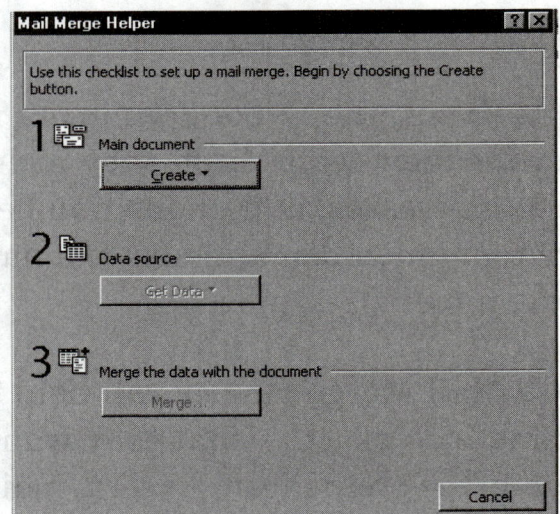

Figure 4-1. The Mail Merge Helper dialog box

3.   Click <u>C</u>reate. *Notice you have four choices, as in Figure 4-2.*

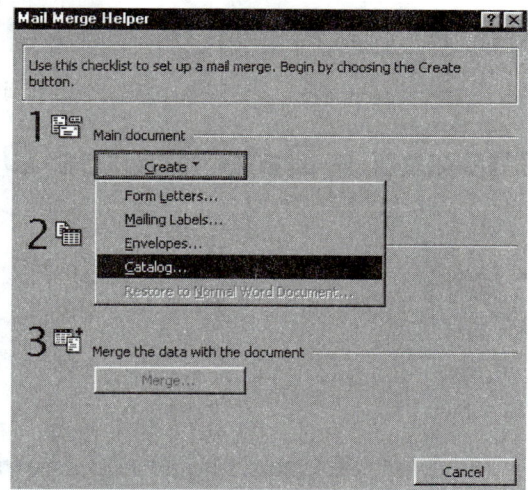

Figure 4-2. In the Create area of the Mail Merge Helper, you can choose Form Letters, Mailing Labels, Envelopes, or Catalog.

4.   Click <u>C</u>atalog.

   A dialog box appears, asking you whether you want to create a catalog using the <u>A</u>ctive Window or a <u>N</u>ew Main Document.

5.   Click <u>A</u>ctive Window.

   Now, see that under Main Document you have selected a Merge type (Catalog) and under this is the title of the Main Document. Since you haven't saved the page yet, you'll see Word's default title: <u>Document1</u> or something similar. See Figure 4-3.

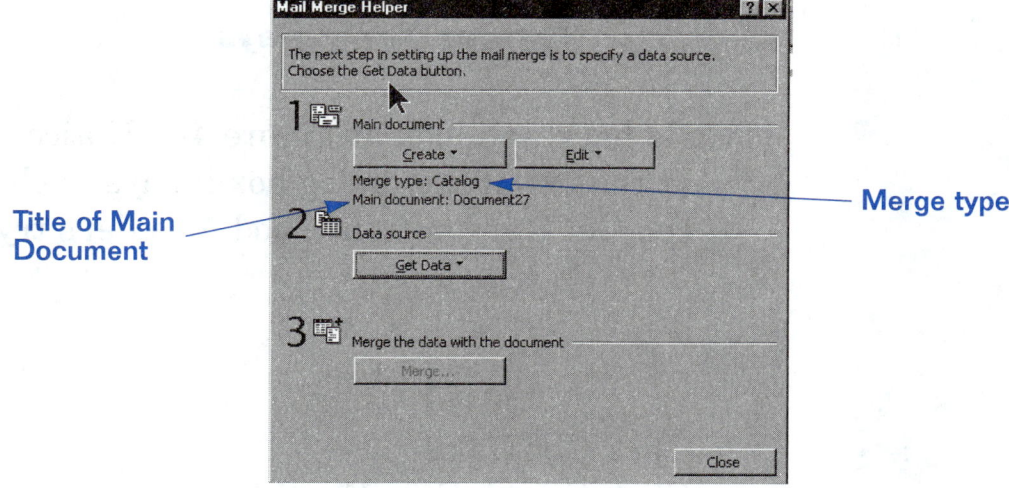

Title of Main Document

Merge type

Figure 4-3. Notice the Mail Merge Helper dialog box displays the Merge type and the Main Document title.

MEG THE MIKE

Data are pieces of information, usually put together in groups.

GETTING YOUR FEET WET

Making a Data Source Document

Coach Carrie Says:

👓 The next step is the Data Source document.

👓 A Data Source document is the document you create to store your data. It's just like drawers in a filing cabinet, where each drawer holds a record, or a group of facts that go together.

Trainer Terry Says:

👓 Go back and look at Figure 4-3. Notice that at the top of the dialog box it says to choose the Get Data button. Good idea, let's try it!

LAP 2

1. Click Get Data.
2. Click Create Data Source.
   The Create Data Source dialog box opens, as in Figure 4-4.

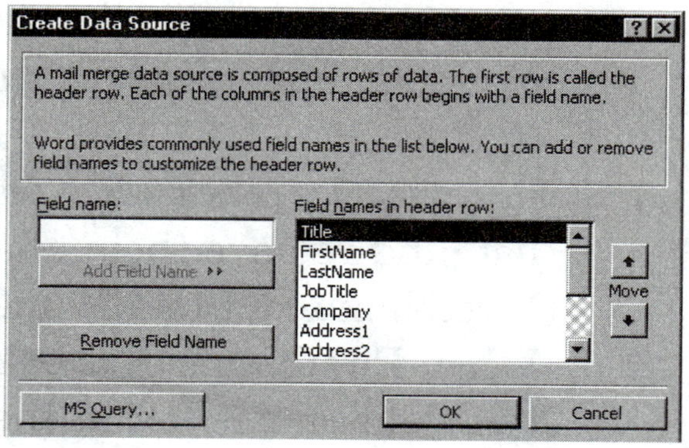

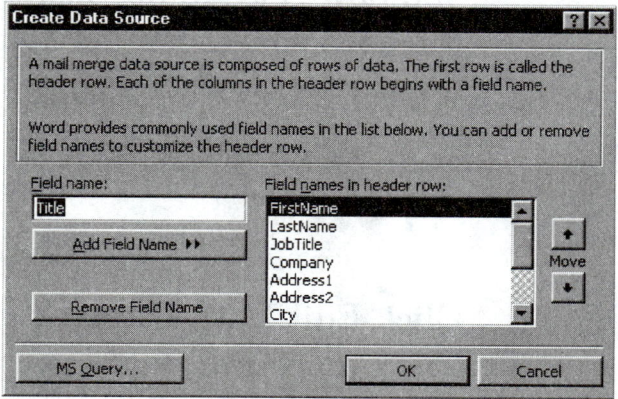

Figure 4-4. Enter data to set up your Data Source document.

👓 In Figure 4-4, Notice the *Field names in header row* list box has a lot of different choices. These field names are names for pieces of data you might put in a list. For example, you might need to have a first name or a last name in a list.

👓 Notice the field names are all one word, so the field last name becomes LastName. Word lets you add or remove field names.

👓 You can remove a field if you don't plan to use it in your merged documents.

3. Click Title and click <u>R</u>emove Field Name.
We're not going to use the field name Title, so we're removing it from the list. Notice that it's in the <u>F</u>ield name text box. Look at the example in Figure 4-5.

Figure 4-5. The field name *Title* is removed from the header row.

MEG THE MIKE

What are *fields*? Fields are like friends holding a place in line for their buddies at the movies. Fields save a space for something that isn't there yet!

A *Title* as used here, means the title of a person—like Mr., Mrs., Dr., and so on.

JEFF THE REF

If you make a mistake and remove a field you need, just enter the word for the field in the Field name text box and click Add Field Name. Then, use the Move arrows to put the field back where you want it!

4.   Click JobTitle and click Remove Field Name. *Now, you have removed two field names from the list.*

5.   For practice, click on every field name in the list, and remove them all except for FirstName and LastName.

6.   When FirstName and LastName are the only two field names left in the list box, click OK. *The Save As dialog box appears.*

7.   Save your document as **workout**.

Trainer Terry Says:

🕶 You now get a dialog box that warns you that the data source you have just created has no data! We have to fix that!

LAP 3

1.   Click Edit Data Source. *The Data Form dialog box appears as in Figure 4-6*

Figure 4-6. The Data Form dialog box

2. Type your own first name in the field *FirstName*.
3. Use the Tab key or the Down Arrow key on your keyboard to move to the next field.
4. Type your own last name in the field *LastName*.
5. Click Add New to add another name.
    You change to a new record. Notice that the record number at the bottom of the Data Form changes.
6. Enter the first and last name of a friend.
7. Click OK.

👓 If you have a blank document in front of you now, you are doing everything right!

GETTING YOUR FEET WET
Making a Main Document (Catalog)

Coach Carrie Says:

When you use Word's Mail Merge function, a special mail merge toolbar appears on your screen. We'll get a chance to use some of these buttons on the next workout. But first, check out Figure 4-7 to get familiar with the mail merge toolbar.

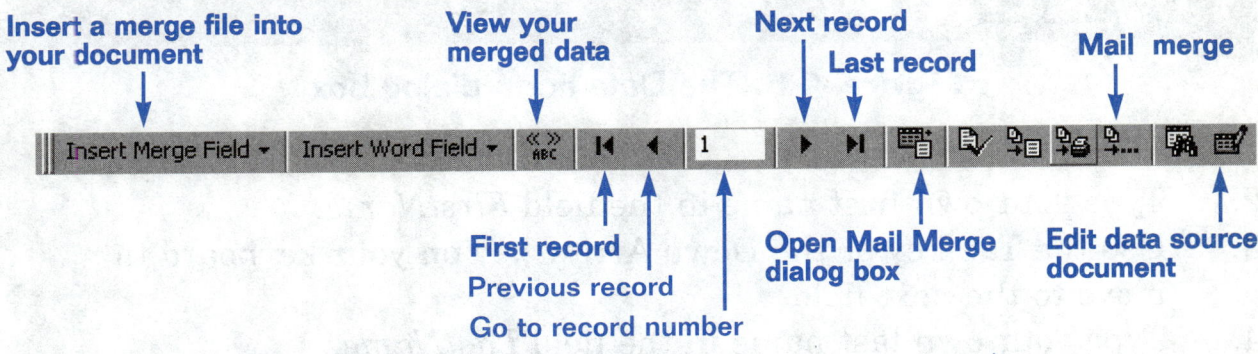

Figure 4-7. The Mail Merge toolbar

Trainer Terry Says:

Time to make a splash with the main document!

LAP 4

1. Click Tools, then click Mail Merge.
   The Mail Merge Helper dialog box opens again.

2. Click <u>E</u>dit in the Main Document area, and then click
    Catalog: Document.
    Your screen should look like the one in Figure 4-8:

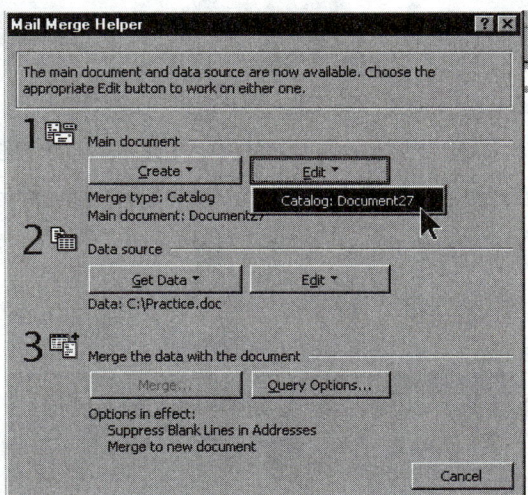

Figure 4-8. The Mail Merge function allows you to edit the Catalog
        document.

3. Click the Insert Merge Field button [Insert Merge Field ▾] on the mail merge
    toolbar.
4. Click FirstName and press the spacebar once to make a space
    after the field in your document.
5. Click the Insert Merge Field button [Insert Merge Field ▾] again.
6. Click LastName and press Enter once to create a space between
    records in your document.

👓 That's it! You're ready to merge your Data Source document and
    your Catalog document in the next Workout.

LAP 5

1. Open the Mail Merge dialog box. (Hint: Click the
    Mail Merge Helper button 🔲 on the Mail Merge toolbar.)

2. Click <u>M</u>erge.
    The Merge Dialog box appears.
3. In the Merge dialog box, click <u>M</u>erge again.
    The Data Source document and the Catalog document merge, and the list of two names should appear. The merged document should look similar to the one in Figure 4-9.

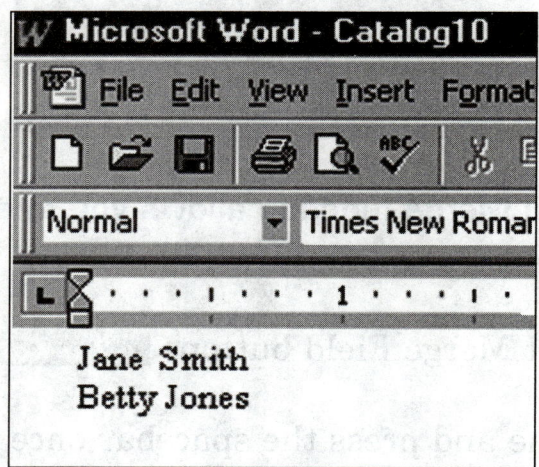

Figure 4-9. Merged document

4. Close the documents without saving them.
    This is just for practice, so you won't need to save them for later.

👓 Great Workouts! You're ready to compete. Now, help those fabulous Cyber Swimmers make a roster. Ready, go!

THE COMPETITION
Merging Documents

Coach Carrie Says:

🥽 In this competition, you're going to learn skills that will not only help you create a roster for the Cyber Swim Team, but will also help you later in other Events.

Trainer Terry Says:

🥽 First, let's use the Catalog function of Mail Merge that you've just learned about in this Event.

LAP 1

1. Open a new document.
2. Click Tools, and then click Mail Merge.
3. In the Main Document section of the Mail Merge Helper dialog box, click Create.
4. Click Catalog.
5. When you see the next dialog box appear, click Active Window.
6. Now, the Mail Merge Helper dialog box tells you to choose the Get Data button. Click Get Data.
7. Click Create Data Source.
   If you are swimming along carefully, you should see the same dialog boxes you saw during your laps.

Now, we're going to make a list of names, addresses, and phone numbers. But first, let's remove Field <u>n</u>ames that we won't need.

8.   Click *JobTitle* and click <u>R</u>emove Field Name.
9.   Click *Company* and click <u>R</u>emove Field Name.
10.   Click *Address2* and click <u>R</u>emove Field Name.
11.   Scroll down and click *Country* and click <u>R</u>emove Field Name.
12.   Click *WorkPhone* and click <u>R</u>emove Field Name.
       Now you have removed all of the fields you don't need in this roster.
13.   *WorkPhone* should be highlighted in the Field name text box. Press Backspace to delete it.
14.   Type the word *Swimmer* in the Field name text box.
       Your screen should look like the one in Figure 4-10.

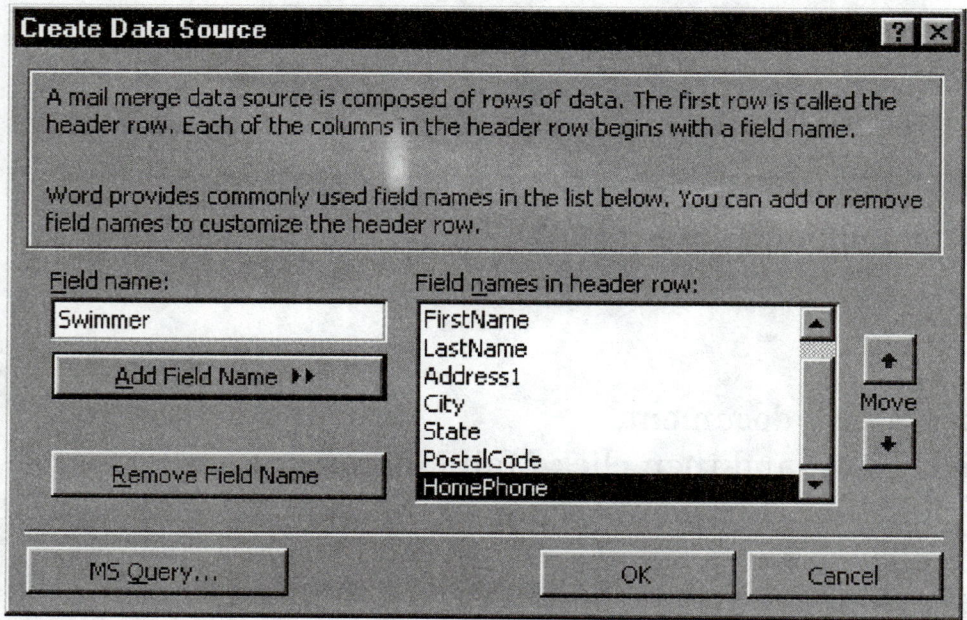

Figure 4-10. Type *Swimmer* in the <u>F</u>ield Name text box.

15.   Click <u>A</u>dd Field Name.
       This makes the field name Swimmer *appear in the list box.*

16. Click on the Move up arrow to the right of the list box to move *Swimmer* up the list.

17. Keep clicking the Move up arrow until you see *Swimmer* after the *LastName* as in Figure 4-11.

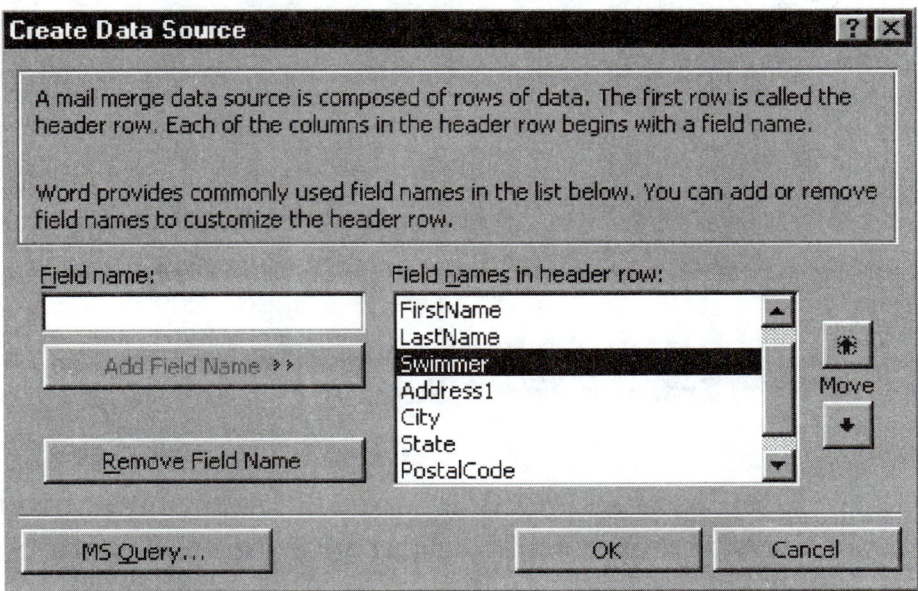

Figure 4-11. The new field *Swimmer* is under the field *LastName.*

18. Click OK.
    The Save As dialog box will appear.

19. Save this document as **datalist.**
    A dialog box will open as in figure 4-12 telling you that your data source contains no records.

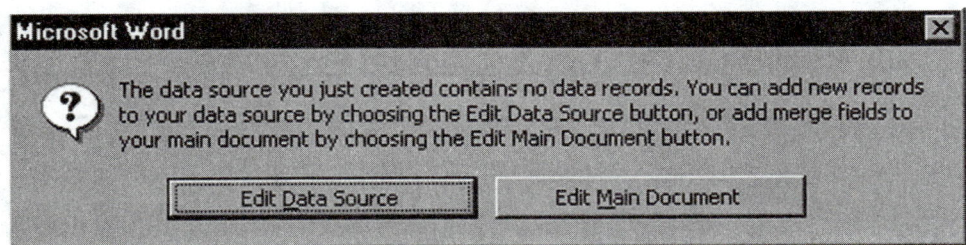

Figure 4-12. Choose to edit your data source or your main document.

20.   Click on <u>E</u>dit Data Source.
           You are now ready to enter the information into your Data Source document.

Trainer Terry Says:

👓 Next, you'll enter the names, addresses, and phone numbers of the Cyber Swimmers and their parents into the Data Source document. Look at the Data Form in Figure 4-13.

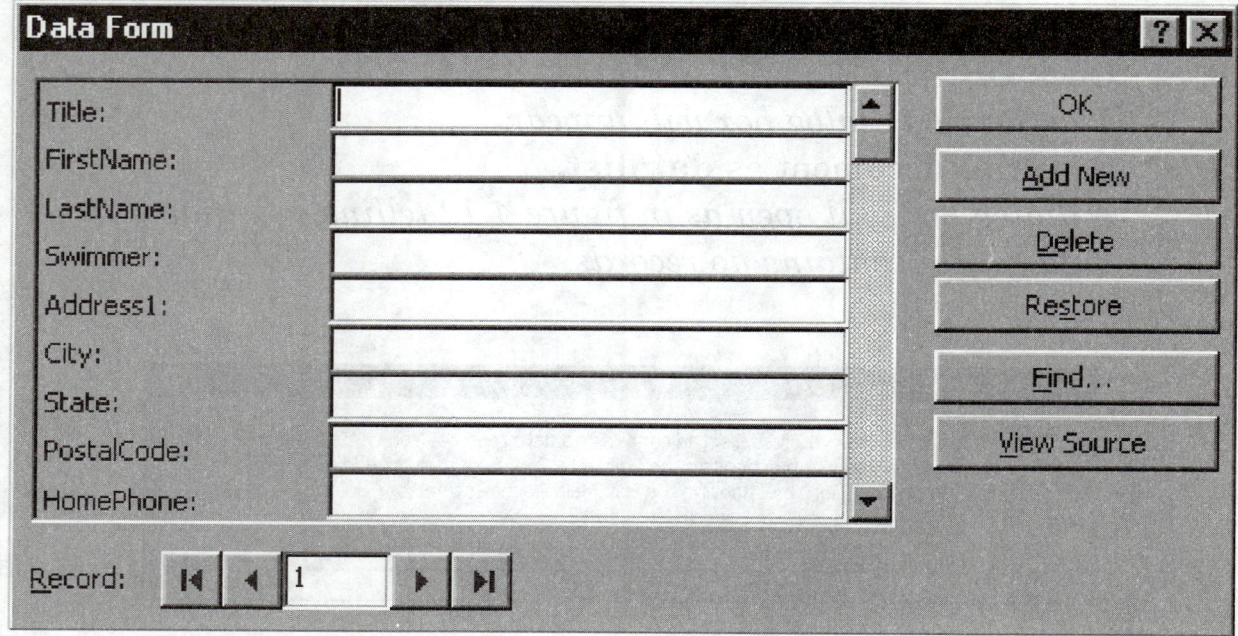

Figure 4-13. The Data Form

LAP 2

Now we'll add names and addresses to the data form. Make sure to proof your work carefully as you go along. Enter Betty Bluewater's roster information step by step:

1. Type *Mrs.* in the Title text box, and press Tab.
2. Type *Veronica* in the FirstName text box, and press Tab.
3. Type *Bluewater* in the LastName text box, and press Tab.
4. Type *Betty Bluewater* in the Swimmer text box, and press Tab.
5. Type *21 Vista Circle* in the Address1 text box, and press Tab.
6. Type *Aqua City* in the City text box, and press Tab.
7. Type *CA* in the State text box, and press Tab.
8. Type *93456* in the PostalCode text box, and press Tab.
9. Type *555-1234* in the HomePhone text box.
   Your first record should look like the one in Figure 4-14.

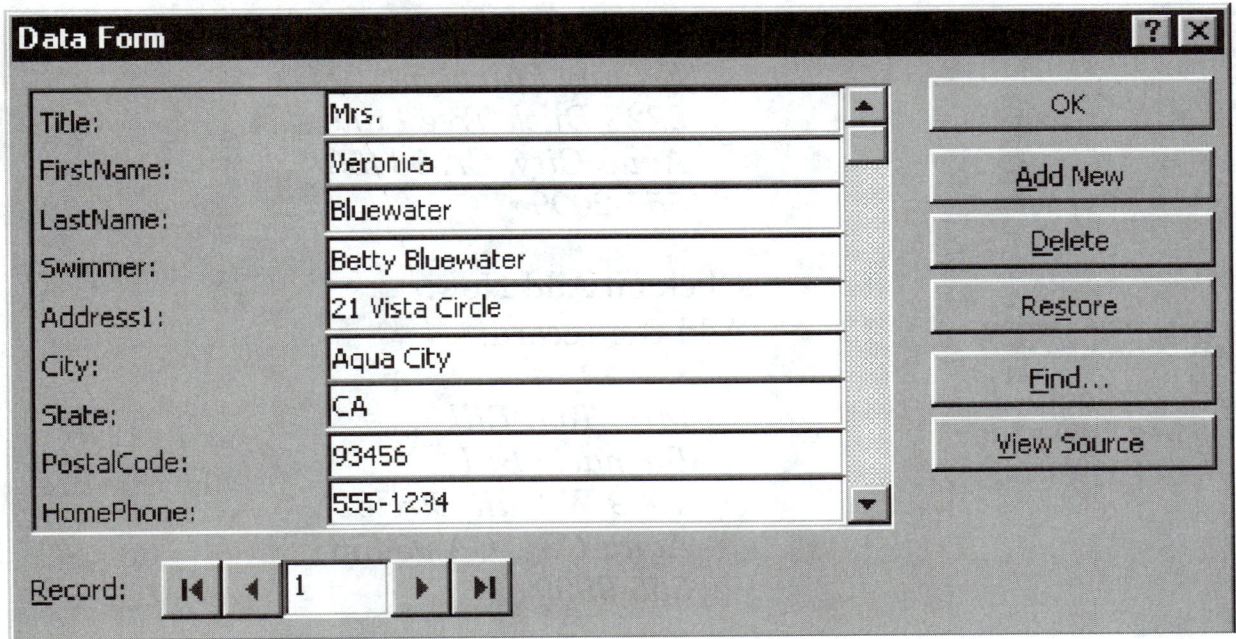

Figure 4-14. Record for Mrs. Veronica Bluewater

JEFF THE REF

If you need to correct a mistake in a record, use the arrow buttons to move from record to record, and to position the cursor with your mouse to change or correct text in a record.

MASCOT MAX

Refer to Figure 4-14 to see how your data form should look.

👓 Congratulations, you have just completed your first record!

👓 Now, lets move on to your second record for the Cyber Swimmer's roster. All the records have the same city, ZIP Code, and state. The swimmers live near each other! That makes it a lot easier to get to swim practice, don't you think?

👓 When you complete each record, look at the bottom of the data form—you'll see the record number change!

10. Click on <u>A</u>dd New.
    This will allow you to add a new record.
11. Add the following record:

    Mr. Robert Fairmont
    Franny Fairmont
    2222 Duck Tree Lane
    Aqua City, CA 93456
    555-2009

12. Click on <u>A</u>dd New.
13. Add the record:

    Mrs. Toni Bill
    Barnacle Bill
    4009 Wetsuit Circle
    Aqua City, CA 93456
    555-9999

14. Click on <u>A</u>dd New.
15. Add the record:

> *Mr. and Mrs. Ron Sammy*
> *Swimmin' Sammy*
> *444 Gurgle Drive*
> *Aqua City, CA 93456*
> *555-0101*

16. Click on <u>A</u>dd New.
17. Add the record:

> *Mrs. Ruth Watterlog*
> *Willie Watterlog*
> *4 Flip Turn Parkway*
> *Aqua City, CA 93456*
> *555-0999*

18. Click OK.
This saves the Data Source document you have just created—your list of swimmers' names and addresses.

👓 Congratulations, you have just completed your first data sheet!

LAP 3

👓 Now, you need to create a main document. This will be the document in which you make your list. You'll merge your Data Source document with this new Catalog document and put into it the information you have entered.

MASCOT MAX

Whew! Come on, swimmers! Go!

JEFF THE REF

If you accidentally exit the Data Form, just open it again by clicking <u>T</u>ools, Mail Merge E<u>d</u>it (Under Data Source) and select **datalist.**

MASCOT MAX

You are almost home. Stroke, stroke, stroke . . .

Trainer Terry Says:

👓 Now let's enter Merge fields into your main document. Think of the fields as placeholders for the information you are going to put into your catalog when you merge it with your Data Source document.

1. Reopen the Mail Merge Helper.
   *Notice that your **datalist** is listed under Data Source and that under Main document it says,* Merge type: Catalog *and* Main document *and lists a document number.*

2. In the Main document section, click Edit. This will allow you to edit your Catalog document. This is the main document. Click Catalog: Document.

3. Now your cursor appears in a blank document. On the Mail Merge toolbar click the Insert Merge Field button [Insert Merge Field ▾].
   You should now see all of the Merge fields you have created—Title, FirstName, LastName, Swimmer, Address1, City, State, PostalCode, and HomePhone. See Figure 4-15.

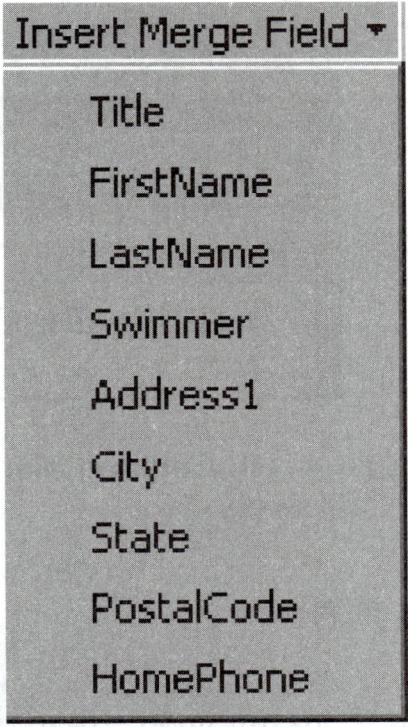

Figure 4-15. Merge Field drop-down menu

4.   Click *Title*.
    <<Title>> appears in your main document. Remember the title is Mr., Mrs., and so forth.

5.   Now, press the spacebar only once.
    You need to make spaces between fields just like you do when you are typing actual words. The space you make puts the cursor in the right place to enter the next field.

6.   Click the Insert Merge Field button [Insert Merge Field ▾].

7.   Click *FirstName*.
    <<FirstName>> appears in your main document.

8.   Press the spacebar once.

9.   Click the Insert Merge Field button [Insert Merge Field ▾].

10.   Click *LastName*.
    <<LastName>> appears in your main document.

11.   Press Enter to start a new line in your main document.
    What you have so far should look like Figure 4-16.

JEFF THE REF

Remember, if you make a mistake, you can delete and re-insert any Merge field. Highlight the field and press delete. Click on the Insert Merge Field button and start again.

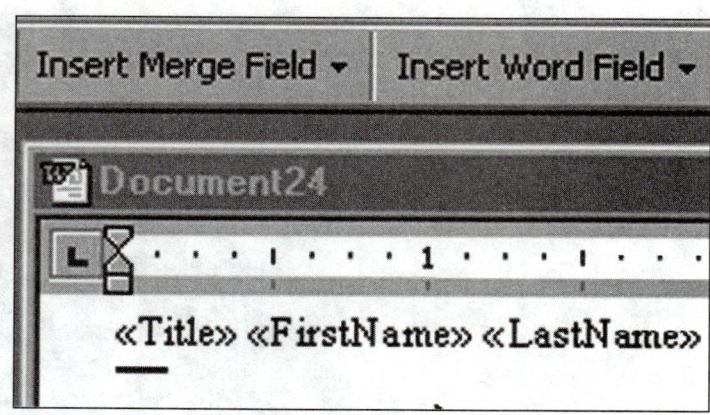

Figure 4-16. Entering Merge Fields into a document

LAP 4

👓 Looking good. Keep going!

1. Click the Insert Merge Field button `Insert Merge Field ▾`.
2. Click *Swimmer*.
   «Swimmer» appears in your main document.
3. Press Enter to start a new line in your main document.
4. Click the Insert Merge Field button `Insert Merge Field ▾`.
5. Click *Address1*.
   «Address1» appears in your main document.
6. Press Enter to start a new line in your main document.
7. Click the Insert Merge Field button `Insert Merge Field ▾`.
8. Click *City*.
   «City» appears in your main document.
9. Press the comma key and then the spacebar once to insert a comma after the *City* field.
10. Click the Insert Merge Field button `Insert Merge Field ▾`.
11. Click *State*.
    «State» appears in your main document.

12. Press the spacebar to insert a space between the State and the PostalCode fields.

13. Click the Insert Merge Field button Insert Merge Field ▾.

14. Click *PostalCode*.
    <<PostalCode>> appears in your main document.

15. Press Enter to start a new line in your main document.

16. Click the Insert Merge Field button Insert Merge Field ▾.

17. Click *HomePhone*.
    <<HomePhone>> appears in your main document.

18. Press Enter two times to leave a space between data records.
    Your document should look like the one in Figure 4-17.

«Title» «FirstName» «LastName»
«Swimmer»
«Address1»
«City», «State» «PostalCode»
«HomePhone»

Figure 4-17. Merge Fields inserted into a document

Coach Carrie Says:

Whew—nice set! While you're catching your breath, let me tell you what's next! Now you have set up your Main document so that when you merge it with your Data Source document, the fields will hold the places for the information you are merging.

LAP 5

Trainer Terry Says:

👓 Now, you're almost done. Here is the fun part—merging! Suddenly, you'll have a completed roster! Follow along for the last few steps.

1. Reopen the Mail Merge Helper. Click <u>T</u>ools and click Mail Me<u>r</u>ge. *You should see the message* The Main document and Data Source are ready to merge.

2. In the third section of the Mail Merge Helper, click <u>M</u>erge. *You should now see the Merge dialog box. The default set up (which is the way it looks normally) is correct. (Notice that you have selected <u>A</u>ll the records to be merged.)*

3. Click <u>M</u>erge again. *You should now see the Cyber Swim Team's finished Catalog document!*

4. Now, check the records and fix any spacing problems you might see. *For example, if you leave an extra space between two fields, the space will still be there when you merge, just as it would be in any regular text document.*

👓 Take a look at Figure 4-18 to see how your Catalog document should look right now.

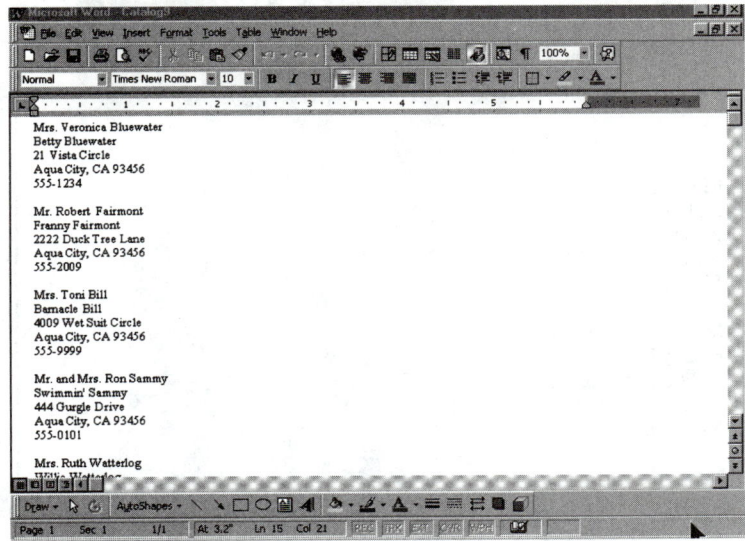

Figure 4-18. The Cyber Roster catalog

👓 I'm proud of you! Now let's change the font size and center a title on the page.

LAP 9

1. On the Menu bar, click <u>E</u>dit, then click Select All.
   This highlights all of the text in your document.
2. Change the font size to 14 point.
3. Place your cursor at the left of the first record, *Mrs. Veronica Bluewater*, and press Enter five times.
4. Return your cursor to the top of the page by pressing the Up Arrow key on your keyboard five times.
5. Click on the Center button ▤ on the Formatting toolbar.
6. Type *Cyber Swimmers' Roster*.
7. Save your document as **cyber**. Save the data source document as **cyberdata**.
8. Close both documents.

👓 Your finished roster should look like Figure 4-19.

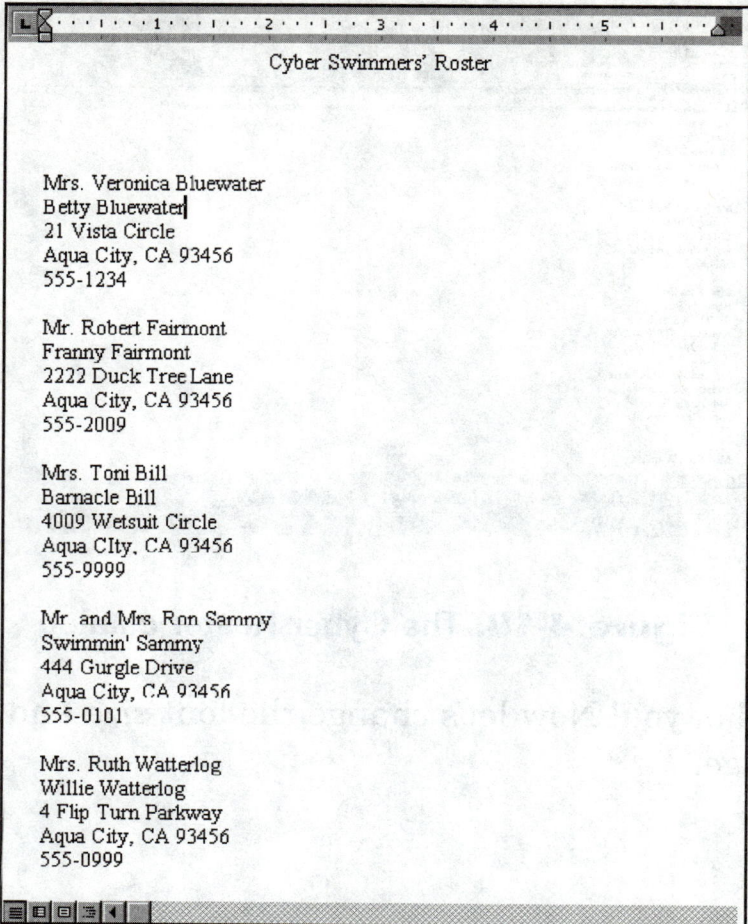

Figure 4-19. The finished roster in Print Preview

Mascot Max Says:

You've done it! The skills you have learned here will help you later in the Season to become a Word pro. Congratulations. After you've caught your breath, let's move on the State Finals.

THE STATE FINALS

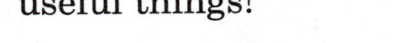 Now that you have learned how to make a catalog, there are many interesting things you can do. For the State Finals, make an address list of your friends. First, gather all the information you want about your friends—their names, addresses, and phone numbers, of course. You might also make a field for their birthdays. You can use a field for anything you want to—birthdays, hobbies, or anything else that you would like to include!

When you're done, print your address list and never miss another friend's birthday again. Another idea is to help your parents clean up their own address book by creating a catalog of your family phone book. Or help your teacher with the class list. (Make sure you ask first!) Now, you have the skills you need to do a lot of useful things!

EVENT #2
THE TEAM FUND-RAISER
POSTER

In this Event, you'll learn how to make a poster that you can customize for your school, club, or team by:

- **Importing Clip Art**
- **Picture Toolbar Fun**
- **Adding Page Borders**

SUIT UP

Importing Clip Art

Coach Carrie Says:

👓 In this Event, you will learn how to use really cool Word functions. You'll find out how to add clip art and use Word Art. During the Competition, you will be part of the "Cyber Swim Team" and will help design their candy sale poster!

👓 Posters are a form of advertising. The idea is to make a poster as eye-catching as possible, to draw attention to your cause. Before you make a poster to advertise an event, however, you need to think about what you are trying to say. Make sure to include the five "W"s (*who, what, where, when, and why*), and the big "H"—*how*, so people know what you want them to do.

👓 Okay, time to get your feet wet. As you may already know, clip art images are public domain pictures you can import into any document. Word has already loaded many clip art options for you. It's also possible to download more images.from the Web.

MEG THE MIKE

Public domain means material, like text or clip art, that you don't need to get permission to copy and use for your own purposes.

Downloading means copying a file from somewhere else, like the Internet or e-mail, and saving it so you can read it on your own computer.

Importing means taking a file, or a piece of clip art in this case, and copying it and inserting it into an existing and open document.

GETTING YOUR FEET WET

Trainer Terry Says:

Toes in the water—let's learn about using clip art!

1. Open a new document in Word.
2. Click <u>I</u>nsert, <u>P</u>icture. Then click <u>C</u>lip Art. *You should now see the Clip Art dialog box, as in Figure 4-20.*

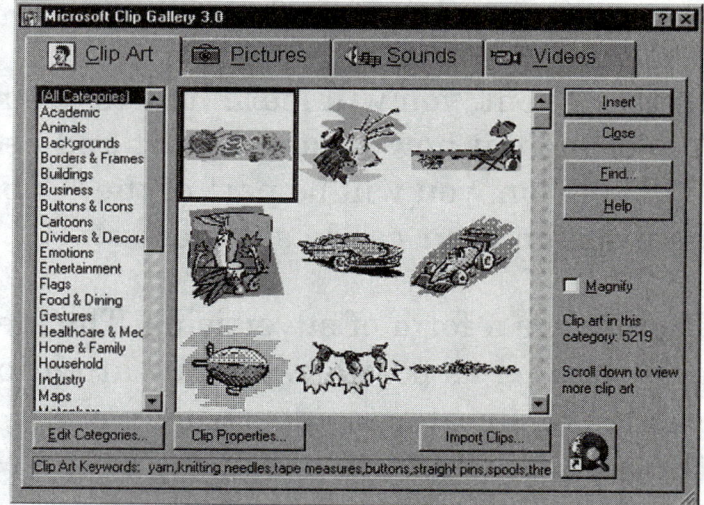

Figure 4-20. The Clip Art dialog box

3. Click on Cartoons in the Clip Art category section of the dialog box.
   This lets you see the cartoons displayed in the box to the left.
4. Click a few different categories.
5. When you find a piece of clip art you like, click on it and then click <u>I</u>nsert.

You have just learned how to import a piece of clip art into your document, without even getting your hair wet! Now that the clip art is in your document, you can change its size and place it wherever you want it in your document. Check out the following Training Table for some clip art basics.

Training Table: Making a Splash with Clip Art

If You Want To:	You Do This:
Move clip art	Click on the edge of the picture and drag after the four-headed arrow appears
Center clip art	Click on clip art and then click on the Center button ▤
Move clip art left	Click on clip and drag it to the left after the four-headed arrow appears
Move clip art right	Click on clip art and drag it to the right after the four-headed arrow appears
Make clip art taller	Click on clip art and then drag the top sizing handle up
Make clip art shorter	Click on clip art and then drag the top sizing handle down
Make clip art wider	Click on clip art and then drag the right or left sizing handle out
Make clip art narrower	Click on clip art and then drag the right or left sizing handle in

MASCOT MAX

Refer to this table when you do the next Workout. You'll soon get the hang of it!

If You Want To:	You Do This:
Make clip art larger all over	Click on clip art and then drag a corner sizing handle out
Make clip art smaller all over	Click on clip art and then drag a corner sizing handle in

Trainer Terry Says:

Now let's size the clip art in your document.

1. Click on the clip art.
    You should see little see-through squares around the edges of the clip art. These are sizing handles. See Figure 4-21.

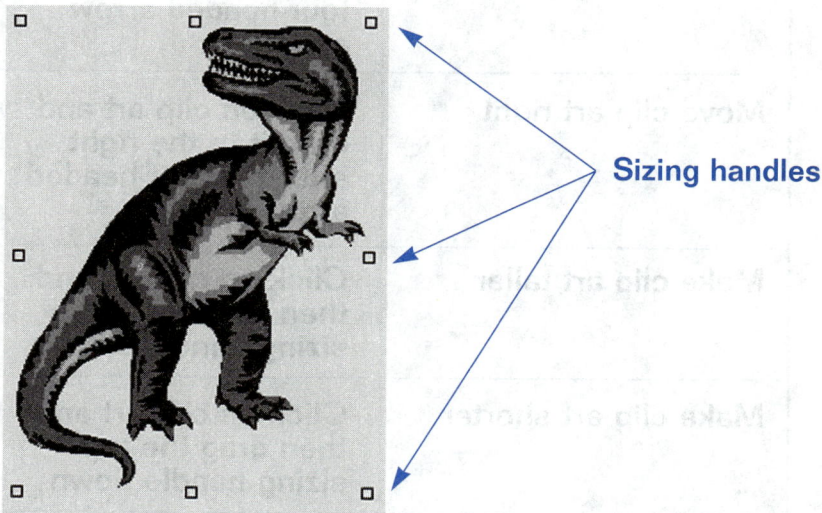

Sizing handles

Figure 4-21. Clip art with sizing handles displayed

2. Click the bottom middle sizing handle and drag the handle down.
    Notice the mouse pointer turns from a double-headed arrow into a cross hair (+) as you do this.

3.   Now, use a corner sizing handle to make the image larger or smaller.

   When you do this, you're making the clip art proportionately larger or smaller.

4.   Move your clip art around by clicking inside the image and dragging.

   You'll see that the pointer changes to a four-headed arrow when you do this.

GETTING YOUR FEET WET
Picture Toolbar fun

Coach Carrie Says:

The Picture toolbar is one of my favorite toolbars. It's called a *floating toolbar*, which means you can move it around wherever you want! This toolbar lets you change the way a piece of clip art looks. As soon as you import a piece of clip art into a document, you can choose <u>V</u>iew, <u>T</u>oolbars and select the Picture toolbar.

Figure 4-22. The Picture toolbar

Now, look at the following Training Table to find out what these buttons do.

MEG THE MIKE

Proportionally means having the same shape, but a different size.

MASCOT MAX

Great Workout! See how easy it is to make your clip art different sizes and to move it around?

MEG THE MIKE

Brightness is when the entire picture becomes lighter or darker.

Contrast is when, within a picture, the dark colors become darker and the light colors become lighter.

Training Table: Picture Toolbar

Button	Name	What It Does
	Insert Picture	Inserts a picture into a file
	Image Control	Changes a picture to black and white, grayscale, or watermark
	More Contrast	Increases the contrast in a picture
	Less Contrast	Decreases the contrast in a picture
	More Brightness	Increases the brightness of a picture
	Less Brightness	Decreases the brightness of a picture
	Crop	Trims a picture, or restores parts of a picture
	Line Style	Reveals line style list
	Text Wrapping	Wraps text around a picture
	Format Picture	Formats a picture
	Set Transparent Color	Formats color for drawings
	Reset Picture	Resets a picture to its original settings

Trainer Terry Says:

👓 Ready for the next workout? Use the same piece of clip art you used before.

1. Click on it so the sizing handles show up.
    Your Picture toolbar should display. If your toolbar doesn't display, click Ⅴiew, Ⅰoolbars, Picture.
2. Click the Image Control button  on the Picture toolbar.
3. Click Ⅰlack & White from the Image Control drop-down menu.
    This makes your piece of clip art black and white, instead of color.

GETTING YOUR FEET WET

Adding Page Borders

Coach Carrie Says:

👓 Borders and shading make your document stand out. A page border is an outline around the edges of a page. You can choose a thick line or a thin line, even a different design. You can also make a shadow appear behind the border so that the page has a "finished" look. You can see what the Borders and Shading dialog box looks like in Figure 4-23.

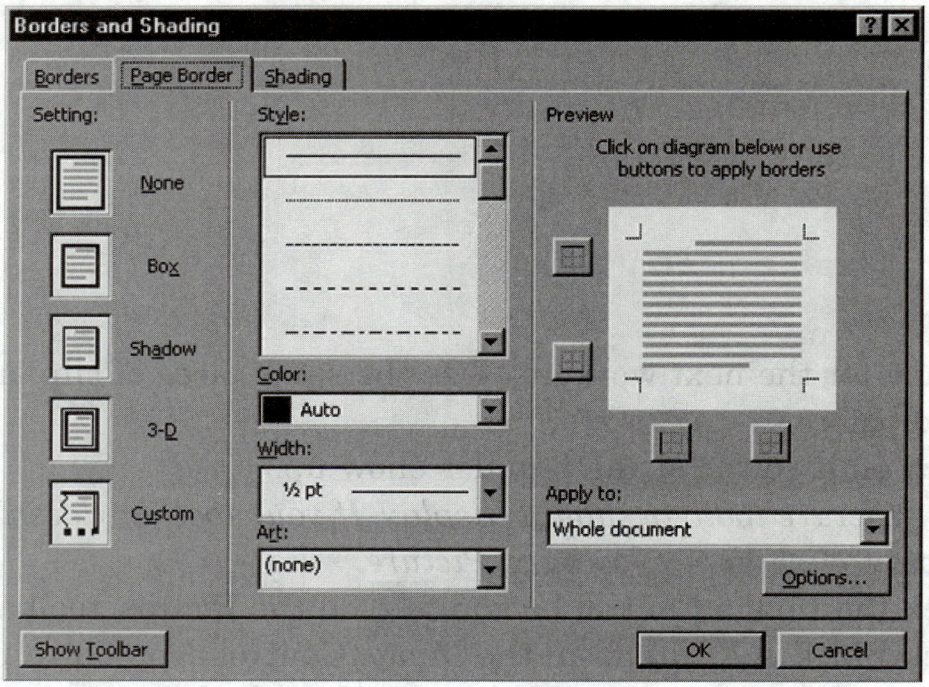

Figure 4-23. Borders and Shading dialog box, Page Border tab

Check out the following Training Table to learn about this dialog box!

Training Table: Page Border Dialog Box

What It Says	What It Does or Allows You To Do
Borders	Creates borders around words, sentences, or paragraphs
Page Border	Creates borders around the edge of a page
Shading	Creates shadows for borders
None	No border
Box	Creates a box around a paragraph or page
Shadow	Creates a shadow around a border
3-D	Creates a 3-D effect
Custom	Creates custom borders you click on in the Preview area
Style:	Click on the border style you want
Color:	Make a color border
Width:	Change how thick the border line is
Art:	Choose a border design
Preview	See how your border will look
Apply to:	What your formatting applies to
Options	More formatting options

Trainer Terry Says:

👓 Now that you have seen the Training Table, let's experiment with <u>P</u>age Borders.

1. Click F<u>o</u>rmat, and then click <u>B</u>orders and Shading.
   Make sure your clip art is not selected!
2. Click the <u>P</u>age Border tab.
3. Click Bo<u>x</u>.
   Look in the Preview area. You should see a preview of how the box border will look around the page.
4. Now, click the <u>W</u>idth down arrow. Click on a couple of different width point sizes and see what happens in the preview area.
5. Now, click the <u>C</u>olor down arrow. Try out a few and see how the border changes colors.
6. Finally, click the A<u>r</u>t down arrow. Try some different borders and see how they look.
7. Pick an A<u>r</u>t Border and then click OK.
   Word takes you back to your document and the border shows up around your document page.

THE COMPETITION

Coach Carrie Says:

👓 Now, you're ready to make a great poster for the Cyber Swimmers. Look at the outline in Figure 4-24 that members of the Cyber Swim Team created before beginning their poster. Use the information in this outline for the Competition.

```
✧ Headline
    ▫ Big Candy Sale!
✧ Who
    ▫ The Cyber Swim Team
✧ What
    ▫ Is Selling Candy --$ 1.00 A Bar!
✧ Where
    ▫ At The Regional Swim Meet At The Cyber Swimmer's
      Booth
✧ When
    ▫ On March 28, 1999
✧ Why
    ▫ The Money Earned Will Help Us Buy New Swimsuits!
✧ How
    ▫ You Can Help Us By Making A Tax-deductible
      Purchase!
```

Figure 4-24. Cyber Swim Team poster outline

👓 In the first part of the Competition, you'll enter and format the text for the Cyber Swim Team Poster. One thing about posters—the lines of text don't have periods!

MEG THE MIKE

Stylistic means a choice based on using a certain style of writing.

Advertising writing is different from the kind of writing you do in a report or story.

The "Headline" is the title of the poster, and it should provide the main idea of the event.

Trainer Terry Says:

👓 Ready swimmers? Let's go!

Lap 1

1. Start Word.
2. Open up a new document.
3. Press Enter three times.
   This provides space for clip art to be added later.
4. Click on the Center button ▤.
5. Click on the Bold button **B**.
6. Type the headline of the poster, *Big Candy Sale!* Press Enter.
7. Click on the Bold button **B** again to turn off the Bold function, and then press Enter.
8. The cursor should be in the center of the page, but if it isn't, click on the Center button ▤ to center the next line of text.
9. Type *The Cyber Swim Team*, and then press Enter.
10. Type *Is Selling Candy—$1.00 A Bar!* and then press Enter.
11. Type *At The Regional Swim Meet At The Cyber Swimmers' Booth*, and then press Enter.
12. Type *On March 28, 1999,* and then press Enter.
13. Type *The Money We Earn Will Help Us Buy New Swimsuits!*
14. Press Enter.
15. Save the document as **poster.**

Coach Carrie Says:

In this part of the Competition, you'll select and import a piece of clip art into the Cyber Swimmers' poster. Have you closed your file? If so, you need to reopen it.

Trainer Terry Says:

Make sure your **poster** document is open on screen, and we'll be swimming quickly toward the finish line!

LAP 2

1. Position the cursor above the lines of text and click the Center button ▤.
2. Click <u>I</u>nsert, <u>P</u>icture. Then, click <u>C</u>lip Art. *Good job! Now, let's do a search for a piece of clip art for the poster.*
3. Click on the <u>C</u>lip Art tab.

JEFF THE REF

Remember, when you see a letter of a button or icon that is underscored, you can also use a keystroke. In this case, you can press Shift+K to position your cursor in the Keywords text box to write your search words.

Using the Magnify button is another cool trick. This allows you to look at a piece of clip art enlarged before you make your selection, so you can see it more clearly!

If you don't have the same clip art on your computer, check with your teacher about choosing an appropriate substitution.

4. Click Find.
   This will let you search for the kind of clip art you want!

5. In the Keywords text box, type swimmer, and then click Find Now.
   Did you get several results? If the Clip Gallery couldn't find any matches, click (All Categories) in the Clip Art tab and pick some clip art that you like.

6. Click on the horizontal swimmer if you have it. Otherwise choose another clip art.

7. Click Insert.
   Your clip art appears where you left your cursor in your document.

8. Click on the clip art.
   Be sure that your Picture toolbar is displayed.

9. If you selected a color clip art, click the Image Control button ◼ on the Picture toolbar and click Black &White from the drop-down menu.

10. Size and position the clip art so it looks good over the text.

👓 Now, let's try the second piece of clip art.

11. Position your cursor at the end of the line *Is Selling Candy—$1.00 a Bar!*
12. Press Enter to create a space after the line.
13. Click <u>I</u>nsert, <u>P</u>icture. Then click <u>C</u>lip Art.
14. Click on the <u>F</u>ind button so you can search again.
15. Type *Candy* in the <u>K</u>eyword text box.
16. Click on the <u>F</u>ind Now button.

👓 If the Clip Gallery couldn't find any matches, click (All Categories) in the <u>C</u>lip Art tab and pick some clip art that you like.

17. Click on the clip art of the unwrapped candy bar if you have it. Otherwise choose another one.
18. Click <u>I</u>nsert.
19. Click the Image Control button 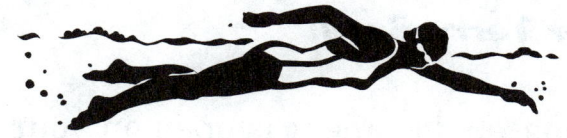 on the Picture toolbar and click <u>B</u>lack &White from the drop-down menu.
20. Size the picture so that it looks good.
    Your document should look similar to Figure 4-25.

Big Candy Sale!

The Cyber Swim Team
Is Selling Candy—$1.00 A Bar!

At The Regional Swim Meet At The Cyber Swimmers' Booth
On March 28,1999
The Money We Earn Will Help Us Buy New Swimsuits!

Figure 4-25. Partial Poster with Candy clip art

Coach Carrie Says:

Good work! Now, it's time to work with fonts. Remember, you can always go back in the book to another Season to remind yourself of important information. Now, let's help the Cyber Swimmers add font sizes and styles to their poster.

Trainer Terry Says:

Make sure the **poster** document is open on your screen.

LAP 3

1.   Select the first line of text—*Big Candy Sale!*
2.   From the Font list box, select Castellar if ou have it.
      If you don't have it, choose another interesting font.
3.   From the Font Size list box, select the point size 72.
      This size will make a nice, readable poster headline, as in Figure 4-26.

BIG CANDY SALE!

Figure 4-26. Castellar, 72

4. Select the two lines of text—*The Cyber Swim Team* and *Is Selling Candy—$1.00 a Bar!*
5. From the Font list box, select Arial Black.
6. From the Font Size list box, select 20.
   Your document should look similar to Figure 4-27.
7. Move and size your clip art to make it look good on the page.

The Cyber Swim Team
Is Selling Candy—$1.00 A Bar!

Figure 4-27. Partial poster

👓 Now, it's time to continue with the next lines of text.

LAP 4

1. Select the next two lines—*At the Regional Swim Meet at the Cyber Swimmers' Booth,* and *On March 28, 1999.*
2. Format the selected text as Arial black, 20 point.
3. Select *The Money We Earn Will Help Us Buy New Swimsuits!*
4. Format this text as Abadi MT Condensed Light, 20 point. If you don't have this font, choose another decorative font.
5. Adjust the clip art as necessary to make sure your poster fits on one page.
6. Click the Print Preview button  to preview your work, then close Print Preview.
    Check your results with Figure 4-28.

Figure 4-28. Sample of completed poster

Trainer Terry Says:

👓 Now, it's time to add the borders. Then the Cyber Swim Team will have a ready-to-use poster.

LAP 5

1. Click F<u>o</u>rmat.
2. Click <u>B</u>orders and Shading.
   Make sure that the clip art is not selected.
3. Click the <u>P</u>age Border tab.
   Don't worry if the settings look funny. You're now going to change them all.
4. Click Bo<u>x</u>.
5. In the St<u>y</u>le box, click on the down arrow until you see the selection with the three horizontal lines. Click on the three horizontal lines.
6. Click on <u>W</u>idth down arrow.
7. Click on 1½ pt.
8. Click OK.
9. Click the Print Preview button [icon] to view your results.
   Do yours match? Great Race!

Figure 4-29. Sample final poster

THE STATE FINALS

👓 Congratulations! You have finished the Cyber Swim Team's poster! Way to go! Now that you are finished with this last step, you are ready to try your own poster. Remember to answer "Who," "What," "Where," "When," "Why," and "How."

👓 Another idea is to take what you have learned here and use it to make a great cover for your next book report or project at school. Use your imagination and make the ideas you learned here work for you!

EVENT #3
THE CLUB NEWSLETTER:
THE UNDERWATER NEWS

In this Event, you'll become a reporter for the Underwater News! (The official newsletter of the Cyber Swim Team!) A newsletter borrows from its big brother—the newspaper. So, think of this as your chance to become an underwater journalist! I hope you have waterproof ink! As an underwater cyber journalist you will learn:

- Newsletter Basics
- Borders and Shading Review
- Working with Columns
- Using the Drawing Toolbar and AutoShapes

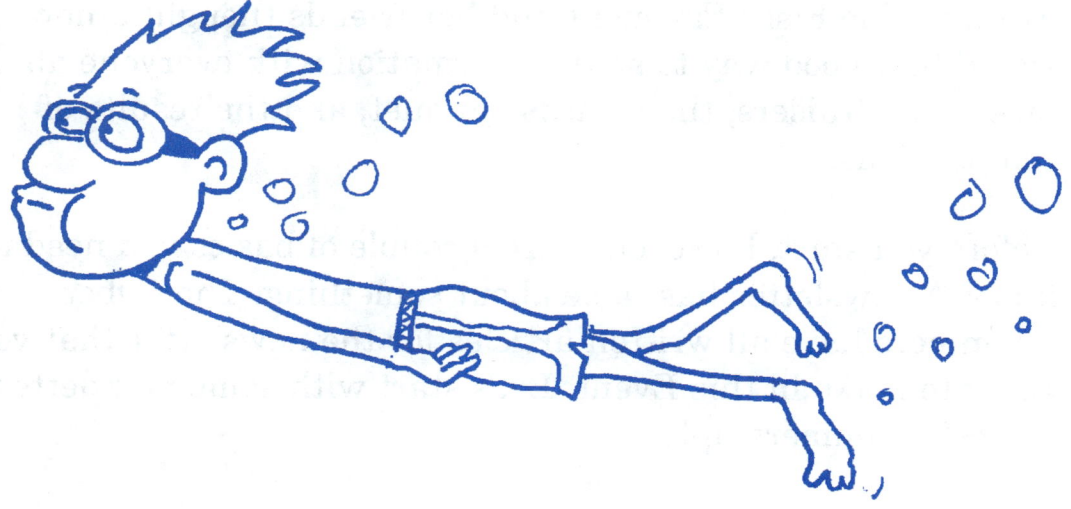

SUIT UP

Coach Carrie Says:

👓 Have you ever wanted to be a journalist or a writer? Well, here is your chance! When you make your own newsletter, you're actually becoming your own newspaper publisher. You can publish your thoughts, ideas, and writing, and share them with the world!

👓 In this Event, you're going to help the famous Cyber Swim Team. Franny (The Fish) Fairmont and her friends thought a newsletter would be a good way to share information with everyone about meets, fundraisers, the awards banquet, and the results of competitions.

👓 Before you start, however, there a couple of basics you need to know. A newsletter has to be about something. The Cyber Swimmers have all written articles for the newsletter that you're going to make in this Event. Let's start with some newsletter basics! Swimmers up!

GETTING YOUR FEET WET
Newsletter Basics

Coach Carrie Says:

Before you start this workout you need to know what you're going to do when you dive in the pool. Here is some shallow-end information for you about newsletter formats. Look at the newsletter mock-up in Figure 4-30 and learn about the parts of a newsletter.

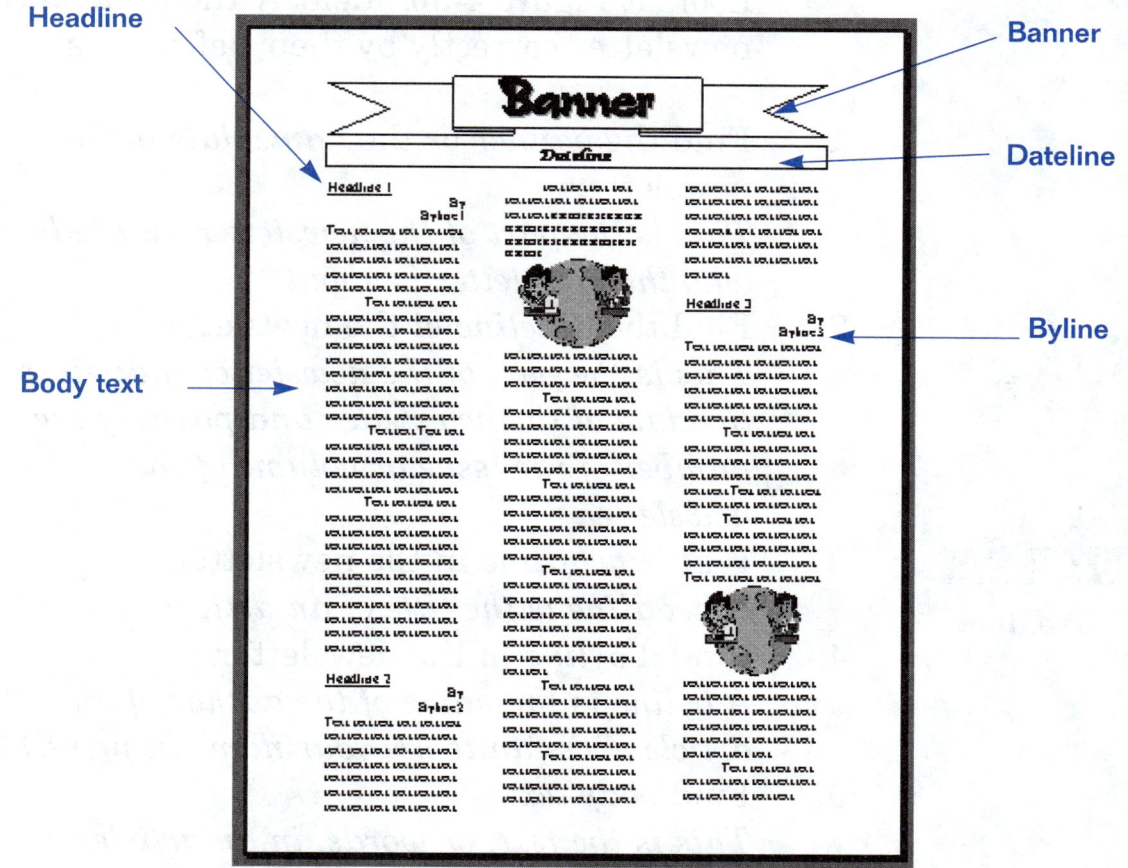

Figure 4-30. Mock newsletter

Trainer Terry Says:

MASCOT MAX

Got it? See, that was easy!

Look at Figure 4-30. Identify the parts of the newsletter correctly by their definitions.

1. Find the *banner* or the *nameplate* of the newsletter.
    This is the part of the newsletter that tells you who the newsletter is about.
2. Find the *dateline* of the newsletter.
    This is the part of the newsletter that gives the date of the newsletter and possibly the number of the issue or volume of the newsletter.
3. Find a *headline* in the newsletter.
    A headline is the title of an article.
4. Find a *byline* in the newsletter.
    A byline is the name of the author of an article. (It's fun to see your name in print!)
5. Find *body text.*
    This is the text, or words, in an article.

GETTING YOUR FEET WET

Borders and Shading Review

Coach Carrie Says:

 In Event 2 you learned how to put a border and shading around a whole page. Here you will learn how to put a border around a line of text. This will help you create a Dateline when you help the Cyber Swim team with their newsletter.

Trainer Terry Says:

 In this Workout, all you need to do is look around. You won't even get a toe wet!

1. Click F̲ormat. Click B̲orders and Shading.
2. Look at the options on the B̲orders tab.
3. Now, click on the Page Border tab of the dialog box and compare them. You will notice that the Borders tab is a little bit different from the P̲age Border tab. How are they different?

MASCOT MAX

If you noticed that the Borders tab of the dialog box is missing the function called Art, you're right! Also the Apply to section changes, as well. Good job!

GETTING YOUR FEET WET
Working with Columns

Coach Carrie Says:

Newspapers use columns to divide the text in articles into easy to read pieces. Word's column feature lets you choose many different combinations of columns. Refer to the Columns Dialog box in Figure 4-31 while you read the following Training Table.

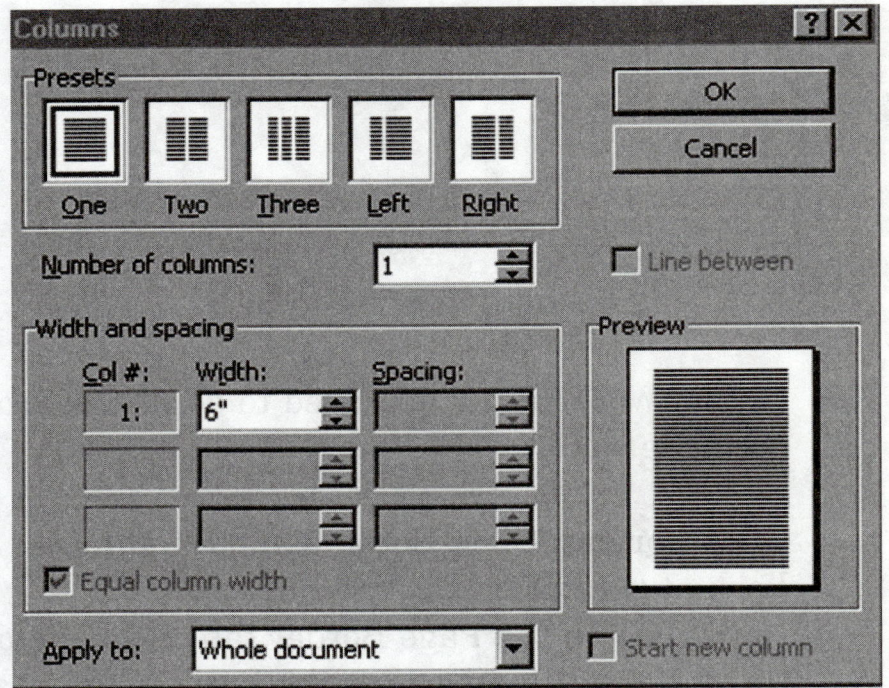

Figure 4-31. Columns dialog box

Training Table: Column Dialog Box

Part Of The Dialog Box	What It Does
Presets:	These are the column formats that are already set for users
One	Click to insert a single column
Two	Click to insert two columns
Three	Click to insert three columns
Left	Click to insert two columns, the left one half as wide as the right
Right	Click to insert two columns, the right one half as wide as the left
Number of columns:	Click on the arrows to select the number of columns
Line between	Click box to add vertical lines between the columns
Width and spacing:	Click to enter the width and spacing measurements for columns
Col #:	The column number
Width:	Click on the arrows to select width
Spacing:	Click on the arrows to select spacing
Equal column width	Click to make columns equal in width
Apply to:	Click to apply the column to selected part of document
Preview	This shows you how your document will look
Start new column	Works with the selection "this point forward" in Apply to box

MASCOT MAX

That was easy. Until you have entered your text, using column functions don't really show you much. You'll be amazed at how quickly your text looks just like a newspaper when you try it later in the Competition!

Trainer Terry Says:

👓 What are you waiting for? Let's do a column lap!

1. Open a new document in Word.
2. Click F*o*rmat, then click *C*olumns.
   Compare what you see on your screen to the Training Table. Can you find all of the things you see in the Training table in the actual dialog box on your screen?
3. Select different options and look at the preview.
   Later, when you have entered text for the Cyber Swimmer's newsletter, you will select *T*hree *columns.*
4. Click Cancel.

GETTING YOUR FEET WET

Using the Drawing Toolbar and AutoShapes

Coach Carrie Says:

Word has lots of options on the Drawing toolbar that make desktop publishing easy and fun. The features make documents look like pages of books and magazines—giving them a published look. (Hey, that's why they call it desktop publishing!)

In this Workout, you will just use the AutoShapes feature of the Drawing toolbar. AutoShapes are pre-made shapes such as circles, lines, arrows, and other symbols that you can insert into your document. Notice the options in the Autoshapes drop-down men as shown in Figure 4-32.

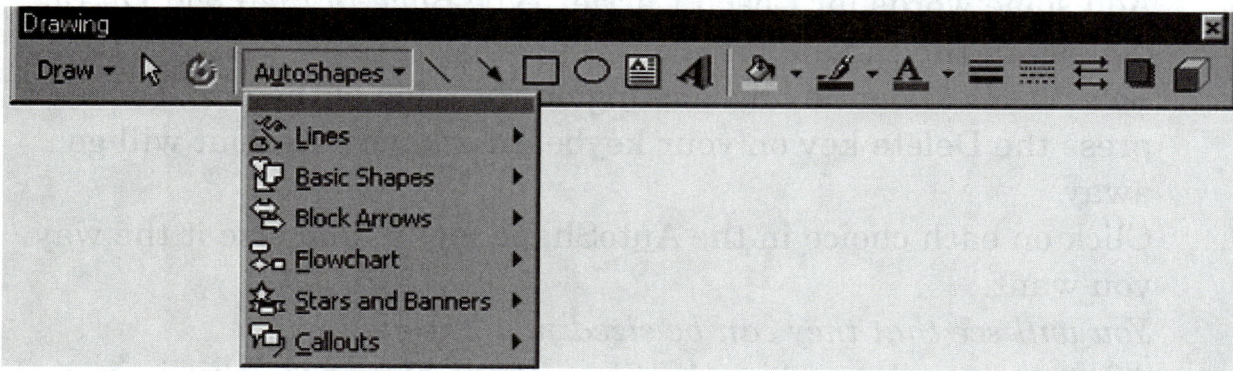

Figure 4-32. AutoShapes drop-down menu

Trainer Terry Says:

Let's start by opening the Drawing toolbar by clicking <u>V</u>iew, <u>T</u>oolbars, and then Drawing.

1.   Click on A<u>u</u>toShapes.
2.   Click on <u>C</u>allouts.
     These things look like the balloons that cartoon characters use when they speak.
3.   Click on one of the <u>C</u>allouts.
     Your mouse pointer will turn into a cross hair (+).
4.   Click and drag to make the callout nice and big in your document.
5.   Add some words for Coach Carrie. Type *Back in the Pool! On the double!* in the callout box.
6.   Select the callout box by clicking on the edge of the box. Then press the Delete key on your keyboard and your callout will go away.
7.   Click on each choice in the A<u>u</u>toShape menu, and size it the way you want.
     You will see that they can be sized just like clip art!
8.   After you are done, close the file without saving it—this is just a practice try!

THE COMPETITION

Coach Carrie Says:

 Hey, you can't spend all day with AutoShapes, swimmers! Back in the pool! On the double! (Where have I heard that before?)

Trainer Terry Says:

Let's dive into the newsletter project. First, we'll set the margins for the newsletter.

LAP 1

1. Open a new document in Word.
2. Save the file as **newslet**.
3. Click <u>F</u>ile and then click Page Set<u>u</u>p.
4. Click <u>M</u>argins.
5. Click the down arrow by the <u>T</u>op box and select 0.5".
6. Click the down arrow by the <u>B</u>ottom box and select 0.5".
7. Click the down arrow by the L<u>e</u>ft box and select 1".
8. Click the down arrow by the <u>R</u>ight box and select 1".
9. Click OK.

Great! Now, enter the text for the Banner of your newsletter.

10. Click the Center button and type *The Underwater News.*
11. Select the text.
12. Click F<u>o</u>rmat, then click <u>F</u>ont.

JEFF THE REF

The fonts suggested in this book are just suggestions. If you don't have a font, use another you like. The computer you use may have a lot more or a lot less fonts, depending on how many have been installed!

MASCOT MAX

Don't worry where the clip art lands. You are now going to change it into a watermark!

13. In the Font dialog box, select:
   - Tempus Sans ITC (or another decorative font)
   - Bold
   - 48 point
   - Shado<u>w</u>

14. Click OK.

👓 Now let's find and import a piece of clip art for the Banner.

LAP 2

1. Click the mouse button to remove highlight from text.
   Depending on the font you used, your text may be on one line or it may have wrapped to two lines.

2. If your text is one one line, press Enter after the word *Underwater* to center *News* on the second line.

3. Click <u>I</u>nsert, click <u>P</u>icture, and then click <u>C</u>lip Art.
   The Cyber Swim Team wants to use the fish clip art called fishscl.

4. So, first click on <u>F</u>ind, then click in the File <u>n</u>ame containing text box.

5. Enter the file name *fishscl*.

6. Click on <u>F</u>ind Now.
   You should see a happy little school of fish. If you don't have the same clip art, choose an appropriate image that you like.

7. Click <u>I</u>nsert.

👓 Now, you have a document with text and a piece of clip art. Next, you'll do a cool clip art trick using the Picture and Drawing toolbars!

LAP 3

1. Click on the clip art and drag it below the text so you can work with it more easily. *If the Picture toolbar doesn't display, click View, Toolbars, Picture.*

2. Click on the Image Control button  on the Picture toolbar.

3. Click on Watermark.

4. Click on the Text Wrapping button .

5. Click None.

6. Click and drag the picture over the text The Underwater News.

7. Size the picture and center it so that it almost covers the text, *The Underwater News. If you can't read the text, that means you're on the right track!*

8. Open the Drawing toolbar by clicking View, Toolbars, and then Drawing.

9. Click on Draw. *The Draw drop-down menu appears.*

10. Click on Order.

11. Click on Send Behind Text. *Now the clip art is behind the text! Looks great, doesn't it? Your screen should look similar to the example shown in Figure 4-33.*

The Underwater News

Figure 4-33. The banner

Now it's time for the Dateline and the text of the newsletter.

JEFF THE REF

Refer to the Picture toolbar Training Table in Event 2 of this Season if necessary.

MASCOT MAX

Well you have set up the banner! That's fantastic.

LAP 4

1.   Position the cursor under the Banner. Press Enter until you see the cursor under the text.

2.   Click the Align Left button ![Align Left button] on the toolbar.

3.   Use the Font dialog box to change the font to Arial, 14 point. Turn off bold and deselect Shadow.

4.   Enter the following text for the Dateline: *Vol.3, No. 3.*

5.   Then press Tab.

6.   Type *The Cyber Swim Team News.*

7.   Then press Tab.

8.   Type *Sept. 1999.*

9.   Press Enter.

10. Select the dateline (including the paragraph mark).
     *Make sure you **don't** select the paragraph mark below the dateline.*

11. Click Format, Borders and Shading.

12. Make sure the Borders tab is selected, then click Shadow.
     Make sure that Color is set to Auto

13. Click OK.

14. Click the Center button ![Center button].

15. Click below the text and see what you've got!
     Your Dateline is done and it should look like Figure 4-34.

The Underwater News

| Vol. 3, No. 3 | The Cyber Swim Team News | Sept. 1999 |

Figure 4-34. The dateline

Now, enter the text of the newsletter. The Cyber Swimmers have written several articles. Keyboarders on you mark, get set, go!

LAP 5

1. Press Enter.
2. Insert a continuous section break (Insert, Break, Continuous).
3. Use Times New Roman, 12 point.
4. Type *Cyber Swim Team Meets Fundraiser Goal!* and press Enter.
5. Type *By* followed by your own name! Then press Enter twice.
6. Type the following paragraph:

> Hey swimmers! Guess what? We did it! We actually raised all of the needed $1,000.00 for our new swimsuits! This means we won't have to wear those old ratty suits from the turn-of-the-century. Think of how we will skim through the water in our brand-new cyber swimsuits! Hey, we should take several seconds off all of our best times. At least! Special thanks goes to our team's parent representative, Mrs. Watterlog, for thinking up the candy idea, and to the readers of *Keyboarding and Word Processing for Kids* for helping us with our nifty poster! Just think, our parents will be eating candy until next summer! Thanks again to everyone who supported our candy fundraiser.

7. Press Enter two times.
8. Type *Awards Banquet Update*.
9. Press Enter.
10. Type *By Swimmin' Sammie*.
11. Press Enter two times.
12. Type the following paragraph:

> We are in desperate need of a restaurant for the banquet. As you may already know, our last year's location—The Sunken Treasure—thought we were too noisy and didn't like the fish cheers. Well, maybe this year we need a banquet hall that is owned by one of our team family members. This way, when we do the fish cheer, the other diners won't get up and leave the restaurant. If you have a suggestion, call Coach Limpicgold and let her know. Hurry, we have only two months until banquet time.

13. Spell check your document.
    Remember, Word spell check doesn't understand names and slang like swimmin'!

👓 .This is good review for all of the keyboarding skills you learned in the first season! Your document should look similar to Figure 4-35.

The Underwater News

Vol. 3, No. 3	The Cyber Swim Team News	Sept. 1999

Cyber Swim Team Meets Fundraiser Goal!
By Your Name

Hey swimmers! Guess what? We did it! We actually raised all of the needed $1,000.00 for our new swimsuits! This means we won't have to wear those old ratty suits from the turn-of-the-century. Think of how we will skim through the water in our brand-new cyber swimsuits! Hey, we should take several seconds off all of our best times. At least! Special thanks goes to our team's parent representative, Mrs. Watterlog, for thinking up the candy idea, and to the readers of *Keyboarding and Word Processing for Kids* for helping us with our nifty poster! Just think, our parents will be eating candy until next summer! Thanks again to everyone who supported our candy fundraiser.

Awards Banquet Update
By Swimmin' Sammie

We are in desperate need of a restaurant for the banquet. As you may already know, our last year's location—The Sunken Treasure—thought we were too noisy and didn't like the fish cheers. Well, maybe this year we need a banquet hall that is owned by one of our team family members. This way, when we do the fish cheer, the other diners won't get up and leave the restaurant. If you have a suggestion, call Coach Limpicgold and let her know. Hurry, we have only two months until banquet time.

Figure 4-35. Partial newsletter document

LAP 6

1. Press Enter two times.
2. Type *Swimmers' Event Line Up—Broadway Invitational Meet* and press Enter.
3. Type *Swimmin' Sammie—100 Freestyle* and press Enter.
4. Type *Barnacle Bob—Individual Medley Relay, Butterfly* and press Enter.
5. Type *Toned Tom—100 Backstroke, 100 Fly, 100 Indo* and press Enter.
6. Type *Betty Bluewater—500 Freestyle* and press Enter.
7. Type *If you haven't seen Coach L. for your meet event assignments, do it today!*
8. Press Enter two times.
9. Press the Save button 🖫 on the toolbar.

Whew! What a workout! Well you are on your last lap of text to enter. You are doing great. Let's see if you can shave a few seconds off your best keyboarding time on this next one!

LAP 7

1. Type *Fishes' Corner* and press Enter.
2. Type *By Franny Fairmont* and press Enter two times.
3. Type the following paragraph:

> Guess which fish has a "clam" to fame? It's Bob! He just found out he is going to be in a commercial playing the part of...a swimmer! (What a concept!) Congratulations to Bob. Will you remember us when you are a big starfish?

4. Press Enter two times.
5. Type the following paragraph:

> Betty's family is moving. Oh-no! We are all going to miss Betty. But luckily, she doesn't leave until the end of the season. Good luck, and don't forget to float by and "sea" us!

6. Press Enter two times.

7. Type the following paragraph:

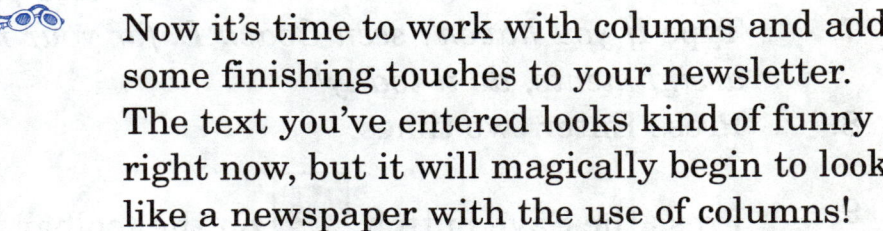

> Have you seen the new team T-shirts?
> They are cool! They are in now, so line
> up with your ten bucks and get one.
> We are all going to wear them on Team
> Spirit Day at school. Don't be left out.

8. Press Enter.
9. Spell check your document again.
10. Save your document.

Now it's time to work with columns and add
some finishing touches to your newsletter.
The text you've entered looks kind of funny
right now, but it will magically begin to look
like a newspaper with the use of columns!

LAP 8

1. Select all the headlines, bylines, and body
   text you have just entered.
2. Click Format and then click Columns.
   *You will see the Column dialog box, as shown
   in Figure 4-36.*

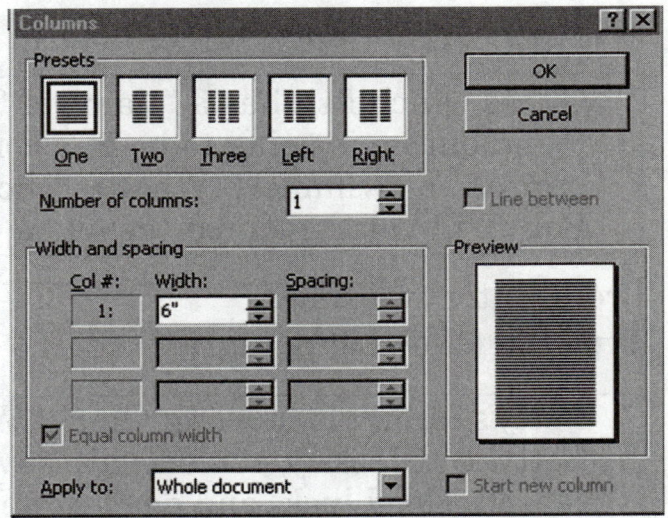

Figure 4-36. Column dialog box

3. Click on <u>T</u>hree.
4. Click on the check box for Line <u>b</u>etween.
5. Click OK.

Does your document look like Figure 4-37? Good job!

The Underwater News

| Vol. 3, No. 3 | The Cyber Swim Team News | Sept. 1999 |

Cyber Swim Team Meets Fundraiser Goal!
By Your Name

Hey swimmers! Guess what? We did it! We actually raised all of the needed $1,000.00 for our new swimsuits! This means we won't have to wear those old ratty suits from the turn-of-the-century. Think of how we will skim through the water in our brand-new cyber swimsuits! Hey, we should take several seconds off all of our best times. At least! Special thanks goes to our team's parent representative, Mrs. Watterlog, for thinking up the candy idea, and to the readers of *Keyboarding and Word Processing for Kids* for helping us with our nifty poster! Just think, our parents will be eating candy until next summer! Thanks again to everyone who supported our candy fundraiser.

Awards Banquet Update
By Swimmin' Sammie

We are in desperate need of a restaurant for the banquet. As you may already know, our last

year's location—The Sunken Treasure—thought we were too noisy and didn't like the fish cheers. Well, maybe this year we need a banquet hall that is owned by one of our team family members. This way, when we do the fish cheer, the other diners won't get up and leave the restaurant. If you have a suggestion, call Coach Limpicgold and let her know. Hurry, we have only two months until banquet time.

Swimmers' Event Line Up—Broadway Invitational Meet
Swimmin' Sammie—100 Freestyle
Barnacle Bob—Individual Medley Relay, Butterfly
Toned Tom—100 Backstroke, 100 Fly, 100 Indo
Betty Bluewater—500 Freestyle
If you haven't seen Coach L. for your meet event assignments, do it today!

Fishes' Corner
By Franny Fairmont

Guess which fish has a "clam" to fame? It's Bob! He just found out he is going to be in a

commercial playing the part of…a swimmer! (What a concept!) Congratulations to Bob. Will you remember us when you are a big starfish?

Betty's family is moving. On-no! We are all going to miss Betty. But luckily, she doesn't leave until the end of the season. Good luck, and don't forget to float by and "sea" us!

Have you seen the new team T-shirts? They are cool! They are in now, so line up with your ten bucks and get one. We are all going to wear them on Team Spirit Day at school. Don't be left out.

Figure 4-37. Columns in newsletter

Now, it's time to add a couple of AutoShapes and font changes, and you're done with the Cyber Swim Team's Newsletter! Let's change the Fonts in the headlines and bylines first.

JEFF THE REF

Now, you can see if you have the newsletter-lingo down! If you need help, check out the first page of this event.

LAP 9

1. Click <u>V</u>iew, <u>Z</u>oom, then click on <u>7</u>5%.
2. Click OK.
   This will make your document small enough to see things a bit more clearly here.
3. Select the first headline in the first column of the newsletter.
4. Format the text as Arial, 12 point, bold.
5. Select the first byline (your name!).
6. Format the text as Arial, 10 point, italic, right-aligned.
7. Now repeat the same steps for every headline and byline.
   They should all look the same.
8. Insert a column break at the end of the first article (<u>I</u>nsert, <u>B</u>reak <u>C</u>olumn Break).
   This will move the second article to the second column! Your newsletter should now look like Figure 4-38. If it isn't quite there, use the Enter key to reposition the text a bit.

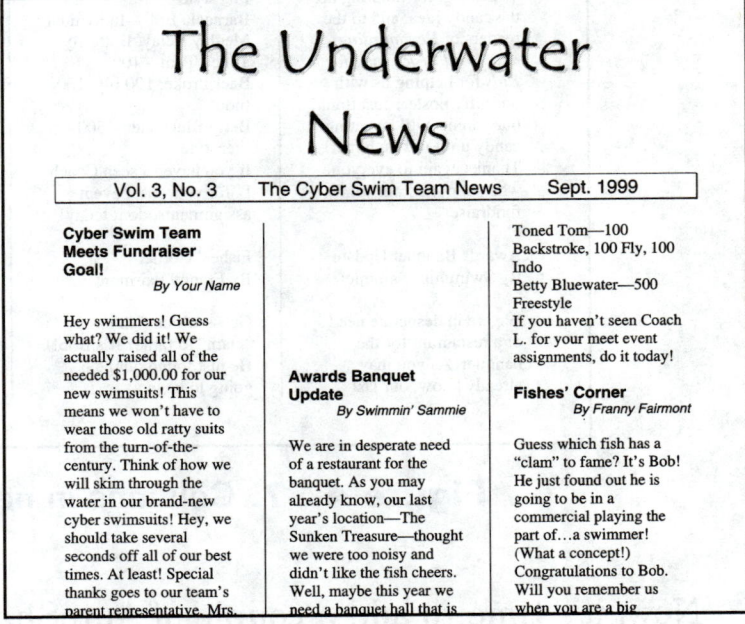

Figure 4-38. The newsletter in its almost complete form

Now you're going to use that extra space you just created to insert AutoShapes. Remember, AutoShapes are part of the Drawing toolbar. Click <u>V</u>iew, <u>T</u>oolbars, and then Drawing to display the toolbar.

MASCOT MAX

Congrats! You did it. The Cyber Swimmers' newsletter is beginning to look great!

LAP 10

1.   Click on A<u>u</u>toShapes on the Drawing toolbar.
2.   Click on <u>B</u>asic Shapes. This will bring up many shapes from which you can choose.
3.   Click on the smiley face.
      Your mouse pointer turns into a cross hair (+).
4.   Position the (+) below the text in the first column.
5.   Click and drag to create the shape.
6.   Now use your skills to center and size the shape in the space!
7.   At the top of the second column, press Enter eight times.
8.   Click A<u>u</u>toShapes, <u>S</u>tars and Banners. Then, click on a star shape.
9.   Position the (+) above the text in the second column of the newsletter.
10.   Click and drag to create the shape.
11.   Size the AutoShape if needed.

12. Click the Print Preview button 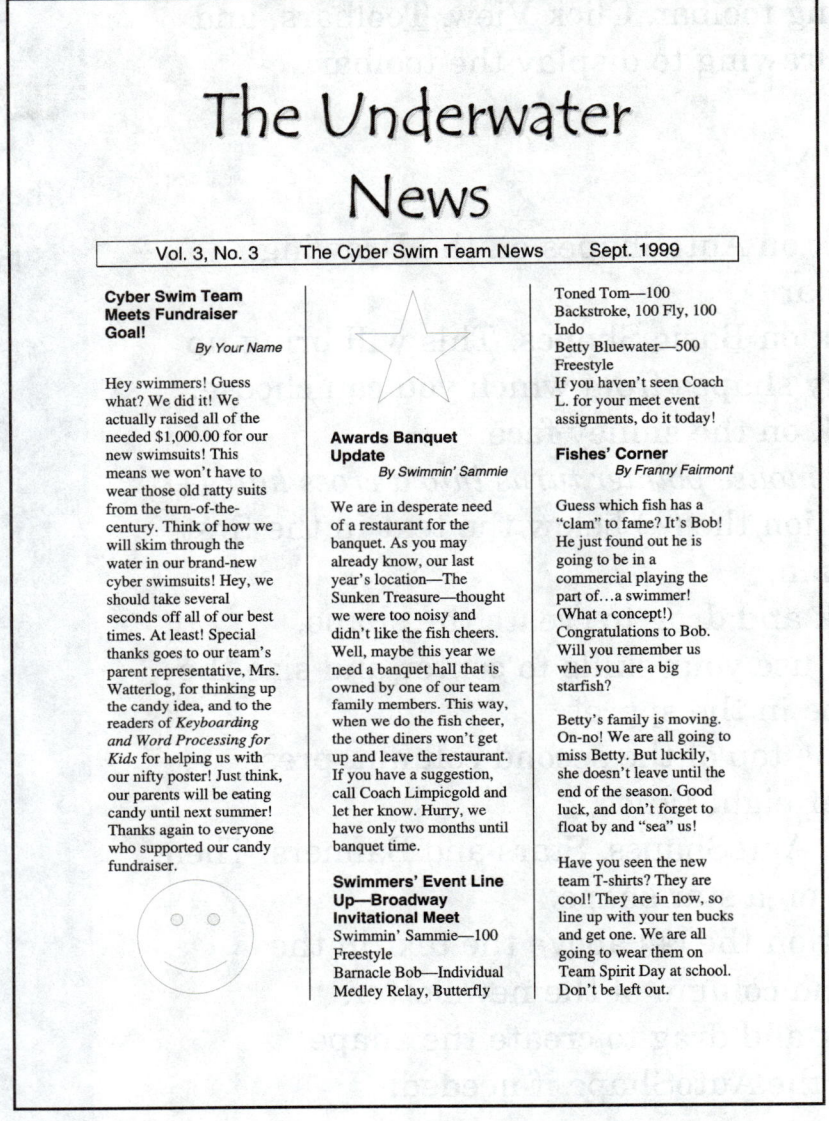 to view your document. *Your newsletter should look like Figure 4-39.*

The Underwater News

| Vol. 3, No. 3 | The Cyber Swim Team News | Sept. 1999 |

Cyber Swim Team Meets Fundraiser Goal!
By Your Name

Hey swimmers! Guess what? We did it! We actually raised all of the needed $1,000.00 for our new swimsuits! This means we won't have to wear those old ratty suits from the turn-of-the-century. Think of how we will skim through the water in our brand-new cyber swimsuits! Hey, we should take several seconds off all of our best times. At least! Special thanks goes to our team's parent representative, Mrs. Watterlog, for thinking up the candy idea, and to the readers of *Keyboarding and Word Processing for Kids* for helping us with our nifty poster! Just think, our parents will be eating candy until next summer! Thanks again to everyone who supported our candy fundraiser.

Awards Banquet Update
By Swimmin' Sammie

We are in desperate need of a restaurant for the banquet. As you may already know, our last year's location—The Sunken Treasure—thought we were too noisy and didn't like the fish cheers. Well, maybe this year we need a banquet hall that is owned by one of our team family members. This way, when we do the fish cheer, the other diners won't get up and leave the restaurant. If you have a suggestion, call Coach Limpicgold and let her know. Hurry, we have only two months until banquet time.

Swimmers' Event Line Up—Broadway Invitational Meet
Swimmin' Sammie—100 Freestyle
Barnacle Bob—Individual Medley Relay, Butterfly

Toned Tom—100 Backstroke, 100 Fly, 100 Indo
Betty Bluewater—500 Freestyle
If you haven't seen Coach L. for your meet event assignments, do it today!

Fishes' Corner
By Franny Fairmont

Guess which fish has a "clam" to fame? It's Bob! He just found out he is going to be in a commercial playing the part of…a swimmer! (What a concept!) Congratulations to Bob. Will you remember us when you are a big starfish?

Betty's family is moving. On-no! We are all going to miss Betty. But luckily, she doesn't leave until the end of the season. Good luck, and don't forget to float by and "sea" us!

Have you seen the new team T-shirts? They are cool! They are in now, so line up with your ten bucks and get one. We are all going to wear them on Team Spirit Day at school. Don't be left out.

Figure 4-39. The completed newsletter

13. Make any adjustments to make your newsletter look good. *Make sure the newsletter stays on one page!*

14. Save your **newslet** document.

Well, you have helped the Cyber Swim Team put together a really great newsletter. You should be proud of your efforts!

THE STATE FINALS

MASCOT MAX

Hey, can I have your autograph? You're that famous newsletter author, aren't you?

Now you're ready to publish your own newsletter! You might want to work with a group of friends, or assign members of your club or team as a committee. Or, work alone—it's up to you!

You'll need to brainstorm and write four articles. Remember to use Word's spell check function to make sure each article is a professional as possible. Then, use the steps in the beginning of the event to create your own newsletter. Did you think you would be a publisher by the end of this Event? Now you are!

EVENT #4
THE PARENT
PARTICIPATION REQUEST
LETTER

In this event you will write a form letter and merge it with a selected mailing list. But, before you start on a letter for your own club, team, or organization, let's help that famous group of swimmers—The Cyber Swim Team—with their parent participation letter. In this event you will learn the following Word skills:

- **Creating a Main Document (Form Letter)**
- **Using Data Source Documents**
- **Inserting Merge Fields**

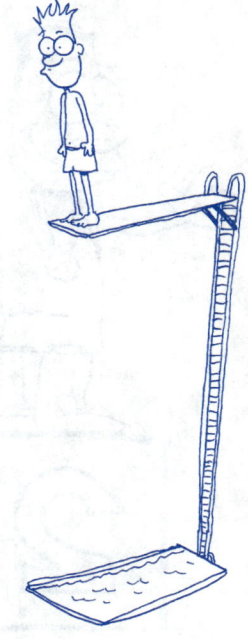

SUIT UP

Coach Carrie Says:

Have you ever needed to send a letter to members of your club, team, or organization? It's amazing how often you need to communicate with other members, parents, or even the community—and letters are a great way to do it.

In this Event, you are going to help the Cyber Swimmers once again. (They are lucky they found you!) This time they are sending a form letter to the parents of the swimmers on their team to ask them to help support their team during the season. The letter is going to ask parents to help participate in a variety of ways.

There are a couple of things you will need to think about as you help the Cyber Swimmers complete their parent letter. First, how could you use a form letter in your own club, team, or organization? What should it be about? Who will it go to? What are the results you want? As you complete the Workouts that follow, be thinking about how you will use the new skills you learn here for yourself or your group.

MEG THE MIKE

Okay, swimmers, time to review some definitions! *Merge*: To combine two things together. In this case, two files. *Data*: A piece or pieces of information.

GETTING YOUR FEET WET

Creating a Main Document (Form Letter)

Coach Carrie Says:

Now, you are ready to review the basic three steps in mail merge! You have already performed a mail merge in Event 1. So, you're about to become a pro. Mail merge really has three main steps: creating a main document, creating a data source document, and inserting merge fields. Now that you know how to do these three steps, you can merge with ease! For a quick review, let's go through these steps again.

MEG THE MIKE

A *form letter* is a letter that is sent to many different people. Each person receives a copy of the same letter, only the names and addresses change.

Trainer Terry Says:

The Main document can be a form letter, a catalog, envelopes, or mailing labels. Let's try making a form letter now!

1. Start Word and open a new document.
2. Click <u>T</u>ools, and then click Mail Merge.
3. Click <u>C</u>reate. Then click Form <u>L</u>etters.
4. Click <u>A</u>ctive Window.

   Now you see the Mail Merge Helper dialog window will have your form letter selection listed as Merge type: Form Letters. You now have two choices; you can edit your form letter, or you can work with your data source. Let's edit our form letter.
5. Click <u>E</u>dit, and then click Form Letter:Document.
6. Type *Dear* and press Enter twice.
7. Type *I am having a birthday party. I hope you can come.*
8. Press Enter twice.
9. Type *Sincerely,* (make sure to include the comma after the word *sincerely*).
10. Press Enter.
11. Type your name.
12. Press Enter.

    This simple, silly form letter will act as your Main document. It should look like Figure 4-40.

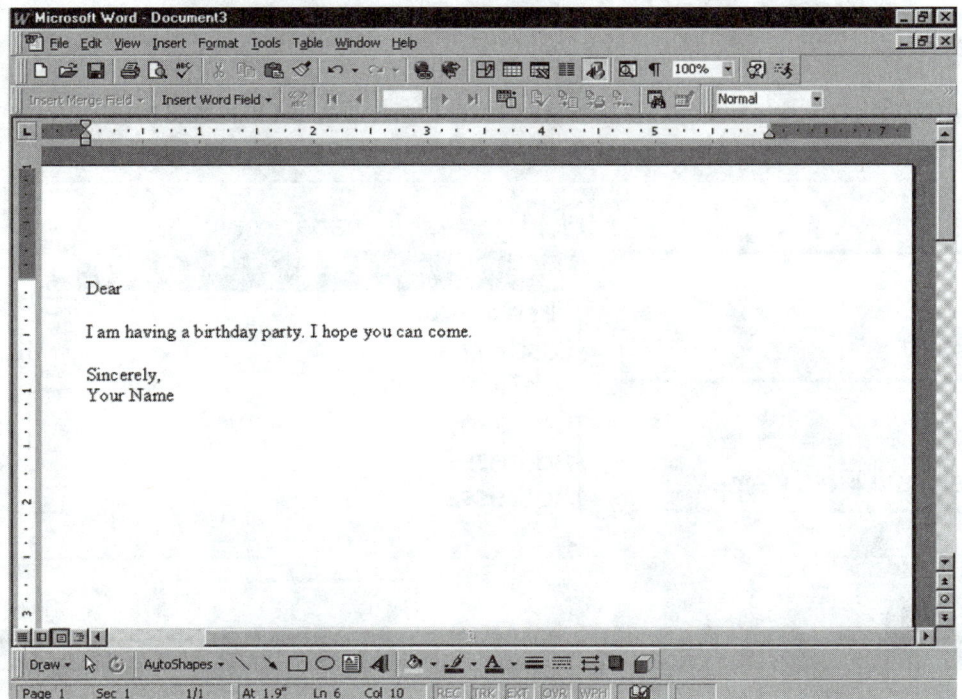

Figure 4-40. Example form letter text

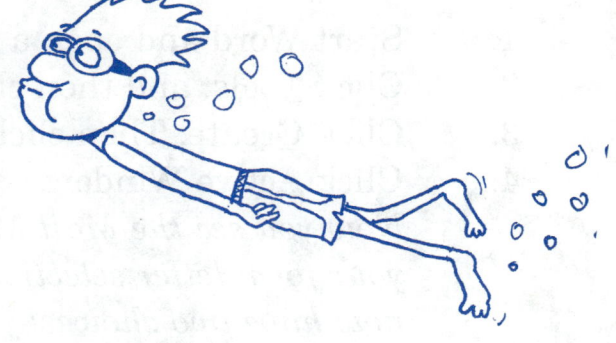

GETTING YOUR FEET WET
Using Data Source Documents

Coach Carrie Says:

Now, you can create a Data Source document and then come back to the form letter document and review inserting merge fields. When you create a data source document, you can choose the fields you would like to include in your main document. Look at Figure 4-41.

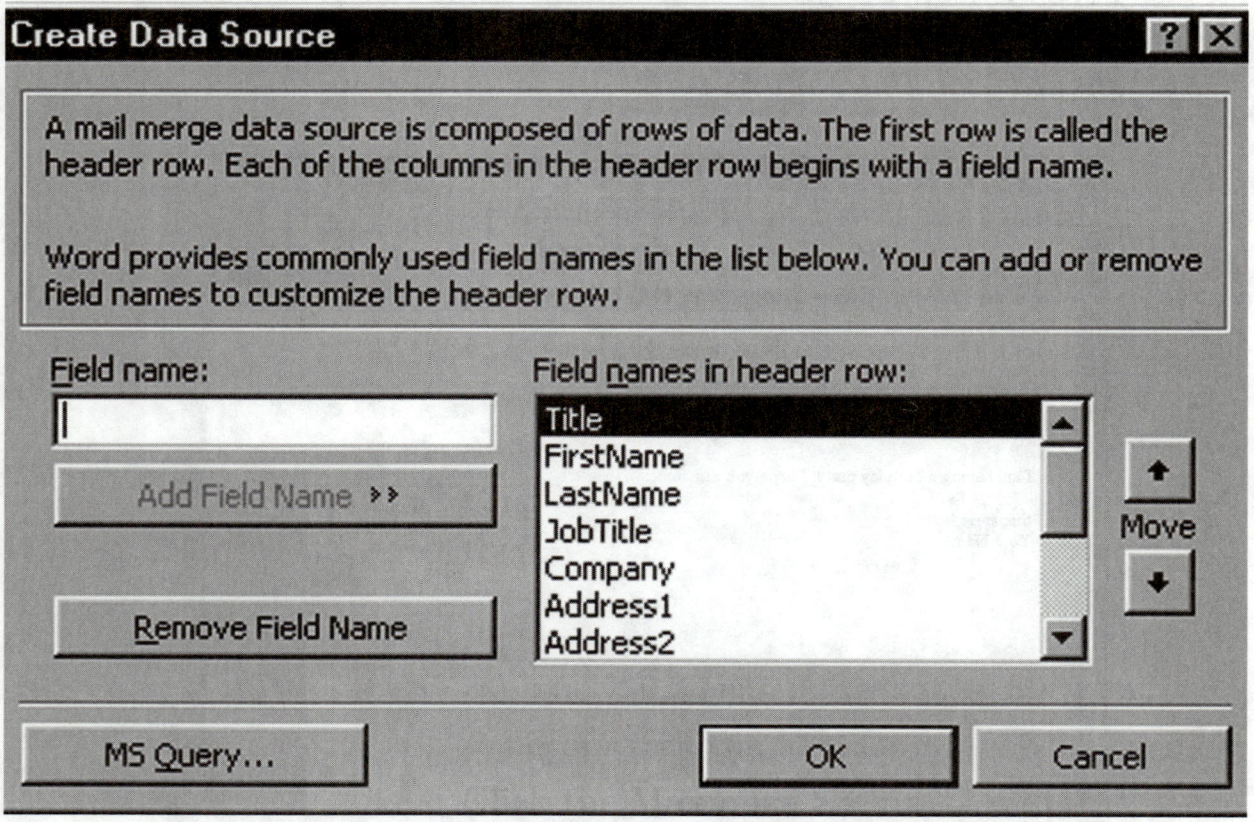

Figure 4-41. The Create Data Source dialog box

You can add and remove fields in the Field names in header row list box. To remove a field, click on the field name in the list box and click Remove Field Name. To add a field name, type the field name in the Field name text box and click Add Field Name. The new field name will appear at the bottom of the Field names in header row list box. Then, you can move the new field name into position by clicking the move arrows, up or down.

Trainer Terry Says:

 Now let's create a data source document.

1. Reopen the Mail Merge Helper by clicking Tools, then Mail Merge.
2. Click Get Data.
3. Click Create Data Source.
4. Click *Title* and remove it, by clicking Remove Field Name.
5. Remove all of the field names except *FirstName*.
   Now you have only one field name in the list box.
6. Click OK.
7. Save the document as **birthday**.
8. Click Edit Data Source.
   Now, you see the Data Form dialog box. This is where you enter the information about each data record.
9. Type *Bill* in the FirstName text box. Click Add New.
   You will now be ready to type your second record.
10. Type *Sandy* in the FirstName text box. Click Add New.
11. Type *Zac* in the FirstName text box. Click Add New.
12. Type *Midori* in the FirstName text box. Click OK to finish adding records to your Data Source document.

That's it! You've finished your data source.

GETTING YOUR FEET WET
Inserting Merge Fields

👓 Now, you will be ready to insert merge fields into your existing form letter. The Insert Merge Field `Insert Merge Field ▾` button on the Mail Merge Toolbar has all the fields you have selected for your main document.

👓 This is a shallow-end drill—wait and see!

1. Make sure your form letter is open and on your screen. Position your cursor right after the word *Dear.* Press the spacebar once.
2. Click the Insert Merge Field button `Insert Merge Field ▾` on the Mail Merge toolbar.
3. Click on FirstName.
   The FirstName merge field will be entered into your document.
4. Add a comma after the <<FirstName>> field.
5. Reopen the Mail Merge Helper by clicking the Mail Merge Helper button 🖼 on the Mail Merge toolbar.
6. Click <u>M</u>erge.
7. In the Merge dialog box, click <u>M</u>erge again.
   Your Data Source document will merge with your Main document like the example in Figure 4-42.

<table>
<tr>
<td>

Dear Bill,

I am having a birthday party. I hope you can come.

Sincerely,
Your Name

</td>
<td>

Dear Sandy,

I am having a birthday party. I hope you can come.

Sincerely,
Your Name

</td>
</tr>
<tr>
<td>

Dear Zac,

I am having a birthday party. I hope you can come.

Sincerely,
Your Name

</td>
<td>

Dear Midori,

I am having a birthday party. I hope you can come.

Sincerely,
Your Name

</td>
</tr>
</table>

Figure 4-42. The completed merge is four pages

8. Close both documents without saving them. This was only practice!

THE COMPETITION

Coach Carrie Says:

It's time to help the Cyber Swim Team create their form letter and perform a mail merge. Remember the **datalist** document you created in Event 1? You are going to use it again for the list of names and addresses you will merge with the Cyber Swimmers' Parent form letter!

LAP 1

Trainer Terry Says:

Let's begin now by creating a form letter for the Cyber Swimmers. This will be our main document.

1. Open a new document.
2. On the menu bar, click <u>T</u>ools and then click Mail Me<u>r</u>ge.
3. In the Main Document section of the Mail Merge Helper dialog box, click <u>C</u>reate.
4. Click Form <u>L</u>etters.
5. Click <u>A</u>ctive Window.
6. Click <u>E</u>dit in the Mail Merge Helper dialog box.
7. Click Form Letter: Document.
   This will allow you to write the form letter.

LAP 2

👓 Now, you are going to use your world-famous keyboarding skills again to enter the text of the form letter.

1. Type *April 30, 1999* and press Enter five times.
2. Type *Dear* and then press Enter.
3. Type *It's that time of year again—fundraiser season! As usual, the Cyber Swimmers are looking for parent support. There are many volunteer opportunities for parents on our team. Some of the Parent Volunteer opportunities include:*
4. Press Enter two times.
5. Type *Team Parents* and press Enter two times.
6. Type *Candy Sale Parent* and press Enter two times.
7. Type *Uniform Parent* and press Enter two times.
8. Type *Banquet Parent Supervisor* and press Enter two times.
9. Type *We hope you will get involved with our swim team this coming year. We are ranked first in our Division. We are very excited about the chance of having an excellent season. I will be sending everyone a swim meet calendar as soon as it is completed. Please let me know if you can volunteer for any of the Parent Jobs. Thank you again for your support.*
10. Press Enter three times.
11. Type *Sincerely,* (and don't forget to include the comma).
12. Press Enter two times.
13. Type *Coach Limpicgold.*
14. Save this letter as **mainletter**.
    Now you have completed the beginning of your form letter. You have the basic text that each parent of the Cyber Swimmers will receive.

LAP 3

Now it's time to use the **datalist** you created in Event 1. Before you merge your documents, you need to insert merge fields into the form letter you just created. This part is simple.

1. Make sure your form letter document, **mainletter** is open.
2. Open the Mail Merge Helper dialog box by clicking <u>T</u>ools and then Mail Me<u>r</u>ge.
3. In the Data Source section of the Mail Merge Helper, click Get Data, then click <u>O</u>pen Data Source.
4. In the Open Data Source dialog box, type **datalist** in the File name text box. Click Open. *If you don't have this file, open **04data** from the student data folder.*
5. Look under <u>G</u>et Data in the Mail Merge Helper and you will now see that the **datalist** is attached to the main document. *Your screen should look like Figure 4-43.*

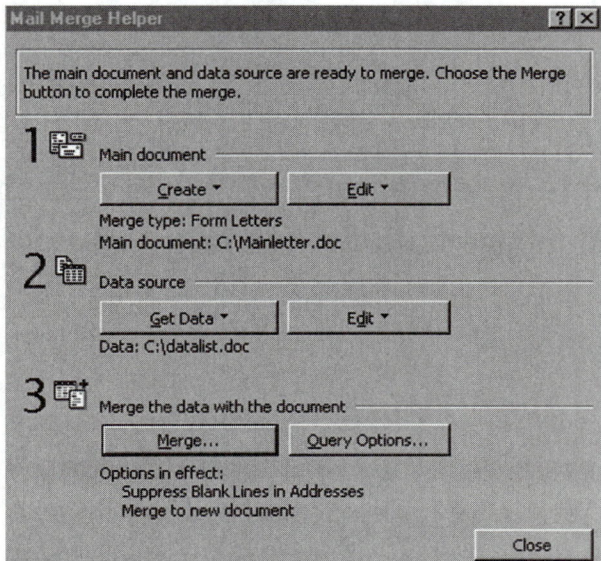

Figure 4-43. Datalist is attached to the main document.

MEG THE MIKE

Okay swimmers! What is a field? And no, I don't mean a grassy piece of land! *Field:* A placeholder for specific data in a Main document file.

LAP 4

Now, let's insert merge fields into your form letter.

1. Click the Insert Merge Field button 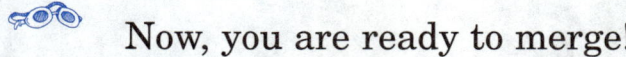 and click *Title*. Press the spacebar once.

2. Click the Insert Merge Field button and click *FirstName* Press the spacebar once.

3. Click the Insert Merge Field button and click *LastName* Press the spacebar once.

4. Press Enter once to start a new line.

5. Click the Insert Merge Field button and click *Swimmer*. Press Enter once.

6. Click the Insert Merge Field button and click *Address1*. Press Enter again to start a new line.

7. Click the Insert Merge Field button and click *City*.

8. Add a comma after <<City>> and press the spacebar.

9. Click the Insert Merge Field button and click *State*. Press the spacebar.

10. Click the Insert Merge Field button and click *PostalCode*. Press Enter.

11. After the word *Dear,* enter the merge field *Title*. Press the spacebar and enter the merge field *LastName*.

Now, you are ready to merge!

LAP 5

Check to make sure you see both your main document and your data source document attached in the Mail Merge Helper dialog box. Your main document will be under Create in the Main document section of the box, and your data source document will be under Get Data in the Data source section of the box.

1. In the Mail Merge Helper dialog box, click the Merge button.

2. In the Merge dialog box that appears, click Merge again.
    Your form letter will appear.

3. Scroll through the document (all five pages) and check your completed form letters.

4. Save this file as **parents**.

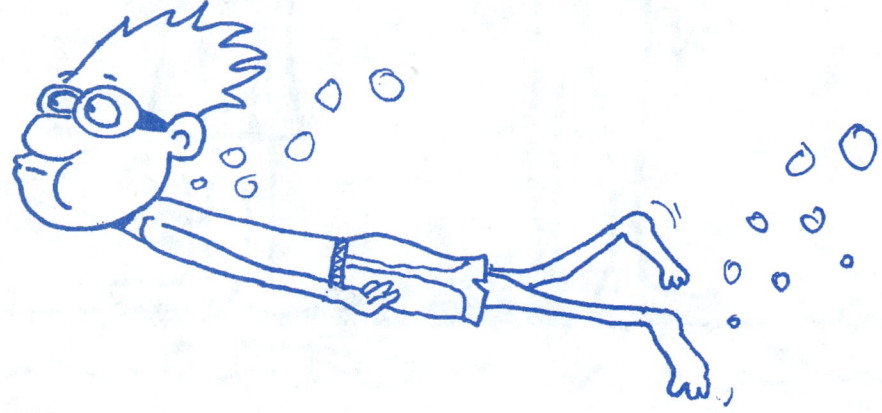

THE STATE FINALS

Now that you have had experience using a data source document and a form letter, why not go further with the mailing list of your friends you made in the State Finals of the Event 1 in this Season? Write a form letter to send to your friends, and merge your pre-existing data source document—just like you did for the swimmers! The results will be a cool form letter you can use to keep in touch with your friends! Why not make birthday party invitations this way? Or, maybe you'll decide to just send a short, informative letter to your friends. Either way, you will be using your new skills to the best advantage!

EVENT #5
THE AWARDS BANQUET
PROGRAM:
IN THE WINNER'S CIRCLE!

In this Event, you'll learn how to make a brochure that you can customize to fit the needs of your own team, club, or organization. Once again, you'll get involved helping that famous group of swimmers—The Cyber Swimmers—as they get ready for their long-awaited Awards Banquet. In this Event, you'll learn how to use:

- Landscape Orientation
- WordArt
- Text Boxes
- Art Borders

SUIT UP

Coach Carrie Says:

Clubs, teams, and different organizations often have special events like a play, or a concert, or a banquet. Often, such events need some kind of a program. A *program* is a small brochure or pamphlet that gives people information about what is going to happen at an event or function, such as the schedule, the speaker, the performers, or even a dinner or lunch menu.

You can make many different kinds of programs. In this Event, the Cyber Swimmers need a program for their Awards Banquet. They don't have much money, so they need to make a program that includes all the info, but is also inexpensive to make.

Franny (the Fish) Fairmont knows how make a one-page program printed on both sides. In this Event you will learn how to print a document in *Landscape* orientation (in other words, sideways!).

You'll also dive into *WordArt*—a feature of Word that lets you make the text you enter look artistic and exciting. You will learn to use *Art Borders*—which lets you add art around the edges of your document. You will use the Drawing toolbar and you'll review lots of Word Processing tricks. Now, it's time to get your feet wet, so let's go swimming in the Workout pool!

GETTING YOUR FEET WET

Landscape Orientation

Coach Carrie Says:

Landscape orientation means horizontal page layout. Most of the time you create documents in *portrait orientation*. Portrait orientation is vertical page layout. This book, for example, has a portrait orientation.

Word's default page layout is portrait orientation. If you want to change paper orientation, you can do so in the Page Setup Dialog box. Just click the <u>F</u>ile menu and click Page Set<u>u</u>p. Then click the Paper <u>S</u>ize tab, as shown in Figure 4-46. For the Cyber Swimmer's Banquet Program you are going to use landscape orientation.

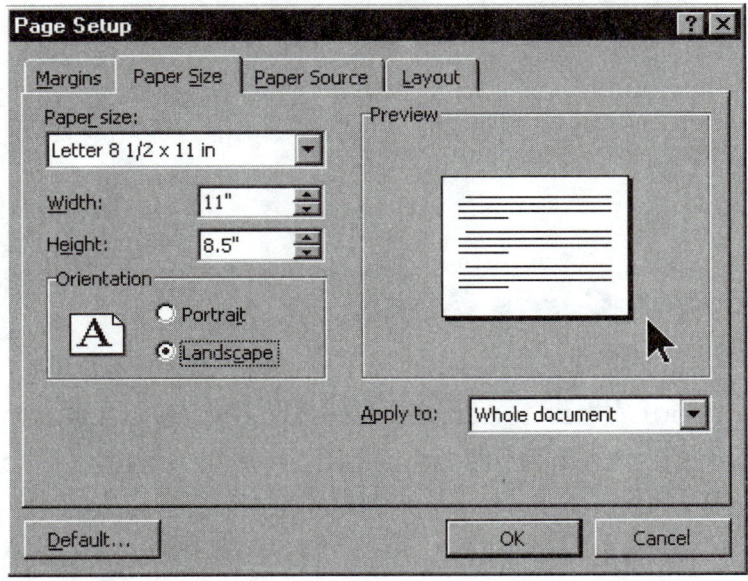

Figure 4-46. Page Setup dialog box, landscape orientation

Trainer Terry Says:

 Let's practice saving a document with landscape orientation.

1. Start Word and open a new document.
2. Click File, then Page Setup, and click on the Paper Size tab.
3. Now, find the Option Button called Landscape and click on it. *This will make the text you enter in this document appear just like in the Preview area. Now you have a document with a landscape page orientation. Good work!*
4. Click OK.
5. Leave the document open for the next Workout.

 Now you're ready to practice with WordArt!

GETTING YOUR FEET WET
WordArt

Coach Carrie Says:

 WordArt is cool. This feature of Word lets you create really creative looking text. But here is the interesting thing—WordArt isn't actually text once it's entered, it is considered a graphic and Word deals with it as if it is one. This means you can move it and size it like a picture. Later in the Competition section of this event, you will use WordArt for the Cyber Swimmers' Program.

Trainer Terry Says:

Back in the water—it's time to become an artist!

1. Make sure your landscape orientation document is still open.
2. Display the Drawing toolbar by clicking <u>V</u>iew, then <u>T</u>oolbars, and then Drawing.
3. Click on the Insert WordArt button ⬛.
    You will see the WordArt Gallery Dialog Box, as in Figure 4-47.

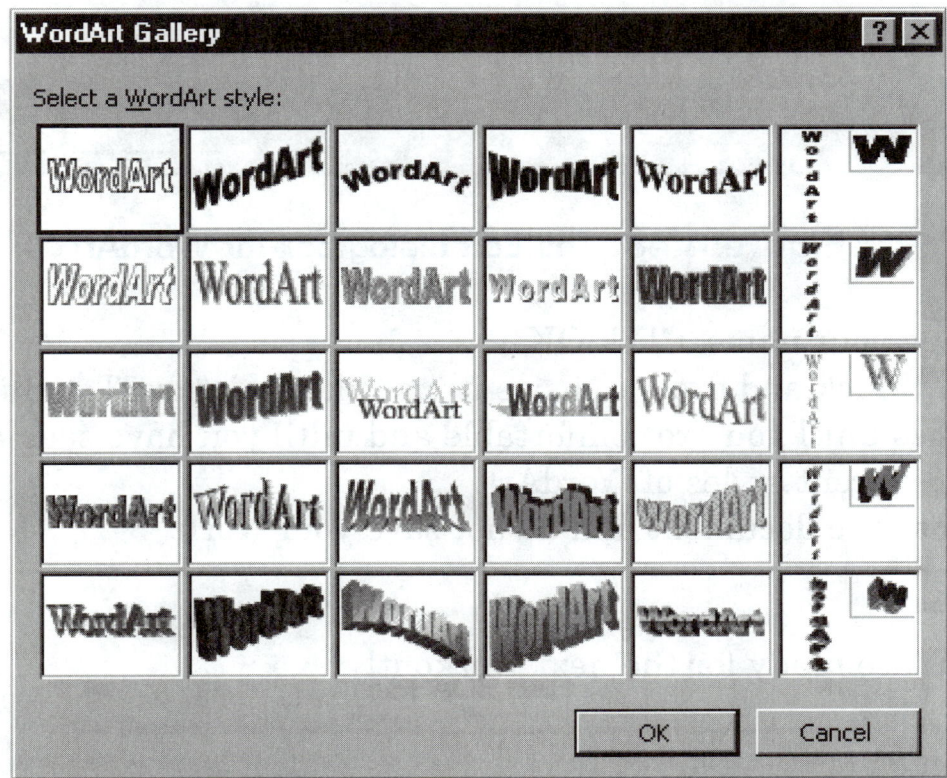

Figure 4-47. WordArt Gallery dialog box

4. Double-click on a piece of WordArt.
    The Edit dialog box for WordArt will open for you to write text that you want magically transformed into art! See Figure 4-48.

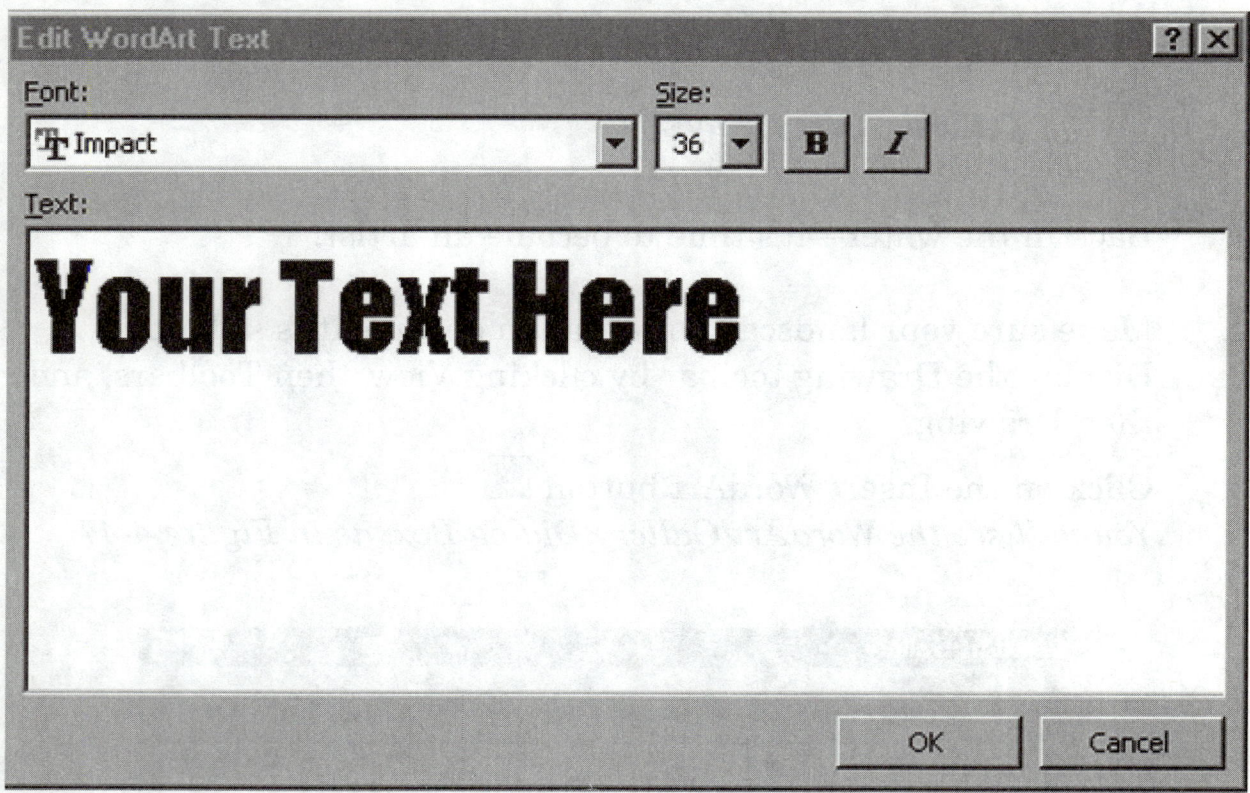

Figure 4-48. The Edit dialog box for WordArt

5. Type your name. Click OK.
6. Now, click and drag and size it just like a picture. Try this a few times until you are comfortable and until you have seen a bunch of different styles of WordArt.
7. Close the document and do not save your work.

You are ready for the next Workout!

GETTING YOUR FEET WET
Text Boxes

Coach Carrie Says:

Now you are going to get your feet wet working with Text Boxes!
Text boxes are boxes you can create right in a document page that
work just like mini-documents. You can position the cursor and
add or paste text into a Text Box in the same way that you would
do it in a document. This works very well when you are making
something artistic—like a program!

Trainer Terry Says:

Okay, swimmers! Let's workout with Text Boxes!

1. Open a new document.

2. On the Drawing toolbar, click on the Text Box button 🄰.
    Your cursor will turn into a cross hair (+).

3. Click and drag until you make a box.

4.	Now, repeat steps 2 and 3 to make more Text Boxes.
5.	Practice resizing the Text Boxes by clicking on the borders dragging them.
6.	Now, practice writing text in the text box and changing font and font sizes.
7.	When you're finished, leave your document open for practice with Art Borders.

Easy, isn't it? One great thing about text boxes is they format just like mini document pages. You can edit the text inside the text box, too.

GETTING YOUR FEET WET
Art Borders

Coach Carrie Says:

You have already learned a lot about borders in the last Event. However, you haven't had a chance to use Art Borders yet! These are really fun and will make a splash on any program.

Trainer Terry Says:

Your Text Box document should be open on your screen. Good! Okay, let's dive in! We'll start by opening the Borders and Shading dialog box.

1. Click F<u>o</u>rmat, then click <u>B</u>orders and Shading.
2. Click the <u>P</u>age Border tab.
3. Click on the down arrow in the A<u>r</u>t list box and select a border you like.
4. Click OK.
5. Try a few!
   Hey, that was easy!

MASCOT MAX

Great Workout swimmers! Now you are ready (once again) to help the Cyber Swimmers. And boy, do they need you here!

THE COMPETITION

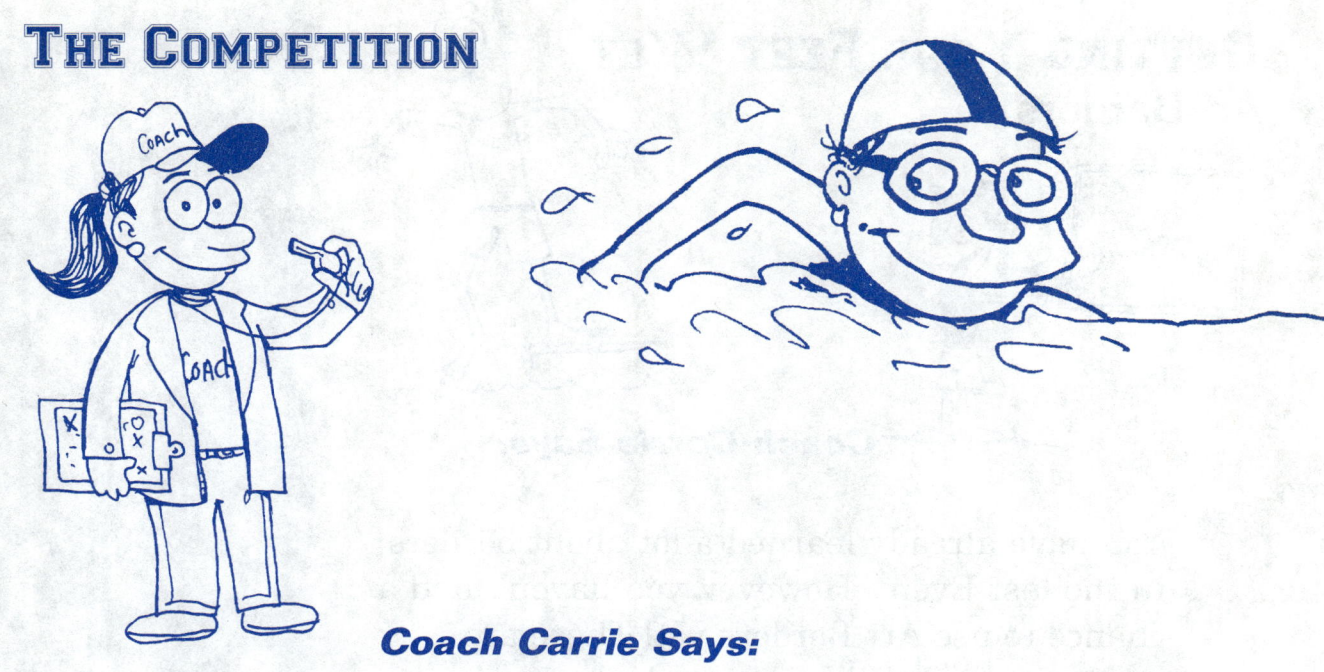

Coach Carrie Says:

In this Event, you'll work out with all the tools you need to make a useful program for the Cyber Swimmers. Now, you are ready to help the Cyber Swim Team make an awesome program for their Awards Banquet!

Now, swimmers, before we start, let's get a picture in our minds about what this program is going to look like. Take a look at Figure 4-49. This shows the outside of the program.

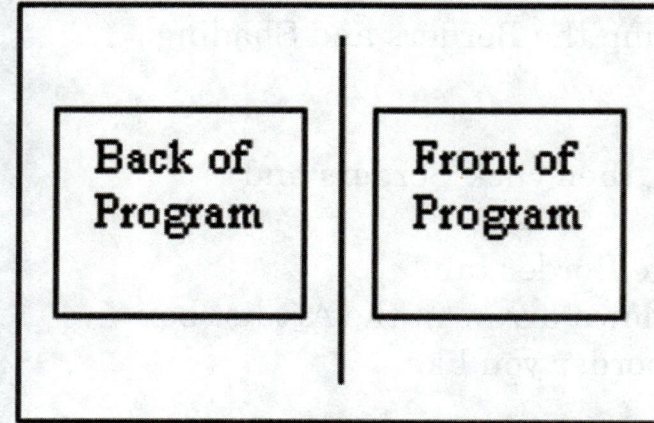

Figure 4-49. Program layout example—outside

Now look at Figure 4-50. This shows the inside of the program.

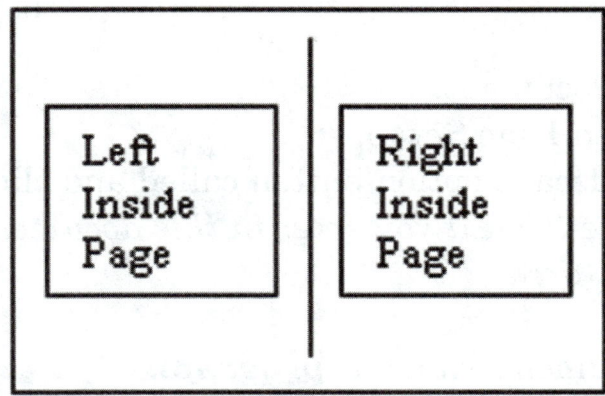

Figure 4-50. Program layout example—inside

As you go on from here, it will be clear which part of the program you are working on. If you have realized the finished program will actually be two formatted pages, you're correct. It is only after you copy them that the program will become one page! Let's move on with the Competition!

Trainer Terry Says:

Swimmers up! Keyboarders and word processors on your mark! First we'll set up the document in landscape orientation.

LAP 1

1. Open a New document.
2. Click <u>F</u>ile, then Page Set<u>u</u>p.
3. Find the Land<u>s</u>cape option button called and click on it.
   This will make the text you enter in this document appear just like in the Preview area.
4. Click OK.
5. Save this document. Name it **program.**

LAP 2

Now, let's work on the front of the program. It needs to be special to draw people's attention to the program and get them to read it. The Cyber Swimmers have decided to use WordArt.

1. Make sure the Drawing toolbar is displayed. If not, click <u>V</u>iew, then <u>T</u>oolbars, and then Picture.

2. Click on the WordArt Button [4] .
   You will see the WordArt Gallery dialog box.

3. Click on the fifth piece of WordArt from the left in the top row (it curves up), and then click OK.

4. In the Edit WordArt text box, type *The Cyber Swimmers'*, and press Enter.

5. Type *20th Annual* and press Enter.

6. Type *Awards Banquet* and click OK.
   *Now your WordArt will be imported into your **program** document.*

7. Click to select the WordArt and position it in the top half of the inside right page of the program, as in Figure 4-51.

Figure 4-51. WordArt position in **program** document

LAP 3

Next, we'll organize the program with text boxes.

1. On the Drawing toolbar, click on the Text Box button .
   You will notice that your cursor looks like a plus sign.
2. Click and drag until you make a box right across from the WordArt in the upper-left outside page of the program. Your document should look like Figure 4-52.

Figure 4-52. Text box example

MASCOT MAX

That was easy! This program is going to make a splash! Ok, moving right along to Text Boxes. You won't believe how easy it is to move text from one document to another with these handy little things!

3. Now, make two more text boxes. Make the first one about the same size, directly below the first text box. Make the second one a little larger, directly below the WordArt.
Your document should look like Figure 4-53.

Figure 4-53. Your **program** document

LAP 4

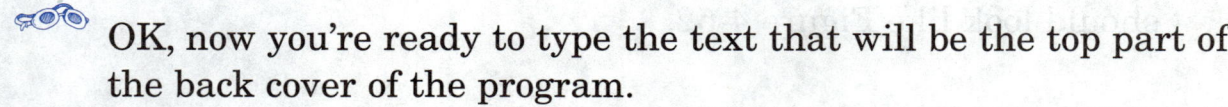 OK, now you're ready to type the text that will be the top part of the back cover of the program.

1. Make sure the insertion point is inserted in the upper-left box.
2. Type *Award Winners* and press Enter.
3. Type *MVP (Most Valuable Player)—Franny Fairmont* and press Enter.
4. Type *Most Improved—Barnacle Bob* and press Enter.
5. Type *Team Spirit Award—Swimmin' Sammie* and press Enter.
6. Type *New Team Captain—Betty Bluewater* and press Enter.
7. Type *Most Valuable Parent—Mrs. Watterlog* and press Enter.

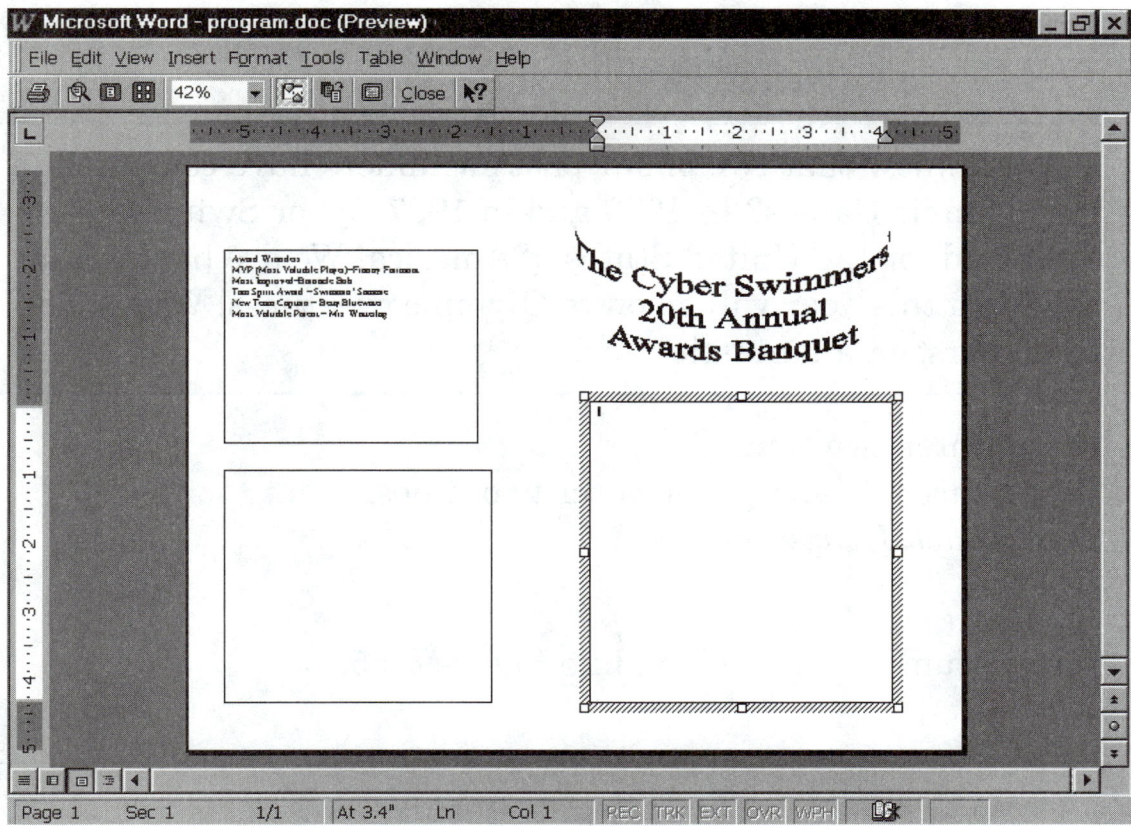

Figure 4-54. Text inserted into first text box

LAP 5

Now, let's add the bottom part of the back cover of the program—a letter from Coach Limpicgold to the Swimmers and their parents.

1. Place the insertion point in the lower left box.
2. Type *Dear Swimmers, Parents, and Friends,* and press Enter two times.
3. Type the following paragraph:

> The Cyber Swim Team started in 1979. This year marks our 20th year as a Swimming force in Aqua City! We are proud to announce that we won our division title this year and that several of our swimmers are going to compete in the nationals!

4.	Press Enter two times.

5.	Type the following paragraph:

> Did you know that two of our past swimmers have competed in the Olympic Games? In 1979 and in 1987 Cyber Swimmers competed for the United States of America! We are hoping that our team this year will go on to Olympic greatness! Way to go, swimmers, on a fantastic year!

6.	Press Enter two times.

7.	Type *Sincerely,* and press Enter two times.

8.	Type *Coach Limpicgold*.

 Your document should look like Figure 4-55.

Award Winners
MVP (Most Valuable Player)—Franny Fairmont
Most Improved—Barnacle Bob
Team Spirit Award—Swimmin' Sammie
New Team Captain—Betty Bluewater
Most Valuable Parent—Mrs. Watterlog

The Cyber Swimmers
20th Annual
Awards Banquet

Dear Swimmers, Parents, and Friends,

The Cyber Swim Team started in 1979. This year marks our 20th year as a Swimming force in Aqua City! We are proud to announce that we won our division title this year and that several of our swimmers are going to compete in the nationals!

Did you know that two of our past swimmers have competed in the Olympic Games? In 1979 and in 1987 Cyber Swimmers competed for the United States of America! We are hoping that our team this year will go on to Olympic greatness! Way to go, swimmers, on a fantastic year!

Sincerely,

Coach Limpicgold

Figure 4-55. Text boxes and text in the **program** document

LAP 6

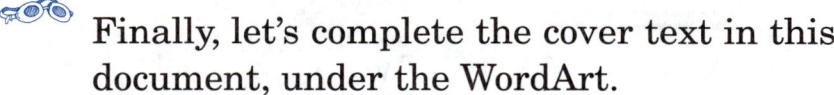

Finally, let's complete the cover text in this document, under the WordArt.

1. Click on the inside of the text box underneath the WordArt.
2. Type *Friday, April 27, 1999* and press Enter two times.
3. Type *The Fish Fry Pavilion* and press Enter two times.
4. Type *Aqua City* and press Enter two times.
5. Select the text in the box, and change the font to Tempus Sans ITC, 20 point. *Use another font if you don't have this one.*
6. With the text still selected, click the Center button ▤ to center your text.

MASCOT MAX

Remember to save your work!

LAP 7

1. Move your insertion point to the second blank line under *Aqua City*. Click the Center button ▤ if the line isn't centered.
2. Click Insert, Picture, and select Clip Art.
3. Now select a piece of fish clip art, and click Insert. Size and position the picture as necessary.
4. Use the Picture toolbar to make the clip art black and white. (Hint: Click the Image Control button ◧.)
5. Save **program** and print it.

Great! You are almost done. Your document should look like Figure 4-56.

Figure 4-56. Program—outside

LAP 8

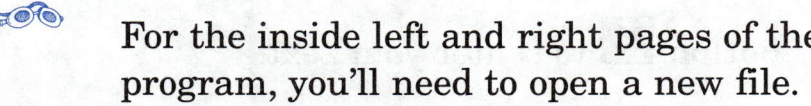 For the inside left and right pages of the program, you'll need to open a new file.

1. Open a new document and save it as **inside**.
2. Set the orientation to Landscape. (Hint: Click <u>F</u>ile, Page Set<u>u</u>p.)
3. Click on the Text Box button ▣ on the Drawing toolbar and create a text box on the left inside page of the program.
4. Make sure the insertion point is in the text box.
5. Type *Tonight's Program Schedule* and press Enter two times.
6. Type *5:00—The Fish Choir* and press Enter two times.
7. Type *5:30—Opening Remarks—Coach Limpicgold* and press Enter two times.
8. Type *6:00—Dinner* and press Enter two times.
9. Type *7:30—Awards Presentation, Franny Fairmont* and press Enter two times.

JEFF THE REF

Remember, if you make a mistake, just click <u>E</u>dit, <u>U</u>ndo to undo what you've done!

10. Type *8:30—Installation of new Team Captain* and press Enter two times.
11. Type *8:45—Team Photo and Good-byes* and press Enter two times.
12. Underline, center, and bold *Tonight's Program Schedule*.
13. Select all the text in the text box by clicking <u>E</u>dit, and then Select <u>A</u>ll.
14. With the text selected, choose Arial, 22 point.
15. Click the Print Preview button [icon] on the toolbar. *Your Left Inside Page should look like Figure 4-57.*

<u>**Tonight's Schedule**</u>

5:00—The Fish Choir

5:30—Opening Remarks—
Coach Limpicgold

6:00—Dinner

7:30—Awards Presentation,
Franny Fairmont

8:30—Installation of new
Team Captain

8:45—Team Photo and
Good-byes

Figure 4-57. Text box—inside left page

JEFF THE REF

Remember, documents will have spell-check underlines in them unless you turn it off. They will show up for proper names and other words that you have chosen on purpose. It won't look like this in the printed document, though!

MASCOT MAX

Great job. Did you spell check and proofread? I knew I could count on you—you're a pro!

LAP 9

These steps will be similar to what you did for the left inside page!

1. Click on the Text Box Button on the Drawing toolbar and create a text box on the right inside page of the program. Make the Text Box look like the one on the left inside page.
2. Make sure the insertion point is in the text box.
3. Type *Banquet Menu* and press Enter two times.
4. Type *Waterside Salad topped with Baby Shrimp* and press Enter two times.
5. Type *Chef's Surprise Clam Chowder* and press Enter two times.
6. Type *Fresh Catch of the Day* and press Enter two times.
7. Type *Browned Baby Potatoes* and press Enter two times.
8. Type *Vegetable Medley with Cheese* and press Enter two times.
9. Type *Chocolate Swimmer Individual Sculpture Cakes* and press Enter two times.
10. Type *Coffee, Tea, Milk, and Soft Drinks*.
11. Underline, center, and bold *Banquet Menu*.
12. Select all the text in the text box by clicking Edit, and then Select All.
13. With the text selected, choose Arial and 22 point.
Your Right Inside Page should look like Figure 4-58.

Banquet Menu

Waterside Salad topped with
Baby Shrimp

Chef's Surprise Clam Chowder

Fresh Catch of the Day

Browned Baby Potatoes

Vegetable Medley with Cheese

Chocolate Swimmer Individual
Sculpture Cakes

Coffee, Tea, Milk, and Soft
Drinks

Figure 4-58. Text box—inside right page

LAP 10

Now, let's add a fancy border, and you are through!

1. Click Format, click on Borders and Shading, click on Page Border.
2. Select an art border from the Art drop-down list. Click on the border you want and then click OK.
   It is a good idea to select a black and white border with clean lines so it will print well later.
3. Save **inside** and print it.
   Your document should look like Figure 4-59.

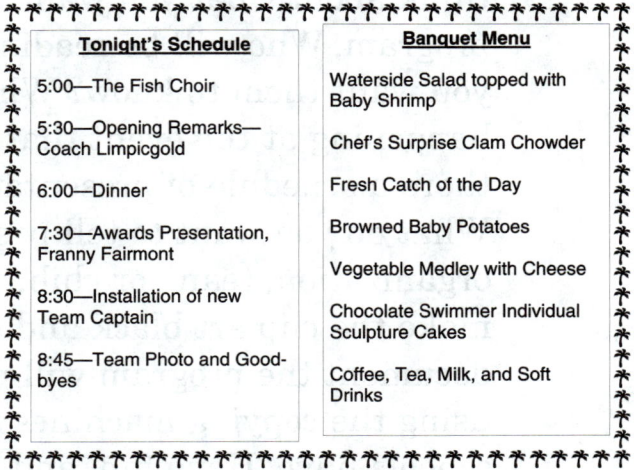

Figure 4-59. Finished inside of program

MASCOT MAX

Wow, what an event! And you even have a beautiful program for your scrapbook!

 When you're ready to print, just do the following steps.

- First, print copies of the **poster** document.
- Second, put the **poster** copies in the copier's paper tray to copy on the *blank* side of the paper.
- Third, put the inside document in the copier and print this.
- Your copies should have the **poster** document on one side and the **inside** document on the other!

 (This can be tricky! So you should try a couple and be sure that you are printing the pages correctly.) Fold, and you are ready for your event!

THE STATE FINALS

 Use what you have learned in this Event to make your own program. Before you start, think about what you want to say with the program. Who will be reading it? What do you want them to know? What will be happening at the event that is important? Is there a schedule of presentations? A menu? What do you want to tell people about your organization, team, or club? Remember, if you make the clip art black and white in your document the program will print more nicely using the copying machines that most schools have. Have fun, and have a great event! Your program will be a souvenir that people will keep for years to come!

460

EVENT #6
THE TEAM WEB PAGE:
WELCOME TO AQUA LAND!

In this final Event, you'll learn how to make a Web page using Word! After finishing this event, you will have all of the skills you need to create your own Web site! As you might have imagined, you'll get involved once more helping that famous group of swimmers—The Cyber Swimmers—as they create their very first team Web page! In this Event you'll learn:

- **Web for Beginners**
- **The Word Web Page Wizard**
- **Selecting a Visual Style**
- **Web Toolbars in Word**
- **Inserting a Hyperlink**

SUIT UP

MEG THE MIKE

OK, swimmers, listen up to some Internet definitions!

E-mail—letters sent electronically over the Internet or an Intranet.

Newsgroups—a group discussion about a specific subject. You can ask a question or put up (post) information and then other people can respond to what you have posted.

Chat—talking to people around the globe. When you chat with someone they respond to your message immediately!

The World Wide Web—the part of the Internet in which Web sites are used.

Coach Carrie Says:

What do you know about the Internet? What do you know about Web pages? In this Event, you are going to learn a lot about both—and you are going to learn all the skills you need to make your own Web page using Word. This final Event is a celebration for a winning season! Congratulations on becoming a Word pro. You will be amazed how valuable learning to make a Web page is and how many different things you can use a Web page for—to connect to your neighborhood, school, and community; even the rest of the world!

The Internet is actually millions of computers hooked together. This is the simple definition. A computer expert could give you days of information about the Internet and how it works. But the basics are simple. Millions of people with computers, all over the world, connect to each other's computers using the Internet. The Internet has lots of different kinds of tools that people have created to use.

 The World Wide Web has millions of Web pages. These are pages that people have created to tell about their school, business, club, idea, or any subject that interests them. People use them to advertise and sell things, and some people use them to express their opinions, or give information.

 Now, it's time to learn the basics about Web pages in the Workout section of this Event. Cyber Swimmers on your mark!

GETTING YOUR FEET WET
Web for Beginners!

— Coach Carrie Says:

 Before you begin to learn how to create a Web page you need to learn a little bit about Web pages. Web pages are created with a language called *HTML* (HyperText Markup Lanuguage). It used to be that you couldn't make a Web page unless you knew this special language. Now, however, many applications, like Microsoft Word, have been developed to make creating Web pages a lot easier. You don't even have to learn HTML! Look at the Training Table on the next page to learn some basic terms that you need to know to understand Web pages.

JEFF THE REF

Be safe online— never give out your real name or address, and always make sure an adult knows if you have any uncomfortable experiences!

Training Table: WWW Basics

Term	It Is...
HTML	HyperText Markup Language: the name of the special language used to make Web pages
HTTP	HyperText Transfer Protocol: the way information is transferred on the Internet
URL	Uniform Resource Locator: the name of a Web site address. URLs can looks like this: www.cyber.com
Web Page	text, graphics, and sometimes audio and video clips that a person or organization creates to represent themselves on the World Wide Web
Web Site	a location on the Internet that represents a company, organization, topic, or individual. A Web site is made up of Web pages
Home Page	the first or beginning page of a Web site
Hyperlinks	the portions of a Web page that connects it, or links it, to another Web page. When you click on a link, you can jump to another Web page
Search Engines	a searching tool designed to search the Web for Web pages that have specific keywords
Web Browsers	a software tool designed to navigate the World Wide Web

Coach Carrie Says:

Think of it like this: The *Internet* is like millions of highways that are connected to each other all over the world. The *World Wide Web* is like all the cities that the highways go through.

A Web *browser* is like the race car you drive in on the Internet. It helps you get to all the places you can visit on the World Wide Web.

Your *Web page* is like your own house, with your own stuff. You can invite people in to look and have them do things while they visit. Your "stuff" can be pictures, sound, text, games, video clips, and more!

A *hyperlink* is a way of quickly going from one place, or page, to another. Think of it like a channel changer—one click and you are on a new page!

A *search engine* is like a guidebook with a really good index. Now, let's look at the special features that Word offers for Web page creation!

GETTING YOUR FEET WET
The Web Page Wizard!

Coach Carrie Says:

Using the Web Page Wizard is a lot of fun—you'll be amazed at all of the features ready for you to use immediately. First, let's take a look at what you see when you use the Web Page Wizard!

MEG THE MIKE

What's a wizard? You may think that a wizard is a magical creature that casts spells! But in computer terms, a *Wizard* is a program that you guides you step-by-step as you create something. There are all kinds of Wizards—such as Fax Wizards, Letter Wizards, and Web Page Wizards.

JEFF THE REF

If you don't have a Web Pages tab in the new dialog box, that means that a complete installation of Word was not done on your computer. Talk to your teacher or parents to have them install Word again.

GETTING YOUR FEET WET

Selecting a Visual Style

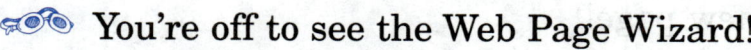

Trainer Terry Says:

You're off to see the Web Page Wizard!

1. Click on File and the New, and then the Web Pages tab in the New document dialog box. *You will see the Web Page Wizard dialog box appear as shown in Figure 4-60.*

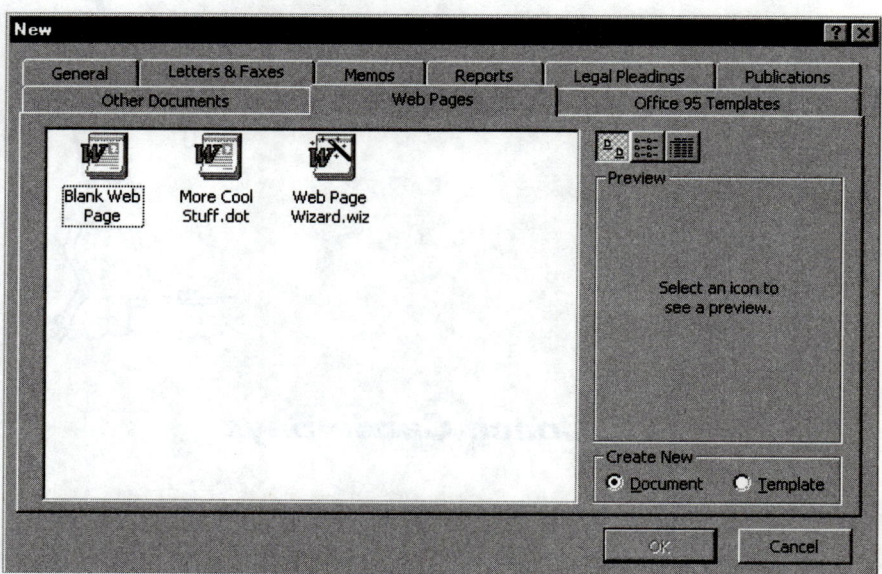

Figure 4-60. The Web Page tab of the New dialog box

2. Click on Web Page Wizard and then OK.
   If you have your modem on, when you click OK, a dialog box opens asking if you want to connect to the Internet.

3. In the Web Page Wizard dialog box that appears, click Centered Layout, and then click <u>N</u>ext.
   You will now see the dialog box that lets you select the Visual Style of your Web page. It looks like the example shown in Figure 4-61.

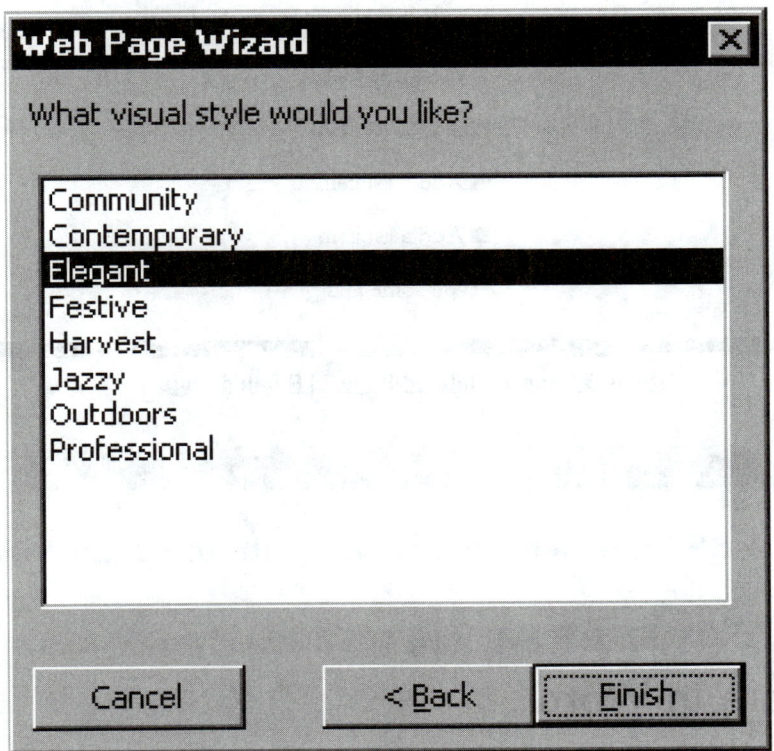

Figure 4-61. You can choose a visual style with the Web Page Wizard.

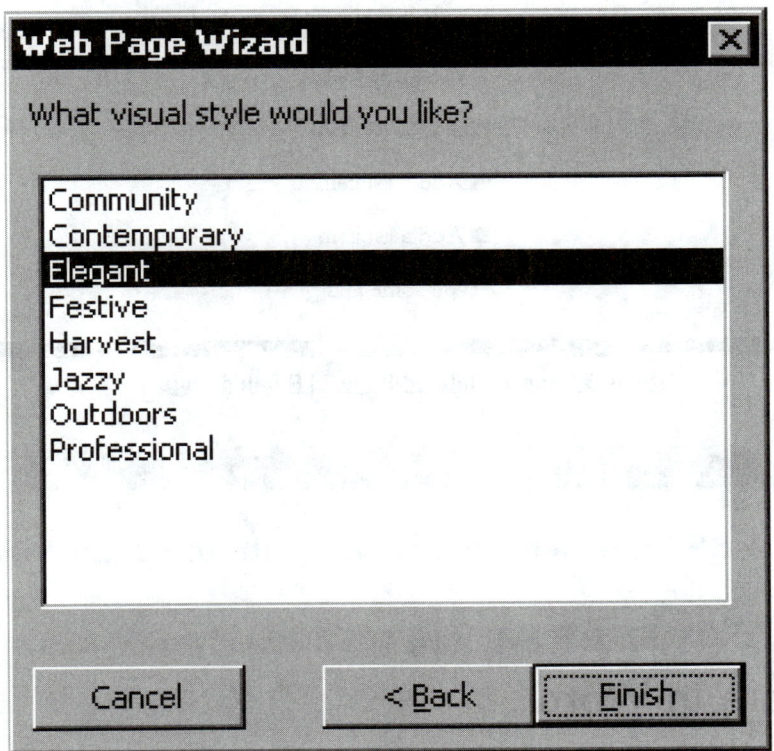 Now, before you choose a visual style, take a look around. Click on all the visual styles and watch the page change!

4. Choose Jazzy and click <u>F</u>inish.
   Your screen should like Figure 4-62.

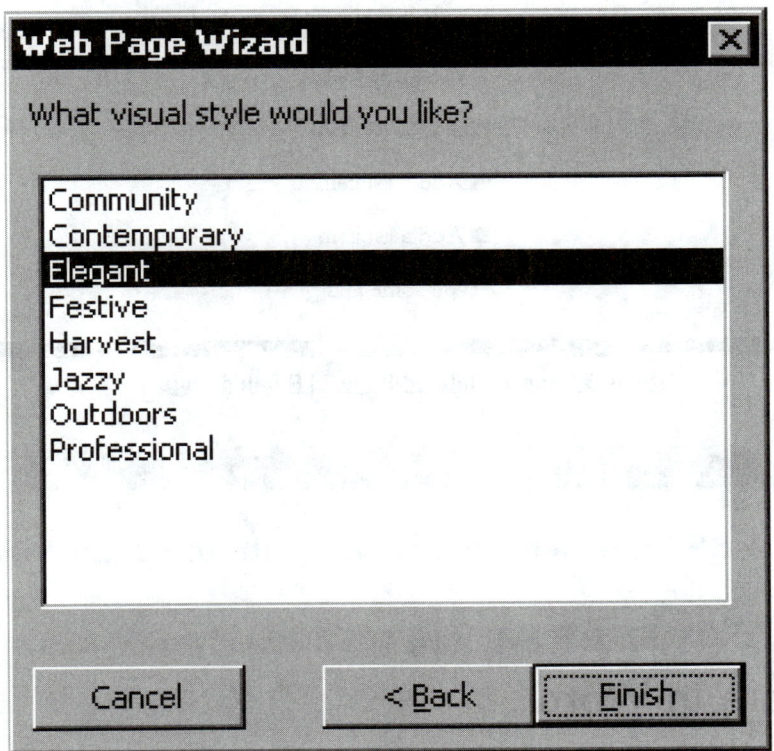 Good job! Now let's learn some cool toolbar tricks.

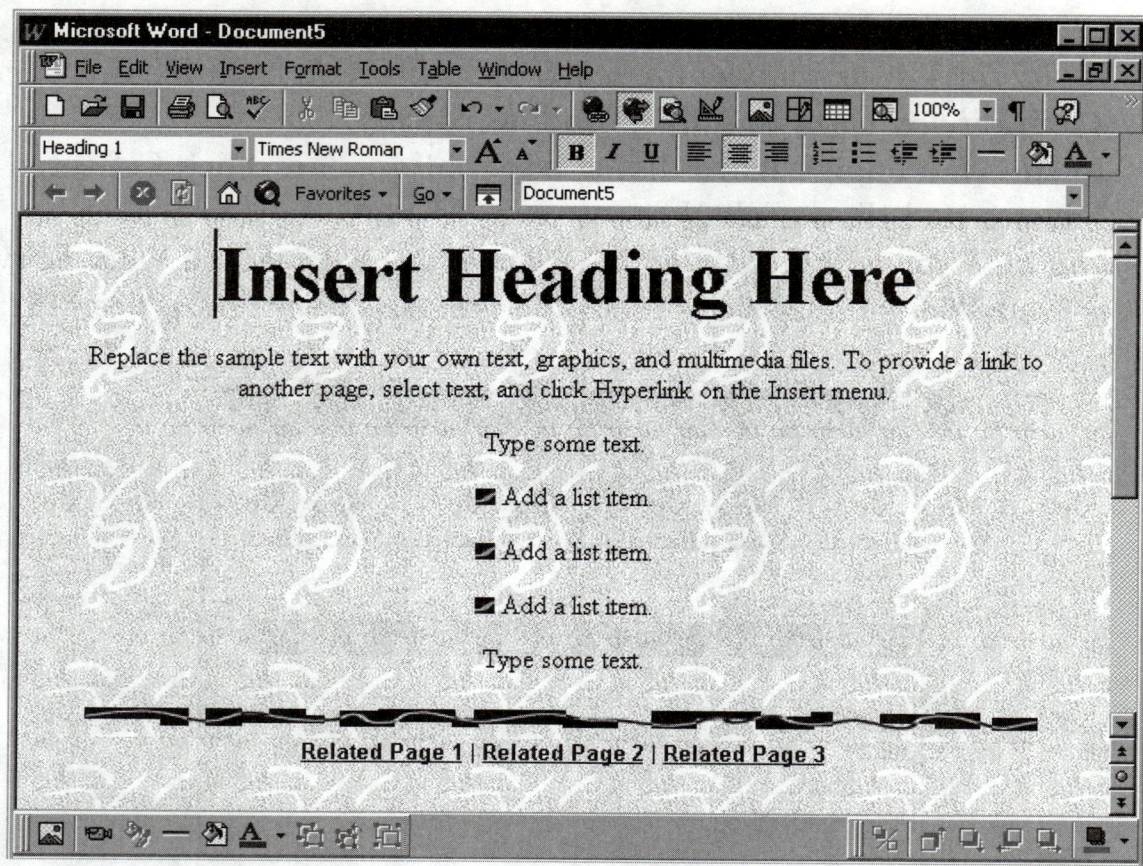

Figure 4-62. The Centered Layout with the Jazzy visual style

GETTING YOUR FEET WET
Web Toolbars in Word

Coach Carrie Says:

When you select the Web page features of Word some very cool stuff happens to the toolbars to make them work for you and help you with the creation of your Web site. To begin with, take a look at the Standard toolbar and the Formatting toolbar and see if you can spot anything new. Give up? Take a look at these changes.

The Standard toolbar

Look at the Standard toolbar after the changes for Web page authoring have been made. See the example below.

Figure 4-63. The Standard toolbar with Web page authoring changes

Trainer Terry Says:

Locate the following buttons on the Standard toolbar by moving your mouse along the toolbar and reading the button title:

1. Find the Insert Hyperlink button 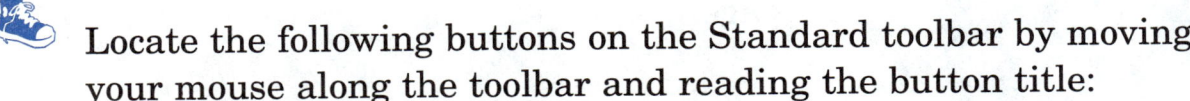. This allows you to insert a hyperlink into a Web page.

2. Find the Web Toolbar button . This makes the Web toolbar appear.

3. Find the Web Page Preview button . This lets you see what your Web page will look like as seen through the Web browser—Microsoft Internet Explorer or Netscape Navigator.

4. Find the Form Design Mode button . This makes a control box appear that lets you add different elements to your Web page.

5. Find the Insert Picture button . This lets you add pictures to your Web page.

Now, look at the Formatting toolbar in Figure 4-64, some buttons have been added or changed for Web page authoring here, too!

MASCOT MAX

If you can identify seven different buttons, you win! Learning these basic changes in the toolbars will help you a lot when you make your own Web page!

Figure 4-64. The Formatting Toolbar

1. Find the Increase Font Size button. This lets you increase the font size of characters in a Web page.

2. Find the Decrease Font Size button. This lets you decrease font size of characters in a Web page.

3. Find the Horizontal Line button. This lets you add horizontal lines to a Web page.

4. Find the Background button. This allows you to make background changes to a Web page.

GETTING YOUR FEET WET
Inserting a Hyperlink

Coach Carrie Says:

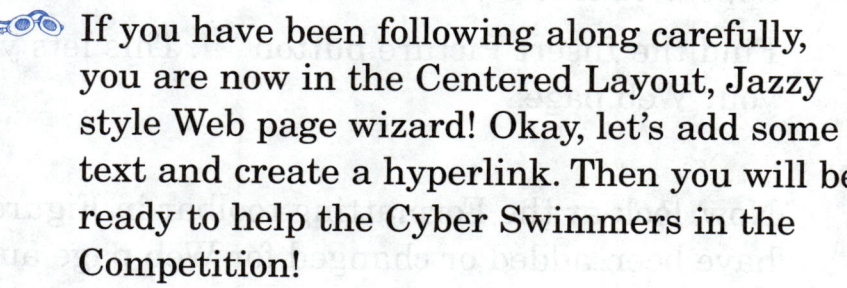

If you have been following along carefully, you are now in the Centered Layout, Jazzy style Web page wizard! Okay, let's add some text and create a hyperlink. Then you will be ready to help the Cyber Swimmers in the Competition!

LAP 1

1. Position your cursor to the left of the text *Insert Heading Here.*
2. Type your first and last name and press Delete on your keyboard until the text *Insert Heading Here* disappears.
3. In front of the text under your name, type *Hi, welcome to my Web page! Find out about me here:*
4. Delete the Web Wizard text up to the first bulleted item.
    Does your Web page example look like Figure 4-65?

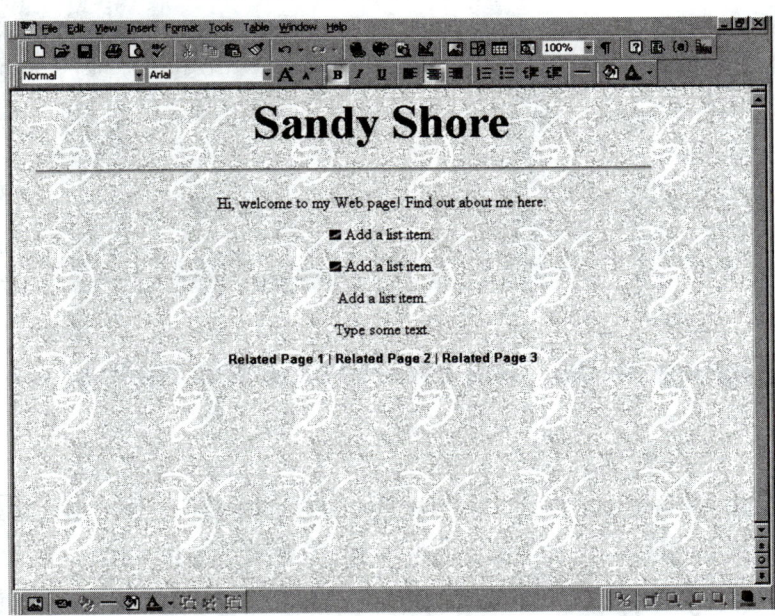

Figure 4-65. Web page example

👓 Now, let's try creating a hyperlink!

LAP 2

1. Select the first bullet in the practice Web page.
2. Click on the Insert Hyperlink button 🖼 on the standard toolbar.
3. You will notice Word asks you to save the Web page. Save it as **web practice.**
4. You will now see the Insert Hyperlink dialog box. It looks like Figure 4-66.

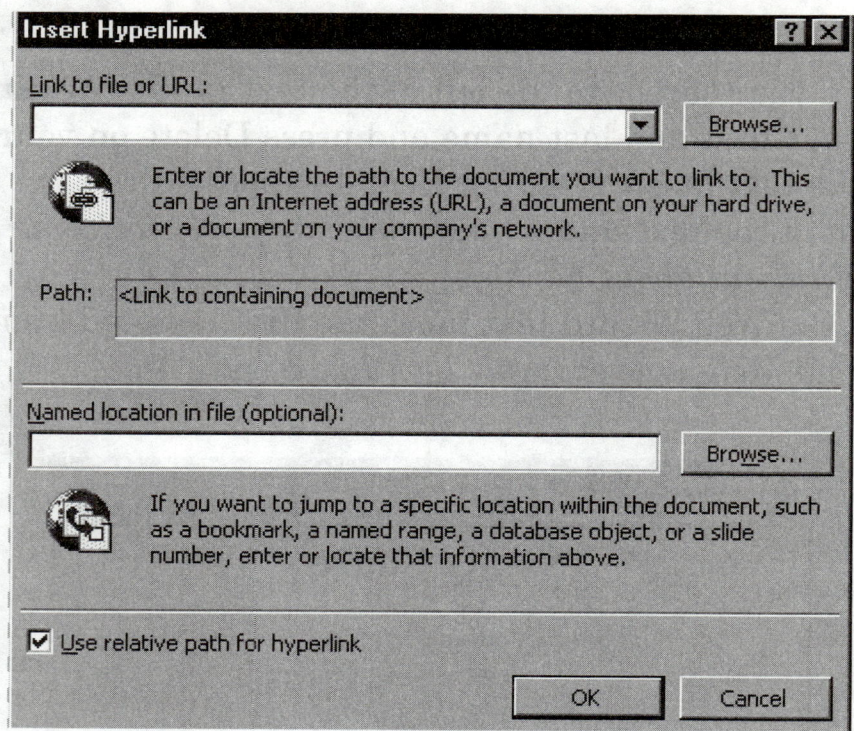

Figure 4-66. The Insert Hyperlink dialog box

Notice that you can link your Web page to a file or URL. There is also a button that lets you browse for a link. You can use a hyperlink to jump from one place to another in your file. But for now, we will work with linking a file from your hard drive or disc.

LAP 3

1. Next to the Link to file or URL text box, click Browse.
2. In the Link to File dialog box, select any file that you previously created to link to the practice Web page.
3. Click OK twice.
4. Point the arrow at the first bullet icon on the practice Web page and you will see the arrow becomes a pointing hand.
   The file will show as linked. Look at the example shown in Figure 4-67.

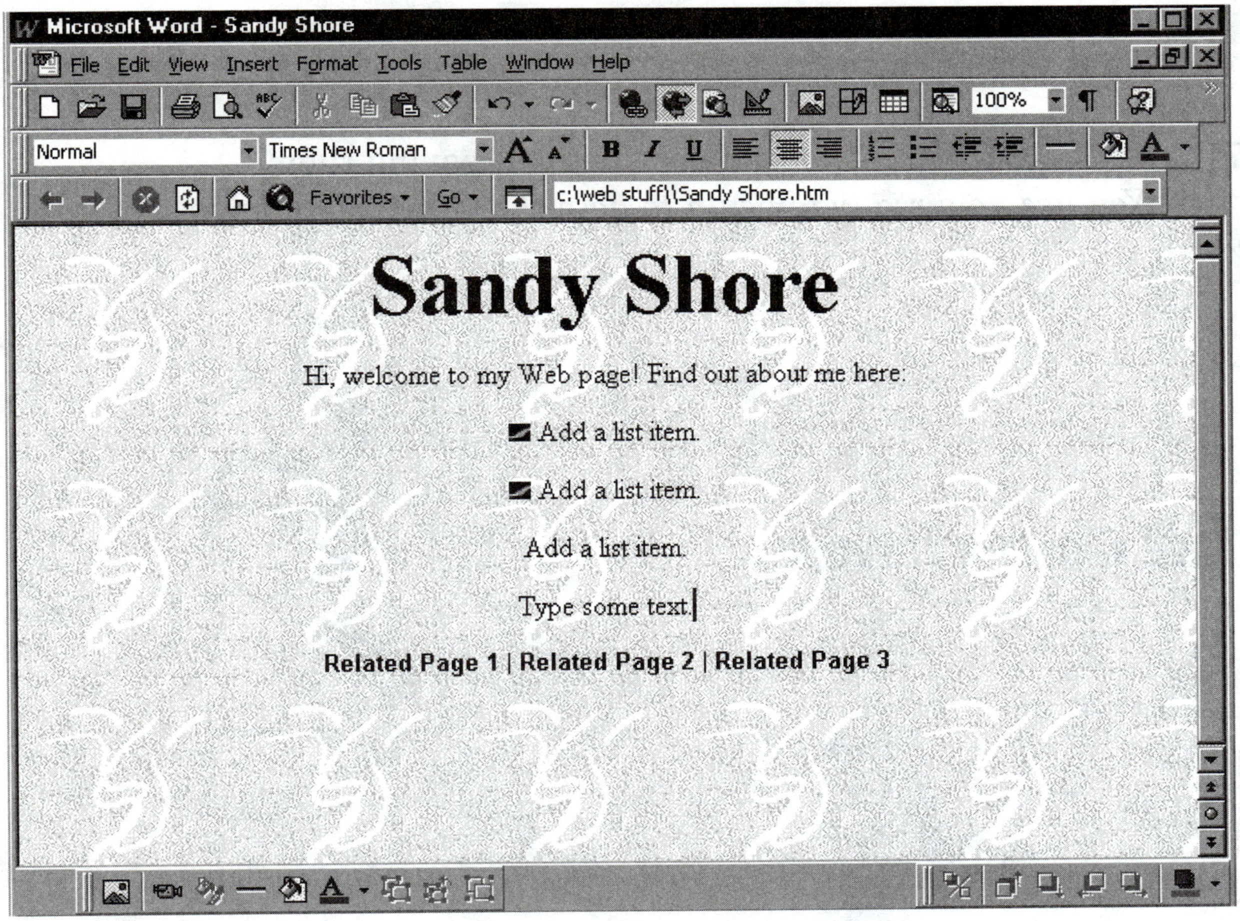
Microsoft Word - Sandy Shore
File Edit View Insert Format Tools Table Window Help
100%
Normal
Times New Roman
Favorites
Go
c:\web stuff\\Sandy Shore.htm
Sandy Shore
Hi, welcome to my Web page! Find out about me here:
Add a list item.
Add a list item.
Add a list item.
Type some text.
Related Page 1 | Related Page 2 | Related Page 3

Figure 4-67. A document link

You just created a hyperlink!

5. Click on the hyperlink and Word will open your linked document.

6. In the Web toolbar, click the Back Arrow button  and return to the Web page.
   Notice the Back Arrow in the toolbar in Figure 4-68.

The Back Arrow
Favorites
Go
c:\web stuff\Team Page.htm

Figure 4-68. The Back Arrow on the Web toolbar

👓 That was awesome, wasn't it?

7. Close your sample documents without saving them.
You are now ready to begin to help the Cyber Swimmers.

THE COMPETITION

Coach Carrie Says:

👓 Now that you have learned the basics about creating a Web page using Word, it is time to try it! Let's help the Cyber Swim Team put together their own team Web page. The Swimmers have chosen the Simple Layout Web Page Wizard to create their Web page document. Let's begin!

Trainer Terry Says:

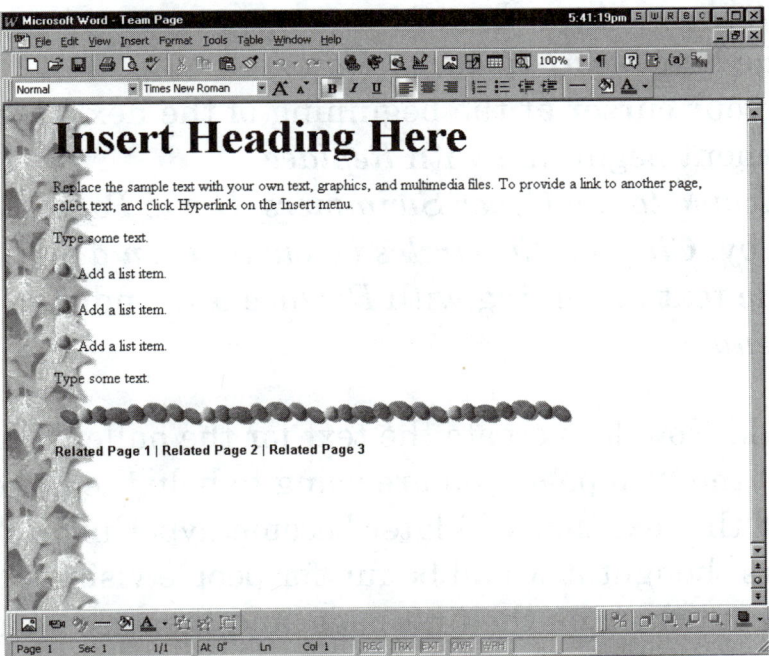 You're off to see the Wizard, again!

LAP 1

1.   Click on <u>F</u>ile, <u>N</u>ew, and then the Web Pages tab in the New
     document dialog box.
     You will see the Web Page Wizard dialog box appear.
2.   Click on Web Page Wizard and then OK.
3.   Click Simple Layout, and then click <u>N</u>ext.
4.   Now choose a visual style for the Swimmers' Web page. Click
     Outdoors, and then click <u>F</u>inish.
     *Look at the picture below in Figure 4-69 to see the Outdoor Web
     Page Wizard visual style:*

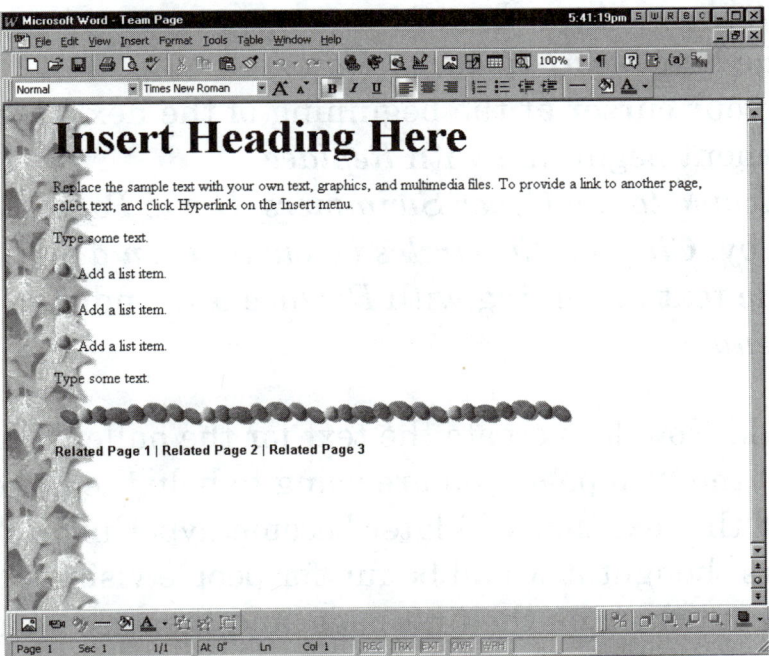

Figure 4-69. The Outdoor Web Page Wizard visual style

Coach Carrie Says:

What you are looking at is the Outdoor Visual style Web Page Wizard selection. This page will be the home page for the Cyber Swim Team's Web site! Now, let's add text to the document. As you did before in the practice Web page Workout, you'll simply add your text and delete the sample text you find in the Web Page Wizard document.

LAP 2

1. Position your cursor so that it is to the left of the text *Insert Heading Here*.
2. Type *Welcome to Aqua Land!*
3. Delete the text *Insert Heading Here*.
4. Position your cursor at the beginning of the next line of text in the document beginning with *Replace*.
5. Type *Welcome to the Cyber Swimmers' Home Page! Thank you for stopping by. Click on the circles below to learn about our team.*
6. Delete the text beginning with *Replace* and ending with *on the Insert menu*.

Good work! Now, let's create the text for the bulleted list. In this portion of the Web page, you are going to help the Cyber Swim Team add the text that will later become hyperlinks. The Cyber Swimmers thought it would be fun for people visiting their Web site to read about them on the first page, and then see a calendar on the second page, and finally, read the newsletter you helped them make on the third page to make the Web site really interesting!

LAP 3

1. Position your cursor to the left of the word *Type* on the next line of text.
2. Type *Check these cool spots out:*
3. Delete the text *Type some text.*
4. Position your cursor to the left of the word *Add* by the first bullet.
5. Type *Team History and Biographies.* Delete the text *Add a list item.*
6. Repeat this step for the next two bullets, first deleting the Web Page Wizard instructions and typing *Swim Meet Calendar,* and then deleting the Web Page Wizard instructions and typing *The Underwater News.*
7. Position your cursor at the left of the text *Type some text.* Type *Swimmers, take your mark!*
8. Press the Delete key and delete the text *Type some text. Check your work. It should look like the example in Figure 4-70.*

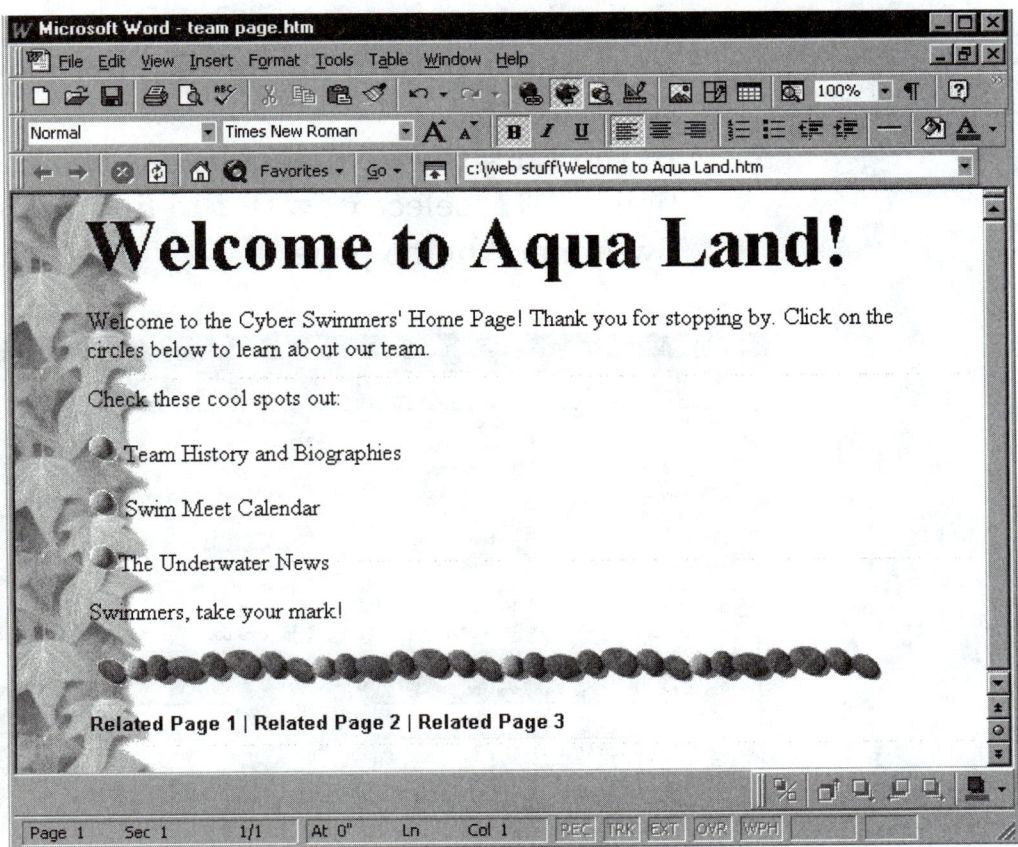

Figure 4-70. Web page example

LAP 4

JEFF THE REF

If you can't find your **newslet** file, ask your teacher or parents for help.

👓 You will use Cyber Swimmers' Newsletter to create a hyperlink to the Cyber Swimmers' home page.

1. Select the third bullet item for the Cyber Swimmers' Newsletter—The Underwater News.

2. Click on the Insert Hyperlink button 🖼 on the Standard toolbar.
    You will notice Word asks you to save the Web page.

3. Save it as **team page**.
    You will now see the Insert Hyperlink dialog box.

4. Next to the Link to file or URL text box, click Browse.

5. In the Link to File dialog box as shown in figure 4-71, select **newslet** to link to the Swimmers' home page.

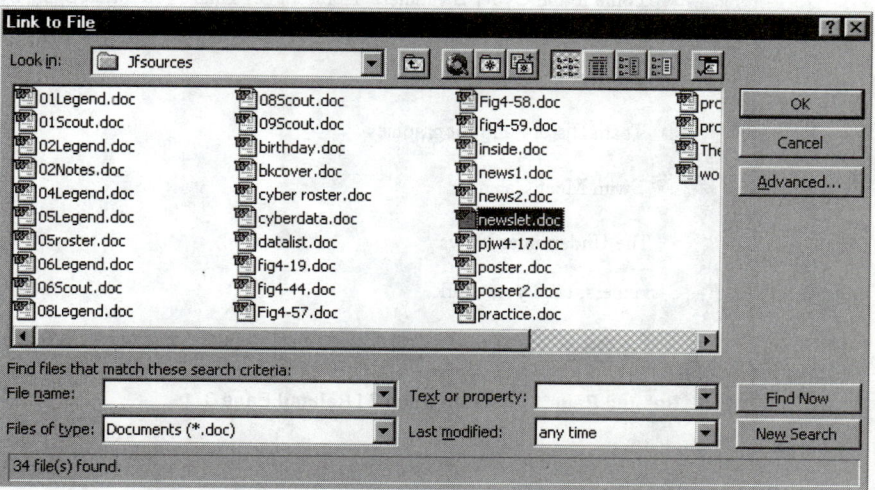

Figure 4-71. Link to File dialog box

6.   Click OK twice.

7.   Point the arrow at the third bullet on the Web page and you will see the arrow becomes a pointing hand. The file will show as linked.

8.   Click on the hyperlink and Word will open the newsletter!

9.   On the Web toolbar, click the Back Arrow button 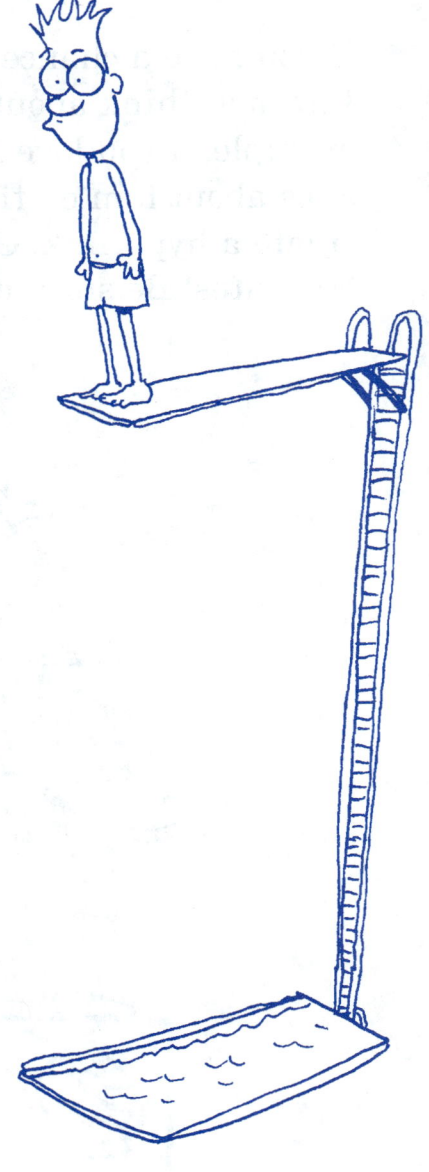 and return to the Web page.

10.   Save and close the Web page.

THE STATE FINALS

👓 Now that you have helped the Cyber Swimmers make their first team Web page, it's time to make your own! Use the Personal Web Page Wizard. You might want to include the following things:

- Information about your school
- Your favorite hobbies or sports
- Your favorite animals
- Your favorite movie stars or other celebrities
- Links to other documents

👓 If you have a chance to actually post your Web site on the Internet, think about including links to your favorite sites. For example, if you love Michael Jordan, you'll find many interesting sites about him on the World Wide Web. Use your favorite and create a hyperlink. Or, add a link to your classmate's or friend's Web sites! Be sure to check with the site before you link to it!

CONGRATULATIONS!
YOU'VE MADE IT!

INDEX

RUN HOME!

W

ABOUT THE AUTHORS

Chris Katsaropoulos is the author and editor of dozens of computer books covering a wide variety of topics. Chris devotes his time to developing top-flight computer textbooks and instructor materials for DDC Publishing. Most recently, he has written *Learning to Create a Web Page with Microsoft Office 97*, *Internet in an Hour for Managers*, *Internet in an Hour for Salespeople*, and *Learning the Internet for Business*, all published by DDC. Other recent titles Chris has written for DDC include *Microsoft Outlook 97 Short Course*, *Microsoft Office 97 Short Course*, and *PowerPoint 97 Quick Reference Guide*.

Chris has held positions as Associate Publisher and Acquisitions Manager for the Que Education & Training and Que imprints of Macmillan Computer Publishing. He also served as Senior Editor in the Office Technology group at Glencoe Publishing, where he was editor of the popular Speedwriting Shorthand series for many years.

Chris lives in Indianapolis, IN with his wife and two children. When he isn't surfing the Web, he enjoys listening to jazz and shooting hoops in the driveway with his kids.

Suzanne Weixel is a self-employed writer and editor specializing in the technology industry. Her experience with computers began in 1974 when she learned to play football on the Dartmouth Time-Sharing terminal her brother installed in a spare bedroom.

Suzanne has written or contributed to more books about how to use computers than she can keep track of. She also likes to write about non-computer-related subjects whenever she has the chance.

Suzanne graduated from Dartmouth College in 1981 with a degree in art history. She currently lives in Marlborough, MA with her husband, Rick, their sons Nathaniel and Evan, and their dog, a Samoyed named Cirrus.

Grace Jasmine is an award-winning author with over 29 current book titles in print. Her most recent title is *The Internet Directory for Teachers*, published by IDG Books/Dummies Press. Grace was awarded the National Parenting 1997 Seal of Approval for two titles written for the series, "Creative Kids." Written extensively for both the parent and teacher market. Other genres include plays, movie treatments, lyrics and poetry, children's poetry, magazines, advertising, professional and business writing, proposals, bids, and resumes.

Grace lives in Costa Mesa, CA with her husband and six-year-old daughter, Daisy.

Ryan Sather grew up in Eugene, Oregon. He has been illustrating books since he was sixteen. Ryan's interests include camping, fishing, hiking, various sports, playing the guitar, and, of course, drawing. He is currently freelancing in Washington state.

PRACTICE KEYBOARD

NOTES

SEE YA LATER!

NOTES

NOTES

Bye for now!

BUSINESS REPLY MAIL
FIRST CLASS MAIL PERMIT NO. 7321 NEW YORK, N.Y.

POSTAGE WILL BE PAID BY ADDRESSEE

275 Madison Avenue
New York, NY 10157-0410

BUSINESS REPLY MAIL
FIRST CLASS MAIL PERMIT NO. 7321 NEW YORK, N.Y.

POSTAGE WILL BE PAID BY ADDRESSEE

275 Madison Avenue
New York, NY 10157-0410

BUSINESS REPLY MAIL
FIRST CLASS MAIL PERMIT NO. 7321 NEW YORK, N.Y.

POSTAGE WILL BE PAID BY ADDRESSEE

275 Madison Avenue
New York, NY 10157-0410